EXILES IN PARIS

BRENDA SQUIRES

THE EATONS Vol 2

Copyright © 2023 Brenda Squires.

The author asserts her moral right under the Copyright, Designs and Patents Act, 1988, to be identified as the author of this work.

All Rights reserved. No part of this publication may be reproduced, copied, stored in a retrieval system, or transmitted, in any form or by any means, without the prior written consent of the copyright holder, nor be otherwise circulated in any form of binding or cover other than that in which it is published and without a similar condition being imposed on the subsequent purchaser.

The characters and events portrayed in this book are fictitious. Any similarity to real persons, living or dead, is coincidental and not intended by the author.

DEDICATION

For Anne Garside and the Rhosy Writers

ACKNOWLEDGMENTS

Anne Garside, historian, helped me enormously in the evocation of the era of the Wall Street Crash. With her detailed knowledge of Russian history and its language and culture she was able to help bring a note of authenticity to the depiction of the émigré population in Paris. As always, she was tireless in reading and rereading drafts. The Rhosy novelists' group has also been extremely supportive in helping me work through various versions of the story. Thorne Moore, one of these writers, has gone the extra mile in formatting the book for me.

Many thanks to all of you.

EXILES IN PARIS

CONTENTS

PART 1 1
PART 2...90
PART 3...174
PART 4...242
PART 5...274
A Distant Call 326
ABOUT THE AUTHOR 327

PART 1

Paris 1929

Chapter One *Derek*

To step off the train at the Gare du Nord in Paris was to engage with another world altogether. Derek could not wait to be back here. Pierre had said to come soon: the best of the studios were being taken. Other artists, seeking freedom and cheap rents and the chance to breathe the same air as Picasso and Braque, were pitching up, if not in droves, then as a steady trickle from all over. Derek had caught only a whiff of this on his previous visit to Paris.

He'd hoped for a studio in La Ruche, the Beehive, but he was too late Pierre told him: the last studios had just been grabbed by a bunch of Russian artists. Derek had grimaced, disappointed he couldn't set up shop in the artists' collective in the heart of Montparnasse. La Ruche continued to give rise to cross-fertilisation amid a constant to-ing and fro-ing. Artists could share models and exhibition space. He'd heard many a tale of it. He'd also heard the rumour that some French art critics sniffed at the place, calling it the School of Paris to distinguish it from the pure French tradition. Despite this, it remained a haven for foreign-born artists of every ilk.

Too bad. He'd have to make do with what he could get.

This time, when he and Mo arrived in Paris, it was no longer a magical spring. Autumn was fast approaching and the days were shortening. In August, Pierre said, the streets had sweltered, shops were shuttered; better-off families headed south or to Brittany to take the sea air, sniff lavender and take picnics under elm trees. Even Picasso and Braque had decamped to seaside farms in Normandy.

Through Pierre he found a lodging in the Marais district, not far from Pierre's studio. It was a mansard apartment with two modest rooms and a tiny, wobbly parapet. The house lay down a cobbled alleyway, which reeked of drains and where the lower windows jutted out and almost touched. From their parapet Mo and Derek had the luxury of looking out over the roofs of the *quartier*, even glimpsing Notre Dame. Up there they often caught an aroma of onions and butter as someone, somewhere, cooked supper.

The rooms were less than he'd hoped for. There'd been an artist living there before: a man from Provence they'd met on their first trip to Paris. When too many days under grey skies left him pining, he'd returned south to the sun and the sound of cicadas. The man had painted the furniture green, daubed shells and fish on the walls and dyed the floor aquamarine. It was like being under the sea.

Mo was at pains to appear cheery and willing to take it all in her stride. Down below they shared a kitchen and rudimentary washing facilities with a family from Odessa. The family, six in all, stank of stale clothes and hogged the range with bubbling dumplings and overcooked, sulphurous cabbage. The water closet was in constant use. The children, ranging from six to twelve, had grey, grim faces with incurious eyes. The mother, Olga, looked worn out. There was no man in view. Derek often wondered how they got by.

To look at Olga made Mo sad. He could tell. Though she said nothing, he knew she regretted their cottage in Malden and her own family. He told her to give it six months, a year, give herself a chance to settle in. Her newly bought Selfridges gown hung limp and neglected in their crammed *garde-robe*.

One morning she returned from market with extra vegetables and gave a bundle of potatoes and carrots to Olga, who could barely believe her eyes. It was Mo's way: once she'd given some of her best outfits to a fellow chorus dancer she felt sorry for.

A few days later they heard shuffling in the night and woke to find Olga and co. had cleared out. When Derek asked the landlord, he said they'd done a moonlight flit and good riddance to them! Not a sou had they paid him in rent and he'd only taken them in out of the goodness of his heart. Bloody refugees. Derek said nothing but made sure they paid their rent on time. It was little enough anyway.

The plight of the downstairs family had stabbed Mo through. He knew she hated poverty. Poverty etched into you like gastric acid. She declared she hated the meanness of it, what it made people do. She hated the going-hungry and the shabbiness. She could not bear to see the pinched faces of Olga's brood. She said nothing but he could tell she was relieved when they moved on. Though Mo might be made for a better life, poverty had a habit of lingering around her.

He never quite fathomed how even as she fled them, Mo's family pulled on her with invisible threads. He sometimes thought they held a negative sway over her. A withering look from Ma bit into her even as she struggled against it. While she'd worked in the West End as a rising star in plays and musicals she'd given them money. Though her parents wouldn't admit it, the East End pub they ran, The Mare's Head, was proving too much: decades of smoking, drinking and hard physical work were taking their toll on them.

* * *

After two weeks in Paris he believed Mo was more at home. The city seemed to retain for her a tinge of the exotic. Outside, she caught the vivacity of the people. She laughed more. This conviviality showed in the cheap but drinkable red wine, the gaiety and melancholy of the street music, the fast vivid talk of the artists and intellectuals; it was a lightness in the air, by the river, in the public squares, wherever they chanced to go. Even poverty here had a Bohemian flavour. The emigré from the Russian intelligentsia, the Spanish artist and the young writer from the American Mid-West were all flocking here to escape tedium and tyranny. As for the Parisians, they carried on much as they had always done.

To see Mo ambling down a Parisian boulevard was a treat, even better was to watch her strolling in the golden September sun along the Tuileries, as if in an Auguste Renoir painting with men in top hats, horse carriages and women with ample cleavages. He laughed at his own romanticism. But whatever way you looked at it, it was a city to be in after the dreariness of London tightening its belt. The bourgeoisie exerted a hefty weight here as they did elsewhere, but he sensed a freedom about the place. The French knew about love, food and wine; but above all they appreciated art.

Despite all that, in Paris things were hard to gauge. In London he'd sensed something in the air. Society was waiting, bating its breath. It noisily declared that nothing had changed when everything had. London was a city where much was hidden away. The upper classes partied, frolicked and entertained then slunk off, when they'd had their fill, to their country piles. They admitted others to their ranks on a whim, if they were talented, amusing or eccentric enough. Above all, The Bright Young Things still wanted to be distracted and titillated. But their parties had started to border on desperation. Although always only on their periphery, he had grown tired of them. The shriek of hysteria was never far away.

He smiled to himself. He should not be lulled by his own wishful thinking or be smitten with his own idea of Paris. He needed to get out there and find out. And Mo would need to get acquainted with the music scene. Pierre recounted stories of the *chanteuses réalistes*. 'With these singers,' he said, 'it's all in their voices. They've been circus performers and street urchins. They've been abandoned. They wander in bedraggled troupes. They have a diet of tobacco, cocaine and cheap red wine. But can they sing! It makes you want to weep. It makes you want to get up and dance.'

After her recent setbacks Mo's confidence was dented. He

knew she would have to muster everything she had to come anywhere near these worldly artists of the soul. She could not claim their extreme indigence. Her lineage was steadier in comparison. Her parents made a sufficient, if precarious, living at The Mare's Head. She had never gone hungry nor had to sing to fill her stomach. She had worn shoes to school and enjoyed a certain, working-class respectability.

What could she say about or to the poor of Paris?

She was an instinctive creature. When they first entered the rooms in Marais with all the fish and blue waves, she'd insisted he paint it over that very night. She could not bear living close to the rocks, as she put it. They made love there and then; she was more desperate, more ardent. There was something in the air freeing them both from inhibition, but that something also unnerved her. She made a stab at adapting her appearance to fit in: she bobbed her hair and looked a delight. But he was not fooled. She needed to perform and there was an end to it.

* * *

'I don't know what I am,' she said one evening. 'I wanted to come here. I want to be with you. London's West End is dead for me. But I don't know myself here.'

It hurt him to hear her distress. They were sitting in a corner café not far from their alley. She sipped her wine and sank into silence. Right then she came across as a poor London waif. He waved to the waiter to bring her something sweet to eat, the house *crème caramel*. That often cheered her up.

He'd spent the day with Pierre, in his studio and mooching around other artists who shared the premises. Pierre said that for the time being he could share his space, for which he was grateful. Now his head was buzzing from the encounters he'd had. He did not want to lose that sensation. Ideas barely glimpsed in Britain were thrown around here. He saw the studio artists playing with colour, form; breaking away with a boldness that thrilled. They spurned handed-down tradition, though many came from its ranks. After his first toe-in-the-water exhibition in Paris a few months before, he hoped he'd settle in quickly. The language of artists was easier than the language of singers. Mo relied on a contact or a musical director, whereas he just needed light, studio space, a set of brushes and oil paints. In Paris, among his painter friends, he felt normal and fed and stimulated all at once. Strange, how shifting a couple of hundred miles switched him into a different gear: he felt both younger and older, more naïve and wiser. Yet nothing was sure. The future was an unknown and choppy sea.

Being here brought back that time, years ago, when he and Mo had first discovered Paris and each other. Then she was raw as sunburnt skin, not bearing to be touched by anyone or anything one minute, fully engaged the next. Not wanting to let him out of her sight, yet in conflict, there, with him, when all family pressure was for respectability and a secure future. And now here they were. She'd thrown in her lot with his and declared herself willing to give their marriage another chance.

He touched her cheek wanting to cheer her: 'Come on,' he said. 'I'm going to take you to all the cafés that count. I'll wangle an invitation to any *vernissage* I can. You know you sparkle in company. It won't be long before you get something…' He looked across at her. She was spooning *crème caramel* into her mouth and looked very far away. She finished the dessert and pushed the bowl away.

Was Paris going to work for them? The question he'd been evading seared through him. How were they going to find their way in this most intriguing of cities? Was it possible even?

Chapter Two *Mo*

Mo wondered if Derek really cared whether or not she found work. He said he did. He knew as well as anyone that singing in West End musicals had brought her no end of accolades. But these were now dispersed like a summer cloud. What was to be done? He could not do her singing for her, nor could he learn her notes. He could only invite her to the parties he was asked to and rap on a few doors.

Pierre and he were busy choosing paintings for another exhibition. Pierre, ever an admirer of hers, kept asking what she was up to. He, above all their French friends, had the measure of her. Derek said he had a heap of work to be getting on with: paintings to finish, practicalities to see to. He was keen to improve his French, too. Too much would pass him by if he didn't. He was working on light. The Machine Age did not appeal to him nor did pure Surrealism. He loved real objects disappearing into the ether. Picasso might rail against the demise of drawing. 'But how,' Derek asked, 'can you hang on to form and solidity when everything is fleeing the centre?'

His preoccupations were beyond her.

One day they were in Pierre's studio. Derek had set up his stuff in one corner. She looked around. Against one wall were rows of jars, beside piles of canvases. The whole place looked like a giant storage shed. The windows were covered in cobwebs. It made her gasp for air it was so dusty.

'So what do you think, Mo?' Pierre was looking at her with a blend of intensity and shyness. 'See,' he continued before she had time to respond. 'I move towards shape, away from the trauma of mutilation.' What she saw on the easel was a picture of a muddy brown background with a blue triangle banged on top of it. To her it was a child's daubing.

'It's bizarre.' She edged away from it. 'Can I have a cigarette?' She suppressed her agitation. Hardly had they stepped inside and she wanted to leave. She wanted to get out in the fresh air and watch the sun sparkling on the river, perhaps see lovers holding hands and laughing as they wove in and out of shadows cast by the plane trees. These paintings only baffled her.

Pierre offered her his packet of Gaulloises.

'I'm impressed by your hard work. I see how busy you've both been…' she attempted to offset her outburst. Pierre looked down at the ground, at once a young boy avid for approval. Derek once said he found women difficult: his mother had died when he was young, leaving him in the clutches of a loveless aunt. Mo touched his arm. 'Pearls before swine, I think.' She gave an awkward laugh.

Derek jumped in and started talking about themes and progress. He went on to bring up issues involved in the upcoming exhibition and the constraints of the space at their disposal. Pierre and he were then off on another tangent as they discussed what pictures to put forward.

Later the three of them went to a *boîte*. It was down a back street somewhere on the hill of Montmartre, its entrance lit by a wonky blue neon sign, Le Cheval Bleu. As they approached raised voices, laughter, the keen shrill of a trumpet burst upon them. Her heart lifted. Squeezing into the narrow, ill-lit building they descended to a low-ceilinged hall. A pall of cigarette smoke hung over a cluster of tables round a stage where four black jazz musicians were giving it their all. When they finished the number riotous applause erupted.

Mo and the men found a table, somewhere near the back, and ordered whisky and wine. Caught up in the hubbub they were unable to talk. Mo sat back, letting the music pulse through her. Never had she heard anything so elemental, so intricate and so free! A few got up and danced with crazed energy between the tables near the musicians. She could not stop moving to the rhythm. Afterwards Derek was gone for several minutes. When he came back his face was set. 'What is it?' she asked. He shrugged. 'Derek?'

'I asked the manager if he would hear you sing.'

'You never did! And what did he say?'

Derek grunted in exasperation. 'He said they had more than enough Parisian balladeers and street singers seeking a spot and he could hardly favour a foreigner over a native speaker...'

'What about the jazz musicians?' quipped Pierre. 'They're not French.'

Again Derek shrugged. 'Mo, you need to get a repertoire of French material.'

'Easier said than done.' It both touched and angered her that he'd approached the man on her behalf.

Pierre looked from one to the other. 'You could find a teacher – some enterprising soul offering conversation classes.'

* * *

In fact, she tried three sessions, sitting in a café in Place de la Bastille with a haughty student from the Sorbonne, who spoke too rapidly for her to catch on. He was constantly thumbing through a dog-eared book searching the English equivalents. When he failed to show for their next session she declared: 'My teacher's bolted. Got bored, I think.'

One day she surprised herself by opening the window and singing her head off. Derek came back early and said he could hear her even as he turned into their alley. 'Good to hear you giving vent.' Derek looked thoughtful. 'Let's make a list of all the nightclubs and go to each of them. We'll get a feel for them and you can pick up a song or two. You've got a good ear. Copy them. And sing your own songs from back home too. You can be the cockney sparrow.'

'You think so?' She knew she could move people to tears when she wanted to. She could hit the notes dead centre, no sliding or vibrato, but jazz singers treated the notes anyway they pleased.

'Most singers just sing – people listen, find it pleasant and then turn back to their drinks. But your voice cuts through.'

She fought back an upsurge of emotion. What did all that amount to if no one was willing to give her a job? 'If I don't find somewhere to sing in the next month, I'm catching the ferry home.' She threw herself down on the sofa, kicking off her shoes and giving a joyless laugh.

Chapter Three *Derek*

Derek could see the destructiveness in Mo. He knew all about that from first hand. They must not go down that path. He feared it much as he had once feared for her sanity after the death of their infant son, Timothy. She was in danger of curling in on herself. If only she would hold out a bit longer, give herself a fighting chance. Sometimes, in the middle of the night, he heard her stirring, muttering under her breath, gasping for air even. It made him feel helpless. She was carrying so much inside. But she refused to talk, it only made her upset: she wanted to look forward not backwards. Work would cure her restlessness, she said.

They should find her something, even if they had to walk down every street in Paris. Trouble was, he needed to be getting on with his own work. When he stopped doing that he grew angry with her, unfairly at times. He became destructive, too, so they circled, a mongoose and a cobra locked in combat. Pierre was a good third party to keep them from baiting each other.

For him, Paris remained the City of Light. Never mind that that was a political designation from the Great War – at a personal level it still held strong. After the war Paris had kicked up its heels and became even gayer and wilder. He felt at home here. He minded less about making a name for himself, though in fact he sold more paintings on French soil than in London. His vague, intangible artistic impulses could be realised here, while his passions were not something to stifle or be ashamed of. Here you could proclaim and strut around and nobody thought ill of you. Perhaps, because of clashing nationalities, artists strove for a vernacular where they could meet. There was less cynicism. Or perhaps, because of his imperfect French, he perceived it less.

How much sadder then to see Mo's troubled face! It stirred his guilt. At times she seemed an exotic songbird plucked from its natural habitat, yet it was the West End that had given her the cold shoulder. It was hardly his fault. After the trauma of the theatre fire, Jonathon Knighton, Mo's mentor and onetime lover, became ambivalent. Knighton would not have been pleased at their reconciliation. He had hinted as much at their last encounter. 'She's a fickle creature,' he'd said, affecting joviality. Enraged, Derek had kept his counsel: what man would not be wounded when Mo walked out on him? She had a way of opening your heart and crawling inside. She was a bolt of lightning that could strike at the heart of a solid oak. Lesser trees she would consume with fire.

The Montparnasse artists' community gave him pause for thought. The women could be bold and brazen. Beside Kiki, the Queen of Montparnasse, Mo was tame. In the eyes of an audience, that was. Mo's voice might be sweeter, her musicality greater, her sense of timing, her movement – all impeccable. Kiki had a streak of vulgarity. She drank too much, sang rude songs and flung off her clothes as easily as she breathed. But over time she had become a star. She sang at Le Boeuf Sur Le Toit, the Bobino Music Hall and The Jockey Club. She'd paired up with Man Ray who immortalised her image. Sometimes she danced the cancan without knickers, kicked her legs so high, all could see. And now she had become an artist, too, and had been invited to exhibit at the Tremois gallery. She had even been persuaded to write her memoirs. She'd sold her book, *Souvenirs de Kiki,* for fifty francs and a kiss with every copy. Derek had heard all about it from Dimitri, his Russian artist friend. Besides all this, Kiki was French, born and bred.

The Surrealists had come and gone. Salvador Dali portrayed what it was to plummet the nether regions of the psyche by sealing himself up in a diving bell suit. He almost died of suffocation when he forgot he needed to breathe! Dali bent clocks into liquid and birthed nightmare landscapes of giant ears in the desert. His was the craziness of an unfettered dream-mind, but it was contained, put out into the world for all to see. Mo was not like that. She was down–to-earth and clear-sighted, a cockney sparrow chirping at noon. Her madness was the occasional sharp note of despair.

When they'd first visited a bar where *chanteuses réalistes* sang, Mo was cast into a trance. The next day she scurried out in search of a songbook. This happened again and again: always this feverish hunting down of the song, the attempt to recapture, recreate what she'd heard. Most of the tunes could not be found, were not yet in print. She tried to reproduce the songs from memory, but her lack of French got in the way. He could see the fire burning – the glitter of talent never far from her eyes.

In several clubs he made an approach to the emcee, explaining what she could sing. But he would be met by a glazed look, as the man shook his head, regretting it was not possible, implying Mo was misplaced. More than once she offered to sing, but to no avail. As he watched her face close in disappointment a gloom passed over his heart. 'So what do I do now?' she would stare glumly into her glass of red wine. Bittersweet when he thought back to her days in The Athena when she'd been fêted with so many flowers and he could not get near her.

The last *boîte* they visited left him feeling as desperate as she looked. 'Mo,' he clasped her chin in his hand and forced her to look at him. She was vulnerable as a kitten and just as skittish. 'Another week and you will have found your feet.'

She frowned. 'Stop spinning fairy stories. Let's go and see Pierre. He might have some ideas.'

Chapter Four

Pierre was surprised to see them again so soon. They went to a café of his choice and ordered mussels, which were just coming into season. They caught a strong whiff of garlic and white wine. It was her favourite dish and he watched her tuck in with relish.

'I've been making enquiries,' said Pierre, spearing a mussel.

Mo asked the waiter for more bread. 'Pierre, you're a sly one. What have you been up to?'

Pierre drew out a flyer. It was crumpled and wine-stained and must have been in his pocket for days. 'A new club's opened up in Montmartre, by Sacré Coeur. L'Etoile. Cabarets have come and gone there. The centre of gravity has shifted elsewhere. But I think you should try it. My cousin works at the bar. Wednesday nights they're open to newcomers.'

She shrugged, saying she had nothing to lose, but later she scooted along the pavement, looking lighter than she had in days, chatting about which songs to perform. They made love that night: once, twice. She exuded an unbounded energy, lay awake, murmuring beside him. 'This could be it,' she said. He loved the brush of her nipples against his chest, her sweet dark wetness, more delicious then than he could ever recall. But he was afraid for her. There was danger in this spurt of unbounded optimism – what if it all came to nothing?

He could hardly concentrate on his own work the next day. In the studio he daubed at a landscape he'd started days before; he worked without drive, too wound up in her story. What if no offer came? He broke off early and returned to their rooms. She had two frocks splayed out on the bed: one powder blue, the other black.

'You're back early.' She seemed surprised to see him.

He looked down at the frocks. 'Getting ready?' In the end she chose the little black one, like those worn by the *chanteuses* of the streets, and plastered her face white after the current vogue. Her eyes and mouth were eager. 'You look adorable,' he said. She twirled around, held out her hands.

'I hope I pull it off.'

'Nothing ventured, nothing gained,' he said calmly.

'What if they don't like me?' Her eyes sought his in a moment of anxiety.

'They will.' He meant it. If they could not appreciate what she had to offer she would be better off elsewhere. But he feared she might become downcast all over again if she did not suit their tastes.

* * *

It was getting late, the sky darkening and the gas-lighters igniting the lamps: that wonderful twilight when shops were still trading – unlike in London – and people drifting out on the town. By the time they reached L'Etoile darkness had fallen. It was more café than nightclub. A straggle of customers was jostling its way inside. Pierre was already there, a glass of claret in his hand. He beckoned the waiter and ordered another carafe. Mo kept glancing around her, fidgeting with a string of beads around her neck. 'I put in a word for you,' said Pierre quietly. 'You can sing. But do you know anything in French? Would increase your chances, I guess.'

'You never said nothing about singing in French.'

They sat through several acts of varying quality, Mo increasingly on edge. After an hour the emcee came over. Inclining his head, he said: 'I believe Madame is a singer?' Mo nodded. 'Then may we hear you?'

She asked Pierre to tell the pianist what she wanted. He looked across, puzzled, ran his fingers up and down the keyboard by way of introduction. No matter. She raised her arms to the audience and started to speak in broken French. '*Mes amis, je ne peux…je ne parle français mais je chante, je chante…'* The audience turned eagerly towards her, willing to give her a chance, liking the look of her in her neat black dress with her pretty, pale face. There was an atmosphere of good will, enjoyment.

Derek looked around. There were the usual down-at-heel artists and intellectual types, workers and artisans, people of the *arrondissement*. Some were boisterous while others chatted quietly. She rolled her eyes and her Rs and the front tables cooed and clapped, egging her on. When she'd exhausted her few French words, she slipped into English. 'For my next song, my friend here will explain.' She whispered in Pierre's ear. Flustered, he got to his feet and exchanged a few words with the pianist and then the audience. The pianist grinned at her; luckily he had spent time in London and often frequented the West End.

> *Though you're only seventeen*
> *Far too much of life you've seen*
> *Syncopated child*
> *Maybe if you only knew*
> *Where your path is leading to*
> *You'd become less wild*
> *But I know it's vain*
> *Trying to explain*
> *While there's this insane*
> *Music in your brain*
>
> *Dance, dance, dance little lady*
> *Youth is fleeting to the rhythm*
> *Beating in your mind*
> *Dance, dance, dance little lady*
> *So obsessed with second best*
> *No rest you'll ever find*
> *Time and tide and trouble*
> *Never, never wait*

Let the cauldron bubble
Justify your fate
Dance, dance, dance little lady
Dance, dance, dance little lady
Leave tomorrow behind

Derek smiled to himself. From Noel Coward's *On with the dance* this song had become one of her favourites. It had done the rounds and now, here in Paris, it seemed to sum up Mo's exuberance, her inability to stay cast down for too long. Her singing was at once strident and sure, tender and ironical, expressing all the pain, humour and unpredictability of modern life. The audience laughed and hummed along as she strutted between tables and waved her arms in mock horror. *'Encore! Encore!'* they yelled when she finished.

She had a mini conference with Pierre. For her next song the pianist was unable to accompany her. She didn't let that deter her. 'Now I sing of dreams. What happens when you watch your dreams.' Pierre translated for her. There was a touch of melancholy in her face: *'I'm forever blowing bubbles, pretty bubbles in the air. They fly so high, nearly reach the sky.'* It was a strain of song unlike the grit of the *chanson réaliste*. This was a song of longing, the heart wanting to soar into the ether. There was a touch of the angelic, the possessed about her, eyes glazed with yearning. He felt vulnerable watching her, afraid for her, afraid for himself, afraid for the plumbers and clerks and laundry girls who were taking all this in.

This was her final song. All hesitation had dropped away. For the moment she was back at the height of her Athena fame, in the lap of the blessed. The emcee came beaming towards her, 'Madame!' He could say no more 'You will come again?' he asked her at length.

'If you pay me!' she piped up. A carafe of red wine had arrived at the table, courtesy of the next and they nodded towards her, all smiles. 'I think I made some friends.'

'Indeed,' said Pierre. He went over and thanked them on her behalf. From another table arrived a single red rose, bought from the gypsy woman hovering in the shadows.

Derek was unable to suppress a growing sense of pride. In the space of one hour Mo had transformed herself: she was a chameleon, a siren to lure sailors onto the reefs. Later, they wound their way through the streets of Montmartre, swaying from the wine, laughing and tugging at each other pausing in recesses for a quick caress, besotted with her success. Pierre lingered behind, never far away but at a distance, allowing them their moment. They stumbled up the stairs of their apartment and called out to Pierre that they would see him soon. For now they needed their bed, their privacy. Who knew how long this joy would last and who might wrench it from them?

Chapter Five *Mo*

It was a start at least. The audience at L'Etoile had warmed to her: after two songs she had them if not eating from her palm, then enticed enough to want more. Jean Luc Fresnais, the proprietor, had asked her to come again, after two weeks. The prospect both thrilled and daunted.

Was this the fresh start she'd been hoping for – her chance to shrug off the past? Of Sandor Olmak she had said very little to Derek. She was not yet ready to talk about her real father. He knew the gist of the story but could only guess the details. He knew about the fire, of course, and Sandor's death. When she'd enquired about Sandor to the police, just before they left for France, she learned he'd been given what amounted to a pauper's funeral. Heavy with guilt and self-recrimination she'd brushed away the connection, the prospect of Paris pushing all else out of her mind.

Still she burned with resentment towards Jonathon Knighton, her former manager. How deluded she'd been to imagine herself a star in her own right! Nothing worked like that. Though she hated to admit it, women were tied and tithed creatures, much as they had ever been. Her speech was like an actress's now and lapsed only in anger or fun. She'd made a lady out of herself, and this was more than surface. But what was she: lady or cockney sparrow? She stood on a cliff edge.

The next day she and Derek were in the Luxembourg Gardens. Trees were shedding leaves, which spiralled down in front of them. A light wind whipped across the grass bringing hints of winter. October marked the onset of the sad time, the turning towards darkness. It was vital to keep her spirits up. Derek was striding and she had a job keeping apace. 'It goes against what the other cafés have been saying…' His words were scattering around her. She wanted to hear everything he had to say. '… a motley bunch – students, people from the *quartier*… not a lot of money around… glad of the distraction.'

'You mean they're so hard up they're grateful for whatever is cast their way?'

He laughed. 'No, not that. They really liked you.'

She swallowed the doubt that these people were undiscerning. Their reaction did not surprise her. Music was visceral, in the human body like the pulse of blood itself. Only in a dried-up, functional fashion could you live without it.

'I told you it would not be long.'

'Did you?'

'Of course, you just didn't hear me.' She smarted only slightly at his tendency to know better.

'He said Saturday after next. That gives me time to prepare.' She had already gone through a list in her head. Nothing seemed quite right. It was true what Derek said: she needed to get a grip on the language and put together a few French songs.

They walked along the straight paths, French parks so much more formal and orderly than English ones. They lingered on a wrought iron bench. She kicked through dried chestnut leaves heaped there. Children were running about on the lawn, watched by bonneted nannies on the gravel paths. As it grew colder, she and Derek left the park and headed in the direction of Derek's latest discovery: Shakespeare and Company, a bookshop run by an American woman, Sylvia Beach.

It was only the second time Mo had been to Sylvia's shop in Rue de l'Odéon, whereas Derek went frequently. Many an impoverished scribbler found his way to the cluttered treasure trove. Sylvia ran a library for members against a small subscription, but if she liked you, she would lend you whatever books you wanted. The place was a lighthouse to the English-speaking world in Paris.

Sylvia asked Derek how his exhibition was coming together. He muttered about disagreements about what should be hung where. He moved off to the music section and fished out a songbook for Mo. She flicked through it but was not inspired. Derek bought it anyway. 'What I really need is another French teacher.' When asked, Sylvia knew of someone. She told Mo to call back. The next day Sylvia introduced her to Daniel Gérome. A student of philosophy and English, he had a pale, wasted look and intense, darting eyes. They arranged to meet at a café on the corner of Montparnasse and Raspail.

***

The place was filled with self-conscious girls in skimpy dresses with bobbed hair and slender young men smoking cheroots. Only later did she learn that this was *the café* where people went in order to be seen.

'I'm a singer, you see,' she said brightly. Daniel peered at her with his sad spaniel eyes and she began to wonder if he was consumptive. She shifted back her chair. 'I need to learn French so I can sing your songs.'

'You have song books – the lyrics?' She reached down for the book Derek had bought. Daniel leafed through it with an air of mild disdain. 'These are street songs.' He had long white hands stained with nicotine between the index and middle fingers. His clothes smelled of tobacco and lack of washing. He was clearly a man to whom the life of the spirit meant more than that of the body.

The next few days she concentrated on learning French. After initial awkwardness Daniel broke out of his reserve. They went to a café on Boulevard Raspail she'd taken a fancy to. It was not far from the *bouquinistes,* the second-hand bookstalls, where she'd started to go browsing. Pierre had mentioned that singers were guarded about their songs. They retained ownership of the lyrics, the tunes, even the songwriters. It was considered bad form to filch another's material. An unspoken copyright agreement existed though no contracts were signed, as nobody could afford a lawyer.

It was the flavour of the street songs, which sparked her sensibility. Nothing was sanitised: it was life itself – raw, ugly and magnificent. Though her French was limited, the songs went into her. The singers, mostly women, came from disturbance and distress. But they spun a poetry, which made her shiver with delight. Pierre told her that Left Bank intellectuals saw this dark seam of magic and laid claim to it, cloaking it in progressive ideas to steal a march over their bourgeois counterparts. They believed this art would elevate the downtrodden.

Tommyrot, of course.

The bedraggled urchins hanging round the streets moved her. She had the urge to voice their untold stories, not to glamorise them, but simply because like anyone else they deserved a place in the light.

Daniel wrote down the new words they had spoken that day and pushed the exercise book towards her. Her head was beginning to throb. She was about to confess that she read only with difficulty when she stopped herself. Was it true? She had forced herself to read at The Athena though it often left her exhausted. She squinted and held the book at arm's length.

'Your eyes are bad,' he said without prevarication.

'I don't know.'

'You don't know? You never had them tested?'

Later that evening she mentioned it to Derek and he suggested that she seek out an optician and hang the cost. 'How come your parents never spotted that?' She caught his undertone of surprise, anger. She shrugged. Why should it bother them? But she felt a twinge of self-pity all the same. Who ever read in her family? The only reading needed was for totting up bills.

A cousin of Pierre's was married to an optician, so an appointment was made, and Mo made her way to the tenth *arrondissement*. It transpired she had a severe stigmatism and was prescribed glasses forthwith: they were needed for reading and needlework. The needlework she could do without, but the reading would usher her into the world of song.

She started borrowing books from Sylvia's library: first the simplest: *Aesop's Fables*, *The Water Babies*. What then caught her attention was poetry, especially the War Poets, who were just coming into vogue. With their rhymes and clever words put together, their poems were the rarest of songs.

'Daniel,' she said one day. 'I have an instinct about people and places. Paris feels like somewhere I could be.' Daniel looked taken aback at the personal revelation. 'In England, men make up all the rules and keep all the best bits to themselves.'

'But you have the Vote – no? French women do not. Have you voted yet?'

'Vote? I'm only just eligible. You've heard of the flapper vote?'

'*Naturellement.*'

'My mother works twice as hard as my … my father, yet he is the one who spouts politics every night in the bar.' She felt guilty, saying this, especially as Pa loved her more than anyone else. She'd hesitated, too, uttering the word 'father'. She'd never be able to use that word again without an undercurrent. She ordered herself another glass of house white.

Chapter Six *Derek*

In L'Atelier Blanc Derek stood back from his pictures and stared at them. He was tired. He'd spent all day transporting his works here from the Marais studio. It had been an arduous task but at last they were getting somewhere. The new painters, the intruders, as Derek thought of them, had been allotted half the original space. They were all Russians, compatriots of Dimitri. So they were the ones that had robbed him of a rightful space in La Ruche! He attempted to suppress his resentment.

Some of the artists hailed from Moscow or Saint Petersburg's upper echelons of society, while others came from provincial towns. They came from every rank of Russian society and every part of the political spectrum: the Civil War that had ravaged the Motherland had ripped through them, too. He did not yet have the measure of them, nor know how this group cohered. All he knew was that many Russians had had to forsake their homeland.

Nor did he have the full story of why the gallery was including them in the show. He guessed Prince Felix Yusupov and his wife, Irina, had given financial backing. The Yusupovs were the acknowledged cultural leaders of the Russian emigrés in Paris. Their generosity was legendary and they'd promised to attend the opening. Derek felt a frisson at the idea of coming face to face with the man who'd murdered Rasputin. The murder of the questionable Holy Man had caused a sensation in the press and apparently the Prince was willing to recount the story to anyone and everyone who came within striking distance.

Derek surmised that there'd been strong outside pressure to support these newcomers. Among the fugitives were some talented but impoverished painters and he suspected that Dimitri was being leaned on to ease their way. Not that this exhibition was sanctioned by the French Academies, not that it could provide a frictionless path into celebrity, but it did mark a point of departure.

Despite his irritation at not acquiring a studio at La Ruche because of them, he decided to offer them guidance, if asked. What point in bearing a grudge? In his time Patrick Shaughnessy, his London friend and mentor, had helped him. He'd shown him a *via negativa,* pointing out everything he was doing wrong: from his attitude through to his compositions. Patrick insisted that in the end you had to kill, symbolically, the one who taught you. How else to find your unique vision – which could never be truly individual anyway, but an amalgam of all you have ever seen, tasted and dreamt?

Dimitri was sorting through the newcomers' work by the entrance. Marc Chagall had been asked to select pictures for the exhibition. Chagall's Modernism and interweaving of Russian folklore sat well amongst these newcomers. He'd shown interest but begged off choosing as he was too busy. Dimitri had hoped Chagall, who'd once said that he'd returned to Paris in 1922 with Russian soil still clinging to his shoes, would relate to the painters better than himself, for he had no recent acquaintance with Mother Russia. His parents, world-travelling Jews used to imbibing the cosmopolitan soul in all cultures, had left Russia when he was in his teens.

In the end Dimitri let the painters pick what they wanted to show, restricting each painter to two exhibits. Now Derek and Dimitri were standing in front of Derek's five paintings. Dimitri was half a foot shorter than Derek and round like a tub, betraying his fondness for the good things of life. His face was rarely still, expressions flitting like clouds across it. He rubbed his chin. 'I like the colours,' he said. Derek had abandoned dull ochres for the vibrancy of spring: acid green and outrageous pinks, splashes and stripes of barely contained exuberance. The paintings were well lit, spotlights above and other lamps illuminating from beneath. The more you looked the more the images drew you in.

The first showed a tree trunk, split by an axe, and oozing

green velvet beside red toadstools, fairy magic unleashed as nature frolicked. The second was of a stag battling another in spiky shadows. The picture unsettled. A tunnel led into the roots of the underworld while the two stags contested territory above. Blood dropped from the antlers and formed into rubies, each one pierced by an eye. 'I wouldn't want that in my rooms,' said Dimitri.

'I saw it as playful,' said Derek.

Dimitri gave an uneasy laugh. 'You found titles for them in the end, I see?'

'Well you told me you wouldn't hang them otherwise, didn't you?'

The third painting was a mountain sliced through, revealing twisted strata of rock: driving forces beneath a tranquil landscape where the trees had almost human form. 'How did you dream that one up?'

'I didn't. It dreamed me. Woke me at three o'clock in the morning. *A cauchemar.* I guess it's how I see society: tranquil meadows above, seething magma below. Why should we differ from the planet itself?'

Dimitri shifted his attention to the fourth picture, watched by Derek, who despite himself was eager to be understood. Few knew the doubt he had to wrestle with before he could proceed at all. In this one, lava poured over hills, rivers and crannies in purple and vermilion, shining a preternatural, eerie light. *Catching fire* the title ran. 'How did you get that luminescent effect?' asked Dimitri.

'I can't recall,' said Derek. 'I was in a trance when I did it. To tell the truth I don't even know which day I finished it.'

Chapter Seven *Mo*

As the time for her next performance approached, Mo was undecided what to wear. What image did she want to create: *femme fatale,* cockney sparrow or professional West End star visiting Paris? Black was anonymous and it was what the *chanteuses réalistes* wore. They painted their faces white and their lips vermilion, so they looked like Chinese dolls.

Derek looked up in surprise as she came out from the bedroom. 'Very chic! The black suits you down to the ground.' He made her turn to see the full effect. She laughed, glanced in the mirror. Would she create the right impression? She knew her round face gave her a young, almost childish look. Her svelte figure fitted easily with the Parisian women, few of whom were stout. Some looked pale with pasty, undernourished skin. Others – the moneyed ones – still embraced the gamin mode, as they had in London, flattening breasts with bands and shearing their hair in boyish crops.

'You are still coming with me, I take it?'

Derek looked away. 'Let's have a drink.' He took a bottle through to their tiny balcony where two seats were wedged together. 'We need to move fast for this exhibition. The gallery owner says he can't wait. We have to get it mounted sooner rather than later. And there's been an influx of other painters. From Russia. He's offering them half the space – being paid to in fact. It's thrown a spanner in the works. The original painters are disgruntled, to put it mildly. But Dimitri – he's the main curator – is adamant. These artists *must* be given the opportunity to show.' He paused, sighed. 'I need to be there to make sure our wishes aren't bulldozed.'

Listening to his rushed words, she guessed what was coming.

She gazed at the alleyway, where the goat man was just disappearing with his nanny goat. A cacophony of klaxons was dying down as people headed home. She could just glimpse a corner of Notre Dame and the Seine under the dying beams of the sun.

She got up and leaned over the shaky balustrade. 'You're going to be so caught up with your paintings – what's going where – that you're not going to have time to come to L'Etoile with me.' She held up her glass towards the glow of the evening light. 'That's the long and short of it.'

'It's one of those unexpected things that crops up just when things are running smoothly.' She felt a sliver of annoyance that it went without saying that his work would take precedence over hers. 'If I can, I'll come. But I can't afford to have my pictures hung in some obscure corner.'

'I'll go on my own. Jean-Luc Fresnais is genial…'

'I'll ask Pierre to go later and accompany you home. He's only showing two pictures this time. He won't need to stay the whole time.' He looked out across the rooftops. 'I only wish I could go with you.'

'I'm sure you do,' she said, quelling a sense of abandonment.

* * *

The next evening Mo walked up the hill of Montmartre in the fading light. There was a chill in the air and she pulled her cape round her. She was nervous, wondering whether they would like her as much as the last time. The street door to L'Etoile had been left ajar. Outside was a flickering neon light in the form of a star. Inside a caretaker was sweeping the floor, last night's revels evident in dog ends, food scraps and smashed glass. He kept banging the legs of the tables as he whisked the broom around with more gusto than precision.

Jean Luc Fresnais was surprised to see her there so early. He invited her into the broom cupboard of a room he used as an office. 'Still getting organised.' He shuffled crates of empty bottles out of the way. She began to have misgivings. Everything was makeshift, from the improvised office to the caretaker who thumped about like a man stung by bees.

Martin, the accompanist, came in and together they ran through the tunes. Luckily, he had some English. The piano had several dud notes. Mo grimaced but put aside her annoyance. The other singer of the night was Dolores Réné. Dolores had a limp handshake, although her darting eyes bespoke a lively mind. Fresnais offered them a glass of wine, which Dolores accepted and Mo declined. Jean Luc was watching them with a keen eye.

Dolores took up her position on the stage and sang a few notes, paused, then struck up again. She had a husky voice, which went up an octave when she got excited. She exuded confidence. All at once Mo felt discouraged: this was not going to be easy. She should be singing in London instead of in some shabby French café.

Dolores came and sat beside her. She drummed her fingernails on the tabletop, looking impatient. Her nail varnish was chipped. When she noticed Mo studying her, she gave a quick smile. 'I'm up first.' She glanced at the habitués filtering into the café. 'I'll warm them up, don't you worry. *Ne vous inquiétez pas.*' She got up, adjusting the dropped waistline of her frock. When Mo looked closer, she saw it was threadbare about the hem, with trailing ends. Clusters of people were arriving now, tables slowly filling. Dolores got to her feet. *'Mesdames, messieurs.'* Chatter faded to a murmur; one man called out: '*Dolores, mon amour.*' Dolores gave a toss of the head and he replied with a throaty laugh. Others joined in.

With a growing din all around Dolores had to make her mark – not a problem with her raucous, full-throated voice. She forced people to turn towards her, partly in admiration, partly annoyance. She could certainly belt it out. Mo wondered what she was singing about. The usual stuff, she supposed: betrayal in love, yearning. When the song ended there were a few cheers, many carried on chatting.

The café was filling up with more people bunched on the pavement outside, laughing and smoking. The lights were dimmed, casting a reddish glow. The walls had been roughly distempered, showing cracks here and there. The menu was fixed, the price low. The food, when she glimpsed it, was rudimentary: soup, sausage and cheese. A working-man's place: a café where the proprietor was glad enough to have a singer to keep people in their seats, drinking. It would be like the Old Music Hall pubs with their function rooms.

Dolores sang another two songs. Hers was not a pretty voice but it was strong and impassioned. Martin did some more trills on the piano. He could really play, that man. Dolores moved back to their table and lit a Gaulloise, inhaling deeply. 'Brava,' said Mo. Dolores ignored her. Sounds rushed into the space she had left. Then it was Mo's turn. Jean Luc Fresnais introduced her. She caught the odd word or two: *moineau,* cockney, Noel Coward. She glanced around: most faces seemed friendly, others dubious.

She'd plumped for an Old Music Hall medley. One could never go wrong with love songs that were melodic and cheerful. Her voice grew stronger with every word. She could feel it doing her good, exercising her musical muscles and her desire to connect with others. *'Sweet dreams till sunbeams find you, sweet dreams that leave all worries behind you.'* People were clapping her now, encouraging her to go on. Next she sang: *Poor little rich girl* from Noel Coward's 1925 Revue. The backing was trickier, but Martin kept the melody.

> *In lives of leisure*
> *The craze for pleasure steadily grows:*
> *Cocktails and laughter.*
> *But what comes after?*
> *Nobody knows!*

You're weaving love into a mad jazz pattern,
Rules by pantaloons
Poor little rich girl,
Don't drop a stitch too soon.

When her numbers were up, she retreated to her table, candles guttering, the wooden floor swaying. Someone banged the table in approval. One or two beamed at her as she passed. *'Encore!'* shouted another. She felt elated but strangely alone; she longed to have Derek alongside. Her head was buzzing the hum of French around her. Dolores poured her a large glass of red wine. *'Bien. Vous avez fait bien,'* she said.

'Thank you,' murmured Mo, feeling like a fish in and out of water: joyous in singing one minute, awkward at table the next.

Jean Luc joined them. 'They liked you.'

All at once, in the corner, voices were raised. A scuffle was breaking out. A large man knocked back a chair. Voices clashed as someone threw a punch, another hit back – within seconds a full-blown fight had erupted.

'Sing. Sing,' urged Jean Luc. 'Distract them!' Dolores and Mo looked at each other and got to their feet. Jean Luc rushed over to the mêlée, joined by a waiter. They managed to pull apart the warring parties. Insults, execrations flew through the air. People shook themselves down, muttering.

Dolores sang, then Mo, cobbling between them a mix of French and English tunes. Martin took it all in his stride, blending melodies as best he could. The fighters slunk back to their tables. It reminded Mo of Friday nights at The Mare's Head, when men had wages in their pockets and heads full of politics and the stupid ways of the world.

The sight of fighting men left a bitter aftertaste. It reeked too much of a past she was striving to push away. It reminded her of dogs penned up without food. It reminded her of the squabbling Russian family in a constant litany of shrieking voices. Physical violence made her ill. Though it was not uncommon for men to beat their wives, Pa did not, as a rule, hit Ma. Despite himself, he respected her too deeply. So the one time violence broke out between them was etched in Mo's mind.

It was not long after she'd fled home to work as a life model in Chelsea Polytechnic and just before she married Derek. She'd entered The Mare's Head by a side door, slipping in when the pub was almost empty. Ma was clearing away, reminding Pa of the casks that needed shifting, empties to be got ready for the draymen. 'Morwenna's in the family way,' she'd started: 'you mark my words, as clear as day.'

Down came his hand across her cheek, like the crack of a whip. She recalled the look of horror on Ma's face, eyes wide, mouth agape. The few remaining bar-huggers had shifted off, sensing trouble. Rage spent, Pa looked sheepish. Until that moment Mo had not realised that a man could strike a woman and get away with it. It shook her to the core.

Now the old sourness curdled in her stomach. As the commotion died down, people were talking and tippling as if nothing had happened. The offending parties steered clear of each other. One left the café, banging into chairs as he went. Jean Luc reappeared. 'Carry on,' he said. 'Just sing.'

'You are my sunshine, my only sunshine,' Mo struck up. It sounded inane, but it was the best she could manage. She repeated the phrase: *'You are my sunshine…'* One or two of the nearby people started mouthing the words.

Later, Jean Luc approached. 'You kept them sweet,' he said and waved a fifty Franc note under her nose. Her neck reddened; this was an order of vulgarity she thought she'd never experience again. But she wanted the money all the same. Without it she was not validated. She took it and folded it into her purse. Last time there had been a rose and glasses of wine. She nodded goodbye to Dolores and Martin and slipped out.

Chapter Eight *Derek*

Derek was surprised to find their rooms empty when he returned from the gallery. He made himself tea in the samovar. He found himself staring at it. Mo had seen it in the flea market by Les Halles and bought it on impulse for the Russian family. 'A piece of home,' she'd said, handing it over. But Olga was not impressed. 'What do I want with all that?' she'd muttered. Mo only laughed and started using the thing herself. Now it sat on the sideboard along with programmes from shows and other salvaged *bric à brac*. She liked to gather items from various places, even the river. Every so often she had a clear out and replaced them with other, equally disparate items. But the samovar stayed on.

As he sat on the sofa listening to the sounds of the night, he pondered the exhibition. His five studies of the post-war mood fit together well enough, considering he hadn't envisaged them as a series. He'd merely stood before his easel and done as Patrick told him to do: trust his daemon and see what emerges. Ideas and images would erupt, coalesce and push him in the true direction.

The paintings of the Russians, however, haunted him.

These people had been mauled by history: uprooted and thrust against the wall. Many were driven from their homes. Others fled. Some had fought against the Germans in the bitter Russian winter without adequate food or ammunition, even without proper boots on their feet, Dimitri had told him, only the baste shoes and *valenki* – peasant leg wrappings; others witnessed mayhem in their streets and villages. They dared not approach that maelstrom head-on. Rather it was in the colours and angles of their work. The totality of the pictures was a volatile mix, not easy to stomach.

It was impossible, if one listened to one's humanity, not to offer them an outlet. They strove to communicate, despite all. They were fighting against the titans of oblivion and suppression. He could not bear too much of it though. He'd always been glad in the end that he escaped the fighting. In London the true story of the war was only just emerging. *Journey's End,* which started as a rehearsed reading in The Apollo Theatre, was pushing people towards the new decade. The play, depicting the futility and madness of the Trenches, offered a stark contrast to Noel Coward's social froth.

But where the blazes was Mo?

He got up and started pacing the rooms. The emptiness gaped back at him, in accusation. Just how safe was a young woman in the darkened streets of Paris? There were many desperate and poor people about. Mo, he whispered. He gave a deep sigh. He'd been so bent on getting things right at the gallery he'd pushed her to one side. But Pierre had left in good time. Perhaps they'd stopped for a drink.

A church bell tolled the hour. Last time the club had given out at eleven. It was now one o'clock. Time enough for them to walk the winding streets down from Montmartre. He pictured her slight figure in a lamp-lit street, tottering on heeled shoes, and was engulfed by a wave of guilt and tenderness. Pierre said the streets were safe. But what did he know? He was a Parisian and a man of sturdy stature.

Chapter Nine *Mo*

Mo started on the downward trek to Marais, wandering along narrow streets. A drunken couple meandered in front of her, hips together, pausing here and there in doorways for a swift embrace, splutters of merriment between the urgency of lust. A crescent moon hung above jagged rooftops, a scattering of fine cloud chasing across it. She passed by restaurants, getting a whiff of wine and roasting meat from open doorways. Further on, where it was darker, a rat scuttled in the gutter. She heard footsteps behind, the deliberate tread of measured strides. She carried on at a brisk pace, in the middle of the street, veering towards better-lit patches. It was madness to be out in this strange city alone. Why wasn't Derek here to protect her, or Pierre?

Still she could still hear the steps echoing hers. She quickened her pace and they grew quicker too. She scurried towards the next lamppost, let out a resolute breath and turned on her heels. Nothing. Only shadows and echoes of laughter higher up the hill, the sound of the trumpet blasting, a blues singer scaling the heights. She scolded herself for being fearful. Night could bring out all manner of goblins if you let it. She walked briskly downhill. She had left Sacré Coeur and its winding paths behind her, together with the mills and ateliers, tumbledown tenements and remnants of artists' hovels. The ground was levelling out. From a side street she saw two men approaching, one with broad shoulders and a Homburg obscuring his face, the other was slight and light on his feet. They passed her by.

And then, as if from nowhere, was a third man. Crossed by his tall shadow, she started. 'Madame,' he said, 'it is not good for you to be out at such an hour.' She pulled away, but before she had time to respond he continued: 'I saw you perform. Allow me to present myself …' He addressed her in English. She counted to ten, much as she did when countering stage fright.

The man drew closer so she could almost feel his breath on her face. 'Can I accompany you – make sure you don't suffer – how do you say – an inconvenience?' The voice was more cultured than she expected. She stepped back to get a better view, but the shadows played over him. Then he turned toward the street light and she caught sight of his face with its intensity of expression.

'Why are you following me?' Her voice was sharp.

'I wanted to speak to you, after you sang. But you left so quickly.' She heard footsteps in the lane that cut across at an angle. She hurried towards them, but the man kept pace. He cleared his throat. 'Sorry Madame, I had no wish to alarm you. Allow me to introduce myself. I am Anton Lensky. This is the second time I heard you sing. I wanted to – forgive the audacity – to make your acquaintance.'

Somewhat relieved, Mo took his proffered hand. It was dry and firm. 'As I said you left so quickly. I wanted Monsieur Fresnais to introduce us…' She put her hands under her cape, wanting to move on and away. The other footsteps faded, leaving them alone.

'Look Monsieur, I need to be getting home, so if you will excuse me…'

'A coffee, a glass of wine – may I invite you?' His tone was urgent. 'I know this is not *convenable* – usual, but I do not want to miss the chance.'

'Monsieur, really I do not think…' She wanted to say she was not what he took her for, but the words failed.

'I have an interest in your voice.'

Others had said the same to her, leading her on but wanting, when all was said and done, to enjoy her body more than her voice. For now, she was eager to get back to Derek and tell him how it had all gone. 'Monsieur, I am tired after my performance.'

'Of course – let me not stop you. I will – if you permit – walk a little way alongside you.' She pushed forward, her heeled shoes tapping the cobblestones. He was striding alongside, throwing glances in her direction.

She stared at the ground, afraid here and there of losing her footing in the dark patches. Eventually they came to a wider boulevard with lights and milling people. She stopped outside a brightly lit restaurant. She would not budge until the man left her side. She fumbled in her clutch bag for a cigarette, but before she could light it he was flicking on a gold lighter, which flared up, revealing his face. He had full cheeks and a sensuous mouth but sensitive, alert eyes. He was well dressed in a grey lounge suit and white silk shirt.

'Please do not mistake my intention,' he repeated. She did not want to hear more. He was being inordinately careful. She'd grown used to the direct French manner and the volatility of exchanges where umbrage turned to anger and swiftly back again. His caution was unnerving. 'It's like this, you see, Madame, I am in the business. I look for singers of talent and promise. Such a one I see in you. Rarely have I heard a talent such as yours.'

Mo held the cigarette to her mouth and blew a long stream of blue smoke. 'So what is it – this fascination with me?' she demanded. 'Is it usual to go stalking a young woman in the dark streets of Paris?'

He laughed. 'No, it is not usual. It is also not usual for such a young woman to be walking home unaccompanied at this hour.'

'Do you fear then for my safety?' She gave a dry little laugh. They could be so wily these men on the prowl.

'In all honesty, yes. Not that someone will fall upon you and rob you, though that, too, is not unknown, but that some man or men might come and pester you.'

'Like you're doing, you mean?'

He was taken aback: 'Do you take me for a scoundrel?' She laughed. The word scoundrel sounded odd on his lips. 'Look, if you don't trust me, I'll go in here and see if they'll get a taxi for you and then give you my card as a token of honesty.'

His quick-wittedness left her speechless. How could she object to such gentlemanly behaviour? His English was impeccable. She paused, uncertain how to proceed. Seeing her hesitancy, he proclaimed: 'That's it. That is exactly what I shall do. Here…' He rifled in a side pocket. 'Here is my card.'

She took it, examined its perfect gilt lettering and put it away in her bag. He opened the door to the restaurant. 'While we wait for your ride will you permit me to buy you a little nightcap, a cognac perhaps? I know this restaurant well.'

She tilted her head to one side, still wary. He held out a chair for her. As she settled herself he called over to the patron. 'Straight away, Monsieur Lensky.' Before she could protest two cognacs had arrived. Lensky looked towards her.

'I visit these cafés with music. There are several in North Paris. It's where you find the new talent – singers not yet part of the established crowd. Talent is what interests me: pure raw talent. I don't want an imitation of what's already going round.'

Mo breathed in her surroundings, noting the warm glow from candles and kerosene lamps, mahogany furniture and the better class of clientele. She caught the rich aroma of ragoût sprinkled with herbs, giving a sense of well-being and autumn. She gazed at bunches of dark red dahlias and late roses on the russet velvet tablecloths. She slipped off her cape. Slid off her shoes, which had begun to pinch. Understandable, she mused, why people grow attached to the things money can buy. Already in her meanderings she'd seen poverty in Paris. You didn't have to go under the bridges of the Seine to see the poor – though there were plenty there – they hung around the cheap drab hotels on the edge of Montmartre and in parts of the Latin Quarter.

Her stomach growled, reminding her she'd not eaten for hours. She glanced across to see whether Lensky had noticed. If he did, he gave no indication of it, but two minutes later waved the menu card in front of her. 'A little something to eat, Madame?'

She blushed. The potent blend of flavours in the air set her gastric juices flowing. 'I'm fine. Thank you,' she said faintly, catching a whiff of pheasant in red wine. My God, she had not witnessed food like that since Claridge's. Light gleamed on the silver of cutlery, the impeccably dressed waiter glided in and out of the diners delivering delectable dishes. Lensky gave a light chuckle.

'The pheasant ragoût is superb. They bring braces in from Fontainebleau. I know the estate.' He spoke with an authority, which benumbed her. She feared all that might go along with the meal. If she said yes to the food, wine would follow and wine on top of cognac on top of the wine she had already drunk was not a good idea. The patron approached. He was smooth-cheeked and had a pleasing blend of knowledge and courtesy. It was like viewing a work of art. But it was a trap. She shifted forward in her seat.

'Have you asked him about the taxi?'

'Ah yes, Madame would like a taxi to take her to…?'

'Marais. Rue Montignac,' she said.

'Very well, Madame.'

There was a pause, the patron looked towards Lensky who waved his hand. 'I'll have the pheasant. Bring two plates. Madame might change her mind.' Mo gave a little sigh. 'Now where were we – ah yes, my search for vocal perfection,' continued Lensky.

Close to, she noticed he had grey-green eyes. They had a certain melancholy about them, shot through with an air of discernment. His mouth betrayed a sensuous, fastidious nature. She grew fearful as she looked at him. She had no wish to get out of her depth. 'Your voice has a rare combination of melody and power. But your technique is poor. Sometimes you run out of breath and strain for notes.'

His critique flummoxed her. How dare he? Seeing her reaction he smiled. 'Forgive the directness, Madame. I see you are not one to be easily persuaded or talked round …' He lifted his hand to embrace all that lay before them in the café. 'You are – if my judgement does not play false – a serious woman. You are a person who prefers the direct approach and SO…'

Before he could expand further the food arrived. Mo was by this time faint with hunger. 'Please be my guest. I am not seeking – if I may put it plainly – to win you round by…'

'Wining and dining,' she added, unable to suppress a smile as he read her so clearly. 'Do you run some sort of music establishment then?' she ventured.

The waiter brought another platter with vegetables and began to serve the ragoût. Without being asked to he put a portion of the pheasant onto her plate. She watched as he lined up the mushrooms on one side and added crisped potatoes. Lensky was silent as the waiter completed his task.

'I do,' he said at length. 'Not quite in the manner of L'Etoile, but along similar lines. It is a *boîte* that offers food while people listen to music and dance. More like a New York nightclub. In fact, we often have jazz musicians. Music is more central to the place. Much as I respect what Fresnais is doing, it's a rough joint. That's not the first time I've seen a fight …And he's only been open a few weeks.' She raised her eyebrows. 'Did it shock you?' he asked. She was about to say that it was run-of-the-mill where she came from but thought better of it.

'*Bref,* I would like to have you come and do a spot for us. See how it works out. I don't want to make any false promises. I have heard your voice and think you might fit in. Though, as I said earlier you need to improve your technique. Would you be willing to do that?'

She bristled. The prospect both excited and irked her. Hadn't she worked hard enough already?

'Don't look so alarmed. You have all the right ingredients.

You just need a little help getting there.' She looked across at him, not knowing what to say. She put a forkful of pheasant goulash into her mouth. It was divine.

* * *

'There is something else I want to tell you,' Lensky said after nearly an hour had elapsed and they'd seen off more wine. By now they had demolished the pot of pheasant ragoût and were lingering over cheese, Mo having abandoned any attempt to resist her hunger. Satiated, the world seemed to her a jollier, more possible place. Lensky's grey-green eyes were shining at her in admiration.

'And that would be?' She tilted her head towards him. I can play this game, she thought. I am in charge of the situation. Her confidence was growing by the minute. What need had she to sing in cafés of dubious repute where fights and violence were the order of the day?

'I am a manager and business man, but in my soul' – here he tapped his chest lightly. 'I am a poet. Words matter. Tunes matter. We are little else but animals if we do not use sensibility and gifts of higher humanity.'

The high-flown words caught her off-guard. 'Where did you learn your English?'

'Ah that. I had an English governess. It was all the fashion.'

'Have you spent time in Britain?

'I went there after the war.'

'Did you like it?'

'It was good for theatre, good for business. But Paris is in my blood. I cannot be away from here for long. It is a magnet, although it has its disadvantages.'

'Monsieur, it's getting late. I need to go.' She was torn between the urge to leave and the urge to stay. A world of opportunity sparkled at her from Lensky, the shadow of misgiving dwindling the longer she remained in his company.

He took out a cigarette. '*Vous permettez,* Madame?' She nodded and pushed away the plate of half-finished cheese. 'I've written songs since I was a boy. Many not fit for consumption.' A businessman and a poet? It was an unlikely combination. 'Beauty, love, suffering – you name it – you don't have to reach far for material. It is all around you.'

But are your songs any good, she wanted to ask. Now he was holding forth, cigarette in one hand, wine in another. It seemed cruel to prick his bubble. 'You write for singers or for yourself?'

'Both. That is, until a couple of years ago.'

'What happened?'

'I didn't want to become a dilettante. So I sing only in private.'

The lateness of the hour was beginning to tell, she barely disguised a yawn and then another. 'So how is it with this taxi?'

Chapter Ten *Mo*

When Mo and Derek eventually found themselves back together there were stories to tell, had they been so minded. Mo though, was squiffy and giggly into the bargain when she finally rolled up in a taxi after one thirty. She saw drunks shuffling by, a couple of prostitutes on the corner with white painted faces, looking desperate with so few clients about. Cabs were coming and going, not down their alley but in the nearby Rue Montignac.

As she stumbled from the taxi she caught sight of Derek by the streetlight. 'So you waited up for me, my precious?'

'Where have you been all this time?'

'Did you fear the big bad wolf might have come for me?'

'Where have you been?'

'Plotting and scheming...'

He was looking at her through his eyebrows. 'What are you talking about, Mo? What have you been up to?'

She laughed. 'You don't mean to tell me you're jealous, do you?' She gave a little twirl and started singing: *'If you were the only boy in the world…'* She caught hold of him by his jacket till he too was forced to swirl around. 'Wait till I tell you what happened. I got followed back from the club...'

They started mounting the stairs. She clattered as she went up, grabbing the banister and humming. 'A damn good meal I had while you were discussing the finer points of art.'

'Mo keep quiet, you'll wake the neighbours.'

'We don't have any.'

'Downstairs I mean. The landlord is here tonight. It's rent day tomorrow, don't forget.'

'I thought it was love day.'

Derek glowered at her. 'Behave yourself, will you. I leave you alone for an evening and you turn up in such a state. I was worried stiff about you. There are so many strangers in Paris. We don't know how safe it is. Where was Pierre?'

She shrugged. They reached their rooms. By now she thought better of stoking his jealousy and became subdued, confused by the events of the evening and longing for bed. Derek sat her down on the sofa and went to fetch a jug of water.

'I want to hear all about it,' he said in a more conciliatory tone, guilt-stricken no doubt that he had left her to her own devices. She felt weariness come over her and her eyelids drooped. She put the half empty glass on the table. 'So what's this you're telling me? Were you really followed?' She snuggled against the sofa wanting to drift off into the darkness of sleep, but Derek was prodding her awake. 'Don't fall asleep there. I want to hear what happened.'

'I sang. They liked me. There was a fight. We sang again I got some money and then I was followed by a man, who wants to offer me work. He runs another club and wants me to do a spot in his nightclub...'

This came out in a breathless rush. Beside her Derek was brooding. Through the haze of her alcoholic stupor she was glad to see she was having an effect on him. She leaned her head onto his shoulder and intertwined her fingers in his. 'Don't worry, I can take care of myself. I took everything he said with a pinch of salt.'

Derek pulled away. 'But he invited you to dinner and plied you with drinks.'

'What of it? I had to wait for a taxi to bring me home. I had a tipple while I waited. And pheasant – mmm – so delicious, I haven't eaten like that in ages.' Derek got to his feet. She could see he was longing to shake her, slap her even. She gave a light laugh.

'Mo you've ... you can't just allow yourself to go with a stranger. Anything could have happened.'

'I can take care of myself,' she repeated and stretched. 'And now I'm longing for my bed. Aren't you? I'm so tired… It's almost two, I think.' She could sense him fuming and for a moment was afraid. She sought to divert him. 'There was a fight, you know. Chairs weren't thrown but punches were. It was tense. Reminded me of the public bar in The Mare's Head on a Friday…'

Derek sighed. 'I'm sorry, Mo. I should have gone with you.' This sudden contrition disarmed her. She was silent. It *was* rash to have allowed herself to be treated to a meal.

'I don't know where it will all lead… He said I needed to learn how – how to control my vocal chords. He was serious about all that.' She started humming: '…*always look on the bright side of life.*' But she was so tired and inebriated she forgot the rest of the words. Derek was pulling on her clothes, hoisting her up from the sofa and propelling her towards the bedroom.

'You need to sleep this off. We can talk in the morning.' He sounded stern. Many a man, she thought, might have lashed out at her.

'Derek darling. I love you. You do know that? No other man comes anywhere near you.' She went to bite his hand in play. He shrugged her off.

'Don't let this happen again,' he growled.

'Why not? I am a free spirit just like you.' He pushed her onto the bed. 'My love,' she pleaded. 'Come here.'

He drew away. 'You stink of cognac.'

Chapter Eleven *Lensky*

Mo Eaton was a delicious creature, there were no two ways about it. The moment he clapped eyes on her he could tell there was a raw energy, a well of talent wanting to gush up and express itself. If not controlled it would spill needlessly, drain away into disparate channels. It was not his habit to follow women in the night. No wonder she'd misconstrued his intentions. It took some persuading to keep her interest, to stop her slipping away into the shadows. She was adaptable and creative. He could tell that by the way she'd handled that ugly scene when violence erupted. Such incidents could wobble an audience and risked escalation. Luckily the spat had been snuffed at source.

He had seen more than enough random scraps leading to flare-ups. Far too many. He drained the rest of his cognac. It was time to be getting home. He asked the management to call a taxi and sat back to enjoy the last of his cigar. He paid the bill, nodded to the maître d'hôte and got into the waiting cab.

Later that night, as he was drifting off to sleep, the anger of the voices in L'Etoile reverberated through him. In them he caught the outrage of the peasant, kept down for far too many centuries, an outrage ready to tag on to any tatter of political belief, any half articulate idiot who could get up and thump a tub, drawing out the toxic hatred.

* * *

Saratov Province was a long way off. He thought he had forsaken forever the ties of Mother Russia but sometimes, woken in the night by the horrid image of his father's favourite thoroughbred horse with its tail aflame with kerosene, he knew he was caught forever in her invisible web. It wasn't just his own family who were affected: when the peasants rioted in the 1905 Revolution they had killed many a master's livestock and torched the horses.

Chapter Twelve *Derek*

Derek was embroiled in getting L'Atelier Blanc up to scratch. It was a larger venue than the warehouse where he and Pierre had exhibited before, was better known and had more floor space. The other galleries on the Left Bank had been alerted. Today he and Pierre had been in since early on, sweeping and rendering the rooms as presentable as possible; meanwhile Dimitri was working on boards, which would provide background notes on the painters.

Derek was excited now about the show: it had such strong links with the movements of the times it would surely spark curiosity. Alexander, the tallest of the Russians, approached Derek and looked at him solemnly. 'You think we will get many to come and see us – we refugees from the East?'

'No, they'll boycott you on account of your beards,' said Derek. The solemnity of the other got to him. They rarely smiled, these Russians; though he'd heard they sometimes laughed till the tears ran down their faces. It was hard to place Alexander. He had the broad, toughened hands of a worker, but his face was fine-chiselled and his closely set eyes gave him a shrewd, slightly shifty look. Just to look at him inspired interest and fear. His French was reasonable so Derek assumed he had been in Paris some time. When he realised that Derek was ragging him, he let out a hearty guffaw.

'I've seen more beards here than whores,' he retorted in a deep voice. Derek wondered why Alexander had been forced to flee the Motherland. He knew a little about the Russians in Paris from Dimitri. He'd told him that there were as many White Russians here as Red, as many left-wing Russians as right-wing. The first influx of emigrés in the nineteenth century brought members of the old liberal intelligentsia, followed by Revolutionaries escaping the Tsar's Secret Police. After the 1917 Revolution emigration swelled into a tidal wave of refugees from every social class – Romanov Grand Dukes and Princes, Imperial ballet dancers, Tsarist officers who'd fought for the Whites in the Civil War and thousands of middle class families, workers and peasants escaping the famines of the 1920s. Berlin and Paris were seething with multitudes of factions and their petty and not so petty hatreds. Even Old Guard Bolsheviks were now fleeing Russia as Stalin imprisoned or murdered anyone who opposed him. He'd heard so many tales in the last few days: tales of arbitrary imprisonments, summary executions and a system of secret police terror. Artists who refused to conform to the officially sanctioned Social Realism were voting with their feet. Yet artists were creative souls who shifted boundaries, so it was hard for him to gauge any individual's political standing.

'They'll come,' he reassured Alexander. 'First out of curiosity and then word will spread. They're disposed to appreciate you.' When Alexander showed puzzlement, he continued. 'There's been such a strong cultural exchange between France and Russia over the years...' Alexander nodded. 'They'll note the originality. See how different these works are. Whether you sell any is another question.'

For some that was the burning issue. The poorer amongst them had tried for jobs as waiters and *plongeurs,* washer-uppers, in the many cafés, but even these jobs were hard to come by. There were just too many hungry foreigners around willing to do anything to scrape by. He liked the way the Russians stuck it out. Several slept in a dosshouse near Rue Montignac in their *quartier*. He came upon them in the evenings, loitering outside. Many did not yet speak French, though some did.

The more educated spoke it fluently. It had long been the language of polite society and even in these post-revolutionary times the habit hung on. The privileged, whose families had led charmed lives under the Tsars, split into subgroups which flared up now and then: some favoured revolution and an upending of the class system, while others had little wish for change. Still others were intellectuals from Moscow and St Petersburg who'd fallen foul of the Bolshevik government. Lenin had died. He was embalmed and venerated as a secular saint while Stalin consolidated his grip on the country. Hopes had faded that there could be any change of regime anytime soon.

He walked through the gallery, while Alexander continued brooding over his own paintings in the largest and best lit of the rooms. Dimitri and Pierre had gone by now. Derek left the gallery soon after. Outside he wound down the sloping path to the Seine. He and Pierre had distributed handbills in the Rôtonde, the Dôme and other popular cafés. They'd visited as many of the ateliers, studios and *vernissages,* as they could. Gertrude Stein, the *grande dame* of art patrons, knew about the exhibition. He'd called on her one evening with Dimitri to oil the way for the Russians, one or two of whom were invited to her next *soirée*. While Alice Toklas, her partner, offered them tea from a samovar and almond cookies, the Russians gaped at the Picassos, Braques and Miros crammed together on the walls.

He'd become so busy that he'd scarcely had time to talk to Mo after her encounter with Anton Lensky. He'd not quite known what to say to her. Not that she had let him down or betrayed him – she'd been forthright about what happened. Pierre was mortified he'd missed her – by just minutes, it transpired. Derek mulled it over: would he prefer her to be depressed and without work or be up there where other men could see her and even lure her away from him? He brushed off the question.

He found a seat at a café overlooking the water, ordered coffee and cognac. The cognac warmed his throat. He tapped his chest, eyes watering. Was he genuine, this man asking Mo to perform for him? He'd have to meet him to find out, once the exhibition was underway there'd be time for that. He heard the heavy tread of someone approaching. He turned. Alexander had tracked him down. 'Coffee? Cognac?' He pulled up a chair for him. The other waved to the waiter and ordered vodka.

'It's like this,' began Alexander, stroking his beard. 'We need an agent to help us. Will you do that for us?' He seemed to have become the self-selected spokesman for the group. Dimitri had sidestepped that role, inferring he was not quite one of them. There were twelve in the core group: The Apostles, they named themselves. Their backgrounds were as diverse as they came.

Alexander wrapped his fist round the vodka and eye-balled Derek. 'Success will come quicker if you are behind us.'

'What about Dimitri? He has lived here longer than I have. He knows the other galleries owners and painters. Even people from the Academies.'

'No, no. It's no good. We want a cool-headed Englishman.'

Derek laughed. Though he might let himself be cast in that light if it suited his purposes, he knew it was not a sound judgement. He waved to the waiter to bring more vodka and cognac.

'We are so – so different,' said Alexander. 'We fight about this and that. We are fatalistic. We'd rather sit over vodka and philosophise than get something started.'

'I doubt that,' said Derek. 'Look at the Revolution...'

'Look, my friend. Russia is a ... a riddle. Too many centuries of servitude, Now too many ideas, too much centralisation. It is a vast place… too many steppes, too many Soviets with too many opinions… and now Stalin, the strongman… the Cheka getting busier every day. Best not to talk about what happens in Russia.'

He looked down at the ground and Derek was momentarily oppressed by his sullen presence. Who knew what Alexander had been forced to witness? What privations he'd suffered?

'You will come tonight to meet the others, yes?' His dark eyes under bushy brows pleaded. Derek would like to know his story, but as always there was no time. He considered his request, was on the point of turning him down, thinking of Mo, but something was tugging at him. 'You look sad,' said Alexander.

'No, not sad. I'm considering.'

'Don't consider too long. Our pockets are empty. We must become known here.'

'I'm not the best person to do that for you.'

'We think you are. We have talked about it. English is good. You have connections in London, no?'

'Barely. I know a few theatre directors and colleges…'

'Perfect. Paris is a good – how do you say – point of arrival but it cannot contain us all.' Derek was tempted by the trust the man was placing in him. Could they see something in him he was unaware of? 'We are meeting in our club. You will come, I think, to talk some more before you make up your mind?'

Derek found it hard to say no. What did it matter whether it was the weight of history leading him on or sheer bravado?

* * *

The club was little more than a cellar down a side street in Montparnasse. The upper storeys looked rickety. A dilapidated fence leaned into the alleyway. As he entered the bar he was hit by a fug of smoke from the *papirosi,* Russian cigarettes, and a cloud from the wood-burning stove. Several tables had been pushed together and bunched around them were the Russian artists. 'You know Ivan, Dimitri, Serge?'

He nodded in response to their openly enquiring expressions. Bottles of vodka and wine were lined up, most of them already empty. Someone was strumming a balalaika. Two or three of the men were singing, their voices down in their boots, harmonising. Others were arguing. Two had their arms locked in a table wrestle.

'So my friends, here we have the man you wanted to meet. Derek Eaton, painter, theatre designer and citizen of Great Britain.' There was an outbreak of laughter and two or three of them banged the table in enthusiasm. Derek glanced around, at once taken by the warmth of their exchanges. They were a colourful crew. Even after a short encounter he'd come to admire their passion, though it also perturbed him. Sometimes these painters seemed mad. They had a tragic outlook on life, yet he'd heard they'd dance and sing as though the devil were in them.

More were coming into place. Amongst them he noticed a couple of women. One was tall and blonde with a broad Slavic face. The other, who had quick, lively movements, caught his interest. Dark-haired, slender and with an upright proud bearing, she reminded him of a gypsy. She flung her head back and laughed at a joke someone had made.

'Ah,' said Alexander, noting the direction of Derek's gaze. 'Let me introduce you to Tanya and her friend, Karine.'

Chapter Thirteen *Mo*

If she was to make progress Mo must see Lensky again, in broad daylight. Wine talks. Pheasant ragoût on an empty stomach talks. The cold clear light of a late October morning would show up all the creases in his proposal. He had given her his card and urged her to contact him.

After her tipsy return home Derek seemed disinclined to discuss Lensky. When she tried to insist he asked her to hold fire until the exhibition was underway. He was not trying to control her with his silence, she concluded; he was just falling deeper into his work. But decisions had to be made: Fresnais had asked her to perform again and there was Lensky with his offer. She had spent enough time cogitating. She was wary of a descent into melancholy for there were times she felt she was clambering up the side of a slimy well. In front of an audience, she became alive. A current passed between her and them, like Mesmerism she'd once heard of. Music melted ice and cut through, arousing the spirit. Who could doubt it?

She surveyed the rumpled sheets of the bed, long since vacated by Derek, and watched the sun streaking shadows through the ancient shutters. She jumped up and thrust them open, threw up her arms as if to welcome in this most female of cities. Ah ah aaaah, she opened her throat and half gargled, half sang until she spluttered into laughter. The city was welcoming her as one of its own. No longer was she an envious onlooker from the sidelines, or a *flâneuse,* seeking to imitate elegant Parisiennes in dress, gestures, or speech. *Arriviste:* Derek had one day called those who sought respectability, acceptance and money. What of it? She would be the *arriviste par excellence.*

She ran downstairs and quickly did her ablutions, for once enjoying the bracing shock of cold water on her skin. As she put on her skirt she noticed it was loose, irregular meals and walking around Paris making her thin. So much the better: she would fit the gamin, flat-chested look of the singers here to perfection. She sent Lensky a *pneumatique* and sat over a café crème rehearsing the questions she needed to ask. He got back to her straightaway and suggested a place on Boulevard Saint Michel. She suppressed butterflies stirring in her stomach as she sped there.

Lensky was frowning as he read *Le Figaro*. By day he looked so very grown-up and serious. He was older than she recalled and that shocked her. She noticed a touch of grey at the temples, lines drawn between his nose and the edges of his mouth. He was a good-looking, self-possessed man: not someone to be trifled with. He was wearing an open-necked blue shirt with a black velvet smoking jacket and had a black hat pushed towards the back of his head.

'Ah Madame, Mademoiselle. I am so delighted to see you again. How beautiful you look today!' He took off his hat and held up her hand to brush it with his lips. Slightly unsettled, she sat down beside him. No one had ever done that before. All the questions she'd lined up fled. 'You will join me for an aperitif, a light lunch?' He touched the menu in front of him. 'The *maître d'hôte* recommends turbot.'

'I'm not hungry,' she said quietly but he only replied:

'You always say that,' as if they were the oldest of acquaintances. His eyes unnerved her with their intelligence.

'One could get confused by the variety of food on offer here,' she said. 'We don't have that at home.'

'At home?' he queried.

'London. But I mean Hackney, East London, where I grew up. And you – where is home for you?' She realised from the slight heaviness of his accent that he might not be purely French. He looked at her from under his brows.

'My mother is from Paris, my father from Moscow.' A shadow passed across his face and he looked uneasy. 'Paris is full of foreigners. It makes me feel quite at home.' The waiter came over with two glasses of champagne. She gasped. 'I ordered them when I saw you coming,' he said.

She was about to say that his nose had been buried in *Le Figaro,* but instead lifted the coupe to her mouth. 'I thought it would be good to go over what we discussed before. I wasn't sure …'

'Whether I was serious?'

'I didn't want you to think… I wanted to clarify…' The more she spoke the more inept she felt. She wished Derek were there. If only he were not so busy. She turned to Lensky: 'A Russian father and a French mother? How exotic. I notice your manners. Kissing the hand.'

'It's ingrained, you know, these traces of civility from another era.' His response intrigued her: she was used to the arch tones of the English upper class, had rubbed shoulders with the middle-class in her theatre work and had grown out of the rough-speaking East End working-class. Half Russian impresarios with French mothers left her baffled. She frowned. What was he expecting from her? These days she trusted few. Derek had betrayed her. Her parents had let her down. Everybody let everybody down in one way or another.

'You look pensive,' remarked Lensky.

She gave a nonchalant shrug. 'We are both setting ourselves up in Paris, my husband and me. But he has a head start. He has contacts here.'

'You are confident before an audience.'

She pictured Ma turning from a careworn publican's wife into saucy artiste in a feathered hat, as she hummed and sang. She recalled Sandor Olmak's tapering fingers hovering over piano keys. 'It's in my blood,' she murmured. She looked across at him. 'So was your father a duke or something?' she asked cheerily.

Lensky gave a rueful smile. 'He was a writer, a Liberal, but yes somewhere in the family there were hectares of land, peasants tied to us for centuries – until the first Revolution.'

'So where did he meet your mother?'

'Here. Or at least in the Midi. He had a villa near the Riviera – and when he met my mother he decided he wanted to try a different life. He always did love Paris.'

'Did?'

'He is no longer… He died several years back.'

'And your mother?'

'She still lives down south. On the Riviera.' Mo could tell by the set of his mouth that he would rather not talk further about his origins. She was curious but thought better of pushing him. 'And you? Cockney sparrow, if I'm not mistaken? Bright as the day is long and just as sweet.'

She gave an uncertain smile. She guessed he must be well over forty, with years of experience behind him. It intrigued her why he should be focusing on her. There were surely many more elegant Frenchwomen about; but the voice, Knighton said it always came back to the voice. She must have been staring hard at him for he looked disconcerted. He tapped on the menu.

'Have you decided what you want yet?'

She sighed. They say the way to a man's heart is through the stomach. She wasn't a man but her appetite for good food was a weak spot in the otherwise set face she presented to the world. 'I'll have the consommé.' She chose the cheapest dish so as not to feel indebted. He nodded to the waiter and placed the order.

'I discussed your proposal with my husband.' She straightened her spine. 'He would like to meet you.' Even as she uttered this, she sensed she was letting power over her life slip through her fingers.

'That would be a good idea,' he replied, a little stiffly then reached down into a briefcase under the table. '*Voilà!* Some songs I thought might be suitable.' He flashed musical scores before her.

'I don't read music,' she said flatly.

He raised an eyebrow. 'I thought you might not, but you do read English, I take it? I got translations.' She bristled. Men so liked to be in control. Instead of snapping on the bait she pulled out her newly acquired spectacles. She hoped they gave her gravitas, for she'd done with the frothy chorus-girl persona. 'I made copies for you. These songs are several years old so there is nothing exclusive about them.'

He started to hum a catchy tune. A couple alongside turned to look, smiling indulgently. 'You have an audience,' she said.

They sank into silence. 'Look,' he said after a while. 'It's obvious you are unsure about me. I hardly blame you. But I had no other way of attracting your attention. You left L'Etoile in such a hurry…'

She threw a sly glance at him, unable, still, to determine whether or not the man was in earnest. The sceptic in her was on high alert. 'I had a manager before,' she fingered the base of her champagne glass. 'He liked my voice. Helped me in my career, but, well, there were complications.'

'Ah,' he said leaning back, 'between men and women there always are.' She sighed. She was tired of these clichés. Why did it have to be so fraught? If only she did not need that sort of help. But for all her experience she was not the best one to negotiate contracts and if she were honest, the last foray at L'Etoile had disappointed her. The set-up was much rougher than she cared for. She felt a stone in the pit of the stomach whenever she thought about it.

'What sort of complications? Artistic, contractual or personal?' His keen eyes were pressing her for an answer.

'I did well.' She paused, reluctant to speak about Knighton.

'And then?' persisted Lensky.

'The atmosphere in the West End started to change. Musicals

became less popular. They've had enough of fluff and distraction.'

'These things always go in circles,' he said. 'But were you not able to adapt what you were doing?'

Mo was pleased to see her consommé arrive. She tucked in, glad of the diversion: it still hurt to mull over the vicissitudes of her career. 'Sometimes managers prefer a new face. You get linked to certain shows or songs and it's not easy to do an about-turn. People don't believe in you if you do.'

'So coming to Paris may be the best thing for you?'

Caught between hunger and eagerness to engage, she spilled her soup. Lensky was working his way patiently through his *salade Niçoise*. She put down her spoon. 'The audience at L'Etoile – how typical was it?'

'I go around a lot of clubs. I get the feel of them. I'd say you could make yourself into whatever you want. You have a chameleon quality. A quickness of spirit and audacity…'

'That's the cockney in me.' This time she was cheered by his words.

'American music, jazz. Swing, negro musicians are all the rage now, alongside the street singers. People have put the war behind them. We lost more young men than you did. We were invaded. Not Paris, but big chunks of Northern France and Belgium. People want to dance, erase all traces of the past. Foreigners are welcome here. *Les Boches* perhaps not, but Americans, the British and Russians. At the moment Paris has open arms. Who knows for how much longer?'

'I hadn't seen it quite like that.'

'There is no time to lose, Madame, no time at all.'

Chapter Fourteen *Derek*

Derek had never met anyone quite like Tanya Sergeyevna. She stood five-foot six high, had the high-sculpted cheekbones of her Slavic forebears and eyes which spoke of an intense personality. She had a firm handshake. *'Enchantée,'* she said, not condescending to smile but measuring Derek with a glance that could cut rock. Who was this woman? She seemed to be assessing and running through him all at once.

'You are not exhibiting,' he said. She shook her head and laughed. He caught sight of her even, white teeth; she looked younger and prettier when she smiled.

'You assume I am a painter?'

'I – er – don't know.'

It would be bourgeois to assume she was here as the wife or mistress of one of the male painters. She must have caught his puzzlement because she went on: 'You may wonder what brings me here. It's true: I paint. I also sculpt and design sets for ballet and theatre. But no, I'm not in this show.'

He wanted to know why she had left Russia but felt reluctant to ask, as though any question was too banal, any observation too commonplace. He found himself staring at her neck as it gave the lie to her steeliness. It betrayed sensitivity, vulnerability. Alexander stood squarely between them, unaware of the mutual appraisal going on.

'Tanya Sergeyevna is one of our most talented sculptors,' he was saying. 'Her parents were both in the arts …her mother in the Itinerant tradition, I believe.' he went to say more but Tanya held up her hand to silence him.

Derek knew several in the group were the spiritual descendants of the Itinerants, those nineteenth-century Russian painters who had defied the restrictions of the Tsarist-controlled Academy of Fine Arts to show Russian life as it really was. Others were avant-garde, including shades of Vorticism, Futurism and Rayonism.

'Let's not get into all that now,' she said as if shutting a door. A flicker of sadness passed across her face at the mention of her mother. Derek guessed that people close to her might well have mouldered in some dank prison in Siberia. Of late he'd heard so many tales of hardship. They seemed to go with the Arctic tundra and sweeping emptiness of vast, wintry Steppes.

'Alexander mentioned you,' she said. 'He thought you might be able to help.'

'Yes, we were talking about…'

'I thought a Frenchman would be better – more in the know. But he convinced me that we need to widen our horizons.' Derek was slightly alarmed at the directness of her manner. It went with the cut-through-rock hazel eyes and a certain underlying impatience and restlessness. He wondered how stable she was. Upheaval did much to undermine one's sense of self.

In the new Russia women were no longer viewed as chattels and breeders of families, according to the official Bolshevik viewpoint. But in reality, he supposed, male insecurity and inertia would prevail. Despite himself, he was curious to find out her status in the group. 'I would like to see your work,' he said. She gazed at him longer than necessary as if gauging his sincerity.

'In time,' she said crisply. 'I am here today to help with the exhibition. To translate if need be. Help put the works into context. Shall we?' She began to walk further into the gallery. She brushed past him and he caught a whiff of musky perfume. Most of her compatriots smelled of sweat and slightly grubby clothing. Tanya took pains with her appearance. She had dangling earrings and a heavy necklace of amber around that vulnerable neck. Her skin was pale as milk.

'I suggest we walk through to gain an overall impression,

perhaps in silence, and then share our ideas afterwards?' Her desire to control was clear. It gave him a frisson of what – curiosity, delight? He wasn't sure. 'Dimitri has asked me to do this,' she said, as if wanting to dispel any doubt as to her right to be taking command. Something in her tone led Derek to believe that they might be lovers, or at least partaking of a deep trust and intimacy.

'I am sure that will be helpful,' he murmured. 'Perhaps we could work out some captions?'

She nodded. As they walked – by now Alexander had left to join a gaggle of artists smoking by the entrance – he wanted to keep glancing at her, wanted to find out more about her, ruffle her self-composure. Instead, compliant, he looked at picture after picture, composing pertinent comments to explain them to the wider public. Some were in the manner of the Itinerant school: often in dull colours, depicting everyday Russian scenes; they were realistic, exact, representational. He lingered by them.

He recalled the movement from his studies. Most Itinerant painters were from lowly backgrounds or were sympathetic to the *Narod,* the dark masses of the Russian peasantry. They had depicted scenes such Volga barge haulers or laundresses toiling in a dingy bathhouse. Most famous was Isaac Levitan's: *The Vladimirka Road.* It appeared to be a simple pastoral view of a featureless road stretching to the far horizon. But all Russians knew it depicted the *via dolorosa* along which thousands of prisoners trudged to exile in Siberia. Other pictures, abstract and harder to decipher, disturbed with their strange juxtapositions.

Tanya sighed, broke her self-imposed silence. 'These paintings reflect our conflicts. We believed it would be better under the Bolsheviks. They promised us *Svetloye Buduscheye* – the Shining Future – but things are worse than ever.' Her breathing became shallow. She calmed herself and moved on. He had the urge to touch her on the arm but restrained himself. She paused before his paintings, turned to him with the glimmer of a smile.

They carried on walking. By the time they had passed though all the rooms his head was buzzing with half-formed questions. But at this stage they were joined by Karine, the blonde woman he'd noticed at his first meeting with Tanya. She'd been waiting in the lobby for Tanya. They went off together.

Chapter Fifteen *Lensky*

Eastern mystery meets Western opportunity, thought Anton Lensky, gazing around Scheherazade. Money enough had been spent on it before, but he'd been happy to fork out for its recent refurbishment. He hoped that in re-opening the nightclub under a new name he was carving a new path, cutting away from the past and its dubious political entanglements. This move signalled his freedom as much as his desire to put music and performance centre-stage, where they belonged. In its former incarnation the club had been more about drinking, with music just thrown in for good measure.

The walls were pale mauve adorned with modish carpet hangings. It reminded him of the Leon Bakst designs for the *ballets russes,* which were still in vogue. How the French still adored the allure of the Orient! Scheherazade was a cut above dives such as L'Étoile, which in his view squandered the talent of its singers in a drive for profit. He glanced at the raised platform below an array of lights, at chairs and tables spaced out around the stage. Behind was a higher level. All in all, a hundred people could squeeze into the nightclub. Only a few weeks underway and already it was attracting a good clientele – people with means who were discerning in their tastes.

It was good to have a trade that was above board, good to retire at the end of the day having totted up the evening's takings knowing he had given satisfaction and promoted music of quality while slowly lining his pockets. He slept better these days. Only occasionally, as he drifted off, did the old fear of being caught out sneak up on him, the rough whisper in his ear that he was needed to undertake one more action for the Motherland, one last piece of the puzzle.

Chapter Sixteen *Derek*

The Russian texts were ready but the translations into French were poor and Pierre had been called in to help. The English was equally bad, so Derek offered to render the display boards comprehensible to the Anglo-Saxon world. For this, he would need to collaborate with Tanya, in order to make sure nothing vital was omitted.

In corners Derek caught whispers among the artists. They were venting their fears: they spoke of a backlash against innovation – Lenin had not been interested in artistic matters, but Stalin was. He had a sophisticated knowledge of music, literature, theatre and poetry. Now he persecuted artists because he knew how powerful they were. The only acceptable style was Social Realism. Artists were expected to churn out paintings celebrating 'the heroic proletariat.' Yet despite this the Russian avant-garde was flourishing and this show proved it.

'You've been pushed to one side by us loud and melodramatic Russians,' said Tanya a day before they were due to open. 'When you planned your exhibition we weren't anywhere in sight.' She spoke with a lilt he found alluring. The accent was softer than a German one, less nuanced than French. He was unsure how to respond to her assertion, for there was truth in it.

'Perhaps your need is greater than ours.'

'*Ladno!* That's noble of you, I'm sure.' She looked at him askance.

He laughed. 'Not noble at all. Some of the work is riveting.' They were standing in the entrance lobby. He hovered. There were things he needed to be getting on with, but he was reluctant to move. It was rare enough to meet female artists, even rarer to come across a sculptress. Tanya, he reckoned, was a woman who would shatter norms with glee. The constraints of being an émigrée and thus dependent on the goodwill of the host country would not daunt her. He imagined she would not be easy to confront. Her skills as organiser he was yet to see.

'Your work intrigues me,' she said. 'It's unusual for an Englishman – considering you have such little connection with Surrealism.'

'Have you been in Paris long?' he asked.

She shrugged. 'My parents brought me to Paris before the Revolution when I was quite young. After the Revolution I got a job as an assistant to Anatoly Lunacharsky.'

Though embarrassed by his ignorance, Derek was curious: 'Who?'

'He was the Soviet People's Commissar for Education but also a playwright and a very cultured man.' She sniffed. 'Probably why he no longer holds that post.'

'I see.'

'My father knew him when he lived in Paris before the Revolution. Later he helped him set up the Bolshoi Drama School. I used to paint sets for the school and one day Anatoly offered me a job in the Ministry as spokesperson for Soviet artists.'

'Sounds important.'

'It was. For a while.' She sighed. 'These days I think of myself more as an internationalist…' Her eyes were restless. He caught a hint of what it must be like crossing borders, at first out of necessity and then because they held no threat, and finally when they became commonplace.

He inhaled slowly, felt a stirring in the loins. He turned away, distracted. He was not here seeking complication. Yet life, damn it, always teemed with possibilities. You could steer your way towards a desired goal and then a bird came fluttering in, singing with such incredible sweetness it was hard not to listen. Tanya was watching him and caught his hesitation.

'So what sort of stuff do you do and why aren't you exhibiting here?' His voice sounded rougher than he intended. She gave a sly smile as though she could read him at a glance.

'I'm working on a project. The pieces are not ready for display.'

'I am sure they'll be worth waiting for,' he murmured.

'What makes you so sure? You know nothing about me.'

'Intuition. It guides me in my work and has been responsible for most of my major decisions.' The more he continued, the wider her smile grew. She was used to having this effect on men, used to seizing what opportunities she could. She was not unlike Mo.

'Describe your work to me.'

She raised her shoulders. 'If I could explain it, I would not need to do it.'

'Granted it's impossible to put a work of art across in words, but I'm curious about the challenges you set yourself.'

'Russia,' she said. 'Old Russia, new Russia, Russia in transition, Russia losing its soul and finding it. The theme goes round and round. The true Russian viewpoint does not believe in progress, more in cycles of nature. It's like Blok's ripples on the canal.'

'Who's Blok?'

For a moment she looked dreamy. 'Alexander Blok was a poet. He wrote about St Petersburg at night, how along the canals in winter the lamps make only a dim light and the water freezes, in ripples. How in life you can go on living for a quarter of a century, but everything will be the same. You think you move forward but you are a ripple frozen on the canal…'

She gave a sad smile. 'What's happening now in Russia is just beginning. Stalin is at the helm. He likes to style himself the great man of steel…' Her eyes flickered and she whispered. 'You know nothing. Nothing.'

'I'm sorry. I didn't mean to upset you. We hear about these

things only from the outside...'

* * *

Two days later they held a *vernissage*, launch party. Dimitri gave a short speech of welcome. He outlined the main features of the Russian display: he hoped it showed the versatility and wide scope of the artists. He hoped the viewers would appreciate the originality of the works. He also spoke of the contribution made by other artists, including Derek Eaton.

Champagne flowed. Tanya and the other Russian woman, whose name he had already forgotten, wandered around with trays of dark bread and French cheese. They'd tried to procure caviar, but the funds did not run to what was available in local stores. Mo put in an appearance, chic in her black dress and cropped hair. She made conversation here and there as she ambled through the rooms, chatting in her primitive French to whoever would listen to her. She seemed a trifle distracted. He was keen to observe the first encounter between Mo and Tanya.

'May I present Tanya Sergeyevna?' he began.

Mo held out her hand. 'Enchantée,' she murmured. 'I have heard a lot about you.'

Tanya nodded in response. 'Your husband has been helpful to us.' She motioned towards the white boards, filled with biographies and interpretations. Mo glanced at the boards, but seemed more taken by the artists themselves as they clustered in doorways or corners, mumbling to each other and weighing up the assorted drift of visitors. The two women eyed each other, passed on and away.

Towards the end of the evening there was a mild flutter as the Yusupovs made an entrance, surrounded by an entourage of friends. Derek watched with bemusement as recognition ran through the *vernissage*. Both Yusupovs were elegantly dressed as befitted the couple who had founded their own fashion house here. Though their enterprise was now in financial straits, one would not have gathered that from their appearance. Prince Felix

Yusupov was wearing a brocade evening jacket in deep purple, matched by heavy purple eyeliner. His wife, Princess Irina, wore a deceptively simple black dress with a string of pearls. Other expensively clad Russians, trailing mink, silk garments and flowing multi-coloured capes, surrounded them.

Only Tanya seemed unmoved by their presence. She was busy chatting to a woman Dimitri told him was Marie Vassilieff. Already Derek knew a little about Maria. Above all, he'd heard she served the Russian artistic community well. Early on, before the war, she'd been a correspondent for several Russian papers. But once here she settled, studying under Matisse and at the Ecole Supérieure des Beaux-Arts. She founded the Académie Vassilieff, where pictures by Chagall and drawings by Picasso hung next to each other.

'Let me introduce you,' said Dimitri. By now Tanya had drifted off to another cluster and Mo was studying one of the larger, darker paintings with a puzzled expression. Derek and Maria shook hands. 'This is the woman who kept the wolf from the door in the war,' said Dimitri.

Maria, a short woman with intense eyes, gave a little nod. 'An interesting exhibition – thank you for helping to get it underway.'

'My pleasure,' said Derek.

'In the war years Maria Ivanovna opened her studio to all and sundry. Artists came pouring in.' Dimitri gave a little laugh. 'She once organised a birthday gathering for Braque, who'd just come back from the Front. Problem was, a drunken Modigliani pitched up, uninvited, and had a go at the man he thought had stolen his lover, Beatrice Hastings. Imagine Maria Ivanovna throwing Modigliani down the stairs!'

Maria Ivanovna gave a dismissive wave of the hand.

'But – seriously – she fed half of Montparnasse during the war… In La Cantine you could get a hot meal, *un petit pot* and the latest gossip of the Ecole de Paris! All for a few centimes.'

'How else could these fugitive artists paint *and* feed themselves?' she murmured.

'They sang and danced and fought and talked until the early hours,' added Dimitri.

Derek recalled that though less renowned than many of her peers, Maria Vassilieff produced a baffling, but effective blend of the avant-garde and the domestic: her doll portraits and furniture pieces no less vital to her than her ambitious Cubist paintings. Certainly a power to be reckoned with, he thought, as he looked down into her earnest yet kind face.

'That's him, that's Anton Lensky!' Mo whispered suddenly in his ear as Maria Vassilieff turned in conversation to one of The Apostles.

'Come on, I'll introduce you.' Mo indicated a man standing near Prince Yusupov, the other side of the room. The man looked urbane and animated as he engaged with people nearby. They moved towards him, but so many people stopped Derek, grasping his hand, patting him on the back, wanting to thank him for all the effort he had put in, that by the time they'd worked their way across, Lensky had left.

Chapter Seventeen *Derek*

The next day Derek and Tanya climbed the winding staircase to her garret studio in Rue Delambre near the Montparnasse cemetery. It was cold and shabby and she'd made little effort to render the space hospitable. 'Do you spend much time here?' he asked.

'Only when I'm obsessed with what I am doing.'

'How often does that happen?"

'At the moment not at all, but I can feel it coming.'

He laughed. 'Yes I know the feeling.'

'Do you? I haven't been able to work for months.'

'Why not?'

She looked away, turned back and pinned him with sad eyes. 'The only way out is for me to work. I've done that in the past, but then I-I scatter myself. I want to build up…'

'A head of steam,' he added.

'Steam?'

'You need the pressure to build. Then the impulse will come of its own accord.'

She gave him a strange look and then laughed. 'You speak for yourself. For me it is different.' He could see it pained her not to be working, it was not enough for her organise and promote the work of others.

'I lose faith in myself when I don't work,' he said. 'Even if I think too much I lose the impetus. I have to force myself to go into the studio. At first nothing comes. I allow myself a mark or two on the canvas. I mix colours. And gradually I start painting again. I can't afford to listen to those old voices that tell me I should be doing something else.'

She led the way in silence to where her sculptures were kept, pulled a cover off what looked like decapitated bodies. Derek gasped. The figures disturbed by their starkness, but more than that it was the ordinary everyday quality they had, much like dressmakers' mannequins, that rendered them distinctly uncanny.

'I call them Stalin's Dolls,' said Tanya. 'I got the idea from an *anekdot* about Stalin. As a young revolutionary he used a safe house in Tiflis. The house was the town's leading fashion atelier and the French couturier who owned it was sympathetic to the revolutionary cause, so Stalin used to hide revolutionary tracts inside the dressmaker dummies. He would be planning a bank raid while the Governor's wife was being fitted for a dress in the next room!'

Derek laughed. He had only a working knowledge of the man they now called Joseph Stalin, who had taken over, by wile and force, the Chairmanship of the Communist Party after Vladimir Ilych Lenin's death. His own earlier enthusiasm for the Bolshevik Revolution was being swiftly eroded after listening to the emigrés, who had fallen foul of it.

'What were you thinking when you created these? Is it satire or a more complex analogy?'

She shrugged. 'It's about the destruction of the individual. Lenin and Stalin believe it is bourgeois to support individuals. Only the urban masses count.'

Derek looked again the mannequins. Their eyes were the most disturbing feature: they were black glass and as the heads were separated from the torsos they glittered with an eerie life–in-death. They haunted. They carried a look of hunger, starvation even, yet spoke of survival beyond the dissolution of the body.

'What are they made of?'

'Plaster over a wicker base. They aren't meant to last. You put them in the Volga. They float, sink, dissolve into mud and waves, like the statues of Saraswati.'

'Who?'

'Saraswati. She's the Indian goddess of wisdom and knowledge. Every year Hindus make elaborate clay statues to her, paint them and cast them into the Ganges. They dissolve in the water.'

'Fascinating!' he said, nonplussed at the notion of female deities and dissolving clay art forms.

Tanya's statues came in varying shapes and sizes. Some loomed in the corners of the studio; some had torsos to the waist only with their heads placed in front of them, connected yet disconnected. They all had a trance-like quality about them, something a nightmare might conjure up.

'They appeared first in my dreams. Many were real people: friends, writers, people who have gone missing. They kept coming to me. I thought I was … crazy. I tried seeing a psychoanalyst when I stopped in Vienna. But it was no use. They were calling to me, the headless ones, demanding I bring them into the world. So I started – sketches, scribbles, – going nowhere. But one thing I've learnt – follow your spirit. It knows what it is doing. Now that is a mystery. Not something comrades Lenin and Stalin would approve of. They want to make sacrifices. The ends justify the means. But for me that's just an excuse to be dark and vile. If you can't care about individuals, how can you care about the masses?'

Derek could see that she would not fit in with the new style of Social Realism, the onwards and upwards of current Soviet art. 'So, you haven't displayed these yet?'

'Of course not! They remind people of things they want to forget. If you question the means of the Revolution you question its basis. No, these have been seen by close friends only – but even then, you never know.'

Remembering what Alexander had said, he asked: 'You think the Security Services are here, in Paris?'

'The Organs, as we call them? Without doubt. They are everywhere. They take art seriously in Russia. They shoot artists they don't agree with.'

Hard to imagine in Britain, he mused: a book might be banned, the Lord Chamberlain might shut down a nightclub, stick an obscenity order on a painting, but the power of art was not challenged head on.

'The Tsars had their secret police and now the Bolsheviks have theirs. We Russians believe everything must be policed. I can't keep up with what they're called. Cheka one minute, OGPU the next. All the same under the surface.'

Downstairs they heard steps.

'Ah, it must be Dimitri.' Her face lit up.

Dimitri joined them. 'You've been viewing Tanya's latest work. Gruesome, aren't they?'

'Very powerful.'

'Not something for The Central Committee of Artists. I told Tanechka they are too risky. One look at these, let alone the writings and poems that go with them, and that would be the end.'

'And to think I was once a spokesperson for the *Nar Kom Pros*. I even had some standing as a painter.'

'You were really a government representative?' Derek was incredulous.

'The early years after the Revolution was a time of artistic freedom. Everyone was experimenting. Then things changed.' She looked wistful. 'So it goes. Now I'm officially *a nonperson*. At liberty in France until they have evidence against me.'

'Which is why she has to be guarded,' said Dimitri looking at her with fervid admiration. 'She is the truest rebel amongst us. Once word gets out about these – and it will if they go on display – there'll be trouble.'

Chapter Eighteen *Mo*

The Folies Bergères was the place you absolutely had to go to. 'They used to put on just ballet, tutus and *pas de deux*,' Lensky told her. 'But it's all changed. You've just got to see what they're up to.' One evening, when the exhibition was well underway, Mo persuaded Derek to take her there.

As they entered the brightly lit foyer Mo was agog at the people milling there: flappers and flat-chested women, well turned-out men in white spats with slicked down centrally-parted hair. She was dazzled by the sheen of pearls, the turn of a delicate ankle, the dress suits and multi-coloured evening wear. In her close-fitting black frock, she drew glances of approval from men nearby. Derek led her towards the cocktail bar and ordered two champagne cocktails. Tonight a French dancer from Martinique was performing a homage to Josephine Baker, who had taken the place by storm three years before.

They took their seats. She remembered the last time she'd been here. That was before marriage and Timothy, before the devastation of his death. How young she'd been then, how impressionable. She would never forget that evening: not only had she witnessed the legendary Josephine Baker, but it had been her first night of passion with Derek.

Now the dancers were bowing and lifting their heads like opening buds. Mo watched their long limbs swaying. She noted their costumes' glitter and sparkle in a flurry of feathers. The jungle scene followed. Mo kept waiting for an explosion of energy, a crescendo of wild dancing, which never came. Without Josephine Baker it was a little tame. There were palm trees, dancers strung out like giant snakes and a higher level where the main dancer gyrated. But it was not the enchantment it had been.

The audience, though, was ecstatic. They applauded, called out and whistled for more.

* * *

That night Mo had strange dreams. She was a leopard stalking through undergrowth, her mottled pelt shiny and elusive, before she morphed into a hunter, in the bushes, pursuing it. Yet when it came to it, she could not do the deed. The leopard was too beautiful to kill. She could only gaze in awe. Next morning when she woke Derek was already reaching for his clothes. She touched his arm. 'Can we…?'

'What is it, Mo?'

She sighed, lay back on the pillows. 'There's us. And then there is you, the painter, and me, the singer. …Derek...'

'Mo,' he looked puzzled. 'Say it, whatever you want to say. It can't be that complicated.'

But it was. She was confused, uncertain what she was asking of him. A commitment? They were already committed: in law, before Church and community. 'I support you … in your work… I want you to do the same for me.' Had he even heard? He was getting dressed now, facing away from her.

'Sounds fine to me,' he muttered then bent down and nuzzled into her neck, kissed her and moved away. 'Got to go now.' The sun was striping through the skylight onto the floorboards, like tall savannah grass, the floor wavered under the effect, which rendered everything fluid, impermanent. She watched the shifting shadows for the sleek of a leopard and wondered if there were things Derek was not telling her.

Chapter Nineteen *Derek*

Derek fled into the early morning streets, striding towards the gallery. He'd left Mo dozing, just waking, mumbling about commitment. No time for breakfast. He'd dropped the habit, downing espresso coffee like the French to get a day started. It was gratifying to see her perk up in recent days though he was none too sure about this Lensky. He could not resist the suspicion that Lensky wanted to bed Mo and that was his sole intention. What man would not want to? But he'd agreed to meet him with her later in the day.

Dimitri greeted him at the gallery. They went back out and took a quick coffee at the corner café. They needed to smooth out a few last-minute ruffles. 'We're expecting more Left-Bankers today,' said Dimitri with a sardonic smile. 'Tanechka did a last minute fly-posting of their cafes. Tried to engage some of them in conversation. Got short shrift but carried on, apparently.'

Derek was forced to smile. He could just imagine her sallying forth in Les Deux Magots and La Clôserie des Lilas, haunts of Sorbonne students and lecturers. Would Sorbonne philosophers be interested in Russian art? They propounded Socialism and workers' rights. Would they sympathise with those critical of the Soviet Union? Dimitri lit a cigarette and passed Derek the packet. Derek declined then changed his mind. A drink and cigarette together often helped cement a connection.

'Are you pleased with how things are going?' he asked.

'We've had enough people coming through.'

After coffee they sauntered back to the gallery. 'How do you know Tanya Sergeyevna?' he asked. Dimitri shuffled his feet through fallen leaves.

'We go back a long time. She's like my sister.'

'Nothing more?'

Dimitri threw him a sidelong glance and took another drag on his cigarette. 'Where I come from you don't sleep with your sister.'

'Never?'

Dimitri broke into a laugh. 'We always fought. But we experimented a bit in our youth. Found we preferred each other as friends. We weren't together that long anyway. My family left for France. I'd kill for her though. She's the only family I have… So don't get any ideas.'

Derek laughed. 'I thought women in Russia were viewed as equals – able to determine their own destinies.'

'In theory, yes. In practice many men are as vile towards women as ever they were. But you're right. I reckon Tanyeshka can take care of herself.'

Chapter Twenty *Mo*

Mo had sent Lensky a *pneumatique*, organising a time when she knew Derek would be free. She sat over coffee on the wobbly balcony, eyeing the goatman and his nanny goat as they jostled and tinkled their way down the alley. A woman approached and he milked the goat, then and there, causing a backlog of traffic. The woman waddled off with her container brimming with milk while the goatman continued on, whistling.

It was one of those absurdities of the *quartier*. They still brought cows into Spitalfields in East London but mostly, these days, the capital's milk arrived by early morning train from Wales. In Paris it was this craziness of cabaret next to goat's milk, windmills next to artists' attics that she so adored: the countryside never far away.

But back to the business in hand: MONEY she wrote on her notepad. Although secondary to her, she knew it was vital. She liked the things money could buy: tasty dishes in the subdued lighting of expensive restaurants, silk underwear, and crêpe de chine dresses. That evening in the Folies Bergères she had observed the affluent French at play. It had whetted her appetite for more *soirées* like that, more sunshine and warmth, more beaded frocks and champagne cocktails and men in dinner jackets. But as for agreeing an hourly rate, she'd leave that to the men to thrash out. Derek had never interfered between Knighton and herself, but then he'd been out of the picture. Now he was taking a proprietorial interest in all she did – in theory at least – in practice, he could barely spare the time.

In the café on Boulevard St Michel Lensky was already sitting at a table, tucked behind a copy of *le Figaro* and wearing a pin-striped suit and crisp white shirt. She dodged behind one of the street pillars, cluttered with dog-eared notices, to catch her breath. He looked so distinguished. Derek was nowhere to be seen. She suppressed a sliver of panic. She wondered how the men would get on. They were chalk and cheese. She stepped forward and hoped the cerise dress and jacket she was wearing would create the right blend of flair and subtlety.

'Ah, Madame Eaton.' He got to his feet as she came forward and greeted her with obvious pleasure.

'My husband is on his way.' She sat down and folded her hands. 'We saw you at the opening but didn't get a chance to talk.'

'Ah, yes …'

'I'd like to hear more about your venue. *Scheherazade,* isn't it?'

'It's been going a few years but we've just restyled it. We intend to attract a more discerning audience…'

A tram squealed to a halt fifty yards away and Derek was rushing towards them. 'Sorry I'm late.' Lensky shook his hand, pulled out a seat for him. 'We ran into problems with the lighting.'

The two men were trying not to look at each other but not making a very good job of it. Derek was clearly impressed by Lensky's tailored looks and maturity. For the first time Mo noticed what well-manicured hands the man had. She wondered if he was married. Derek, by contrast, looked dishevelled after hurrying to get there. Yet there was an attractive exuberance about him. He was watching Lensky like a sparrow hawk.

'My wife tells me you heard her sing and would like to offer her a contract?' Lensky raised an eyebrow at this snatching of the moment. 'She worked in one of the top West End theatres in Noël Coward productions. She will have told you all this?'

'She mentioned it. But tell me more. Which theatre would that have been? And which musical company?'

For Mo this turn in conversation was unwelcome: she did not

want to be reminded of Knighton and The Athena theatre. Derek nevertheless filled in the details of what he knew. Mo sat back and eyed the two men. It was like watching a poker game, neither willing to give much away. They got round to discussing Scheherazade. This time Lensky mentioned its track record as well as how the place had undergone refurbishment.

'You said something about further vocal training?' Derek challenged him. Lensky glanced over his shoulder and ordered a large cognac.

'You will join me, Monsieur Eaton?' Derek nodded that he would.

'She has a splendid voice. I had some training in the conservatory in Moscow. Pre-Revolution. I have high standards. That's why I suggested it.'

'It's not exactly L'Opéra de Paris we're talking about, is it?'

'She?' Mo said. 'Am I not sitting here right now between you?' Derek glanced at her, looking uncertain.

Lensky laughed: 'Forgive us. It is the way of men,' he began. 'It is usual for these things to be sorted out by a third party.'

'Well, I have no agent.'

Lensky signalled over his shoulder for another two cognacs and inclined his head towards Mo, asking what she might like. 'Yes, why not? Cognac please.' She paused. 'Can we come and see Scheherazade then?' She looked from one man to the other: Derek ever lean and hungry, dark eyes signalling an intensity that never left him, never failed to stir her; and Lensky older, more measured, with greying temples and eyes, which despite their sharpness were often veiled with something between tenderness and sympathy.

'*Naturellement,* you shall see the venue. I like my artists to be involved in setting the tone. This is theatre as much as music.' She thrilled to hear the agreement becoming more concrete.

'You have many other singers there?' she asked.

'A few. Sometimes I arrange for them to sing at other places.

They have sung for Fresnais at L'Etoile, some even at Folies Bergères and Le Chat Noir.'

After a few minutes Mo excused herself to go to the ladies. 'You're on your way, girl,' she whispered to her image over the hand basin. When she returned the men were talking about money. Much as she liked to think she could determine her own life, she hated haggling. She downed the rest of her brandy and told the men she wanted to stretch her legs. They nodded assent.

She strolled towards the river, the air cool in her face, the slow movement of the water calming her. When she returned they were shaking hands. Lensky nodded and left.

'I think we have an agreement' said Derek. 'The man's intentions are honest enough. He knows a lot about music.'

'Did you fix a time to see Scheherazade?'

'Tomorrow. No time to waste, he says, and who am I to disagree? He'd like you to sing then. Just a song or two – so go prepared.'

'Will you come with me?'

'Of course.'

Chapter Twenty-one

The next day, though, Derek was again unable to keep his word. A number of Americans were putting in an appearance and he needed to be on hand. One of the visitors owned a gallery in New York and was considering investing in Russian émigré art, if the calibre was high enough.

Buoyed by the previous meeting, Mo minded less than she might have done. Derek had cleared the way for her, virtually securing a deal with Lensky. Above all, by his presence they'd given the signal that she was not to be trifled with.

Scheherazade was in Pigalle, not far from the Folies Bergères. She recognised the place, having passed it on the way back from L'Etoile. It was in a dingy backstreet, its lights glinting alongside two other cafes. From the outside it looked nondescript; Lensky's promises of a better class of establishment seemed farfetched. She pushed aside this judgement: good music often emerged from dowdy venues.

She had no desire to return to l'Etoile. She'd been back once since the fracas. Fresnais, unshaven and dejected, had lost that earlier spark which had led her to believe she was onto a good thing. Pierre's cousin had stopped working behind the bar. Over coffee Dolores gave Mo the lowdown. Mo managed to piece together the story from a mix of gestures and odd French words she knew.

There had been another bust-up. Some ruffians were threatening to do the place over again if Jean did not cough up protection money. The place belonged to his brother, who had run up debts and was now serving time for having a go at one of his creditors with a knife. Mo need hear no more. That sort of sordid brawling she wanted no part of. Dolores's skin had the coarse, pasty look that comes from malnutrition. Mo wondered how old she was and how long she'd been singing in bars.

* * *

Lensky was not around when she arrived at Scheherazade, but there was a young woman who said yes, she was expected, and to come in and wait. 'I'm Lisette. Monsieur Lensky asked me to look out for you. He's been delayed.'

Mo glanced around. It was larger than l'Etoile. She took out a cigarette from a mother-of-pearl cigarette case and offered one to Lisette. 'Have you been working with him for long?'

'Just over a year.'

'And you enjoy it?'

Lisette shrugged. 'I come from the south. My folks don't have much money and my dad's out of work. I met Monsieur Lensky when I was working in another *boîte*. An old bloke was playing the accordion. There I was, singing as I doled out beer. Lensky caught me by the wrist. I nearly spilled the beer down his trousers. He said I had a good voice and would I call round and see him. Well, I was sceptical, I can tell you. So I took a friend along. I got the story about the Russian Conservatory. I think he was trying to win me round…'

Mo's French just about seized the gist of the story. Lisette had sharp features in an oval face, which changed expression every second or so. She was about twenty.

'Is he married?'

'So he says. Never seen her though. They say she's a semi-invalid, see.'

'But he's a good boss?'

She shrugged. 'There are worse.'

By the time Lensky arrived Mo's curiosity was aroused but she kept her counsel as he showed her round the venue. He glanced at her. 'Tonight you will sing. Not the main act, but a couple of songs.'

She barely had time to change before the evening kicked off.

She sat through Lisette's songs. She had a plaintive voice that made you look at her slight figure and wistful face and want to wrap her in approval. Then she began to stomp about the stage, giving members of the audience a cheeky stare. They erupted in laughter and egged her on. She reminded Mo a little of herself when she was starting out. She looked around. The clients were a notch up from those of L'Etoile. Mostly they were couples relishing a night out. The place had a contented and more secure feel to it. She could not imagine fights erupting here.

Before she knew it Lensky was introducing her to the audience. They looked at her with blank faces but once she'd started turned to her with interest. Time fled as she performed *'Poor little rich girl'* again. Were they clapping as loudly for her they had for Lisette? Would they welcome her back? Lensky put his hand in the small of her back, guiding her towards a barstool.

'Brava,' he said. 'A good start.' He pushed a glass of wine towards her. She looked towards him: whether she liked it or not, she sensed that right now he had her career in Paris in the palm of his hand.

'What happens now?' she asked.

'You did well tonight. They liked you. This is the second time I've seen you perform and I'm not disappointed. A short rehearsal. We go through more songs together, okay?' They agreed to meet after a couple of days.

A wave of tiredness came over her, she did not want to sit and hear more voices. She was longing to get back to Derek and tell him how it had gone. She bade Lensky goodnight and slipped out into the street. It was starting to drizzle and she drew her jacket round her. The rain made the cobblestones slippery and she had to pick her way. When she reached home and there was no sign of Derek, she felt strangely bereft. She threw herself onto the bed, fully clothed. She dozed a while and woke when she heard Derek on the stairs. He was looking very chipper. 'A successful day?' she asked.

'Very. All the problems have been ironed out. Dimitri is fine for advising on the paintings, but when it comes down to practicalities like sorting out the electricity supply, he's useless.'

'And the Americans?'

'The New York connection could be useful. Wouldn't surprise me if they didn't want to take the whole exhibition over there.'

'Quite a turn-up for the books.'

'And you? So sorry I couldn't be there.'

'He wants me to do more. We're meeting up soon to go through the numbers.'

'Let's go and celebrate.'

'What now?'

'Why not? The night is young and we're in Paris.'

They discovered a low-lit bar with music in the *quartier*. Derek exchanged a few words with the maître d' who led them to a secluded table overlooking the stage.

The place throbbed with life as people chatted, laughed and called out to each other across tables. A different bunch again from Scheherazade: more sophisticated, racier, younger – *hommes d'affaires* with their young mistresses and chic women from the better *arrondissements*. The music had a raw vitality, which dazzled and deafened her. Jelly Roll Morton had set the ball rolling. Here was that same wildness of clashing, competing instruments and the rhythms of Swing, which made her want to tear down the barriers which kept people apart.

Jazz had found a home-from-home in Paris. Black musicians from the States, many of them soldiers left over from the war, flocked here. They knew what it was to be at the bottom of the heap and without hope of rising, except through music. Music let them ascend, ever higher. She grew intoxicated just listening to them. How could they do it? Surely their lungs would burst, their hearts give out, their brains sizzle to a cinder. How did they turn misery and despair into pure fire and air?

You just had to get up and swing. Move every muscle you had, shake out fustiness and fear and inhibition. If they could do it, so could she. If they could boogie their way into the fibre of Paris, so could she. As she watched the four musicians bending and straining to make music and dancers on the small platform gyrating, she was transfixed.

She and Derek danced. She let the music take her. Here they were together again, a dangerous volatile combination, everything hanging in the air, everything possible. She could not stop. She wanted the music to go and on forever. You can't dwell in the shadow of death. Life pushes you forward, makes you breathe with the pulse of the universe.

Chapter Twenty-two

Mo was woken the next day by an insistent banging on their door. Still half asleep, she rubbed her eyes. After Derek had left she'd snuggled back down under the blankets. Puzzled, she pulled on her peignoir and glanced at the clock. It was just after nine. When she opened the door the irate landlord stood before her.

'I've been knocking several minutes,' he complained.

She gave the man a weak smile and brushed the hair from her face. He thrust a telegram into her hand and promptly withdrew.

'Misery guts,' she whispered to his retreating back. The man only ever seemed interested in money. He went out his way to let them know that by rights he could demand a higher rent. Her hand trembled as she took the envelope back into their sitting room. Telegrams were harbingers of death. She recalled the black-edged ones that came thick and fast around the time of the Somme when she was a child.

'Mother ill. Come soonest.' Was the bald statement when she tore open the envelope. She could not stop herself shaking. Within seconds her world telescoped within itself, no distance between here and there. She sat on the sofa staring into space, absorbing the news, seeing her mother's pale face under a pall of exhaustion. In the next moment she got to her feet, resolved to go home. This sent her into a flurry of activity. An old ferry timetable was stashed away in a pile of books by the stove. These she now rummaged through, growing frantic as her search proved fruitless. Finally she came upon it, tucked behind the clock.

There was no time to lose. If she caught a train this morning, she might just reach an afternoon ferry and be in London by nightfall. She threw a few clothes into a battered small case. With no time for breakfast, she felt giddy as she rushed through the streets towards the gallery. She had barely enough on her for a train ticket to Calais, let alone the price of ferry and train from Dover to London.

Derek was busy chatting to a group of artists in the lobby when she pitched up, breathless. They were laughing and joking. Derek looked shocked to see her.

'Mo?'

She thrust the telegram towards him. 'I have to go.'

He excused himself from the others. 'Shall I come with you?'

'No. You stay here.'

His eyes searched her face. She felt disconcerted. Of course, she would rather have him with her: even now her legs were liquid and the blood was leaving her head. But it was clear that he was so embroiled here: a key opportunity, he'd said. To get entangled with her family was the last thing he needed. He grasped her arms. 'Sit down.'

He signalled to Dimitri, who was watching. Dimitri brought a chair. She put her head between her knees until she felt herself steadying.

'I want to go back, but I need more funds,' she said.

Derek fumbled in his pocket and produced a wad of notes. He took out a five-pound note and unfolded it carefully. 'This should see you through.' She tucked the money into her purse. The others had faded away and Mo, calmer now, began to feel restless. She needed to leave as soon as she could. She pulled the small suitcase towards her and began rooting in it for the rest of her money.

'Will you hail a taxi for me?' He nodded and disappeared into the street.

'I'll come to the Gare du Nord with you. That's the least I can do.'

PART 2

Chapter Twenty-three *Mo*

The clackety-clack of the train made Mo drowsy, yet the telegram kept startling her awake, urging her onwards to Hackney. At Calais she had to wait two hours for a ferry. She drank cups of tea and ate bacon sandwiches in the dockside cafeteria: a bit of home, she thought. The foot passengers boarded through a side gate. She watched her fellow passengers: a jolly though squabbling family, a bored-looking businessman reading *The Times*, a couple so enmeshed they seemed one creature. The ship's crew was craning a car and umpteen crates aboard.

On the ferry she searched out a window seat. The engines whirred, the water churned, and the bow thrust away from the quay, where a few lone figures waved off departing friends. The wake trailed shrieking seagulls. As they left the coast of France she had an unshakeable sense of foreboding. Her mother often suffered from patchy health, though rarely gave in to the infections that sent others scurrying to their beds.

The cliffs of Dover were visible as grey, enshrouded monsters. She disembarked. The customs sheds were desolate. She wandered through without being stopped and trudged the short distance to the train station where two trains were leaving for London within the hour. By late afternoon she was in Hackney. The pub appeared closed. She went round the back alley and let herself in. The house was empty. 'Come soonest' the telegram had run and yet where was everybody? With accelerating heartbeat, she searched the rooms. The old bedroom she'd shared with her sisters looked tinier than ever. She felt she no longer had a connection here, yet she'd been pulled back as surely as if she still inhabited the place. From downstairs she heard a door opening. 'Morwenna!' Pa was standing at the foot of the stairs. He was unshaven, his shoulders slumped, but his face brightened on seeing her. 'Morwenna – you came. I never fought you would.'

'Is she...?'

'She gave us a proper fright. We thought we'd lost her.'

Mo leaned against the banister as she came downstairs. She gave Pa a quick hug. 'Where is she?'

'Hackney hospital. But they won't be keeping her.'

He made a pot of thick tea and handed her an enamel mug. He told her how Ma had collapsed and seemed on the brink but had pulled through. She'd been muttering Morwenna this and Morwenna that. All things considered, they thought it a good idea to send for her. After all, Paris was not Timbuktu and she'd be able to catch the ferryboat.

Mo asked about clean clothes and hospital expenses. Should they not go and fetch her as soon as they could? 'Yes, yes,' he said, but looked dazed. He was lost without Ma. She had ever been the practical one. Fortified by the tea, Mo quickly gathered a small bundle for Ma and they took the bus to Hackney hospital.

Ma Dobson looked small and helpless, shrivelled almost, in the large frame of the hospital bed. Her eyes were shut as they approached the bed. Seeing her pale, slightly hollow cheeks, Mo realised how old and used up Ma had become in the space of weeks. 'Ma,' she said gently, touching her hand. Ma's eyes shot open. The look was clear and penetrating as though she had been awaiting this moment.

'Morwenna.' Then she shut her eyes again. 'I'm tired, pet. But I'm glad you come. I didn't think you would – what with your new life and all.' Mo squeezed her hand, overcome by a confusion of emotions.

The nurse came to the end of the bed, picked up a chart and placed the thermometer in Ma's mouth. 'Isn't it grand you have your third daughter now, Mrs Dobson?' she said, busy and crinkling around in her starched uniform.

Ma muttered something incomprehensible. When the thermometer had been taken out of her mouth and the nurse had moved to the other end of the ward, Ma started up again: 'There are things I wanted to tell you. In case… '

'Shsh,' said Mo. 'I'm here.' Ma closed her eyes, her lips curling in a smile of relief.

Chapter Twenty-four *Lensky*

Strange how sense impressions linger in the mind. Lensky thought he was finished with all that: shivers in the night, the tendency to look over his shoulder, fearing every movement in the gloom of evening and the pervasive sense of being watched. It had been years now. He had come to believe they were leaving him alone.

It was the sound of a familiar shuffle, not a limp quite, but the dragging of a foot that caused his throat to go dry and the years to concertina into moments. The rasp as the other cleared his throat. *'Tovarich'* he called. The blood began to drain from Lensky's head. He half turned.

'Yes, it's me, Ivan Ivanovich.' As if the other would give his real name. 'It's been a long time.'

Lensky said nothing, hoping the other would evaporate – just a chimera of his anxious mind. The shadow fell across him as he pulled down the shutter protecting Scheherazade and slid the padlock into place.

'Nice place you've got there. Very *kulturniy*.'

'What do you want?'

'Come now, not so brusque.'

If only he'd been less headstrong as a youth, less enamoured of the crazy ideas of equality and idealism doing the rounds; if only he had not had such fellow feeling for his family's retainers, their loyal eyes full of devotion, resignation, but, above all, the extinction of hope.

When Lensky moved away from the door the other laid a hand on his arm. 'It's nothing much. No harm will come to anyone. A little information. That's all.' As if that would ever be enough. The breath of the other was laced with tobacco and rancid oil. Lensky felt himself becoming queasy.

Chapter Twenty-five *Derek*

The first group of Americans included a surly reporter from the *Chicago Tribune*. They wandered through the rooms and left soon after, without comment, puzzlement on their faces. In the second group was Samuel Goldman, who ran a prestigious gallery in New York and had connections with the Metropolitan Museum of Art. Though his Jewish grandfather had fled the pogroms instigated by the Tsarist Secret Police in the 1880s, he'd still yearned for a connection with Mother Russia, and this he'd passed on to his family.

In the end Derek had agreed to mediate for he sympathised with the emigrés' unease at presenting themselves to the international art world. Not that he knew much better; but their fear, often disguised as bluster, could be off-putting. The Russian artists were a sensitive bunch who needed to grow an extra skin to be able to deal with their western cousins.

Now, when both White and Red Russians were seeking refuge here, it was more complex than he could grasp. Former aristocrats linked up with remnants of the French *ancien régime* while those of a liberal bent sought out the fractured avant-garde. London had had its share of Russian anarchists plotting in the East End and setting off bombs, but much of that had fizzled out with the coming of the Great War. These days he could not hope to penetrate the labyrinth of what constituted the Union of Soviet Socialist Republics: enough to catch the sparks of ice and fire that flew off from it.

* * *

Derek and Tanya were in the furthest room of the exhibition. It was almost closing time, though this was an arbitrary cut-off point depending on who was wandering through. After dropping

Mo at the Gare du Nord, he'd thrust himself into doing what he could to further the event. He needed to distract himself. He was torn, knowing in his gut that he should have travelled with her, but unable to resist the urge to plumb the spirit of these troubled émigrés.

'Where did you get your idea of mannequins and decapitation from?' he asked Tanya.

She shrugged, lit a cheroot, and started pacing around the dim room. He wanted to get up and switch on a light yet was fascinated by the shadows playing about her. 'Where does anything come from when you're an artist? I thought I explained. The more I work the more I trust my instinct. If I think about it too much, it disappears.'

This, he supposed, was the clearest answer he was going to get.

'What moves *you* then?' She skewered him with her dark, truth-seeking eyes. He let out a long sigh. This woman could take him to dangerous places.

'Once I grasped the fundamentals of composition, drawing and colour, I wanted to imitate all and sundry. No one can paint skies like Constable or trees like Corot. But what's the point?' He paused, watching her silhouette. Her face changed the more he looked at it, switching between an impenetrable veil and guileless curiosity.

He went on, almost to himself. 'I began to paint out of desperation – not caring who saw it, what school of painting it was. I didn't give a brass monkey. Everything had already been done. I worked out of necessity. I wanted to live again.' As he spoke he felt himself growing restless. He had never uttered this before, not even to Mo. His solar plexus tingled.

Tanya laughed. 'Then we are not so very different, my friend.'

'It took the death of my son, actually,' he whispered. She moved closer to him, quieter now. 'He died of diphtheria. The worst was…' he was unable to continue. He'd grown so used to being the strong one who kept things steady.

'I know what it's like,' she said hoarsely. 'I lost my whole family. In Russia life can be cheap. Really cheap.'

He was trembling. A tumult held back for so long was longing for release. His chest was cut with pain, his throat thick with perilous memories. She took him gently by the hand and laid her cheek against his neck. 'Life goes on my friend – as it must. We grieve. We must never forget those we have loved and lost. They come through in our work, in our dreams, in every decision we make…' She paused, drew apart from him. 'Look, it's getting dark. Shall we close up now and go and find the others?'

He nodded, relieved she was distancing herself from him. Steps were echoing in from the next room. Dimitri stood on the threshold.

'What's happening here?' he said, switching on the light. The ghosts fled.

'Oh nothing,' said Tanya with a laugh. 'We were discussing creativity and where it came from…'

'So I see,' said Dimitri. 'It's time to shut up now. Leave the rooms…'

'To the wraiths,' added Derek.

'Wraiths. What are wraiths?'

'Wisps in the wind,' he said. 'Whispers from another world.'

'I'm done with ghosts. I'll leave that to the priests and the *babushkas*,' said Dimitri. 'Several of us are heading to the club. Want to join us?'

Tanya threw a glance around the room to make sure everything was in order. Out on the street three of the artists were standing by the gas light, smoking. With their rough serge jackets and workers' caps they reminded Derek of Lenin, whose signature cap had replaced the bowler hat he once wore.

They approached a cafe by the river. With its glimmer of red lights and an awning that flapped, it was almost full. Derek caught the familiar whiff of seasoned meat and garlic, the buzz of animated talk and laughter. He thought of Mo: anxiety in her face, helpless but spiked with determination to get home. What if Ma Dobson died? He walked on, suppressing the thought. He had shone the Russians in a favourable light. Samuel Goldman had expressed interest not only in their work but also in his own. He would contact Mo as soon as he could.

As they entered the cafe basement, which served as the Russians' club, voices were rising in a crescendo of excitement: they would be promised contracts, sales – great things lay ahead. There was no end to the hyperbole and grand designs. The clashing din continued to build as the wine and vodka flowed. Faces became red; at one stage a fight threatened, quickly averted by Dimitri, who was trying to keep the whole thing under control.

A slim, dark young man whom Derek knew only as Tengiz got to his feet. *'Rebyata* I hate the Cossacks and all they stand for,' he yelled out. 'But they know how to dance.' He thrust chairs to one side and as the others slowly clapped he folded his arms and attempted to dance, kicking out his legs from bent knees and toppling over, which led to a roar of laughter.

'Tengiz is from the Caucasus,' Dimitri explained. 'They're a wild bunch down there.'

These were good days for them, Derek mused. They were at last coming together, gaining the cohesion and recognition they deserved.

'They can't get over it,' said Tanya. 'It's the first time many of them have seen their pictures on a wall.' This reminded Derek of his first portfolio show at the Chelsea Polytechnic, with students drunk on their own success, however minor. Yet he was beginning to feel tired. This was not his party, not his celebration. The American gallery owner had just come in.

'They're like children,' murmured Tanya. 'I've never seen them so excited. We Russians always think the worst is going to happen. It often does. We've been pushed down too many times.'

Now others had got up to do their own version of Cossack dancing.

Samuel Goldman joined them at table. 'They certainly know how to cut a rug,' he said.

'It's all show,' said Tanya quietly. 'Underneath they're nervous.' Goldman smiled but seemed unwilling to open up. Tanya nodded to take her leave and drifted over to join a cluster, deep in talk by the bar.

When Derek steered the conversation around to possible purchases and dates for a New York showing, the man grew evasive: 'I don't want to go into that here. It's a teeter-totter.'

Derek was bewildered. 'A teeter-totter?'

'What you Brits call a seesaw. It means I'm still weighing things up. I need to match paintings with potential buyers.' As if sensing his reaction, the American went on: 'The market is jittery now. There's been too much buying on margin.'

'On margin?'

'What you call buying on credit. We had Calvin Coolidge as president until last year. He always said the business of America is business. But there's been too little regulation. The Stock Market is going to fall out of bed sometime soon.'

Warming to this theme Goldman continued: 'Cal wasn't a bad president. He knew when to keep his mouth shut. He was called Silent Cal. Once someone sitting next to him at a reception said: 'I bet someone I could get more than two words out of you.' Cal replied. 'You lose' and didn't open his mouth again all evening.'

Derek smiled. Was Goldman a betting man? Was buying art like backing horses to him? Goldman's skin looked too tight for him, as if something wanted to burst out but was kept strictly in check.

'Have you come across much Russian stuff before?' Derek asked.

'Some. I travelled to Moscow and St Petersburg before the Revolution.' Derek eyed him again. He must be older than he seemed or have travelled when very young.

'I went there with my parents. My mother's father was from Odessa but saw fit to leave after one pogrom too many.'

Derek intuited there were layers of attachment and disgust in his relationship with the country. He was only just beginning to untangle these complications with regard to Tanya. Goldman would have his own web. But he would be keen on acquisition, Derek surmised: keen to keep the link with Russia vibrant.

The American seemed about to leave. 'Perhaps we can meet in the morning?'

'Yes, that would be good,' said Derek. 'There is a rawness in some of the images. In others great subtlety and blending of old traditions, in yet others an otherworldly, mystical element unique to the Russian spirit.'

'If you say so,' said Goldman and looked at his watch.

Chapter Twenty-six *Mo*

Within an hour of Mo arriving at Hackney hospital the ward sister had handed her a discharge note and her mother's belongings. Among them was a crunched photo of Timothy, which made her start. Rarely had she and her mother discussed him. She'd assumed her mother had taken it all in her stride. Ma had a way about her that made it difficult to talk feelings. The past was the past was the past, over and done with. Only the present counted, only the tasks at hand.

Ma had undergone a metamorphosis. As she stood beside Mo her whole body seemed smaller, frailer and her arms and legs had become stick-like. She'd always been a strong woman: wiry, able to shift barrels and pull pints for hours on end. Now her skin was papery and her eyes sunken. There was no cure or treatment for pneumonia. You had to be kept warm and hydrated until you reached the crisis and then your fate was in the lap of the gods. Some inner fire of determination had seen Ma Dobson through. She gripped her daughter's arm and nodded vaguely in the direction of the ward sister. 'Thank you, nurse,' she said and stared ahead.

The ward sister was already stripping the bed in preparation for the next patient. Pa stood by, long arms dangling. He seemed mightily relieved Mo had arrived to take over. This, she guessed, was the real motive behind the telegram. Mo insisted they took a taxi home. They squeezed into the back of a Hackney cab, Pa uneasy at the novelty, Ma still too faint to notice. Once back in The Mare's Head, Mo set about lighting a fire in the kitchen parlour and inspecting her parents' bedroom. She pulled fresh bed sheets out of the dresser: they smelled moth-balled but were clean enough. She settled her mother in the one good armchair by the fire and began making a barley broth from the meagre selection of vegetables she found in the larder. When she'd put this on the range to simmer she took a broom and swept through the rooms, taking care not to raise dust, which would only aggravate her mother's chest.

Her sisters, Cissy and Tilda, who lived nearby, put in an appearance; they had been too tied up before, they excused themselves. Mo did not give it another thought. She fed Ma soup from a chipped bowl then added the scrag end of lamb, which Cissy had brought, into the mixture and put it back on the hob. The meat would thicken it up and give Ma strength.

'There's my girl.' Mo caught a flicker of rare affection in her mother's eyes. The others stayed on for tea. Tilda had brought some Bath buns. They sat around munching and watched the shifting embers, not knowing what to say.

'A near thing.' Pa chewed on his pipe. 'I thought we'd lost you. I really did.'

'I'm not so easy to get rid of,' murmured Ma, her eyes drooping. She needed to rest, sleep. Cissy and Tilda took the hint and bade her goodbye: they'd be back soon bearing more meat, bread, milk, whatever she needed. Mo led her upstairs, helped her into a clean nightie and edged her towards the bed. Ma gave her a weak smile. 'Where's your husband?'

'He couldn't come. He's too busy. He's …'

'Don't worry. 'E never did like me.'

'But…'

'You can't fool me. Can't say I blame 'im. 'E thinks I've been too 'ard on you. And it's true. I didn't want you to end up like me.'

'Hush Ma. You need to rest. Sleep.'

* * *

True to their word the sisters returned the next day bearing milk, bread and meat, albeit scrawny. Ma was sleeping and the three sisters sat downstairs. Mo pushed mugs of freshly brewed tea towards them. Cissy looked drawn. 'How's the stall going?' asked Mo. Cissy gave a shrug and cupped her hands round the mug.

'People are getting poorer. Not spending more than they need to.'

'And how's Sam these days? Quite an 'andful, I imagine?' Mo affected jollity, not wanting to be contaminated by Cissy's low spirits. 'At school yet?'

''E started a few weeks ago. I thought you knew.'

'It's hard to keep track...' She went back into the scullery to top up her mug. Though she'd swept through the place the day before, she noticed how grubby it was. The walls were lined with grease, the lino blackened and cups on the table chipped. Ma had been particular about cleanliness. She'd nagged them enough about it when they were young.

Cissy looked sullen. That would be marriage to Bob Scratchett. He was sly – she would never have trusted him with any savings – and she guessed he remained a womaniser. Cissy thought she was the queen bee to have landed him back in the days when the three sisters squabbled in the room above where they were now sitting. It had given her a sparkle of superiority to be walking out on the arm of the cocky stallholder. Her eyes had shone with pride. Now they emitted a dull disappointment. Her skin was pallid. Not enough good food, thought Mo, who'd seen that look of just getting by on faces in Paris. Yet there they at least had cheap wine and art.

She took the remainder of yesterday's buns, toasted them and handed them round. Tilda smiled at her. She, in contrast to Cissie, had improved with age. Now she no longer tried to copy everything Mo did, she had become more cheerful and self-possessed. Marriage seemed to suit her. She had grown a little plump, but in an attractive, womanly way. Mo could barely recognise in her the whining brat of a younger sister from the past. She had a one-year old, Victoria, whom she'd left with a neighbour. 'Don't want 'er to catch nuffin,' she whispered.

'Pneumonia's not catching,' said Mo with an air of knowing what she was talking about when she didn't. 'So how is she?'

'She's well.' It was obvious Tilda was not used to being asked about her daughter's welfare. "'Ow long you staying?' she shot out.

Only as long as necessary, Mo wanted to say, but bit it back. 'Better see if Ma's awake yet.' She took a browning bun off the range and lavished a thick wallop of butter onto it.

'They could do with you 'ere,' said Cissy.

'I've a lot further to come than you two,' retorted Mo.

'Yeah, but you're better off, ain't you? And you're not working now, are you?' Her voice had an edge of malice.

'As a matter of fact, I am. I have a contract to sing in…'

'Get you. So high and mighty – with your contracts and singing in gay Paree.' Cissy laughed and bit into her bun with greedy delight. Mo reddened. She would not rise to the bait.

Tilda piped up: 'Do tell us, Mo. It sounds exciting. I'm jealous. I'd love to go to Paris. I think you was born under a lucky star.'

'Maybe.' Mo picked up the buttered bun and took it upstairs. She heard fierce whispering behind her. Perhaps Tilda was defending her.

Ma's eyes flickered open as she entered her bedroom. It was chilly in there, a draught blowing though the rattling window. Mo pulled the curtain across. She'd once loved these red velveteen curtains as they'd reminded her of Music Hall and Ma's days as a performer. Now they were threadbare and let in the light. Ma gave her a weak smile and attempted to hoist herself up.

Mo put the plate on the chest-of-drawers and arranged pillows so Ma could sit up. 'There now, I'll fetch a shawl. Where…?'

'In the bottom drawer.' Mo pulled out the green shawl she recalled from childhood. Though faded, it was thick and warm. She arranged it round her mother's shoulders. 'I'm going to cook you something proper. They brought some more lamb. But this will tide you over.'

'You're a good girl,' said Ma hoarsely.

Mo found herself near to tears. Ma had never praised her before, never seemed to acknowledge her even. Illness must be making her soft. She'd almost prefer to see her brittle, battling self. 'Got to get your strength back…'

'Don't worry, I will.' She closed her eyes again, making Mo suddenly afraid.

'So.' The eyes opened again, watery and far away. 'I want to hear about Paris, Mo. And Derek. What's he up to now? I'm glad you're back together.'

'Here.' Mo put the bun, oozing butter to her mouth, cupping her chin in her hand to steady her. Ma took a nibble, chewed and swallowed.

'You'll look after Pa, Mo, if anything happens?'

The suddenness of the question took Mo aback. 'Come on Ma. Nothing's going to 'appen. You're right as rain.'

'But you will, won't you?'

'The others…'

'I know they're just around the corner. But they don't care like you do.'

Mo felt heavy.

'Please, promise me.'

'I promise,' said Mo, seeing her mother getting distressed.

'Besides, they've got their families to look after.'

'And I don't have?'

'Yes, but you and Derek are different. You're independent, the two of you. You'll both make your own way. And there's something else…'

'Come on, I want you to finish this bun and then I'm going downstairs to make more stew. The best you ever tasted.' Mo sensed a mesh of obligation drawing over her. She was impatient to shrug it off. She wanted to ask Ma about that other self: Maisy, the dancer and Music Hall singer, Maisy, the impassioned lover, Maisy who would throw all caution to the wind to ride high with

Sandor Olmak, the musician from Vienna.

'No, listen, Morwenna. It's something you need to know...' Ma whispered. But whatever it was, it would have to wait. Ma's head was sliding back onto the pillow, her eyes closing in exhaustion. The life had been sucked out of her. She was pale as dawn mist and just as insubstantial. Most of her forty-six years had been lived for others. Only one gleaming year had been for herself, one year of dangerous delight amongst so much duty and self-denial.

Mo left her, shutting the door quietly behind her and creeping down the stairs.

Chapter Twenty-seven *Derek*

When Derek woke he thought he was dead. These Russians could drink him under the table, even the women. Vodka was not a beverage he was accustomed to and he had downed a fair quantity. His head was throbbing horribly, a tight band across where his higher faculties should be. It all rolled back, bit by bit, the day and evening in the club: the euphoria of it, the comments which sent the painters into paroxysms of hope. Fantasies proliferated as the alcohol flowed. He wondered how many of The Twelve would be morose this morning, nursing a hangover and no sales.

As he staggered up, he noticed he was still wearing his trousers and socks. He must have slumped semi-conscious onto the bed. He tripped on the ruffled rug – *'Merde!'* – and grabbed hold of the dresser to prevent himself hurtling headlong onto the floor. He took care descending to the kitchen, gripping the banister. He lit the gas and watched the flickering blue flame a second or two before filling the saucepan with cold water, which stung his hands. He splashed some onto his face to wake himself up. 'Yes, I know,' he muttered to himself, feeling that if Mo were here she would disapprove of his shambolic state.

He drank a gallon of strong coffee, sniffed his armpits and considered that if indeed he wanted to make an impression on the New York gallery owner, he should at least wash himself, however inconvenient. That meant heating a large saucepan of water on the stove. But he had time: it was still early. The birds squawking and flapping around the balcony had woken him. He could tell by the position of the sun that dawn had not long given way to day.

Samuel Goldman was the one whose attention he needed to

catch. His sidekick from a lesser gallery had the dull look of someone who knew he was second-rate. Derek couldn't even remember his name. The caffeine was starting to have its effect. His heart was pounding as he started to shave. As he lathered his chin, his hand trembled but once he was skimming the razor across his cheeks, he felt calmer, more in charge. He brushed his hair. After a quick wash and with a fresh shirt, he was presentable enough. After all, people did not expect painters and their agents to look like tax inspectors.

He had agreed to meet Goldman at ten on Boulevard St Michel, known by locals as Boul Mich. The man was staying in a hotel near the large department stores on Boulevard Haussmann. Derek had not been able to find out much about him: only that there were money and good connections in the family. That was enough: definitely a man worth cultivating.

In all this he had been pushing the interests of the Russians; only now as he wandered through the early morning streets, did he think that he should be directing the man towards his own work as well. He watched lorries collecting night soil from the blocks with no proper sanitation. Elsewhere housewives were sluicing down the cobblestones in front of their dwellings. He reached the wider thoroughfare with relief. The stench of Paris drains and night soil was hard to stomach even for someone used to the slums of London's East End. There was a light mist shrouding the trees in the boulevard.

Yesterday he'd accompanied Goldman through the first rooms before Goldman requested time alone with the paintings: they needed to communicate with him without the agency of another human being. Derek had said he merely wanted to be at hand in case the other had any questions, but he'd made himself scarce.

He'd heard on the wireless that the Stock Market on Wall Street had crashed, swallowing billions of dollars. He wondered how Black Tuesday, as it was already being called, would play out in France and Great Britain. Would it affect Goldman's business? They'd be less money around for investment, that was certain, but paintings might hold their own in an unstable market. In the next breath he wondered when Mo would be returning. He'd had a letter that morning saying she'd get away as soon as she could. The danger seemed to be over, Ma Dobson was out of hospital and making a reasonable recovery.

The pavement tables were empty due to the cooler weather. He caught sight of Goldman at the second café from the corner, just inside the door, perusing the international edition of *The Chicago Tribune*. It had tombstone headlines about the Wall Street Crash. He laid the paper aside as Derek joined him.

'Well, the party's over,' Goldman remarked. 'The boom times are past. We've gone bust. America really will be singing The Blues now.' He folded the paper away. 'Good of you to come.' They shook hands. There was a civility and ease about Goldman, which suggested ingrained custom. In spite of the gloomy financial news he was wearing a candy-striped shirt and a tie that was a fraction too loud.

Derek ordered an espresso and whatever pastries they had. When two croissants arrived he wolfed them down without ceremony. Goldman smoked a cheroot. 'Quite some shindig, last night,' he remarked.

'It's their first collection in Paris. It means a lot to them.'

'So I gather,' he paused, eyed him askance, the hint of a sardonic smile across his sleek face. 'And you, Mister Eaton, what does it all mean to you? You seem awfully keen to be their mouthpiece.'

Derek sensed himself under scrutiny. He began to dislike the man. 'Most of them have had a rough deal. Alexander for instance…'

'That doesn't, of itself, make their work any better.'

'Of course not. But you asked why I …'

'There's no need to go into detail. I don't mean to pry.' Ah, these delicacies of feeling: empires can crash and wars rage but civilised society must continue with its niceties. As he sipped the last of his coffee Goldman offered him a cheroot. He took it.

'Mmm, Turkish I think,' he said waving it in the air.

'No, Moroccan,' corrected Goldman. 'I prefer the tang to the American brands these days. A hint of the exotic.' Derek was unsure how to proceed.

Goldman laughed. 'Don't look so confounded, my good man. Just because I'm not leaping at the prospect of taking on your Soviet friends, that doesn't mean…'

'They're not Soviets,' retorted Derek. 'They're Russians. Most of them have suffered under the Bolsheviks.'

'Yes, yes. I wasn't meaning to be offensive. I'm – well let's say over time I've grown cautious. It's not just my money. Others depend on my judgement. It's not about personal taste.'

The words were spoken in an even, measured way as though they had been uttered before – at board meetings, family conferences, shareholder conventions. This converting of art into a product with a price tag was something Derek was getting used to, but Goldman's air of superiority grated.

'Before the Revolution there was of course so much traffic and communication between the art worlds of Russia and France you could barely tell them apart,' Goldman was saying.

'There was a lot of dove-tailing, it must be admitted,' answered Derek. Goldman reminded him of one of the students at the Chelsea Polytechnic who did little work but appeared to be in the know about every school of painting, every last piece of sculpture. He supposed Goldman's family had a couple of Repin and Levitan paintings stowed away, and some priceless icons. Maybe even a Matisse from pre-Revolution Moscow.

'How long will you be in Paris?' He veered onto another tack.

Goldman blew a smoke ring into the air, watched it disappear and smiled at Derek. 'No definite timetable. I'm yet to make a few calls. I thought I'd take a bit of a vacation. Go down south to St Moritz if I get time. There's a writer called Ernest Hemingway. My uncle's in publishing, you see.'

'You seem to have all the arts well covered between you.'

'Not really.'

'So are you interested in these painters or not?' Derek was growing impatient with the prevarication, which came so naturally to Goldman. He beckoned a passing waiter and asked for another coffee.

'As a job lot, no. There's too much that's dull and mediocre mixed in with odd glints of … something more interesting. It would be naïve to go for the lot just because the painters have been jostled together in Paris. One must be discerning, after all...'

'Which of them makes the grade as far as you're concerned?'

Goldman referred to his scribblings. 'Some I note are very much in the *Blaue Reiter* mould. Some very avant-garde. Others have been sucked into Social Realism. Too pedantic and didactic, but as I say, here and there, I observed nuggets of originality. Roman Kurovsky, for example. Something in his use of colour and flatness appealed to me – primitive art but with a difference. I don't want to raise expectations. And I don't want to do what you Brits do so well.'

'And that would be?'

'Don't they say that about the politics of Empire? Divide and Rule. Keep everybody guessing.'

Derek failed to see the connection. 'Kurovsky was there last night.'

'I know. I spoke to him. Didn't get very far. The man doesn't speak English.'

'And you don't speak Russian?'

'I speak French but that didn't help. The man is a bit of a peasant. You know who I mean, I take it?'

'The man's a recluse. That's why you couldn't get much out of him.'

He recalled that when he and Tanya had worked on the

captions, they had found Kurovsky reluctant to talk. Tanya had explained that many of the artists where fearful of saying anything in case it got picked up by the OGPU. The Organs could get back them through hurting friends or relatives back home.

'So you want to buy some of Kurovsky's work?'

'Maybe. I admit I'm interested in his work. One or two others sparked my interest. I'm surprised they haven't been lapped up by Gertrude Stein.'

Goldman and Derek agreed to hold a further meeting with Dimitri to discuss how they might move forward. In the meantime could Derek put together some notes on the man and the paintings he'd put into the exhibition?

* * *

Derek headed back to the gallery to see how things were faring. Dimitri was standing by the entrance with a grin on his face. 'Guess who came calling?' His face was wide with delight. 'Pablo Picasso. He was visiting a friend nearby and had heard about us. Wanted to take a look for himself. He stayed almost an hour.'

'And?'

'That's it.'

'Did he buy anything or make any comment?'

'He just came and stood and stared and left as suddenly as he'd appeared.' Derek failed to see what Dimitri was so cheerful about. It went without saying that artists were curious about each other's work. In and of itself it meant nothing.

Alexander was tidying papers on the reception desk. When Derek asked him who had visited that morning he looked blank, then remembered there had been a troupe of students from the Sorbonne who spoke a lot to each other but barely looked at the pictures. He also mentioned Picasso: the short man with powerful eyes, was how he described him.

There was an open bottle of wine in the furthest room and an ashtray full of cigarette stubs. Tanya was in a corner, frowning.

She did not register his presence.

'I'm not disturbing you, am I?'

'Oh, I didn't see you.'

'You're looking tired,' he uttered without thinking as he moved towards her. It was more than that. She looked troubled, preoccupied. 'Is anything the matter?'

She gave a light sigh and started rooting around in her handbag. She pulled out a packet of cigarettes and lit up. 'The long arm of the OGPU,' she half laughed. 'Even if I say nothing, keep as quiet as the grave, it seems I'm causing trouble. Those in high places don't like me nor what I do.'

Derek had grown used to this cast of paranoia among the Russians. It went with the vodka and winter boots. She eyed him, tilting her head to one side. 'I can see you don't believe a word I'm saying.'

'What can I say? I don't know what you're referring to.'

'No-one who has not lived in Russia can possibly understand – really understand – in their soul and gut, what's going on there.'

He felt smacked into place. How could his unruffled life possibly compare to the complexity of hers? 'I dare say, you're right. But I'll understand even less if you don't tell me …'

'It doesn't serve you in the least to get tangled up with the likes of me. I am a bringer of bad luck.'

He laughed. 'You certainly take yourself very seriously.'

She got up and started striding around, puffing energetically and avoiding eye contact. He realised he might have offended her or else she was carrying an anger that had nothing to do with him. Oh, but she perplexed him now. He wanted to crawl inside that head of hers and find out what was going on there. He wanted to stop her in her tracks and force her to look at him.

'Stop this pacing around. It's making me nervous,' he burst out then realising how ridiculous this sounded, started to laugh. A deep belly laugh. She looked across in astonishment.

'What's there to laugh about?'

'You. You're like a cat about to spring.' Once he'd said that he fell silent. She was having an effect on him. And that did make him nervous. She stopped pacing and approached.

'I'm afraid,' she almost whispered. 'I thought I was safe here in Paris where there are so many other refugees. So much mingling and mixing – that I would not stand out. But they have sent spies. Even here. I don't know how to extricate myself. I don't want to involve Dimitri. He has done enough for me. He'd do anything for me and already has.'

Her eyes were filling with tears. Something in her snapped then. 'So you see, Mister cool-headed Englishman I am not just imagining these things. I am being followed.' She was standing a couple feet away from him. He saw the fragility of her arms, the sinews of her neck, and had an irresistible urge to touch her.

'Who is following you?'

'I caught only a glimpse. One was pock-marked – *a chomura*. The other looked like a bouncer in a low-class nightclub. I think of them as Platon and Gomer.'

'Platon and Gomer?'

She gave a little laugh. 'That's Russian for Plato and Homer.'

Chapter Twenty-eight *Mo*

Over the next day or so Ma perked up, sitting up in bed for longer spells and then insisting on getting up and with Mo's assistance having a wash-down. She was weak on her legs but determined. When she started finding fault with everything that Mo was trying to do for her, Mo knew she was on the mend.

'Can you scrub the scullery out, it looks disgusting.' This triggered a desire to escape, she was not their skivvy and her darling sisters were getting off scot-free. Meanwhile Pa had distanced himself, claiming he needed to run the pub, which was of course true, but even then he kept asking Mo to tot up the evening's takings and lend a hand when she could.

Slipping back into this world was like putting on a grubby old glove: it fitted her hand to perfection, yet she itched to get it off. She was ashamed to feel that way, but she couldn't help it. Day by day she was becoming a prisoner.

At first, she'd been happy to repay any emotional debt she owed, happy to swab down floors, singing as she did so. She'd never liked housework, but it was a way of channelling her restlessness. She liked to gaze at the result: to decipher patterns in the linoleum or the original grain in the wood. In the bar she buffed taps and shone the copper counter so it displayed all the extravagance of a former era. The stain glass windows began to tell their stories of flowers and birds as daylight broke through.

At the end of each day she penned a letter to Derek, telling him what she was up to and how things were going with her mother. She was delighted to hear back from him. His letter ran:

'Darlingest Mo, my darling wife,

If I had the time I would say I missed you beyond measure, but it would be an exaggeration. At the end of each day I am dog-tired. The exhibition has been a success. It has gained attention from an American gallery owner with a Russian grandfather. A regular crowd comes through: other artists and gallery owners, students from the Sorbonne and grandes dames of the bourgeoisie, who poke their noises in and take quick flight... So I'm kept very busy. The Russians have installed me as intermediary in their dealings with the Anglo-Saxon world. It's all very exciting, but I do miss you, my love. The nights are very long without you. I sit on our wonky balcony and look out over the roofs, more often glistening with rain now or battered by autumn winds and wish I could fly over to you like a pigeon and rest my head on your breast, hear it softly beating, And so much more... Come soon, my love.'

It was after this letter, that Mo decided she must see about getting back to France. Ma was quite active now: in a day or so she would be able to resume light duties in the pub. Mo had worked hard getting the place presentable: the downstairs scullery and sitting room were as clean and tidy as they were going to be.

She called round to Cissy's place. She lived four streets away in a terraced house, which had a back outside privy and running water inside. In the years since she'd last been there it seemed even more cluttered with the bric-à-brac Cissie loved to collect. The mock Meissen lady and gentleman were still there, bedside the coronation mug of George V. At first, the rooms gave Mo a sense of continuity but after an hour she longed to break out. Now as she and Cissy sat either side of the range, like two bookends, it crossed her mind that had they not been family they would have nothing in common. She sipped her tea. 'Bit strong this. Got any sugar?'

Cissie got up and came back with a bowl. 'Getting refined in your tastes, are you?' she said as she spooned two teaspoons of sugar into the khaki brew.

'Ma's a lot better,' began Mo. 'She's eating properly and starting to pick holes in everything. That's a sure sign…'

Cissy gave a little laugh. 'She's a tough one, that's for sure. I never reckoned she'd pull through.'

'I need to get back to Paris. Otherwise I'll lose my work there.'

'Is that so?' replied Cissy with no show of interest. 'I would've thought with Derek selling paintings it didn't matter anymore.'

Mo inhaled sharply to contain her annoyance. 'It matters to me.'

Cissy shrugged. 'But it's not a matter of life or death, is it – your work?'

Again Mo felt she was being made the indulgent one, the seeker of dreams, when everyone else around her had their feet planted firmly on the ground. How could she ever explain any of this to Cissie, who had married the stallholder round the corner and now had a strapping five-year old and another on the way?

'How's it going?' She indicated Cissy's bump. Cissy stroked it with an air or resignation. 'The doctor told me to eat more greens and put my feet up. Fat chance of that. What about you? Anything?'

Mo shook her head. This was not a conversation she wanted to embark on. 'As I was saying I need to get back to Paris. I was wondering if you could look in on Ma and Pa, once or twice a week. Make sure she doesn't overdo it.'

'So you're off, are you? Swanning back to gay Paree…'

'It's where I live, Cissy. I'm not going there on holiday.'

Mo tried to ignore the sour expression on her sister's face that implied she was hard done by. She got to her feet. She went to kiss her on either cheek as she'd grown used to doing in France. Cissy gave her a strange look. Just then there was a rap at the door and in rushed Sam, face aglow, back from school. Mo's heart beat strangely. He looked adorable. 'Best be on my way,' she said crisply, planting a kiss on the top of his head. 'Do you like school, Sam?'

''S'll right,' he said. 'Got any bread and jam, mum?'

Mo walked on towards Tilda's place a few streets further near Kingsland High Rd. There she received a warmer reception and

Tilda promised she would call by The Mare's Head at least twice a week. This, Mo knew, would require effort as she kept the books for her husband's decorating business as well as taking in odd jobs sewing to make ends meet. Next on Mo's list was getting in enough groceries for her parents for the coming days.

    She caught the afternoon train to Dover, feeling lonely as she left Victoria station, with no one to wave her off. She arrived in Dover and made her way to the ferry port where she was dismayed to learn there were no ferries that day: the wind had picked up and the big sea meant the vessels would roll and pitch to a dangerous degree. She resigned herself to finding cheap lodgings for the night. She booked into the first reasonable-looking guesthouse she came across. She went to the post-office to put through a telegram to Derek but it had already closed. Chilled from the sharp wind, she trudged back to the guesthouse and took herself off to bed.

Chapter Twenty-nine *Derek*

The last letter Derek received from Mo informed him that Ma Dobson was getting tetchy and therefore well on the way to recovery. He smiled as he read Mo's familiar scrawl, heartened that the crisis was over. He fingered the light paper, imagining Mo as she struggled not to show emotion, keeping a practical even tone, much as her mother did when under pressure.

The exhibition had settled into itself with a steady flow of the interested and the curious passing through. Critics had appeared and written up their mainly favourable reviews in *Gil Blas* or *Le feuilleton*, though he did not expect these to affect sales vastly. The American connection was proving fruitful, though tricky to negotiate. Goldman insisted on saying as little as possible and masking any enthusiasm. The man clearly wanted as much of Kurovsky's work as he could get hold of. His eyes flickered when he looked at Derek's work, as though still making up his mind about it. The bulk of the Russian work would remain unsold – appreciated, ogled but not sought out for galleries or private collections.

Derek folded up the sheet of Mo's letter and stuffed it into his jacket pocket for safekeeping. He wrote a list of things he had to do that day. His encounter with the Americans had given him an appetite to deal, even when unsure of the market value of a particular piece of art. He'd been back to Gertrude Stein's for cake and art talk, together with Dimitri. Tanya had declined to get involved. It seemed she did not trust to show herself in public, even in the gallery.

He was trying not to think about her too much. She was unsettled and unsettling, a puzzle that begged to be unravelled. While he disapproved of Picasso's entanglements with women, part of him yearned for the same license. The letter burnt in his pocket. Already he'd thought the unforgiveable and betrayed Mo in his mind. Only he hadn't, had he? Even as an artist Tanya weighed heavy upon him. She wanted to get the Russians represented, but what of her own work stashed away in the attic? Would she ever get to air *Stalin Dolls,* as startling as they were?

He arrived at the gallery soon after it opened. Dimitri and Alexander were already there, hugging the entrance, chain-smoking, watching every gallery visitor with fervid appraisal. Derek nodded a greeting, wanting to pass between them. Their sullen response should have alerted him.

'Goldman came in early,' started Dimitri. 'He left soon after. He asked for Kurovsky. Apparently wants to interview him with an interpreter.' The voice sounded clipped. Was he angry, wondered Derek? You could never tell with these Russians. He started whistling, moving about, wanting to create an air of business as usual.

'Tanya's gone,' said Dimitri.

Derek's heart thumped erratically. 'What do you mean – gone?'

'I haven't seen her in forty-eight hours. Her studio has been ransacked.' Derek felt the blood leaving his head. Dimitri offered him a cigarette, which he took. He inhaled deeply, digesting the news. It seemed only moments ago he'd drawn in that musky smell of her perfume, wanting and not wanting to embrace her otherness, her familiarity. How could she have just vanished into the streets of Paris?

Questions bombarded him. 'Watch out for the long arm of the OGPU,' he'd joked a couple of days ago. 'What's going on?' he almost shouted. 'She must have said something. You must know something.'

'All we know was that she was going to meet an old friend. She didn't say who it was.'

Derek was angry that Dimitri had let himself be taken in; he was otherwise so protective of Tanya. 'Have you been to the police?'

'They won't care about a bunch of Russians.'

'But they might know something…' he baulked at mentioning bodies fished out of the Seine or crushed below the Eiffel Tower. He felt a hollowing out. 'When was the last time you saw her? What exactly did she say?'

'I just told you.' Dimitri's patience seemed at its limit. He sucked on his cigarette, looked at it, threw it onto the gravel outside and crunched it with his foot. 'Don't know where to start,' he muttered.

'Can we go to her studio?' said Derek, warding off the helplessness he felt coming from Dimitri. 'The intruders might have left something behind – some trace.' They went back inside. Alexander was in the foyer, shuffling through the brochures. He offered to stay and greet any visitors.

As Derek and Dimitri walked towards her studio, Derek was revisiting every conversation he'd had ever had with her, every exchange. It was conceivable she'd met a friend from back then; but that did not explain why her studio had been targeted. As they arrived he saw that even the street door had been attacked. It swung off its hinges and creaked in the morning wind. He had a growing sense of dread. They moved quickly up the steps. Dimitri pushed back the door into the attic.

Devastation. Chairs toppled, tables upended, marks against the wall as if the butt of someone in fury. The scene spoke of violence, a ruthless disregard of what had been here. Derek leant against a beam, as if winded. The two stared at each other, bereft of language, as if they, too, had descended to the place of animals. Derek felt a sickness in his stomach, in his bones. Had Tanya been here when the intruders burst in?

The mannequins had been smashed and trampled. One, on its side, seemed to stare at him in consternation. Who were these men? What did they want? And more to the point what did they fear? Of late he'd learnt that fear was the most savage motivator. It fuelled rage. It fuelled random chaos. Tanya, he whispered. He looked across at Dimitri. 'What do you know?' he mumbled. 'What has been happening?' He paused. 'I hope to God she wasn't here when they came.'

Dimitri gave a helpless shrug. 'She hasn't been working much lately.' He kicked over a crushed carcass of a Stalin doll. 'Tanya knows lots of people. She trusts everyone and no one. Never wants to limit her experience but gives herself into no one's keeping…' He seemed to be speaking to himself.

They moved silently through the space, shuffling through the debris, each guarding his thoughts, pushing away the darkest of fears. 'Shouldn't we tell the police?' asked Derek at last, exhausted by the useless scouting around. Again Dimitri shrugged. Derek could not understand Dimitri's disinclination to inform the local gendarmerie. They would keep a list of missing people together with descriptions.

He gaped at the desecrated studio. It was hard to tell if there'd been a struggle. Despite himself he looked for signs of blood, a struggle, fragments of torn clothes. But there was no trace of Tanya. Dimitri was looking pale as death. His hand was shaking as he picked up a shard, wired mesh covered in now cracked plaster.

'She said she'd been followed,' said Dimitri in a whisper. 'I tried to reassure her. We get so used to looking over our shoulders, we Russians. Part of the new social order, you might say. She's been followed before. She was hauled in front of a local Soviet just before she left Moscow. She talked her way out of it. Had a friend or two in high places…'

'Who should we be talking to about this?' Derek paced back through the attic. Dimitri looked down at the ground, at that moment as lost as a child. Derek recalled what Dimitri had said about Tanya being like family, his sister. 'Do we go to the police?' he repeated.

'Not yet.' Dimitri snapped to, gazing straight at Derek. 'We don't want to jeopardise her. There may be something they want. Something we can give them.'

'That sounds like blackmail to me.'

'It might do. But you don't know our ways.'

'When was the last time you saw her?' asked Derek.

'Two days ago. She said she had to see someone. I was busy. I didn't pay her much attention.'

'Did she say anything more? About where she was going? Did she seem frightened?'

'As I said, she was her usual self. A bit distracted, perhaps.'

They had not been in the attic for more than a few minutes when they heard noises below. Then feet rushing up the stairs. They looked at each other, quickly signalling that they should stay silent. Derek flattened himself against the wall by the door. Dimitri dodged behind a vertical beam. The footsteps got closer. It was clearly more than one person.

As if sensing their presence the intruders hesitated, steps slowing as they neared the top of the flight. Derek could scarcely breathe. He wondered for what reason they'd be returning to the massacred artwork. The first of them kicked against the door so it wobbled, threatening to fall. He yelled something in Russian. Dimitri stifled a gasp. And then the man was in the space. Derek caught a side view of him: he was around five foot ten with close-cropped hair and a heavy jaw. His eyes shifted, chameleon-like around the attic. 'I know you're there,' he said in thickly accented English. And two others followed, rushing in. 'Ivan,' he spewed out words in Russian. The burly broad-shouldered men filled the attic with their bulk, barging about and discovering Dimitri and Derek within seconds. On seeing one of them was pock-marked, Derek went cold.

They shoved them roughly into the centre. There was a fast exchange in Russian. Dimitri looked angry and frightened in turns. He shifted from one foot to the other, glanced towards the stairwell as if gauging the feasibility of escape.

'What did they say?' urged Derek when there was a break in the torrent of words.

'They told us to get out of here. To mind our own business and then no harm would come to us.'

'What about Tanya?' Dimitri shot him a dark look to the effect that he should not mention her name. 'What happened?' whispered Derek fiercely. The crew-cut man approached and yelled something. He drew out a knife – a long, old-fashioned dagger with a pointed blade – and held it close to Dimitri's throat. Derek stiffened: these were henchmen of the first order who would not flinch at slitting throats.

The man lowered the blade.

'What are they saying?' Derek whispered in desperation.

'We need to get out of here. Walk and keep walking and don't look back,' snarled Dimitri. The crew-cut man drew back, grinned at Dimitri, showing yellowing teeth. He gave a coarse laugh and said something to the other over his shoulder.

'What do they want with her?' insisted Derek, unable to let it rest. Dimitri said nothing. Crew cut shouted something at him, then Dimitri started towards the stairs and signalled to Derek to do likewise. They trod slowly down, not daring a backwards glance. Out on the street Dimitri paced away and kept looking over his shoulder until he was certain the others were not in pursuit. He opened a packet of cigarettes. With trembling fingers he lit one and offered another to Derek.

'Did they say anything about Tanya?'

Dimitri shrugged, still too shaken to speak. Finally he said: 'they seemed worried about what we might have found. Asked if we had taken any of her pieces. I asked about her – as occupant of the attic – but they were not giving anything away.'

'Who were they?' he asked. 'Not anybody you know? Who were they acting for? Did you pick anything up?'

'I assume they're connected to the OGPU. How or on

whose command or in what capacity I don't know. They looked like thugs to me, lowlifes called in to do someone else's dirty work.'

'So what do we do now?'

The question was rhetorical. It was incredible to Derek that Tanya could be whipped away from a studio in the heart of Paris. The streets looked so innocent, the cars and houses and cafes carrying on just as before. But who knew what viciousness lurked just beneath the surface?

He glanced at Dimitri. He was still pale.

'Where was she staying?' he asked, aware that he knew very little about her. Dimitri seemed too numbed to think clearly. He himself would have to gather what intelligence he could, scour the city if need be. The haunted look, the shadows playing over Tanya's face were images that kept recurring. She was the truest rebel of them all: the most authentic artist and upholder of the truth. He vowed that he would do everything in his power to track her down.

'With me, until three days ago. She moved out of her own apartment weeks ago. Said she didn't feel safe there.'

'Did you question her about it? Did she take anything with her when she left?'

'There wasn't much to take. She was living out of a suitcase.'

'We should ask the others. Perhaps one of them knows something. '

Dimitri looked at him askance. 'They're already uncertain about Paris. This will only stoke their fears.'

Derek paused. 'Let's go back and see what we can find at your place. She may have left an address book, a diary.'

Dimitri drew deep on his cigarette, frowning. 'Unlikely. She's always been secretive. As a girl she kept a journal under lock and key. One day, fearing it might be read, she set light to it. She can be very drastic.'

The two made haste to reach Dimitri's rooms. He lived not

far from Derek and Mo's place in a ground floor apartment beside a *Tabac*. Traffic passed constantly before his door. A tramline ran down the nearby boulevard. Opening the street door they entered a dark crowded space. Dimitri picked up mail lying on the mat. He creaked back a shutter. Derek noted dusty surfaces, no time given to order the room and make it welcoming.

'She slept in there,' said Dimitri gruffly. Derek opened the door onto another room, little more than a cupboard, a box room. Here the bed was neatly made. Some blankets had been folded at the end of it. He pulled out a drawer, caught his breath when he glimpsed her silk underwear. He banged the drawer shut. In the wardrobe hung one or two day dresses in pastel shades and one evening gown in a deep, glossy blue. On the ledge was a bottle of Chanel scent next to an English-French dictionary and a copy of short stories by Anton Chekhov. The air felt still and empty: an uncanny silence as though she had died. Dimitri slowly turned back the bed covers, then his actions became hurried, desperate, as he thrust himself about the room 'Tanechka Tanechka,' he whispered and gave an almost inaudible whimper like a dog searching its master. Watching him fuelled Derek's own sense of futility. He sat on the bed.

'Look Dimitri, we can't do this on our own. We need to call in the police.' Dimitri said nothing, glanced at Derek in the pitted mirror, avoiding direct eye contact. His shoulders slumped.

'There is another way,' said Dimitri.

'Is there?'

'Someone in the wider Russian community might know something. Everybody is enmeshed in the politics back home, one way or another.'

'One minute you want to involve them, the next not.'

'We need to be careful, that's all. Many won't even know she's here. Her first exhibition won acclaim. There was a short space of time when there was tolerance, time for self-expression in the name of the greater good. But not any more…'

'Yes yes. But tell me –Tanya fell out of favour as a result of what? Stalin's Dolls haven't been shown yet.'

'No, they haven't. Look, it's a long story. Ties up with her father. Plus I think there was envy from some of the Politburo wives.'

'I thought you were supposed to be past all that?'

Dimitri gave a short bitter laugh. 'For all the wonderful ideas about Socialism, meanness still creeps in. Ideas of revolution can be interpreted anyway you choose.'

'Maybe you *should* sound out the others. Though I don't want us to make things worse than they are.'

Dimitri raised his shoulders. 'There's nothing here. Let's get over to the gallery.'

Chapter Thirty *Mo*

There were strange octopus creatures all around, flailing tentacles with poisonous tips, glaring at her with red eyes. Mo pressed towards the surface, broke through. She woke with a start, fighting off tangled bedclothes, gazing around in bewilderment until she realised where she was. The room was dark, smelled vaguely of damp carpets. It was the best and cheapest she could find at that time of night, and she'd hardly given the place a second glance. Now she took in the antique dresser, missing a handle, and the mahogany wardrobe. Soon she would be in Paris again, back with Derek; but the sensation of displacement persisted. The visit home had perturbed her. Ma would rally and life at The Mare's Head would resume, albeit unsteadily. Yet concern at Ma's illness only compounded her sense of two worlds jarring within.

To whom did she owe more loyalty?

She threw back the covers and put her feet to the cold floorboards. The wind had picked up again: the window was rattling in its frame, a branch snagged and whipped across the pane. It was unlikely that the ferries would sail today. She parted the curtains and peered out over tidy privet hedges, neatly kept gardens and trees now almost bare of leaves. This was a landscape she knew little of. She pivoted between London and Paris, the buzzing, teeming cities. Here, on the outskirts of Dover, people would lead quiet, routine lives, bound by the annual rhythm of church fêtes, births, deaths and marriages. It was an England that scared her. For she felt shut out from it, forever on the periphery, looking in with a mixture of disdain and longing.

She gathered her sponge bag and towel and went to the

bathroom. The landlady had said she could run a bath if she did it before eight and did not use up too much water. She watched the steam curl up as the Ascot flared. She dropped in a few bath crystals, which coloured the water pink. What luxury! She could tell the landlady had a taste for extravagance from the seashells round the mirror and the porcelain figurines on the landing.

The dining room was half full. Only commercial salesmen travelled at this time of year. Underneath a frilled pinafore the landlady was wearing a pink dress with a single row of pearls. Her hair was swept back off her face. She took Mo's order for scrambled eggs and toast, adding that the marmalade and jam were home-made. Mo wondered if she was a widow.

After breakfast Mo wandered down to the ferry port. The place was desolate. The wind was gaining force and swept in gusts around the terminus. She drew her coat around her. A notice announced that they were expecting to run ferries the next day. She walked into town to send a telegram to Derek, informing him of the delay. She found the library in Dover and settled in a corner, strangely out of time, lost in a space of her own. She looked for songbooks but came across nothing. She was on the hunt for something new: exciting material to push her boundaries.

She wanted to be back in Paris, getting on with things. Though it had crept up on her and then startled her, she did not rue the decision to have Derek back in her life. When she thought of Jonathon Knighton, she was glad that that particular episode was over. Derek pulled at her like a wind, a fairground ride. He made her delve into herself as no one else did. With him she could be delighted, overwhelmed, furious, but never bored.

She sprang to her feet, startling an old man dozing behind a copy of *The Times*. She left the library, impatient to get moving. She'd make one last call home before she left for Paris, before she booked another night at the guest-house. She tried calling from a K1, a public phone box, but the lines to London were busy. When she did get through she half wished she hadn't.

'You need to get back 'ere,' rasped Pa. 'She's taken a turn for the worst.'

Chapter Thirty-one *Derek*

Derek arranged to meet Anton Lensky again. When Lensky suggested a cafe on Boulevard Raspail Derek began to wonder whether the man actually had an office: he always seemed to be hanging around cafes and *boîtes*. Derek was not in the mood for alcohol or heavy meals. He ordered coffee. He told Lensky what he needed to know about Mo and her trip home. He said he was not sure what day she'd be back in Paris as she'd sent a telegram to say the ferries were not currently operating.

Derek wondered how many other young women Lensky had lined up. Someone who tracked down a singer after a performance would leave nothing to chance. 'She has a rare voice, your wife. But she shouldn't waste it. She needs guidance.'

'You've told her that in no uncertain terms.'

'I don't mean to undermine her. It's just when an audience is enthusiastic one can get carried away.'

'I'm sure that wouldn't happen. Mo's a professional.'

'No doubt – I'm just saying – as a musician.'

'So, will she be able to continue to sing for you when she gets back?'

'Oh yes. Very much so.'

'Good. She'll be happy to hear that.'

Derek found himself reluctant to broach the second reason he'd wanted to see Lensky. He pondered a moment whether it would be rash to continue, for he barely knew the man. He glanced at him: there was shrewdness in his eyes, a sense of having seen much of life. He had an evenness of manner, which denoted a man not easily thrown into panic.

Desperation to unearth Tanya was gnawing away at him. He considered Lensky's grave demeanour and decided to take a chance. 'There's something else I wanted to ask you about. It's delicate – not a scandal – but politically speaking.'

'And that would be?'

Derek exhaled and stared at Lensky. 'There's someone gone missing. She was helping to organise the exhibition. She was there the other night. I don't know whether you met?'

'Oh?' Lensky's curiosity was whetted, though he affected nonchalance.

'The sculptress. I fear for her safety. That she might have fallen foul of the powers-that-be.'

'Not difficult these days.'

'The thing is – the place where she worked was ransacked…'

Lensky leaned back, staring with concentration into his empty glass, his mouth set. After a while he cleared his throat, said his Russian contacts in the city were not extensive, but he'd find out what he could. Dimitri had also vowed to put out feelers, Derek recalled. The knot in his stomach tightened. He resolved that if they had not heard anything by the next morning he would go to the gendarmes. The image of pock face and his cronies in the attic made him nervous: if the Russian secret service was involved, they were clearly out of their depth.

He and Lensky parted company soon after.

* * *

It had been a long day. He'd been wading through mud. His mind kept reverting to Tanya. At the exhibition he'd hardly heeded the flow of viewers. He'd made a few calls, set up another meeting with Goldman and fiddled with the exhibition notes. Walking through the gallery rooms he tried to reassure himself that everything was in order. Dimitri and Alexander were in a huddle. He caught the urgency of their hushed voices, saw the alarm on Dimitri's face, and wanted to distance himself from the ongoing drama. He wanted more than anything not to care, but he could not fool himself.

Slowly he approached his rooms in Marais, wondering as he

kicked out at a scrap of litter, when Mo would be back. He had not heard from her in two days. The rooms seemed dark and empty without her. It reminded him so much of the early days after Timothy's death, when Mo was away doing what she needed to do.

There was a shadow by the street door. He blinked hard. His eyes were deceiving him. As he drew closer he realised that his first instinct had been correct. It was Tanya! Relief flooded him in a surge of joy. He rushed forward and wrapped his arms around her. She clutched at him then pulled away. She was gulping for air, struggling.

'I don't want…' she began but was unable to continue.

'We went to your studio. Saw …'

'They ruined them. Before they've even been shown anywhere…'

He could hear the anger in her voice. Nothing so destroyed an artist as to tamper with their work. 'Who were they? Who were these men?'

'I have no time to spare. They may know your connection to me. And now they've seen your face. They'll track you down.' She cast her eyes about, scanning the street. 'I came here because…' she began, 'I had your address from the gallery. I need to disappear. I thought you might be able – you might know someone, somewhere …'

She wants to stay in my place, he thought. And it's not possible.

'Were they chasing you?'

'I heard them coming. There's a fire escape nobody knows about behind the chimneybreast. Hasn't been used in decades because nobody lives in that space anymore. They've been watching me – from a distance. I don't know how but word has got out about my work. *Stalin's Dolls* have stirred things up. I should have known better. …' Her words failed. She was trembling. He put his arms around her, wanting to shake off the nightmares pursuing her. He was trembling too. He pulled back.

'I don't know who to trust,' said Tanya. Her face looked drawn in the half-light cast by the gas lamp in the street. Defiance never left her eyes but her body and her mouth were slack with the effort of resistance. From what he knew of Russian methods of persuasion she was lucky to be standing there, alone, without anyone behind her.

He glanced up and down the alleyway, eyes lingering over the recesses by doorways. Her pursuers would not necessarily be as thuggish as Pockface and his accomplices. They could be watching slyly, further down the passage, awaiting their moment. 'You can't stay here,' died on his lips. How could he thrust her out into the night? Her life was in danger. He took a step towards her. 'My wife…' the words failed to emerge. This was an emergency. They moved out of the shadows into the circle of light, while he looked up and down, harkened for any noise, any shift in the low hum of late traffic fading on the boulevards. He laid his hand on her wrist. Her skin felt cold to the touch. 'Tonight you stay here. Tomorrow we see.'

She gulped back whatever she'd been about to say, sighing in relief. He put his hand on her shoulder. It felt thin to the touch – so much fire in so delicate a vessel. He fished in his pocket for the key and quietly let them into the house. He wasn't sure whether or not the landlord was here. He sometimes dropped in on odd days in the month to check everything was in order.

He did not put on the light in the stairwell but groped upwards, using a sliver of light from the street. Their steps creaked on the stairs. He opened the door to the rooms, smiled as if to welcome her in. He thought of the tiny balcony where he and Mo drank wine and glimpsed Notre Dame, he thought of their brass bed beside the long, shuttered windows overlooking the shadowy alley.

'You'll be safe here. It's a bird's nest. No one ever comes up here.' The sitting room was in disarray with items of clothing and newspapers strewn around, a couple of enamel mugs on the table with dregs of coffee in them. 'Forgive the mess. I was going to have a tidy up...'

For the first time this evening Tanya smiled. 'No need to apologise. I'm grateful. I wouldn't be here if I … I just didn't know what to do. The others are being watched. You, too, maybe. But for one night I think we'll be safe.'

'Sit down. Sit down.' He cleared away a crumpled shirt and scattered pages of a newspaper from the sofa. He picked up a sock or two from the floor. 'Would you like a glass of wine. Or I've got cognac. Coffee.'

'Whatever you have,' she said quietly, eyeing the space around her. 'So where is your wife?'

'London. Her mother took sick.'

'When is she back?'

Derek gave a little shrug. 'Any time. She's been delayed by the weather.'

He took a bottle from the cupboard and pulled out the cork. 'Wine's easier than coffee. I'd have to go down to the kitchen for that.' He handed her a large glass of claret and sat down beside her on the sofa. They sipped.

She touched him lightly on the knee. 'Not everyone would take this risk,' she said. He felt a shot of electricity go through him. He shifted away.

'I'll sleep here,' he said. 'You can have our bed.'

'No, I'm fine here. I'm much smaller than you are.'

He took her hand in his. He wanted to say he'd be her friend, be there whenever she needed him, but his mind went blank. He felt awkward, not knowing how to broach the dereliction of her work nor her fugitive status. He was just aware of her there, breathing quietly, an intense, intelligent presence beside him. He released her hand, already he could feel a stirring in his loins. He took a stride towards the bottle in the cupboard, refilled their glasses.

'Come and look at the view,' he said. 'We even get a glimpse of the Seine and Notre Dame.' His voice was brusque, almost severe, as though commanding her. She said nothing but got to her feet and moved towards the balcony. She saw the two cast iron chairs, tucked against the railing.

'She's very beautiful, your wife.'

'And a talented singer. Look, can you see the towers?' The moon had slid out from between scudding clouds, illuminating the sky with a pale luminescence, casting silver over the rooftops. 'What happened?' he murmured. 'We saw your studio, Dimitri and I. We were afraid for your safety. Three men came. One had a knife…'

She sighed, leaned over the railing. 'I was living a time that was not mine.'

'How long have they been on to you?'

'Ever since I was born.' She gave a little laugh. 'My father was a writer – a playwright with Liberal tendencies. He had a very critical, speculating mind. Always annoying people in power. Reminding them of their inconsistencies. He had a problem with orthodoxy, with dogma.' She stared into her glass. 'The last time I saw him was just before they took him off for questioning.' She went silent, fingering the stem of her glass, lost in the dark memory.

'What happened?'

'Oh, he was shot. Along with his assistant, the stage manager and a couple of actors for good measure. As I said before, life is cheap when it's not your own.'

He could feel his heart thumping wildly. He wanted to crush her against his body, shield her from the cruelty and injustice of it all. He managed to steer himself back to the conversation.

'And your mother – what happened to her?'

'She was very independent. They were made for each but just too fierce together. She had carved out a life for herself as an artist – in the Itinerant mould. She loved observing scenes of

Russian life, sketching everything. But she knew enough to keep safe. Never did anything too daring or too provocative.'

'I see.'

'Well, she had us – didn't she – my brother and me? She became the mistress of a Kommissar. I believe she did it in order to protect us. Or because she was tired of bloodshed. She realised the least said, the better.' Tanya took a long draught of wine. 'She died too, though, in the end. Caught dysentery when she was in the provinces. Then cholera. Half starved she was. My brother went to join the Revolutionaries and I never heard from him again. I took off for Moscow. Hung around artists. Learned a thing or two.'

'You take after your father, I think.'

'Maybe. Or maybe I'm just driven. I don't feel I have a choice.' She gave a long yawn. Her eyelids began to droop. 'I need to sleep.'

'Yes, of course.' He went through to the bedroom to give it a quick inspection. The sheets were clean enough, though not freshly laundered. He cleared away more strewn clothes. He thrust open the windows and shutters. 'Here, you'll be fine here,' he called out.

When he heard no reply he went back to the sitting room. 'I said I'd be fine here on the sofa.' She had curled up like a cat on the cushions. Within minutes she was sleeping. He touched her lightly on the head. All her liveliness and angst softened by exhaustion. He ran a light finger across her cheek. What an extraordinary woman she was. He fetched a spare blanket and laid it gently over her. He sighed and returned to the bedroom.

* * *

He could not sleep. His head swam with the possibilities before him, the sheer tantalising mystery of her. He stared up at the stripes thrown by the half open shutter. He kicked away the sheets. Tanya had come to him. She had entrusted him with her safety. She was lying just feet away. He listened for the sounds of movement, her breathing, imagining her as she lay coiled on the sofa. She must surely be uncomfortable. By now she'd have a crick in the neck. He smiled to himself – a crick in her neck, in that beautiful vulnerable neck of hers, which bothered him a lot less than the rest of her. He turned over. She was a defenceless woman in the prey of dark political forces beyond her control and not of her making. She was in a predicament. He would not exploit that. Besides he had made a vow. Mo had let him back into her life. He'd be the greatest of fools to jeopardise that. Mo was the one who counted. The one he'd chosen, been chosen by, the woman he'd pledged his loyalty to, again.

And yet there was Tanya with her dark questing eyes and penetrating intelligence, her artistic integrity, the deep imponderability of her. He stirred, turned over. Tried to shut off his mind. Mo would never forgive him a second time. There was no question of it. His bedroom door would stay firmly shut. He looked at the pale moonlight falling across the blanket, the table where he'd stacked his books: Dostoyevsky and Tolstoy and others as he tried to come to terms with the Russians. It was impossible and there was an end to it. He would never understand them, just as he would never fathom Tanya.

He imagined he heard a creak from next door. Listened hard. Nothing. He took a slug of wine from the bottle he'd brought into the room with him, thinking it would help him sleep. It tasted metallic. He had the urge to spit it out. He swallowed it, groaned and turned over. What was he going to do with Tanya? He smiled again at his presumption. What, rather, was she going to do now? Who could help her? He thought of Lensky. The man had more to him than met the eye. He slid between the cracks in a fragmented culture and found a path through. He was the arch deal broker. Wheeler-dealer. Cultured, well-connected, suave, urbane, musical, he understood the Russians as few did.

His mind grew tired, thoughts going round in circles and not getting anywhere. He drifted into broken snatches of sleep. He saw Mo forcing open the street door, blasting him for Tanya's presence. He saw Tanya tied to a stake, waiting to be shot, incinerated. He woke with a start.

His door creaked open. There at the foot of his bed was Tanya. She had discarded her skirt and blouse and stood in a simple shift. She had set loose her hair. 'I couldn't sleep,' she said. She approached. 'I'm afraid.' With a sweep of his hand he pulled back the covers, drew her in. She slid in beside him. He kissed the top of her head, drew in the musky smell of her, a whiff of lemon in her hair. He felt the frailty of her arms, the slightest tremoring in her body. 'Just for a while,' she said. She leant her head against his chest. He enfolded her in his arms.

'You're safe now,' he murmured. 'No harm will come to you.' His heart was racing. It would be easy, so easy. Breaking trust was the easiest thing in the world. Just yielding to the moment, to the instincts sweeping through him. He held back, about to burst, strained, taut, unable to bear the tension. And then she wrapped her arms around his waist, felt down towards his groin and then there was no stopping. They kissed, tore at each other, discarding clothes, sheets, hungry, desperate, mindless. In no time he was inside her, moving, loving her, unable not to. Plunging. All lost now, all discretion, caution, sense – only their bodies together, only the moment, only the fever.

Afterwards he kept her in his arms, nuzzling his mouth into her hair, taking in the fragrance, the animal nearness. For now, Mo was a distant planet, not to be thought of. He slept. She shifted out of his grasp towards an empty space in the bed. Towards morning she moved again, got up out of the bed and went back next door. Alone, he stared at the ceiling. He had not meant this to happen. He had not sought her out, but had offered her his protection, his bed. But the experience of loving her had changed all that. He could not bear to think of Mo now, upset and in London, even on her way towards him. What now, he thought? But he could not bear to think. He turned, kicked off the blanket, listened out for the sound of Tanya through the wall, half afraid to go in and see her; afraid of what her eyes might say to him. Afraid.

Chapter Thirty-two *Mo*

Ma had been fine when Mo left her. Was Pa exaggerating, just wanting Mo back as it eased things and put less of a burden on him? She half believed that was the case. But her heart was racing horribly, suspecting that Ma really had taken a turn for the worse. The Hackney hospital discharge note had said very little, but the ward sister had told Mo to keep an eye out: Ma was not in good health and her lungs were weak after numerous attacks of pleurisy and bronchitis. Mo knew that was true: Ma was sick virtually every winter but never took to her bed. Her diet was inadequate and she was always too long on feet and gnawed by the anxiety of keeping The Mare's Head together.

Mo gathered up her things and headed for Dover station. By early afternoon she was in Hackney. She found a note pinned up in the back yard of the pub. The door had been left open. Clutching the scrap of paper, she wandered into the empty scullery and through to the Public Bar, which stank of spilled beer and nicotine. She sank onto a chair by a table, which still had dirty glasses on it. So Pa had had to hold the fort on his own: Ma was particular about gathering and washing glasses for the next day and she always swabbed the floors with bleach last thing at night.

Mo fingered the message, which told her that he had taken Ma back to the Hackney hospital. Families like theirs rarely went near hospitals unless desperate. Was it a recurrence of pneumonia? Pa had not said. Could one have two bouts of the illness in quick succession? She fetched a glass of water and sat sipping it. One of the last conversations she'd had with Ma kept running through her mind. Her mother had wrung a promise from her. Look after Pa. That meant Pa and The Mare's Head.

Was she to move back to Hackney? It was the last, the very last thing she wanted to do. Why did the other sisters get off so lightly? Why was everyone so keen to clip her wings and send her plummeting to earth? She tapped the table with the flat of her hand. Best get over to the Hackney and see just how bad things were.

Maisy Dobson had been put in another ward. Pa was there, in the corridor, looking grey and shrunken. Cissy and Tilda looked relieved to see her. 'They're in with her now, the doctor and nurse,' Pa mumbled. 'But it's not looking hopeful. She 'ad another turn.' He ran his hand over his forehead. Mo had the urge to shake him. Why had he let things get so bad? Why had he driven his wife into illness? She shook off the thought. He looked as guileless as a child.

'What sort of turn?'

'She was clutching her chest. Couldn't breathe proper…'

Mo walked to the threshold of the ward where she could hear the medical staff muttering. Oh, how she hated hospitals with their ammonium and bleach, with their all-pervasive smell of dread, of so much that was left unsaid. She thought she was done with all that. She was tired of grief and regret. For goodness' sake, she was not yet twenty-five! She sniffed, gave a quick smile to her siblings and watched the medical staff coming towards them.

The doctor, who was handsome in an austere sort of way and not much older than herself, flicked back his hair and addressed Pa. 'We've done what we can. Given her some morphine to ease the pain.'

'So – so what is the problem?' interjected Mo, knowing no one else would have the gumption to ask.

The doctor eyed her with surprise. 'She's had a relapse. Her lungs are badly infected.' He seemed on the point of saying there was nothing they could do, but looked around the small anxious-looking group and decided the less said the better.

'Can we go in now? Can we see her?' asked Cissy.

The doctor waved them through without speaking and hurried off down the corridor. One look at Ma and Mo sensed the rapid deterioration that had happened. They'd placed an oxygen mask over her face and her eyes were closed. Her skin had the colour of dried parchment. She looked ancient. Surfacing momentarily into consciousness, her eyes flickered open then she sank back into the depths. Mo could scarcely bear to watch her. She clutched her hand. 'Ma it's me, Mo.'

Chapter Thirty-three *Derek*

Derek and Tanya sat nursing coffee cups side by side on the tiny balcony. Neither spoke. Derek watched pigeons flap towards them, heard them cooing on a nearby balcony. The sun was slanting across, the last gift of autumn, despite the chill in the air. She had taken last night's blanket out with her and pulled it round her as she bent forward, her nose close to the rim of the cup.

'These last days have stirred memories,' she almost whispered. 'My father – always knew too much. I didn't tell you the full story.'

'No.' Derek was curious but hesitated to push her.

'He was touring the provinces with the Bolshoi Drama Theatre, back in the early twenties. He saw what was going on…'

'That was the time of the famine, wasn't it?'

She nodded, sipped more coffee. 'They snatched the grain from the peasants for the cities. Let them starve. They couldn't even sow seeds for the next crop. Imagine that. He saw it. It made him weep. But more than that it made him angry. When he came back to Moscow he wrote about it. Couldn't stop himself.'

Derek whistled lightly through his teeth. Tanya seemed lost in the past.

'He wrote a scene about an old peasant making his own coffin and lying down in it to die. My father knew he could never put on such a play but he talked about it – to trusted friends. Someone leaked it. I don't know to this day who it was.' She looked out over the rooftops, got up and leaned on the balustrade.

'Careful,' said Derek. 'I don't know how safe that is.'

She gave him a gentle smile, sat back down.

'They told me he was executed as a counter revolutionary.

They made it sound very official. I was already established as an artist by then. Had some acclaim. Official approval. But I couldn't carry on. My eyes had been opened.'

'So what happened?'

'I started doing my artwork in secret. As the daughter of *an enemy of the people* I was suspect. But I was good at the daytime job in the Ministry. Good at talking, writing reports. Then one day my boss invited me to take a walk along the bank of the Volga.'

"Tanechka,' he said. It was Lucharsky, remember? 'Tanechka, I was a close friend of your father. I admired him.' Lucharsky paused. Looked at me. 'I am concerned about you.' When the People's Commissar for Education says this to you, you take notice. 'I am going to send you abroad as a member of a delegation. The government is short of foreign currency so the Politburo has decided that my Ministry should negotiate the loan of some of our French masterpieces to museums in Paris, like the Louvre, for cash. As a fluent French speaker who knows Paris, it will be natural for you to be in the delegation. I can arrange the necessary visa for you.'

'When was that?' asked Derek.

She waved her hand. 'A few years ago. In the meantime I've been making my living as a translator. But always involved with the art world. He was a true friend, Anatoly Vasilyevich Lucharsky. He said: 'When you get to Paris, stay there. Don't come back. I have friends in Paris who will help you.' But as you know, the man is no longer in office.'

'We'll find you somewhere safe,' Derek said.

She nodded. 'I know I can't stay here. I don't want to make life difficult for you.' She looked at him directly, 'Last night – I didn't know where else to go.'

'I know someone who might be able to help.'

'Someone you trust?'

He sighed. 'I hardly know him. But he seems resourceful. I'd say he has good connections in the city. You do want to stay in

Paris, I take it?'

She leaned back, glanced across. 'I don't know where else to go.'

Derek finished his coffee and got to his feet. 'We need to move quickly on this. I'll send a message. You wait here. I'll go down to the *Tabac* and send a *pneumatique*. I'll fetch some croissants while I'm at it.' She barely seemed to register what he was saying. She seemed in a state of shock. He left her on the balcony and bounded downstairs three steps at a time. He almost collided with the landlord by the street door. The other looked towards him with a disgruntled air.

'This just came for you, Monsieur.' He thrust a flimsy envelope towards Derek and slammed back into the room where he stayed when visiting. Derek fingered the telegram then tore it open. It ran: *'Staying on. Ma very ill. Come if you can.'*

He put it into his jacket pocket and slipped out into the street, heart racing. He crossed from the alley into the thoroughfare and entered the *Tabac* where two men were leaning on the counter, arguing. He brushed past them and pointed to two croissants behind the glass, then asked the proprietor if he could send a message. The man nodded and led him towards the back of the café.

Having despatched the message Derek retraced his steps. He would have to return to London. He wanted to, he realised. This was no time to be leaving Mo alone. There had already been so much to break her and still she had come through, skirting despair, plumbing darkness but always resurfacing, always ready to take on the next day and the next. But this might be the tipping point.

What was their marriage if he was not there for her?

And Tanya? He owed Tanya a lot less loyalty than he did Mo. She was new in his life, barely over the horizon. Yet there was that same brittle helplessness in her, disguised though it might be by a will of steel. She was determined to come through, to carry on with her work. There'd be no giving up for her. That would signal victory to her enemies, victory to those who had carted off her father and slaughtered him for daring to mirror what was going on. She had an appetite for life, but also, he suspected, for danger. It was in her bloodstream, part of her worldview. The croissants were freshly baked, still warm in the paper bag. Catching a whiff of butter and almonds, he bounded up the steps to the apartment.

* * *

Lensky had reached the café on the corner of Boulevards Raspail and Saint Michel ahead of them. As always he was propped behind a copy of *Le Figaro,* leafing through with an earnest look about him. He was sitting by the entrance with his coat collar turned up against the chill. Derek surmised he preferred an outside table for the sake of discretion. Or maybe he just wanted to avoid the fug of too many bodies and swirling nicotine clouds.

'May I present …' Derek found himself falling into the formality of introductions as he tried to observe what these two Russians were making of each other. Tanya had borrowed one of Mo's cloche hats and had rammed it right down around her ears and pulled up her collar so little of her face was visible. Lensky raised her gloved hand as if to kiss it then looked fleetingly into her eyes.

'Enchanté,' he said.

She nodded, the wisp of a smile on her lips and took a seat. Derek wondered how to broach the subject. He had said little in his missive. 'I've had word from Mo. Her mother is gravely ill. She won't be back in a hurry. I need to go to London.'

Lensky regarded him levelly, his grey-green eyes measuring him and every word he said. 'How terrible for her. She is still young.'

'Yes, it's hard.' Derek had no energy to explain just how hard, coming on the heels of all that had gone before. 'I don't know when we'll be back.'

Derek became aware of Tanya sitting alongside, watching them, taking in every word. He glanced at her. She was looking pale. He remembered their passionate love-making. He took a deep breath. He realised just how much he'd wanted it even as he longed to stay true to the renewed vows he and Mo had shared.

Lensky leaned back and took in the two of them at one glance, as if to say: there is more going on here than meets the eye. 'So?' He opened his palms in a gesture of enquiry. Derek was about to frame the meeting, gradually lead on to Tanya and what she might need, but she leaned forward and started talking in Russian. There was warmth in her voice as she cupped her face in her hands and engaged Lensky in a fast flow of words. Lensky broke into a smile, lightly touched her arm.

After a few minutes they turned to Derek. 'Forgive us,' said Lensky. 'We were sounding each other out. It's a habit that dies hard. It's tricky for an outsider to gauge. There are so many Russias within Russia, like those fat Babushka dolls. Our paths have crossed. Obliquely, you might say. I know her father's theatre. May even have met him. Certainly my father would have. Moscow is a small place, all said and done.'

Derek eyed Tanya to see if this chimed with her expression. Was she looking more or less relaxed? Now she had taken a cigarette from the gold cigarette case Lensky was proffering. Still Derek hesitated. Having brought them together he should let her do the telling. It was her life, after all. Yet he found it impossible not to feel responsibility towards her. After all, he barely knew Lensky, this man so suave and charming, who crossed and recrossed borders. For a moment Derek felt he was floundering in treacherous waters with no idea of the currents. 'Tanya Sergeyevna needs to make herself scarce,' he ventured, hoping to cut through the confusion.

Tanya smiled. 'Derek has been a good friend,' she said. 'But now his wife needs him. It is true what he says, I need to go under for a while…' Lensky nodded. Derek had no idea how much she had divulged of *Stalin's Dolls* or her current status as non-person, or even whether she had gone into the whys and wherefores of the exhibition and her former role as spokesperson.

'Yes,' said Lensky. 'I do not doubt it. People have become very edgy. The dear leader of the Russian people especially. Do not fear, I will be able to offer shelter to Tanya Sergeyevna – for the time being at least.'

Chapter Thirty-four *Derek*

With cross Channel ferries back in operation Derek arrived in Hackney by the end of the day. He learnt that Ma's condition had worsened: her lungs had become re-infected just when they thought she was making a slight improvement. She'd also had a minor stroke.

He came upon a family gathering in the lounge bar of The Mare's Head. The pub had shut, with a hand-written note saying: *Closure due to family illness,* though this did not stop curious regulars peering inside. Mo got up, exchanged a few words with them so they went on their way, shaking their heads. She drew together the faded velvet curtains, plunging the bar into gloom while Tilda lit the paraffin lamp to provide a glimmer of light. Derek looked round the dazed faces and felt a stranger. He wondered how best to help but could think of nothing useful to do or say. He went and sat next to Mo and clasped her hand. She bristled slightly, unaccustomed to any display of affection in front of her family.

She seemed to be leading the discussion.

'The doctors said she'll be lucky to pull through. The lungs are … there's internal bleeding.' Her voice was flat and matter-of-fact. 'If she does … if they do allow her home … we need to make sure she has a good rest. It might mean bringing in extra help.' He wondered who would pay for that. No doubt Mo would offer but in her own right she did not have much, just savings from her Athena days, plus income from L'Étoile and Scheherazade, which she kept in a jar, for women were not entitled to run their own bank accounts.

It was the family's petty quibbling over money she'd want to avoid. It was a way of thinking, she claimed: if you think poor, you stay poor. If you think mean, you become mean. But it was not a problem: he was there to support her. After his recent sales his bank balance was sounder than it had been in years. In fact, he'd been on the point of suggesting they move to a more spacious flat in Paris, though he'd developed a sneaking attachment to their eyrie with its rooftop views. He noticed the others staring at him. Had someone asked a question? Before he could react Mo stepped in.

'Kind of you to offer, Cissy. But there's a lot needs sorting out here. Pa, are you feeling all right?' Pa had slumped back in his chair. For a split second Derek thought he'd had a stroke and had the awful urge to laugh: it was becoming a Greek tragedy.

Mo was getting to her feet. 'We've had a long day. We need to eat. I'll look in the pantry to see what we've got. Once the word gets out there'll be a trail of people offering pies.'

Derek knew she was right. Adversity in these streets would never be a private affair; the habits of suburbia had not yet crept in. He could hear Mo rattling pans and opening and closing the pantry door. He went to help her. She looked over her shoulder as he entered the scullery. He nuzzled into her neck and she gave a deep sigh. 'Are you okay?' he murmured in her ear.

'She's still so young. Worn out before her time. Like an old nag.' She fetched a knife and started peeling and chopping onions. Her eyes were watering.

'D'you want me to get anything? Meat? More vegetables?'

'There's not much here. A bit of meat wouldn't go amiss. Strengthen it up. Pa looks washed out. This has really done him in. You know where the nearest butcher's is?'

'On Mare St?'

'Yes. Turn to your left. Go to the second one, not the first. He has better stuff. And get some more potatoes.'

* * *

On the street Derek wondered how much the eruption of Sandor Olmak into her life had contributed towards Ma's condition. She always seemed so tough and resilient, but it was clear her brittleness covered a more vulnerable self. Nobody spoke these days of a broken heart, everyone had become so sharp and witty that such notions reeked of Victorian sentimentality. But heart, spirit, soul – whatever one chose to call it – played a more crucial role than everyday common sense allowed.

Mo negotiated for them to stay at Tilda's place. For this he was relieved. He knew Mo preferred her company to Cissy's. The first night they stayed in The Mare's Head, to keep Pa company. Mo would not hear of them taking his bed so they'd scrambled together on the mattress on the floor in the room next door. The scratch of mice in the skirting boards and Mo's restless movements kept him awake most of the night.

Tilda's place was cramped but felt more private. They were sleeping in Victoria's bedroom at the back, while Victoria's cot was pushed onto the landing. They'd rigged up a camp bed. In this narrow space he held Mo close, kissing the top of her head and murmuring. She was cold to the touch and a little rigid, though she nestled into him. Exhausted from lack of sleep, they drifted off. He came to in the night and could hear her muffled cries into the pillow. She was turning away, trying not to disturb him. 'Oh, Mo, my darling Mo. You've been through so much.' This made her start sobbing. He held her tight against his chest. He could feel her heart throbbing. He kissed her and she returned the kiss passionately until they were making love in the cramped bed. She almost fell out at one stage and he was relieved to hear her laugh. 'Thank God you're here,' she whispered in his ear.

The next morning, when he woke, she was struggling to get dressed. She kept bumping into the walls. 'No room to swing a cat.'

He eyed her sleepily. 'You are so beautiful – the brightest star of your family.'

She gave a wistful smile. 'No – the brightest star has been eclipsed.'

He took hold of her hand.

'I need to sort through Ma's stuff.' She released her hand from his. 'I promised her I'd sort things out.'

'What do you mean?'

'The pub and all. She didn't think Pa would be up to it. She talked about it – before like...' Her words filled him with apprehension: he sensed her entanglement with The Mare's Head would not be ending anytime soon.

Chapter Thirty-five *Mo*

Tilda was doing her best to make them feel at home. Tilda had always been the gentlest sister, the one who admired Mo the most and took no pains to hide it. As a young girl she'd clung to her like a limpet, annoyingly so, catching her words and spinning them till they became her own. She smiled as Mo entered the kitchen. 'I'm glad you're 'ere. Wouldn't know what to do with Pa. 'E's all over the shop.'

Mo sat down with a sigh. 'Give 'im time…'

'Toast? D'you want some toast?'

'I'll wait for Derek.' She looked round the kitchen, which was scrubbed clean but showed signs of scarcity in the stringy curtains, the holes in the linoleum. For all that, it exuded warmth and homeliness. Tilda looked content with her lot, she was a capable housewife and manager of her husband's accounts. Bill Parker had a reputation for diligence and reliability and was never short of work.

Victoria was struggling to get out of her highchair by grabbing Mo's hair. 'Stop it! Leave aunt Morwenna's hair alone. Or she'll smack you one.'

Mo laughed and grasped Victoria's chubby raised wrist. 'Maybe she doesn't like being shoved out of her room. Can I help you with that porridge, Vicky? It looks yummy.' She drew the bowl towards her and attempted to spoon the mash into the toddler's mouth. Victoria moved her face from side to side. 'Maybe you've 'ad enough already?'

'She's just playing up. She's a little tinker, that's wot.'

Bill came into the room with his work overalls on and gave a wide grin. 'She likes an audience.'

'You've got your packed lunch?' asked Tilda. 'I put it on the dresser.'

Bill nodded and patted his canvas bag. He had an open face with a smattering of freckles across his nose and thick, strong hands. Mo felt more at ease in his company than in Bob Scratchett's. Simple in his needs and outlook, he was a man Mo felt she could trust, though he would have bored her silly.

No sooner had the front door slammed shut than Derek put in an appearance. He was unshaven and a bit tousled. Some men always verge on scruffiness – it was as though their unruly thoughts burst out through their wayward hair. He stood looking around, at once too tall and too much of a presence for the small space.

'Sit down! Sit down,' fussed Tilda, colouring slightly.

Mo pulled out the chair alongside her. 'Toast?'

He nodded and sat down.

'Tilda says she's worried about Pa,' said Mo without preamble.

'It's just... 'e never really listens to us. You have more influence.'

When Derek showed no reaction, Mo shrugged.

'Ma did so much in recent years,' continued Tilda. 'We can't just leave 'im to it, not now.'

Mo felt a sudden deadening. 'You're here, you and Cissy. I'm not.' A hectoring tone crept into her voice. She hated herself for it, but surely she shouldn't have to defend herself against her family? Derek had a mischievous glint in his eye. He was not about to spring in and champion her, yet he was on her side in this. 'You don't expect me to leave Paris and come back here?'

Tilda glanced around as if seeking protection. 'No, it's not like that...'

The dead feeling did not leave Mo. That was exactly what everybody was expecting. She looked towards Derek. 'I have my obligations, too, you know.'

'I weren't saying that you didn't 'ave...' Tilda was growing flustered.

'We need to get together and have a chat about this.' Mo shrugged. Who would call such a family gathering, if not her? Ma's words resounded in her head. She'd extracted a promise from her, an oath almost.

At The Mare's Head Mo felt like tearing down the heavy curtains, still drawn against the daylight to ward off punters. She wanted to thrust open the doors and sluice down the floors with carbolic soap. It all felt so tainted with the past. The next moment she longed to run upstairs and rifle through her mother's frocks and ancient pots of powder to get the merest whiff of her, to call back any disappearing trace of the woman she had been.

Pa reeled off what he knew about the running of the pub. He attempted to take them through the accounts. Previous years were in order, with income and outgoings clearly marked and the business turning over a small profit. The most recent figures were a shambles, though, with arrows darting here and there and no clear columns.

Pa rubbed his forehead. 'She wasn't 'erself – not since you lost your little one. But really bad recently.'

This brought Mo up sharp. What was the connection? Why had he said that? Ma hardly ever mentioned Timothy and hadn't seen that much of him when he was alive. 'She thought she'd lost you, too. Sort of …' Pa spoke in a monotone, as if to himself.

'That's news to me.' It angered her that he was unwittingly drawing her back into the web.

'She adores the ground you walk on.'

Again Mo smarted. What rubbish! She changed tack. 'So, is there someone from the brewery who oversees the account? You have to produce an annual tally, I take it?'

'Yes, there is.' He shook his head as if it were all too much for him.

'Tilda's a whizz at figures. I'm not. She should be the one going through all this with you,' she said.

Pa cast Mo a sideways glance. His shoulders sagged. She felt like smacking him. But he also made her want to cry. This was the man who had nurtured her and looked up to her; his eyes had always lit up on seeing her; he'd led her, more than anyone else, to believe in herself.

Derek was flicking through the accounts, jotting down notes here and there. 'Nothing a decent book-keeper couldn't sort out,' he mumbled. 'Are there any debts we should know about?' His voice was level and calm, injecting a little objectivity into the proceedings. Mo felt a rush of gratitude. Though Derek was not a trader, he could grasp the wider pattern and was pragmatic enough to run a sound business. After all, Fingal's Cave, his theatre props business, had been a moderately successful venture, given that his true ambition had lain elsewhere.

'What I suggest is this,' continued Derek. 'We get Tilda to sit down with us and go through the last two years. In the meantime, Pa, you can perhaps think about any other expenses, debts or bills that might be outstanding.'

Pa lifted his head and smiled. 'Thanks son,' he said. 'That's a good idea.'

The meeting was arranged for the next day.

Chapter Thirty-six

Mo braced herself to go through her mother's things. Ma had requested this in her first bout of illness: she wanted to clear the decks, she'd said. Even if Ma did return from the hospital, she would not need most of her clothes or jewellery. This sorting Mo wanted to do alone. She wanted the space to dwell on a shrivelled boa, a faded velvet frock, a glistening belt or droplets of old earrings.

Ma's bits and pieces were crammed into the bottom drawers of the dressing table. Mo had only ever glimpsed them before for that place had always had an aura of the forbidden. Even now she felt she was trespassing on private, even sacred ground. She sat on the bed, heavy with misgiving. Pa was in the pub below, with Derek and Tilda. They had plenty to be getting on with.

Mo laid the contents of the drawers out on the counterpane. She fingered an ancient fan, thin to the touch and almost falling apart. She glanced at the tangle of necklaces, bracelets and earrings, all of them paste. There were several odd earrings. She came across a bundle of old cards and photos, wedged into a corner. Other things lurked, but she could not sort through everything. She'd do that another day.

She clutched a string of enmeshed necklaces, holding it aloft. Sparkling and clinking together, tawdry, broken yet bright things, they suggested glamour, the stage, a well-turned heel and a cheerful voice singing a Music Hall favourite. *'Daisy Daisy give me your answer do, I'm half crazy, all for the love of you. I don't need a horse and carriage ...'*

Maisy Aurora. What a strange, highfalutin name! Mo's throat tugged as she imagined Ma swishing around in the now faded velvet dress, entrancing the rows in front of her, be it at a Variety theatre or in the function room of a public house. Did she kick her legs up and egg them on with an upward gesture of her arms or did she lull them into submission with the sweetness of her voice? Was Sandor accompanying her or watching her with admiration from the sidelines?

She would bundle up what she could for a local thrift shop. Perhaps someone might get a penny or two for them. When all was said and done, what price for our dreams, what price for what's left behind, she mused with a touch of bitterness. She opened the wardrobe and took out Ma's clothes: first, the old Music Hall ones, which she sniffed. They smelled of dust and must: they could not have been worn in years. She heaped them together through her tears, growing angry. She shouldn't be here, moping, courting a past that could never return. Why hadn't Ma thrown them all out years ago? Was she clinging to a self, eclipsed by events, which she hoped might one day come roaring back? Or had she merely stashed them away and forgotten about them? Or if not forgotten, did the sight of them bring only pain?

With growing frustration Mo tipped out the motley contents of the wardrobe and dressing table, the three-legged chest-of-drawers. There were skirts, stockings, cardigans, shawls and underwear. She lifted them up and dropped them, letting them scatter as they would. Ragged stuff, much of it not worth passing on, just fodder for the rag-and-bone man: Ma rarely spent money on herself in recent years. Mo sometimes brought her a colourful frock from Fingal's Cave, but even then she seemed to prefer her dowdy old cardigans and skirts.

Mo sifted through the strewn garments, no longer allowing her mind to linger. She had a job of work to do. She held things up to the light, inspecting them for ladders or holes and sorted them into neat piles. The tattered and torn she scrunched into a ball and tied with an old belt. The salvageable she put in a second cardboard box. After an hour she had created a sort of order. She placed the bundle of photos into her handbag for safekeeping.

* * *

Downstairs Derek, Tilda and Pa were sitting with ledgers and a pile of bills in front of them. Pa looked more relaxed than he had in days. The colour had returned to his cheeks. Tilda was busy sorting out paid and unpaid bills according to dates. Derek was scrutinising the columns of figures.

'So,' said Mo with mock cheerfulness. 'One job done. I've sorted through Ma's things.' A shadow passed across Pa's face.

'You didn't waste much time.'

If that was intended as criticism, Mo let it wash over her. 'There's a bundle or two for the rag-and-bone man, some things can be passed on or sold. I didn't find any jewellery of any value.'

Even Tilda looked slighted at her words. Was she being just too quick and forthright? For her it was the best way of driving through difficult emotions; the others, though, seemed to be finding her insensitive. Derek gave her the flicker of a smile. 'Are you making much headway with the books?' she asked.

'We're getting there.'

'Anything I can do to help?'

'Tilda's done a great job getting all the paperwork sorted,' said Derek. 'There is not so much in the way of debts. This month's figures are still unclear.'

'So nothing too much to worry about?'

'We are not out of the woods yet,' said Tilda. 'I don't really understand it. Until a few weeks ago everything looks clear. Then suddenly – well it's like a big hole in the accounting. Maybe she was sick already…'

'Pa?' Mo turned to her father.

He shrugged. 'She done all that.'

'Nothing we can't sort out,' said Derek with finality. Mo was touched that he was getting involved to the extent that he was. Previously she sensed that he tolerated trips to The Mare's Head rather than enjoyed them. She couldn't blame him. Only in the last weeks, after their reconciliation, had he been made to feel welcome.

'We've done about as much as we can for now,' said Derek. 'Pa, you need to get in touch with the brewery. Get them to send a representative. We need to clarify the contract. That is, if we – rather you – want to make any changes.'

He looked towards Pa and Tilda, then at Mo. He was urging them to take on responsibility. They seemed in awe of him. Perhaps it was the middle-class tone of voice, his air of decisiveness. Tilda became perplexed in his presence.

Tilda had brought a thick vegetable soup with her. They cleared away the ledgers while she disappeared to the scullery to warm it on the range. Mo went back upstairs and brought down the things she'd sorted. These she placed by the back door, ready for disposal. They ate their soup in silence. She became aware of Pa chewing on his bread; he seemed ravenous. He would not have eaten properly in days. She kept her bag close to her leg. Her mind reverted to the bundle of photos. Her head throbbed. The foray into her mother's past was throwing up so many unresolved issues.

Later when she and Derek were sitting in a Lyons Corner house enjoying a little respite, she said: 'Rummaging through Ma's things brought back memories. We think we know someone – but we don't.' He frowned as she continued with a wistful air. 'We just skim the surface.'

He tipped more sugar into his tea and stirred. 'How did the sorting go?'

'I've done the clothes. Found a few photos and cards I haven't had time to look at. I'll go through the rest when I get a minute.'

He finished his tea and pushed away the cup, looking at Mo with dark concentration. 'Good. I'd like to go back to France as soon as possible. I've had a telegram from Dimitri.'

Chapter Thirty-seven

The next day Derek had another meeting with Pa and Tilda to further disentangle The Mare's Head finances. Mo sat in but contributed little. A Mr Daniels came from the brewery, clutching papers. Everything had always been on Pa's name but the brewery was fully aware who had run the business. At the brewery's request there was to be a financial appraisal before anybody signed the renewal of contract. This, in itself, was unusual. Daniels was pleased to note that an up-to-date audit had already been set in motion. Pa was only too glad to leave them to it: he was spending more time in the bar, soaking up the sympathy and stories of clients who came flooding back once the doors were open.

Later that morning Mo was due to return to Hackney hospital to check how Ma was doing. Every time she thought of her mother she felt heavy, knowing there was scant chance of recovery. To see Ma's prone, pale form with eyes vacant of recognition was sad beyond words. She put off going as long as she could.

Now, alone in Tilda's front room, she tipped out the box of photos and cards onto the floor. She was disconcerted to discover a photo of herself next to Knighton at a reception in the Savoy. How on earth did that get there? Knighton had a proprietorial arm around her shoulder and was gazing at her with a mixture of admiration and pride. She cast it to one side.

There were other faded snapshots. She rifled through them. She came across one that looked distinctly like Ma, and sure enough scrawled in one corner was: *Maisy Aurora 1904*. She peered at it. Maisy was throwing her head back, laughing. She was wearing a satin dress with a scooped neckline. An abundance of wavy hair reached the base of her neck. Her cheeks were full, her mouth slightly open and tilting forward. She was lit up, her eyes brimming with a *joie de vivre* Mo had never seen in her. Mo touched the photo with her fingers, outlining the contours of the young woman her mother had been. She began searching through the other photos, avid to see what else she could uncover. She gasped. There was one of Sandor and Ma! She turned it over. *Grecian Saloon, The Eagle 1905* was scribbled on the back. The Eagle was an old Music Hall venue in London. She gazed at the photo, wanting it to speak, to tell of the relationship it had witnessed, the birth it had led to. She took it to the light by the window. Turned it this way, then that. Her heart pounded against her ribs: if only, if only… kept going through her mind.

She felt a shadow of shame delving like this but was spurred by anger that so much had been hushed up. They looked so young, her parents: young and in love. Sandor was gazing down at Maisy and smiling. She looked so free and easy, her body curved in towards him. She was wearing that velvet frock, the one Mo loved to dress up in when she was little. It was fresh then and hugged Maisy's gentle form to perfection. Sandor was wearing a dark suit with tails, and what looked like a stiff white shirt and collar. They were the cat's miaow: beautiful young people at the height of their powers.

*　*　*

Ma's eyes flickered open. The nurse said she thought there'd been some progress. Ma was able to sip water and had asked to see her family. At least, that's what the nurse surmised. Ma's mouth was drawn down on one side together with her cheek and the folds of her eye. That side of the body was quite slack and Mo found it hard to decipher her slurred stabs at communication. Forcing a smile she grasped her mother's hand: 'They say, you're on the mend,' and gave it a gentle squeeze. The eye of a fish was watching her, unblinking, cold, grey. Ma turned her face towards the pillow, gasped something Mo did not understand. The nurse, who was hovering nearby and checking charts, approached.

'Is it a drink, you're wanting, Mrs Dobson?' Ma inclined her head. The nurse poured from a jug of water and cupped Ma's chin in her hand. 'There you go.' Mo watched as Ma slurped through a straw but managed to get something down her throat. 'She's come round, she has, – no longer in a coma. She's doing grand, so she is.'

The professional cheerfulness of the nurse from Sligo helped filled the void Mo did not know how to bridge. For once she felt thankful for the procedures and rituals of hospital. How else to struggle through the tragedy of this middle-aged woman, immobile and unable to fend for herself? Mo stayed by her mother's side until she was asked to leave as they were wanting to give Mrs Dobson a blanket bath.

Chapter Thirty-eight *Derek*

Paris now seemed far away, but Derek was unable to stop himself thinking about Tanya. He'd tried to rationalise that she'd flung herself at him, entering his bedroom as she did, in her simple shift, her hair loose about her shoulders, whispering that she was afraid. He had not willed it. He had not sought her out. She'd just happened. And maybe what passed between them had meant nothing at all to her. After all, she was a free spirit, an artist and a woman of the new post-Tsarist era.

But he could not forget so easily, try as he might. Since arriving in London he'd been all the more helpful to Mo, more willing than ever to enter the fray of her demanding family, willing to goad her passive father into the practicalities of commerce. The man was not stupid: he'd merely passed his wife the reins so he could have an easy existence. Now that possibility had been whipped away from him.

He felt a sliver of apprehension. God forbid that Mo ever discover what had gone on between Tanya and himself. That would be the end of their marriage. The two women must never be allowed to be at the same gathering again. Mo had an uncanny knack of reading beneath the surface of things, even when she didn't know she was doing it. The best strategy was to act as if the encounter with Tanya had never happened: it was just something he'd dreamt up.

In the meantime, there were things to be getting on with. The figures seemed to tally now, but he wanted to be sure. There was no huge leakage of funds. Most of the stock was accounted for. Clients had started calling at the pub again. There was no reason why it might not turn a profit in the coming year. He wanted to make sure everything was as watertight as possible so he and Mo could to return to Paris, with no cracks and fissures in the vessel. Otherwise it would be all too easy for Pa and the others to draw Mo back, away from him. On the face of it everything seemed straightforward. But would that be enough? He sensed that Pa's heart was no longer in it. Once the others had departed back to their various lives would he just allow himself to drift? There was no quick solution to inertia.

He was sitting in Tilda and Bill's tiny front parlour, reading Bill's *Daily Mirror*. He flicked through the pages. There was more talk of the instability of the financial markets. There were several commentaries on the speculation and ensuing disastrous run on shares in Wall Street, but right now there seemed to be more interest in the invention of moving images: the first television studio was opening in Soho. John Logie Baird was heralding a great new era of communication.

He heard a knock on the door and Tilda poked her head round looking coy, as though she were a parlour maid. He smiled to put her at ease. She seemed to enjoy working side-by-side with him over the books, as they'd done for the last couple of days. She blushed when he spoke to her, which made him think he should not be too friendly with her.

'Tea – would you like some tea?'

He looked at his watch. It was nearly four o'clock. Mo should be back by now. 'That would be nice.' Tilda disappeared and he heard a clattering of tea things. She reappeared with a laden tray with fresh scones on it. She was making quite an effort. Just then he heard the front door opening. Mo came in and sank down into the easy chair opposite him.

'How's your mother?' he asked.

'She opened her eyes. The staff say she's making progress.' Her voice sounded flat as though it was an effort to speak. Tilda came in and seeing Mo disappeared to get another cup and plate. She nodded as Mo told of her hospital visit.

'I'll go tomorrow,' she said.

As the three of them sat over their tea and scones, Derek couldn't help comparing the two sisters. Tilda belonged here, in this respectable household with its small but scrupulously clean rooms, her husband nearby earning their bread by the use of his hands; whereas even in repose Mo had a restlessness about her. It was hard to define. Certainly, she was darker than her siblings and her fine features gave her an exotic appearance. The eyes were rarely still. They sparkled and delighted even as they penetrated and searched. Her hands were fine and long-fingered as befitted an artist. In Tilda's parlour she looked out of place: a bird of paradise flitting through.

Warmth expanded his chest. How he missed her when she was not around! How glad he was to have her in his life. It made absolute sense to him that she was the love child of this chance alliance between a sometime Music Hall performer and the wandering and gifted musician from Vienna: two empires about to collapse; two human beings crossing boundaries, pursuing an impossible love.

'Shall I clear away?' asked Tilda.

'Please do,' said Mo, a touch of the lady about her. When Tilda had disappeared with the tray, Mo turned to him. 'Poor Tilda, she doesn't know what's hit her. She's quite infatuated with you.'

He gave a weak smile, forced, once again, to acknowledge Mo's casual but unerring power of observation.

Chapter Thirty-nine

Mo was in love with the past, with a story she was spinning of her parents' young love. As soon as Derek came back from his meeting at the brewery she was agog to show him the photos. Never mind the contract he had completed, on her behalf, between Pa and the brewery, or the agreement he'd wrested from Tilda – needing to flirt mildly with her into the bargain – that she would undertake the book-keeping on a fortnightly basis. Bill had grumbled that that would leave her insufficient time for his decorating business. Over a pork-pie lunch he and Derek had thrashed it out. Derek promised that she would be adequately recompensed for her efforts. In the end they'd shaken hands on it, Tilda sitting by and nodding her assent. In short, he'd been tireless in making sure that as many of the ends were tied up as possible, leaving Mo free to pursue her career once they got back to Paris. Until now he'd assumed that was of paramount importance to her. After all, it was what she pined for, what she had striven for since their arrival there.

Yet now he perceived a subtle change in her.

'Look!' She was holding out two photos for his inspection. 'How beautiful she was! What a star. You can see it in the tilt of her head, her confident smile. A born performer! I always knew there were things she was not saying. This proves it.'

As he looked across at Mo, he could see she was entranced. It was evening and they'd slipped away from Tilda and Bill's house to have the chance to speak alone. They'd walked some distance down Mare Street to find a pub away from the family's usual haunts. Her eyes were glittering. 'Don't you see, they loved each other.' She put the photos back into her bag. 'No doubt he had to go to preserve her reputation.'

What of it, Derek wanted to ask. Perhaps Olmak was just escaping the snare where his lust had led him. Mo was idealising their connection. She must know as well as he did that the entertainment business led to transitory liaisons: they were par for the course. Wherever men and women were thrown together it would happen, but especially where the conventions of wider society did not pertain. He held his tongue. This was a fragile business. She had always felt tolerated rather than loved in her family. These photos rendered her birth special, rather than an inconvenient accident.

Derek rubbed the back of her hand.

They were sitting up by the bar and now a cluster of men came crowding in, laughing and pushing. They all seemed to know each other, were part of a regular bunch. He caught the smell of sweat and men out for a good evening. He glanced over towards the wall where a poster announced that tonight there was to be a darts' match. The bar was filling from both ends. The rival team were already lifting glasses and joshing each other in the far corner. It was going to get increasingly noisy.

'Mo, shall we move on?'

As he led the way out of the pub he said: 'Don't say anything to the family… about the photos.'

'Derek, I'm not a child. I don't even know if Pa knew about Sandor Olmak. I presumed he did, if he and Ma were performing together. But maybe he didn't.'

They were ambling towards the terrace where Tilda and Bill lived. The roadway glowed faintly in the blue light from the gas lamps. Someone had dropped a newspaper in the gutter where it flapped like a white bat. A cat slunk across the street in front of them, a quick, disappearing shadow. Derek had the odd sensation that their lives were about to be turned upside down. He put his arm round her, pulled her towards him.

'I want to explore… I've always felt at odds with the world. I'm beginning to understand why,' she said.

'That's not how I see it.'

'What do you mean?'

'You're an artist. It's the role of the artist to stand back, never get too swallowed up in the story. Stories change. They always change. Yesterday's stories are not today's stories. We need to keep distance – not get too caught up …'

She threw him a sideways glance. 'Derek, I'm not sure I know what you're talking about. For me, it's much simpler. I need to know where I come from.' He sighed as she continued: 'I'm tired of living on the edge.'

'You hardly live on the edge.'

'All right then, I'm tired of living in the shadows. Your shadow, for instance. I need to stand in my own light.' And with that she strode ahead of him and took out the key to Tilda and Bill's front door.

* * *

Mo steeled herself for departure. Derek was insisting they go back to Paris, otherwise he'd lose too many opportunities. Ma was making a very gradual recovery. She would never be the woman she was, never do what she had once done. But she was getting back a little speech, some mobility. At Derek's insistence and with his funds they would pay a neighbour, who'd worked as a nurse before marrying, to come in and see to Ma every morning. There was money enough for a year. After that they would review the situation. Perhaps by then The Mare's Head would be earning its keep.

Mo was sceptical. But she could not allow her imagination to conjure up all the things that could go wrong. They had made their decision and would stick to it. Tomorrow they would catch the boat train to Dover and take a ferry returning them to France and the life they were building there.

Pa was even more reticent than usual. It could not be helped. They were all having to cope, one way or another. She was tired of the mind-draining ache of trauma. She wanted to shake it off much as one threw off a shabby winter coat when the first sprouts of spring arrived. She had work to be getting on with. She would head back to Lensky's Scheherazade, hoping to slot back in where she'd left off and not trouble herself with alternatives right now.

Derek was tracking her like an eagle. Did he fear her melancholy might come creeping back? Was her apparent cheeriness a trifle forced? He could see into her like no one else. There were times she feared the shrewdness of his gaze. He had exerted himself on her behalf, shielding her from the neediness of her father, the demands of her sisters. For that, she was grateful and more than a little surprised. This was the responsible trader who had run Fingal's Cave, rather than the self-absorbed artist to whom all else was secondary.

'You're looking pensive,' he said, as they prepared for bed. After the pub they'd had a supper of cocoa and biscuits with Bill and Tilda and told them of their travel plans. Over the digestive biscuits conversation soon ran dry. Bill and Tilda expressed no curiosity about their lives in Paris. Perhaps they'd dared not ask. They seemed too modest to talk of their own lives apart from everyday specifics such as getting in the right sort of paint or how soon they could fulfil orders. Tilda kept looking towards Derek with expectation. In turn, Bill was watching his wife with bemusement. She and Derek had never been at such close quarters with them before. Mo would catch a certain look in Tilda's eyes and be puzzled. As a child she was simpler to read. Tilda liked things to run along known grooves and could not cope with the unexpected. Derek she would be unable to fathom. She suspected Bill would be relieved when they left.

Later, Mo was sitting by the bedroom window, brushing her hair.

'Are you pleased to be going back to Paris?' Derek asked.

'I couldn't wait … but now I'm not so sure. Ma's so poorly. I'd like to see her settled at home. Lensky will surely wait.'

Derek drew in his breath sharply. 'I can't afford another day. Goldman is pressing us.'

She shrugged. 'I'm glad Tilda is going to lend a hand. That'll make a difference. Though I hardly know her these days.'

'She feels out of her depth. With you, I mean.'

'Why should she?'

'You don't even talk like them anymore. Sometimes you slip back, but mostly you're from a different planet.'

'No going back then?' There was a tinge of sadness in her voice.

* * *

Derek watched Mo as she lay sleeping. Her mouth was slightly parted, the breath coming and going then a sudden light shudder, as if she were facing down a dragon. The mention of Lensky had brought him up sharp. Now as they prepared for their re-entry into Paris his mind was racing ahead. What accommodation had Lensky made for Tanya? Goldman was awaiting his return: what paintings would he buy and what exhibitions would he want to mount?

Mo would be keen to put the last cruel weeks behind her. Work suited her. She thrived when she performed and dwindled when she didn't. Only that collapse at The Athena disturbed him. She was more sensitive than she cared to admit. Rooted in her emotions, distress pushed her off balance. Yet she needed depth of experience to be the singer she was. She almost attracted trouble, he'd once thought.

He could not sleep. A sliver of wan light crept in from the gaslight in the street. It zigzagged across the counterpane, across her undulating form. It lit the glass of water beside her bed and highlighted a family picture on the wall. To have had so much upheaval in such a short space of time would perturb anyone. But Mo? She was fired with ambition. Of Sandor Olmak and her mother she wanted to track down every trace, sniff the animal spoor. But where would that lead?

He continued to gaze at her sleeping face. She sighed, turned over, almost as if she were experiencing the weight of his mind while his fears stirred. He would be there as she wished. Stand behind her, beside her, lift her up when she needed to be raised, calm her down when she needed to be stilled.

But what of Tanya?

PART 3

Chapter Forty *Derek*

Their rooms seemed airless when they arrived back in Marais. Mo wasted no time thrusting open the windows, jamming wide the creaky door to the balcony. She seemed impatient, rooting around like a dog marking its territory. Derek watched, hoping that there was no whiff of Tanya in the air. He'd left in a hurry, throwing clothes pell-mell into a weekend bag and rushing down the stairs without a backwards glance. 'Sorry, it's a mess. I wanted to catch the first ferry I could.'

'No matter.' She picked up two wine glasses with a remnant of red dregs in them. She held them up to the light. 'Had company, did you?' she said nonchalantly. His heart thumped. He'd overlooked them.

'Too busy. Didn't get around to washing glasses.'

She came across a plate with crumbs and a smear of Camembert. 'That's how you get mice.' She piled them all together and took them to the communal kitchen on the floor below.

Derek went through to the bedroom and pulled the sheets together in a heap. Before Mo returned he had them scrunched up in the corner and was searching for the spare set of bed linen she kept at the bottom of the wardrobe. He pulled them out and attempted to make the bed. When she came in and saw him, she laughed.

'Here, let me.' With a couple of deft movements she'd made up the bed. If she had any suspicions, she was keeping them to herself. He added a pile of grubby clothes to bed linen and rolled them up into a ball.

'My turn to go to the washerwoman,' he said. 'I'll drop them off. I need to go out and check at the gallery what's happening.'

'I thought the exhibition was over?'

'It is. But I need to see Goldman, the American collector. He's been travelling. Came back a couple of days ago. I won't be long.'

Mo nodded. 'I'll sort things out here. Get some food in. I need to get used to being here again. I'll go and see Lensky tomorrow.'

Derek took the steps down two at a time and was soon out in the alleyway, whistling, hands in his pockets. It felt good to back in Paris. The streets had a different smell to those in London. The hint of drains was there but above it the pleasing smells of ground coffee and freshly baked bread. And always, everywhere, the essence of garlic: it got under the skin, into the stonework of the old buildings.

He started thinking about Tanya and wondering how she was doing. She and Lensky seemed to have hit it off. It seemed they already knew each other, or certainly knew enough about the circles they both moved in to feel comfortable with each other. But from what he'd heard of the Russian Security Services they would not give up so easily. He told himself he'd done his bit to protect her, that it was no concern of his what she got up to next. But his thoughts kept wandering back to her, a melody that hung in the air, not wanting to go away. He went down Rue Montignac, doubled back towards the Seine and the gallery.

He crossed the river by Pont Neuf, watched ducks scooting towards the bank. The sun glinted on their backs – verdigris, purple. He'd pulled Mo along this same bridge their first time in Paris – kissing in full view of passers-by, no one minding them in the least.

It seemed a century ago.

* * *

Goldman looked in fine fettle. His sojourn in Saint Moritz and his business trips to Zurich and Vienna had gone off well. He looked more relaxed, less guarded than before. They met at Café

Dorndt, a stone's throw from L'Atelier Blanc.

'Good to see you, Mr Eaton.' Derek ordered tea with lemon. 'Thank goodness you're back. I've been tearing my hair out with the Russians. I had another meeting with them. Only Dimitri speaks reasonable English. Kurovsky has gone deeper into his shell. The others were pestering me via Dimitri to take another look at their works.' He leaned back and took out silver cigarette case containing cheroots. He offered one to Derek.

'I'm fine. Thank you.'

'But I mustn't bombard you. I believe you've just got back from London. You had a fruitful trip?'

'It was a family matter. My mother-in-law is gravely ill.'

'Oh, sorry to hear that.'

'It kept me busy one way or another. I haven't had time to dwell on things here.'

'Understandably.'

'The last time we met you expressed interest in Kurovsky's work. Said you needed to consult others before you committed. A matter of investment, I believe.'

'I never like to be rushed into anything, unless of course one has to move fast to beat the competition. But that's not the case here. I said before, I can't take the whole exhibition as a job lot.'

'No, of course not.'

'Kurovsky's pieces interest me. And some of your own.'

'That's good to hear.' Derek suppressed a smile.

'I had a conversation with Dimitri. He told me about Tanya Sergeyevna's work. Granted, I haven't seen the pieces yet. But from the sound of it they are ground-breaking. It's unusual enough to have a female sculptor. But to have someone who is creating a critique in sculpture of the Soviet Union is way more interesting.'

'He told you that, did he?' Derek attempted to contain his shock. Tanya had wanted to keep the nature of her work under wraps. What had possessed Dimitri to go blabbing around the place about what she was up to?

'Don't look so alarmed, my dear fellow. I'm sworn to secrecy. I assured Dimitri of my family lineage. And my loyalty. There is no way I would want any harm to come to her. Besides, we'd have to think carefully about curating such a show – the timing, the venue. All sorts of things.'

'We'd need to establish trust,' said Derek almost to himself. 'I don't know how much Dimitri told you, but much of her work has been destroyed.'

'Yes, I heard that. But if she's done it once, she can do it again.'

'Art doesn't quite work like that.' He glanced across at Goldman. The man looked mildly amused. The comment had been naïve. Who was he to lecture an art connoisseur about where art came from?

'He says Tanya Sergeyevna has been working furiously, though he wouldn't take me to her new studio. He's protective, I suppose, after what happened. Apparently what she's doing now ties in more with the émigré experience in Paris. So that gives it an added interest. Many Americans wouldn't be too bothered about the inner workings of the new Soviet Union. Some of the Labour unions might be, but not the general populace. And certainly not the people who flock to art exhibitions.'

'You just said her critique was ground-breaking?' This was moving too fast for Derek's liking. The man was above all a businessman, though he held the wider view: a sense of how things fitted together and how people were influenced and what they yearned for. 'Has anything been said to Tanya Sergeyevna about any of this?'

'Dimitri was going to fix a meeting. If she's willing, that is. Dimitri said he'd try and persuade her.'

Derek leaned back, sipped his tepid lemon tea and appraised Goodman.

'I am sure Tanya Sergeyevna is capable of handling her own affairs.'

'She might be. But I still need a go-between, a bridge – someone to safeguard the interests of both parties. And that, my dear fellow, is where you come in.'

Chapter Forty-one *Mo*

They'd arrived in their rooms in the early afternoon. Derek seemed fidgety, longing to get out there on the streets, re-establish links with his art world and pick up the trail of the recent exhibition. His listlessness did not surprise her. He'd had to ditch everything and race to London once he'd heard her news. He'd made no attempt to tidy or clean up after himself, but that was not unusual. There was something else, though, which she could not quite put her finger on. It wasn't the dirty glasses or the bundling together of the bed sheets, which she chose not to dwell on. It was rather the sense that life was more real, more vital for him on French soil. His soul had been on hold until he got back here. And that puzzled her. It had not always been so.

She looked round the rooms, which by now she had aired and swept clean till they became more how she'd left them. She sat on the balcony clutching a cup of watered-down coffee, gazing over the rooftops at the late sun on the towers of Notre Dame. She'd gone out to fetch a few groceries, the bare essentials, and had bought a couple of bottles of red wine. Enough housekeeping for the moment – right now she wanted to absorb the fact she was back here, in Paris, and what that meant. She'd been so intent on getting here, summoning ruthlessness towards Pa and the family. And now here she was, on the balcony, alone, and beginning to wonder if she wasn't interrupting Derek's life. The thought flitted through her mind and was gone. It was nonsense. He'd done everything he could to clear her passage back here.

A pigeon came fluttering onto the railing, then another. Their wings rustled and they took off, gliding through the still air. She watched their flight, saw them alight on a parapet further along. She smiled to herself. She loved the muted greys of the rooftops, the skeleton shapes etched against each other, the murmur of traffic and hum of voices drifting up from the streets below. It was like being on a mountain. How she had striven to get here, to climb until exhausted, her mind weary. Now, above the world, she was seeing through the eyes of a soaring lark.

The next minute tears were trickling down her face. Here they were allowed, here they could be both salve and relief and need concern no one. Today she wanted to be gentle with herself, not only for what she had been through, but for the tough times she intuited ahead. She thought of Sandor, consumed by toxic fumes; she thought of Ma, wasted, and hanging onto life by a thread. She thought of the vibrant, glowing couple she and Sandor had been. And at last she allowed herself to think of Timothy, her darling son.

She cried without inhibition. The tears were warm on her cheeks. The next moment she let her voice sound the scales, quietly, then ever louder until her chest was reverberating with the notes. She stretched out her arms, as if embracing the city and sang out again:

> *'As I wash my dishes, I'll be following a plan*
> *Till I see the brightness in every pot and pan*
> *I am sure this point of view will ease the daily grind*
> *So I'll keep repeating in my mind.'*
> *Look for the silver lining,*
> *Whenever a cloud appears in the blue*
> *Remember somewhere the sun is shining*
> *And so the right thing to do is make it shine for you…'*
> *A heart full of joy and gladness*
> *Will always banish sadness and strife*
> *So always look for the silver lining*
> *And try to find the sunny side of life.'*

The tears continued to flow. She went back inside, feeling calmer than she had in days. In the bedroom she took out her mother's photos and laid them on the bed. The one of Sandor and Maisy at The Eagle she placed above: a star and magnet to attract all the elements.

When Derek had not returned by five, she followed a desire to go out and feel Paris around her. She strolled down cobblestone alleyways and passed into Rue de Rivoli where shops were still plying a lively trade. She heard vendors calling out to each other. Others were laughing and raising their voices as they moved along: shoppers, lovers, and housewives laden with shopping bags. She crossed into Rue D'Arcole that would lead her near Notre Dame.

How strange it was to see this mighty edifice from below, with its mighty flying buttresses and long windows. It was a giant. She imagined people thronging here during the Middle Ages, seeking sanctuary. She slipped inside. She wandered down the dark nave and around the back of the high altar and stared up at the magnificent rose window, luminous with deep blue. One side chapel with a weeping saint drew her attention. In the dim light the figure looked ghoulish, but the more she gazed at it the more comfort she felt. It was permissible to mourn, to feel sad. She sat in a pew before flickering candles and allowed herself the hollowness of loss. She slotted coins into the metal container, lit three candles and watched the straight yellow flames burning without smoke.

Outside she welcomed the lingering light of the sun on her body. She tilted her face upwards to magnify the effect. Some days she switched so fast between sadness and joy. Everything was keener: colours glowed, sounds penetrated: her body was a finely tuned instrument absorbing everything around her.

She had no desire to return home yet. She crossed the Seine, looking down into the swirling water. A lone angler stood on the bank, casting his line. The low sun sparkled on a patch of water. She wandered towards Jardin du Luxembourg, wanting the fading golds of autumn around her as she retraced her steps to places where she and Derek had walked. There was a growing chill in the air as she crossed the formal garden. Few people were about: it was the time office workers started returning home.

She was not far from Sylvia Beach's store: Shakespeare and Co. Sylvia had always been friendly to her, helpful even. She decided to call in. In the music section she found a book with Music Hall songs her mother might have sung. She paused, suppressing a stab of pain as she flipped through it. Sylvia emerged from the back and beamed a welcome. She looked grave for an instant. 'I heard about your mother. How is she?'

'On the mend.' Mo grimaced. 'But it's good to be in Paris again,' she said, not knowing what else to say.

'And now,' said Sylvia, 'you're going to be performing again?' She cast around, picking up the odd fallen book or stray glass. 'Just tidying up. We had a party here last night.' She explained that they'd been celebrating James Joyce's latest book, *Shem and Shaun*. Mo knew writers-in-exile often found refuge and concrete help here. 'Half the writers in Paris were here!' said Sylvia and carried on creating order.

'Have you ever been to Vienna?' Mo asked.

Sylvia tilted her head, a little surprised. 'Not yet I haven't. Why do you ask?'

'My father was from there.'

'Oh?' Sylvia had a way of imparting interest without seeming to pry.

'I'd love to go there.' Mo studied the collar of Sylvia's blouse, which was clean but rather worn. 'And sooner rather than later.' Sylvia gazed at Mo as if awaiting more details.

* * *

Back in Marais Derek was sprawled on the sofa with the balcony doors open. He'd opened one of the bottles of wine and the wireless was blasting out jazz. 'There you are! I was beginning to wonder where you'd got to.' He made space for her on the sofa. 'Look, let's go out. Get something to eat and take in a bit of jazz.' He looked nonchalant, exuding a confident, devil-may-care attitude, but she suspected there was more going on with him than he cared to admit.

She put on the little black frock she wore to perform in. It reached the middle of her knees, a look that had taken off here but was still considered fast in London. She twirled around so its fringe of a hem swished. She painted her mouth red. Already she felt different, getting herself into the mood for the nightlife of Paris. No time to look back, no time for regrets. Paris was in the moment and for the moment, energetic and exuberant. Her eyes glittered back at her from the antique mirror wedged at the back of the dressing table. Derek smiled when he saw the transformation.

They returned to the *boîte* nearby, Le Coin Caché. Derek led the way. Even as they approached it via an alley, strains of music rang out – the insistent beat that went through you, into your muscles, set your heart thrumming. 'Oh, it's good to be away from the dreariness of London,' said Derek.

She said nothing, neither agreeing nor disagreeing with him.

It was hot inside the nightclub, even the walls seem to be sweltering. It was packed to capacity. Three black musicians were blasting out: a trumpeter, saxophonist and a drummer. Those dancing were ecstatic, swinging with the tempo, crushed before a collection of tables, gyrating from the hips, with flailing arms and feet never still.

So many black musicians had been attracted to the capital that they were now commonplace. At home Mo had felt the lash of discrimination: if you weren't the right class it was hard to make your way. How much harder then if your skin was dark! But the French had taken Josephine Baker to their hearts. Only the diehards and conservatives disapproved of her.

The dancers and musicians oozed life, totally at ease with themselves. She'd spent so much effort trying to fit in, shedding signs of where she came from. Theatre directors had demanded it of her, told her she was in the West End now not some smoky den in the East End. And she'd complied. But what good had it done her? Now the music was urging her to abandon control, to give in and enjoy. Derek pulled her through the throng and found a table, not far from the musicians. 'Are you okay? You look a bit solemn,' he said. 'Do you want to dance?'

'Why not?'

They moved into the cramped space where bodies were swaying together, restless and turbulent as a storm-struck sea. She let go, allowing the throb of the music to take over. Derek was throwing off whatever had been playing on his mind. And so it should be, she thought: just us, here, now, with the music and the people of Paris, the wanderers, artists, free spirits and Bohemians, just as it had been when they'd first discovered each other here. The instruments were blaring in unison then working against each other, coming back into crazy harmony, higher and higher, louder and louder. And then it was over. An outburst of applause, feet stamping, cries of 'Encore! Encore!'

They returned to their table. Derek went in search of food. He came back with two glasses of wine. 'Not much selection. Shall we go somewhere else? The musicians are having a break now.'

They wandered down the alleyway onto an adjoining street where they found a bistro and ordered steak and a bottle of Bordeaux. 'You were going to tell me about your meeting with Goldman,' she began.

He looked across, chinked glasses with her. 'He wants me to act as middleman between him and the Russians.'

'Haven't you been doing that already? What's different now?'

'There are two artists he is particularly interested in.'

'Would I know them?'

'One you met. The other was there the night of the opening but you probably wouldn't remember.'

Mo had an uneasy feeling in her stomach. 'It's not the woman, is it? The dark one who looks like a gypsy?'

Derek laughed, poured them both more wine. 'Tanya Sergeyevna?'

'Is that her name?'

'She has done some fascinating work that's got her into trouble. She was a spokesperson for Russian culture at one time. Now – well she has to watch her step.'

'You're not about to get involved, are you Derek?'

His eyes shifted away, over his shoulder as if to see if the food was on its way, then he looked back at her, held her gaze. 'It's hard to turn your back on someone who's been through as much as she has.'

What exactly was he trying to tell her? Did he even know himself? 'Don't you think you've got enough on your plate already? I am sure there are plenty of her fellow countrymen who'd be willing to help.'

'One already is,' he replied. 'Anton Lensky.'

Mo felt herself go cold.

Chapter Forty-two *Derek*

Derek lay awake, staring at the ceiling. Mo was beside him, curled away towards the wall. He stroked the back of her head. These had been such draining days for her. She was sleeping as she had not slept in an age. The cramped bed at Tilda's had been a hindrance, as had all the anxieties she was carrying. Last night had washed some of that away. After dinner they'd returned to le Coin Caché, danced and drunk till the early hours and then wandered back here, laughing, bodies entwined like the old days.

He would go out and hunt for breakfast, bring back warm croissants. While he was at it, he'd send off a *petit bleu* and set up a meeting with Lensky. Part of him shrank from the task. Without Lensky, Mo's singing career in Paris would be stymied, but Lensky had become, for better or worse, Tanya's protector. It hadn't been too clever of him, had it, to go straight to Lensky when he needed someone to shoulder that responsibility? He obviously hadn't been thinking clearly.

Downstairs the alley stank. The sluicing down had not yet begun. He remembered reading somewhere that there'd been an outbreak of bubonic plague in some insanitary settlement in Paris earlier in the decade. They were lucky to have an indoor closet and running water. For all that, it was probably time to seek somewhere better. Somewhere Tanya did not know about.

When he returned to their rooms Mo had woken and was sitting on the balcony with a coat wrapped round her, sipping water. 'Look, fresh as they come!' he said. They sat side by side, munching and dipping their croissants into milky coffee.

* * *

Anton Lensky was sporting a tweed jacket and chartreuse shirt, which gave him the look of an English country squire. He was matching himself to his surroundings, thought Derek as he glanced round the interior of Café Dôme with its dull gold walls. The place was humming with a hundred muted and not so muted conversations. More people kept arriving. It had been Lensky's suggestion. Derek would have preferred somewhere quieter. Mo gazed around, taking it all in.

'When did you get back?' Lensky asked them. For a moment or two they went over familiar ground till it felt like the social niceties had been observed and they could get on with the matter at hand. Only he wasn't sure what that was. All he knew was that he did not want to discuss Tanya Sergeyevna in Mo's hearing.

Mo was holding back, but she'd want to know where she stood. Recent days had forced her to adopt the mantle of dutiful daughter and it would take a different energy to place herself centre-stage. 'Monsieur Lensky,' he began, 'as you know my wife had to return to London at short notice…' Lensky grunted acknowledgement and leaned back, eyed the two of them. 'We understand you have a business to run, a clientele to satisfy. And as you've pointed out before, you have to be on top of things…' Mo's smile became fixed. She was enough of a professional to keep *stumm*. But the tension was getting to her. She kept fiddling with the lapels of her jacket or drumming her fingers on the table.

He turned to Lensky. 'We appreciate your need to maintain a supply of singers. Any impresario worth his salt would do the same. But there are other offers under consideration and we wanted to give you first refusal…'

Mo glanced at him then quickly away again. Was he ladling it on too thick? Lensky had the grace to give a little laugh. 'What hasn't changed is my admiration for your voice, Madame Eaton, or your ability to delight an audience. I'd be delighted if you came to sing for us again.'

Mo stopped fiddling with her hands. We're not home and dry yet, Derek wanted to say: terms of agreement were everything. He knew the performer in Mo couldn't care less as long as she could get up there and do what she felt she was born to do. Mo excused herself to go to the Ladies. After she'd left the two men looked at each other. Lensky poured himself a glass of water. 'I'll draw up an agreement for you to have a look at. I'm keen to have your wife sing for us, but I wouldn't want to push her too hard at the moment.'

Derek nodded.

'But I do need to talk to you about Tanya Sergeyevna.'

Derek was alarmed. 'Not now, surely?'

'Well I can't wait too long. Things are getting critical.'

Just then they spotted Mo weaving her way towards them.

Chapter Forty-three *Mo*

Mo scolded herself for her lack of sang-froid. Sometimes she allowed herself to be caught on the hop, to become again that ever-insecure young singer. Stupid, she knew. Yet she wasn't alone in this: she'd heard of actors at the pinnacle of their powers who vomited every time they had to go on stage. Maybe it was necessary, this dying a death before flaring into life before an audience.

Now she wanted to get away from these two. She sensed they would haggle a bit, cross swords and come up with an agreement, which they'd both decided on before anyway. She wasn't averse to Derek bargaining on her behalf; in fact, she liked it. It demonstrated his growing maturity and commitment to her. There was a time when he seemed opposed to her career altogether. Though she hadn't believed that either. It had just been his own vulnerability.

'So,' she said cheerfully as she drew level with them. 'I'm going to love and leave you. I'm sure you will iron out the differences. I'm keen to sing for you, Monsieur Lensky, but not,' she added with a coquettish tilt of her head, 'at any price.'

Surprised, Lensky got to his feet, kissed her lightly on either cheek. Derek nodded, giving her a searching look.

* * *

Pierre had told her about Gustav Klimt, the leader of the Secessionists in Vienna at the turn of the century. Before she plunged back into her singing career in Paris she wanted to explore in her imagination the city of her father, dwell on the ambience of the early years of his life. After all, it was her heritage.

Pierre had given her a few pointers. He told her about the

Beethoven Frieze.

At Shakespeare and Company Sylvia was nowhere to be seen. Mo moved around the shelves, picking out and mulling over the odd tome. Books were stacked from floor to ceiling. In the corner, where the larger atlases and art books were displayed, she found what she'd hoped for. She flipped over pages until she came to an illustration of the frieze. She looked round for a space where she could squat and view the pictures at leisure. She found a low stool.

The Beethoven Frieze was unlike anything she had ever seen: writhing snakes, Gorgon heads, genii, a huge ape – Typhoeus – representing evil, images of death, sickness – all challenged by the golden knight. The finale was a display of heaven-bound genii and entwined lovers in the *Kiss to the Whole World*. She sat staring at the golden, decorative images, at the rippled snakeskin, the gold leaf and the swooning ethereal beings. She began to read.

The Frieze appeared in 1902 in the fourteenth Vienna Secession Exhibition. It portrayed the human longing for happiness amongst suffering. This masterpiece of the Secession movement celebrated the beauty of art, love and music. The artists of the Vienna Secession had seen Beethoven as a hero. This was at a time when Otto von Bismark was forming the modern state of Germany and making it the dominant power in Europe. The Austro-Hungarian Empire, with its Hapsburg monarchy, was a splendid and sophisticated society, but critics said it was cracking apart. With nationalist factions in its member states urging for independence, its days were numbered. The Secessionists decided they would honour the great composer, for more than any other he foreshadowed the Gesamtkunstwerk, a key concept in their movement: Gesamtkunstwerk meant a total work of art. Beethoven had achieved a Gesamtkunstwerk with the Ninth Symphony: Schiller's verses in Ode to Joy combined with orchestral harmony, the human voice and the colour of verbal imagery...

Mo sat staring at the images of the Beethoven Frieze. She laid the book at her feet.

Something was shifting in her; something she was not yet ready to take on board. It was as if she'd stumbled into a maze; a door opened to reveal a new set of rooms in a house she thought she knew.

She replaced the tome onto the shelf.

Her father had been part of all that. Perhaps he had personally known Gustav Klimt, the inspired father and creator of the frieze. Perhaps he had been part of the Secessionist Movement. He had spoken with enthusiasm of Gustav Mahler, who had performed Beethoven's Ninth Symphony when the Secessionist exhibition opened.

Her father.

She wandered back to Marais, thoughts jumbling, dispersing, reassembling. She climbed the stairs to their apartment and went through to the balcony with a cup of coffee. Unbidden, unwelcome, other sensations started to impinge on her. She recalled the night of the fire in The Athena theatre. Each image, each impression was the stab of a knife, a splinter of ice needling its way into her awareness.

* * *

She was in the dressing room, removing her stage make-up. In a corner a candle was flickering. She was downing whisky, one glass after another. And why shouldn't she? She was courting oblivion, wanting to float away, disembodied, like the genii in the frieze; above all, keen to take herself out of the struggle, leave her troubles and grief behind, slough them off like dead snakeskin.

She'd left the candle burning in the corner. The scripts were heaped, higgledly-piggledly, next to the naked flame. She had taken the bottle and glass and moved to an adjacent room where she lit the kerosene lamp and sank onto the crumpled sofa. What did she care? She was a star. She was an artist. She was suffering. What need had she to worry about the consequences of a night spent alone in an empty theatre?

… And then she was being dragged away, roused, slapped in the face, given water, loaded onto a stretcher, siren-wailing taken to the nearest casualty department. Her mother anxious beside her bed, flowers from God-knew-who. And Knighton – whom she avoided as best she could – what right did he have to be angry with her?

But but but…

If she had not chosen to go her own sweet way, to lie down on the soft cushions, throw her cares to the wind and drink until her mind clouded over, how might things have turned out differently? So deep in inebriated sleep that she didn't hear papers crinkling in the room next door as they caught fire, did not hear the whoosh of air as the curtains and screen fed the flames. Her door was firmly shut, just yards away.

Mo stared in horror over the grey roofs of the *quartier*. She felt a sickness in her stomach. She wanted to throw up, empty her body of all that it was trying to digest, float away like one of the genii. She had not known. Did not do it on purpose.

Was she cursed with a touch of evil? She had not had Timothy inoculated. She had left him with a neighbour to pursue her own ambition. He had died. He had died. He had died. And then she had caused the fire that destroyed The Athena. Burnt a theatre down and killed her own father. Never mind that the police said the fire was caused by a burnt-out stage light. If she had not been there, he would not have died. The fire would not have been as bad as it was. She was a witch. Lady Macbeth had nothing on her. Her child and her father! She might not have willed it, but her carelessness, her self-absorption had been the trigger, the means by which the dark forces of Typhoeus entered and wreaked their vengeance. She was the bringer of evil. The Jonah in the boat. The rotten apple. The snake in the garden of paradise.

She rushed down the flight of stairs, almost falling headlong as she went, and retched into the toilet bowl, again and again, until there was nothing left in her stomach but bile.

Chapter Forty-four *Derek*

Though Derek was relieved to have Mo out of the way when Lensky broached the subject of Tanya Sergeyevna, he was peeved that she had made such a hasty departure. It verged on rudeness. She wasn't a child, for goodness' sake, although at times she acted like one. She considered it vulgar to have to haggle over her talent. He could understand that. But she might have forewarned him. They could have worked out a strategy. Now she was gone, leaving Lensky and himself disconcerted.

Sometimes she was the most exasperating person in the world.

Lensky was beckoning to the waiter for a menu. It was after one o'clock and all around them people had started ordering food. He was not hungry. He wanted to get matters settled and find out just what was going on with Mo. But before that he needed to meet with Goldman and push things forward. For the sake of form he ordered an endive salad and glass of Sauvignon Blanc. Lensky ordered *foie gras*.

'My wife – I am sorry she had to leave – she is still upset. About her mother...'

Lensky nodded. 'Are they close?'

Derek shrugged. How to describe the fraught but passionate relationship between Mo and Ma Dobson? In its own way it was as intense as any. 'They've grown closer in recent months.'

'I see. Anyway, what with everything that's going on I thought I would offer your wife two slots a week at Scheherazade – at our normal rates. I want to keep her on the books. She has a lovely voice. If that works out, I may offer her more slots.'

Derek smiled. 'That would be fine – for a start at least. She shouldn't overtire herself just now.'

'That's what I thought.'

When their food arrived they consumed it in silence. Derek

glanced up and saw that Lensky was watching him. He had a shrewd, curious look in his eyes, as if he were assessing him. 'I wanted to talk to you about Tanya Sergeyevna.'

'Go ahead.' Derek was aware of his chest tightening.

'*Eh bien*, to put in bluntly in asking me to take on responsibility for her you were handing me – how do you British say? – a poisoned chalice.'

'Where is she now?'

'She's staying near my family home. I found a sort of studio for her.'

'That was good of you.'

'Let's not beat about the bush. It's a volatile situation. I already have my share of responsibilities.'

'Well yes, I realise that. But I thought you had more contacts in the city than anyone else I know.'

'Do you believe her life is in danger then?'

'I believe so. In Russia they are killing people left, right and centre…'

Lensky grunted. 'You don't need to tell me this.'

Derek sighed. 'One day she's a spokesperson for Russian culture, the next they are raiding her studio…'

'Some might say she brought it on herself.'

'Meaning?' Derek glared at him for a moment, a nugget of pure rage gathering in his throat. Lensky deflected the gaze.

'Not my opinion, necessarily, you understand. But you've put me in a fix. I don't want to endanger my family, any more than you want to endanger your marriage.'

Derek winced at the broadside. He leaned back, stared at the residue of oil on his plate. 'What's to be done, Monsieur Lensky? We can't just abandon her to her fate. As a fellow artist I appreciate what she is trying to do.'

'We need to speak to some of her fellow artists. Discreetly.'

'Have you heard about Goldman?'

'The art dealer? Tanya Sergeyevna told me about him. He

came to view the recent exhibition, but I wasn't introduced to him.'

'Well, he's keen to see her latest work. Dimitri told him about it. He is contemplating an exhibition. In New York.'

Lensky raised an eyebrow. 'You believe him?'

'He represents the family firm. Old money. Russian connections. They invest in art and culture. I would say he means business. He made no false promises to the other painters. He has a good, quick eye and knows what he wants and doesn't want.'

'Mm,' Lensky signalled to the waiter. 'Would you like a coffee?' He took out a cheroot and offered the case to Derek, who declined. 'Why don't you come and talk to Tanya Sergeyevna? See what she has to say about all this.'

Though constructive, the notion filled Derek with apprehension. He needed a wall between himself and the disturbing, enigmatic Russian sculptress. 'Very well,' he said. 'I'm seeing Goldman later. Be good to have something to report.'

* * *

Anton Lensky's substantial residence in Boulogne Billancourt was a turreted villa overlooking the Seine. With its wrought iron railing and a density of shrubbery it reminded Derek of a Bournemouth boarding house. The rooms were high ceilinged and adorned with ancient prints and art nouveau pieces. In the first reception room was a gleaming Steinway grand piano. 'You play?' asked Derek.

'It has been known,' said Lensky with a half-smile. A maid in a frilly apron presented herself. 'Would you fetch some tea with lemon?' he instructed her.

Derek was slightly fazed by the solidly bourgeois circumstances of Lensky's life. How long had he lived here? Where was his wife from? How had he made his money? The maid entered with a tray, which she unloaded onto the round table between the two sofas of plush blue silk.

Steps echoed outside and there, standing in the doorway in an artist's smock and with her hair round her face like a dark halo, was Tanya. She started when she saw Derek, giving Lensky a baffled look.

'Monsieur Derek Eaton, we meet again.' He took her proffered hand. Since they last met her cheeks had filled and the haunted look had left her eyes. As they arranged themselves on the sofas Lensky poured tea.

'So how have you been keeping, Tanya Sergeyevna?' asked Derek.

'Very well, thank you. Monsieur Lensky found me a space where I can work.' She gave the glimmer of a smile. 'Would you like to come and see my latest pieces?'

'I would, yes. They reflect your experience in Paris, I believe?' He felt strangely reserved in her company as though they scarcely knew each other.

She gave a little shrug him. 'News travels fast.'

Tanya's studio, hidden by a high hawthorn hedge, was an outhouse on what looked like wasteland, half a mile away. 'You're very private here,' remarked Derek as they approached.

Tanya smiled. 'It's been a godsend.'

'Somewhere to tide you over,' Lensky murmured. His voice sounded tight, as though he were forcing himself to be civil. Derek glanced at him. He had not yet met Lensky's wife but could imagine the presence of this independent-minded and attractive artist would disrupt any well-ordered household. No wonder Tanya was tucked out of sight.

She creaked open the double doors to the outhouse. There was a faint smell of overripe apples. She switched on the lights to reveal a large space with a mezzanine level, akin to a small barn. The faint apple smell gave way to fumes of oil and turpentine as they moved into the body of the building. Derek caught his breath. There in front of him was a painting several meters high. The colours were lurid as was the clash of elements within the work itself. Just looking at it gave him a queasy sensation.

Tanya laughed to see his reaction. Lensky was frowning, as if puzzling something out. 'It's not finished,' she said. 'It's an impression of the warring factions among the Russians in Paris. Nothing of harmony or reconciliation about it. It's a preparatory canvas for other works.'

An effect of dissonance was achieved by jagged diagonals cutting across the main area while faces and figures, interacting or solitary, were moving in different directions so you didn't quite know where to look. None of the colours harmonised or balanced each other.

'So, it's one huge sketch, is it?' Derek ventured.

She shrugged. 'It is what it is. I'm allowing anything just to see what emerges.'

'Has Dimitri seen the work?'

She nodded. 'He's been urging me to carry on in the same vein.'

As Derek continued to stare, he let it take him over. He wondered whether Dimitri had described this piece to Goldman. The uneasy feeling did not go away; rather it morphed into a sense of displacement, dislocation, as though he had to wobble his head to recall just who and where he was. As an expression of the émigré experience it was brilliant.

On either side were charcoal figure drawings: some in flight, leaning outwards and away; others clustered so close that their lower halves merged like tree roots; others exuded pain through angular gestures or anguished faces; still others had a bemused, dreamlike state as if hypnotised.

'You've certainly caught something here,' said Derek.

'It's not meant to be pretty.'

'I can see that. Has Dimitri told you about his conversation with Goldman?'

A shadow crossed her face. 'He mentioned him. And the

exhibition he'd like me to put together. I'm not sure I'm ready for that.'

Derek took his leave soon after. Taking advantage of seclusion, Tanya was giving full vent to her Parisian encounter. Now that she no longer need concern herself organising other people or running from the Russian Secret Services, she seemed inordinately free. But Derek asked himself just how illusory this respite might be.

* * *

He found Dimitri at the Russians' basement club. He was in a buoyant mood. 'So there you are. I was wondering when you'd be back.' They came out from the gloomy interior and wandered along the banks of the Seine. A light wind was ruffling the trees and sending patterns shivering across the water.

'I've just been to see Tanya.'

'And? Did you see what she's been getting up to? Good idea getting her fixed up there.'

'But it can't last. Lensky wants her out.'

Dimitri tilted his head in surprise. 'I thought they were getting on.'

Derek shrugged. 'That's not the point.'

'Then, what is?'

'It's a temporary solution. How many people know she's there?'

Dimitri shrugged. 'Some of the group, I guess.'

'You told them?'

'No. But they seem to know.'

'How?' As Dimitri shrugged his ignorance, Derek felt disquiet. 'And Goldman, does he know?'

'Not exactly.'

'What d'you mean, 'not exactly'?' Derek was irked by Dimitri's nonchalance. The man had seen the harm the OGPU could wreak if they had a mind to. Today Dimitri seemed lulled into a false security. Had he forgotten so soon? 'You go discussing her with Goldman. Did you even ask her permission to do that?'

Dimitri gazed into the middle distance. 'Things have quietened down. I think the Organs have given up on her.'

'Who?'

Dimitri laughed. 'It's what we call the Secret Service.'

Derek was not convinced. 'Do you know anything about Lensky? Apart from the fact he's well-heeled and seems to have good connections.'

'Derek, you were the one who introduced them, don't forget.' He paused. 'Their families knew each other. Old Russia lives on.'

'I saw her work. It's disturbing – but vital. I see why you think it should get an airing. I'm just concerned about exposing her to more danger.'

Dimitri patted Derek on the back. 'Touched that you care. I guess being a Russian artist is about being willing to take a risk.'

Chapter Forty-five *Lensky*

Tanya Sergeyevna was a drive of nature. It was no wonder that the current powers-that-be feared her influence, especially given her father's history. They would not want her volatile contribution in the mix of politics. There was no telling where she would set her sights next. It was understandable, too, that she had once been cultural spokesperson for she was bright, articulate and sharp as mountain air. Derek Eaton did not know what he was playing with. To him it was all art and expression, disquiet at the squashing of freedom, at strictures the larger force exerted on the lesser. What did he know? He was the child of a lethargic, law-abiding people.

Lensky watched him slope away, back to the centre of Paris. Tanya left soon after, too, pulled by the sketches and scrawls of her fervid creating. She wanted to be alone. She'd said that from the outset and he'd agreed to respect her wishes. For all that, she was about as safe as a can of paraffin in a blazing warehouse. Let her have her borrowed time, let her indulge her rampant gift, her tireless energy. He would not bring about her downfall. If he could possibly help her on her way, he would do so. If he was allowed to, that is.

He sighed and watched as the maid tidied away the tea things in the salon. Her neck was pink, he noticed. Had she been listening in on their earlier conversation? Or was she just flushed from rushing around? He brushed away the questions. Since when had maidservants made him edgy?

From the hallway he could hear the stamp of small feet, giggles and excited voices as the nanny returned with the children from their walk in the park. Anna, his wife, would come soon and join him for an aperitif before dinner, her dull eyes flitting over him and away as though he was just too much for her to bear in her current state of health. He sighed again. What price a quiet life? What price duplicity?

He had fended off the shadows, the undesirable connections, which reeked of the past and Mother Russia. Tanya reminded him of his youth. There was a cynicism, which veiled only thinly an idealism that could not quite die or be tempered with pragmatism. Once, he'd been like that. Once he'd wanted to better the lot of his fellow man.

* * *

In the winter of 1905, he'd been horrified at the mowing down of unarmed petitioners as they marched on the Winter Palace to present the Tsar with their plea for reforms. Such barbarism! Bloody Sunday, they named it. Without hesitation he'd sided with the luckless workers. He was a young man then, studying music at the St Petersburg Conservatory. Outraged, he joined the throng of protesting students from the academies and university faculties. They did what they could. Joined strikes and demonstrations, formed societies, talked late into the night and dodged the Cheka, the Tsarist Security Service. Some plotted revenge.

But when the reprisals came, they were just as ugly. Unrest spread across Russia. There were peasant rebellions: nearly two thousand Tsarist governors, generals and officials were murdered. The peasants set fire to the gentry's manor houses, slayed landlords and destroyed crops and livestock.

In Saratov Province, where the family estate lay, it was particularly acute. By a stroke of luck his parents had been wintering at their residence in the Riviera. That saved them. The reprisals put an end to his own political involvement. Power relations were a nasty business: it was a maze where you could lose your mind.

His father's connections and assets in the South of France were a godsend. They worked the stronger magic. Art called him.

Music became his mistress, poetry his weakness. He sighed and got to his feet. Even as he whispered these words, he realised what romantic notions he was peddling.

He moved towards the lobby where Sergei came rushing into his arms. 'Papa, papa we saw a duck with her babies. There were five of them!' He tousled his son's curly locks and smiled at his daughter who was looking rather solemn.

'And you, Ludmila, what did you see?'

'Nothing. There was a man kept following us. I didn't like him.'

'Nonsense, my dear,' said Mademoiselle Grignon, their nanny. 'He sat on the bench and was reading the paper.'

'No,' insisted Ludmila. 'He kept looking at us.'

'Maybe that was because you were making such a noise,' she remonstrated.

Chapter Forty-six *Derek*

Derek left his meeting with Dimitri disconcerted. When Goldman called the gallery to defer their meeting, stating the need to make several trunk calls to the United States, Derek was glad. He needed time to consider how the strands were coming together or pulling apart. Besides, he was looking forward to seeing Mo and forgetting for a while this whole Russian fiasco.

He took the steps in their Marais *immeuble* two at a time, impatient to see Mo. She'd left the late morning meeting with Lensky in a cheerful frame of mind, and he was eager to give her the good news about the contract for singing at Scheherazade again. But when he opened the door to their rooms he was met by a strange silence. She must still be out. He moved towards the balcony and saw a lone cup on the floor there. When he entered their bedroom, he found her crumpled on the bed in a foetal position. He stared at her for a moment, wondering whether she was drunk. He scolded himself for the thought: these days she drank little and then only socially. He hesitated before drawing closer. She looked towards him with blank eyes.

'What is it? What's happened?' he asked. 'Is it your mother?' She turned over to face the wall. 'Mo? Are you alright?'

'I've been sick,' she murmured.

He sat down on the bed and stroked her shoulder. 'Are you in pain?'

'If only it were that simple,' she almost whispered. Now she was beginning to worry him. She looked as pale as milk.

'What is it?' What's wrong?'

She shivered shaking her head.

'Here, let me…' he drew the blanket round her. 'Maybe you are ailing for something. Or a touch of food poisoning? Or you're not…?'

'No, no.' She sighed again. 'Derek, do you think I'm evil?'

He laughed. 'What's got into you, Mo? Of course you aren't evil. Why ever d'you say that?'

'Sometimes I think I am cursed.'

'Mo, you're making no sense. You left us looking confident. I come home and find you looking like death warmed up. What's going on?'

She gathered the blanket up around her knees, then cast it to one side. 'I'll get up now.' She got unsteadily to her feet. 'Will you bring me some water. I'll go through to the balcony.' Derek went to fetch two glasses of water. When he returned she was ensconced on the balcony, wrapped in the same blanket. She took the water from him.

'Where did you dash off to? Lensky was shocked at the abrupt way you left. He thought he'd offended you. We were just about to talk about your contract.'

'You know how I hate discussing money.'

'Somebody has to.'

'What did he say then? What's the contract?'

'He's willing to offer you two slots. Usual rates. To start with, that is. You can acclimatise yourself, work at your own pace…' When Mo said nothing but sat hugging her knees, he moved closer to her. 'Mo, what is it?'

She was swaying gently, as if rocking herself asleep. He felt a sliver of fear. It was hard to keep up with her moods. He put his hand on her knee to steady her, transmit his support. She took his hand. 'Derek, I didn't want you to find me like this. It just came over me. I couldn't stop the thoughts …'

He took her hand in his. It was cold to the touch. 'This morning you were radiant. With Lensky you didn't seem to have a care in the world.'

'I'm like that these days. I hardly know myself. One minute I'm light and ready to take on the world, the next …'

'You've had a lot to contend with.'

'I went to Sylvia's again. I wanted to – to connect with Sandor through his life in Vienna. It's like thread that's been tangled up. I'm trying to undo it. Pierre told me about the Beethoven Frieze. I found a book about it. I was completely taken by it. And then I started thinking about evil. And it all came back to me…'

'What did?'

'Oh Derek. You have no idea.'

He went to pull her towards him. 'Come here.'

She resisted. 'Derek, I am monstrous.'

'Mo, what on earth are you talking about?'

'It was my fault Timothy died. It was my fault the theatre burnt down. I killed my own father. I am evil.'

She started sobbing. There was a ferocity burning through her. Her body was rigid. The sobs wracked her chest. He waited helplessly until the sobs grew quieter and she allowed him to hold her. 'Mo, it was never your intention to harm anyone. That's what counts, in the end. Besides, the police concluded it was an accident. They found a burnt-out light.'

She lifted her tear-smeared face towards him. 'But I made it worse. I had a candle burning, a kerosene lamp…'

'Mo, it wasn't your fault.'

'But it was because of me Sandor came into the theatre.'

'Listen – you are not to blame. You're innocent. You meant no one any harm.'

'Do you really think so?' Her voice was little more than a whisper.

* * *

Later that evening he made them a simple supper from the food she'd bought earlier. She sat over the bread, pâté and cheese, silently chewing. She seemed calmer. They were at the small table wedged into the corner of the sitting room, their knees almost touching. He poured her a glass of red wine.

'Anton Lensky said you can start work whenever you want to.

Have you thought any more about it?'

'Sooner rather than later, I would've thought. Gives me less time to torment myself. How about tomorrow?'

'Not too soon for you?'

She shrugged. 'I don't want to be spending too much time on my own.'

'Fair enough.' He poured himself more wine.

She gave him a weak smile. 'You can't blame me for thinking a lot about Sandor Olmak. I met him. We were getting to know each other. He was trying to make amends – for not being around when I was growing up. I am sure of it.'

Derek looked at her without speaking, feeling a tender concern. She needed to calm down. She needed to feel the ground beneath her feet. 'I'm here,' he said.

'Are you?' she asked. She looked wistful. 'So many times in the past you've made promises and then not been around.' He looked at her without replying.

Chapter Forty-seven

The next morning he left while he she was still sleeping. It shocked him to see the state she'd got herself into. Until yesterday she seemed to be coping: showing sadness, yes, but not this self-flagellation.

Yet, when he pondered it, he could not blame her.

There had been little discussion of culpability as far as the fire was concerned. The metropolitan police were happy to write it off as an accident, a charred lamp offered as evidence. The insurers had been in, viewed the sight and allowed compensation payments to go ahead without undue wrangling. Theatre fires were not uncommon. Electric wiring was either non-existent or faulty. The premiums were set accordingly high. There'd been no whiff of a court proceeding to prove individual negligence.

But all this did not alter the fact that had she not been there Sandor Olmak would not have died. He himself had assumed she was still tied up with Knighton at the time and therefore living in the Aldwych flat. Why had she chosen to sleep in The Athena Theatre when she had other options? Why did Garfield, the stage manager, allow it? Had he even known about it? And what of the night watchman, who locked up after everyone had departed – was he in the know? Just what had been going on with her?

A bundle of his own stage sets had been burnt to a cinder. Not that he cared that much about them. He'd been paid for them and could turn his hand to more at any time. But above and beyond all this was the issue of Sandor Olmak's death. He had attempted to rescue her. Later, Mo related how she'd heard him shouting out her name. He must've known she sometimes stayed there. That, in itself, was strange. Tragic, ironical, almost, for him to be trapped, suffocated by fumes and burnt alive at the very moment his daughter was escaping through a rarely used side entrance.

Derek attempted to push these intruding thoughts aside. He'd reassured Mo. But how indeed did one live with that sort of guilt? One just didn't, normally. One pushed it out of awareness, rationalised it away or blamed someone else. He'd meant what he said. She had intended no harm. For now, those words consoled her, but he suspected the spectre of the fire and its aftermath would continue to haunt her.

He moved down the alleyway and merged with the flow of workers going to their jobs. Dimitri was surprised to see him so early. 'Shall we take a coffee?' suggested Derek and the two ambled to a corner place not far from the L'Atelier Blanc. Dimitri was in a more sombre mood today.

'I thought about what you said,' Dimitri began. 'I was distracted yesterday. Three more painters sold pieces to latecomers. Their delight spilled over. I was not thinking straight – about Tanya, I mean. Everything has gone so quiet I assumed she was out of danger. But you're right. We need to be vigilant.'

'She says she's happy to exhibit, but not in Paris. A lot of what she is doing is preparatory. More will follow,' said Derek.

'The white-hot fire of creativity?' replied Dimitri with affection. 'That's my Tanyushka. Once she gets going there's no stopping her.'

'Have you found out any more about the thugs who destroyed her work?'

Dimitri shrugged. 'They seem to have disappeared.'

Derek sipped his espresso and looked at Dimitri askance. 'Nothing picked up on the grapevine?'

'Names are not important. It's not a personal thing.'

'But are they likely to strike again?' He paused. 'I'm seeing Goldman later. He wants to view her work. Tanya is in agreement. I need to work out how to proceed.'

'She's still vulnerable. I agree that we should exercise caution.'

Derek frowned at him. 'Do you have anything concrete to add? You understand Russian politics a hell of a lot better than I do.'

'You seem to be doing a fine job.'

Derek felt a surge of impatience. 'I think you need to take over.'

'Oh?' Dimitri tilted his head in curiosity.

'If I make an arrangement for Goldman to go and see Tanya's work and we reach some sort of agreement, will you be able to take it from there? I think Tanya needs support after what's happened.'

'I've been keeping an eye out for her for years. But yes, in answer to your question, I'll be there. I'd appreciate you and Tanya cutting the deal with Goldman first though. So we know where we stand.'

Chapter Forty-eight *Mo*

My time has come, Mo told herself, as she stared at her wan image in the mirror, which was lit by a side lamp throwing jagged shadows across the room. She pinched her cheeks, dusted them with tinted powder and pursed her lips. She'd only sung at Scheherazade once before. That was weeks ago. She was a different person now.

Shadows crossed the pale lilac walls, bedecked with *Ballets Russes* wall hangings. The tables still clustered, under starched white tablecloths, around the main podium, where the guests – up to a hundred of them with hopeful, glistening faces – were hungry for entertainment. She could hear Lisette's plaintive tones. She would be finishing her act any minute. What was the mood of the audience tonight? An audience, though made up of disparate individuals, became one creature to the performer: a cold, judgmental being that could destroy you or an embracing, open partner that took you to its heart.

Lensky had told her she could sing what she wanted. This she had heard through Derek for she had not seen Lensky since their morning meeting. Singing in English was not a problem, he said, as there were now so many English-speaking musicians and visitors in the city. Everywhere in the clubs, French *chansons réalistes* vied with American jazz. People didn't care anymore. They had been won over. She recalled her early struggles, just weeks before, to learn a few French songs so she could stay on a par with these singers of the street, not to ape them but to bring her own take on poverty, struggle, defiance. She must have been trying the wrong places. Now she could just be herself. Sing Noel Coward if she wanted to, or Cole Porter or Ivor Novello.

Lensky would be in the audience along with Derek. They had

had a late meeting with Goldman about the Russian artists. She peeped out from the shadows and could just make out their silhouettes beyond the far end of the podium.

The pianist was beckoning to her. And then she was out there. Lisette brushed past her with a smile. 'They're in a strange mood tonight,' she whispered. Mo swept on to the podium and smiled towards this unknowable, pliable creature. Faces turned towards her in expectation. She had chosen songs from Broadway musicals. By rights she should have had an orchestra or at least a jazz band to back her, but she would do what she could. The pianist would do his bit. After all, it was all about illusion.

She started with '*Singing in the rain.*' By arrangement one of the waiters threw her an umbrella, which she caught with aplomb. She looked towards the ceiling as if expecting a downpour and burst into song. The audience lapped it up, clapping as she tapped her brolly and swivelled round an imaginary lamppost. Then she sang: '*I'm nobody's baby now,*' pouting and giving the men at the front tables the eye.

Her last song, also made famous by Ruth Etting, was: '*I'll get by.*'

'*I'll get by as long as I have you. There may be rain and darkness too, I'll not complain…*'

She was in love with the audience as they rewarded her with shouts of approval. Then it was over. She stepped from the podium as the next singer, someone she'd never seen before, came forward. She changed out of her shimmering black dress and slipped quietly among the tables, searching out Derek and Lensky.

'Congratulations,' said Lensky, beckoning to the waiter for champagne. 'You were a delight, my dear, a sheer delight.' Mo nodded her thanks. Derek was smiling towards her. She was still high from singing. Always it took her by surprise, this sense of a different world, plucking fire from the gods, she'd once heard an actor say. She wasn't sure about that, but she did know when she performed something else came over her. All her fears, hopes, skills and aspirations balled together.

She was surprised to see a third man with them. Derek introduced them. So this was Goldman! He got up and kissed her hand, making her laugh for he had a slight mischievous twist to his mouth and sparkle about him. 'What a true Chantoosie,' he said.

'What's a chantoosie when it's at home?' she quipped.

'A *chanteuse*, they'd say here. What a voice! You'd be totally at ease in a New York jazz club. Or in operetta even.' He kept up a steady flow of comments – some irreverent – on the act that followed. 'A few bum notes there,' he whispered, and she couldn't help giggling. They carried on chatting. She was intrigued, too, that he knew so much about music. He'd seen the premiere of Noel Coward's *Bittersweet* in London. To her amusement he hummed a tune from it. His voice carried. Lensky frowned at him, and he shut up. He talked about operas and operettas he'd experienced elsewhere. He had connections in Vienna, Zurich – all over the place, it seemed. He came from a scattered family, he told her. Though he breathed no word about persecution, she guessed why. That he was Jewish only added spice to the mixture – there was still so much about Sandor and his heritage that she longed to explore.

After a while he glanced at his watch and excused himself: there was a call from New York he'd arranged to take at his hotel. Lensky moved off to circulate amongst the other tables. Derek glanced across at her. His eyes were full of admiration, tenderness. She sipped more champagne and leaned back. All doubts became wisps in the azure of the sky.

'Derek,' she said. 'I can't get that frieze out of my mind. Do you know about *fin de siècle* and all that?'

He looked at her in surprise. 'Who doesn't? The most important era in Viennese cultural history.'

'I'd like to go to Vienna. Can we plan a trip there? I want to see the place for myself.' She felt her neck growing warm. 'Well?'

'What's brought this on?'

She shrugged. 'Shall we plan a trip there?'

Derek looked at her sharply. 'Can we settle back into Paris first?' When she said nothing, he took her hand. 'One day we can go. But not right now.' He looked at his watch. 'It's time we went home.'

The walk back from Scheherazade in the fresh night air was bracing. In Marais Mo gazed out from the balcony. A sliver of moonlight was glistening on the parapets as clouds scudded across it. 'You caused quite a stir tonight,' said Derek.

'I'm glad you were there.'

'You once said my being there made you nervous?' he laughed. 'Make up your mind.'

'I need to know you support me.'

'I've just sorted out the finances at The Mare's Head. I got a contract with Lensky. Don't these things count?'

'I'm immensely grateful. You know I am.'

'Then?'

She smiled to herself. A remnant of self-pity was exerting itself. She wanted none of it. Later, as she closed her eyes to sleep, she thought fleetingly of her father and Vienna. She was aquiver with possibility. The gig, Vienna, Samuel Goldman, the connection with Sandor Olmak…

Chapter Forty-nine *Derek*

The more Derek saw of Samuel Goldman the more he knew not to underestimate him. Not only could Goldman not be pushed or cajoled on a business front, but he had reserves of taste and humanity Derek had been inclined to overlook. He was a complex but not unsympathetic man. He revealed himself to Derek more by what he did not say, more in his ability to stay the course, speak when he needed to and ask the right questions.

His chauffeur took the two of them out to Billancourt to view Tanya Sergeyevna's work. Derek looked out at the passing boulevards, the scraps of trees and allotments on the fringes of the city, out through angular neo-modern buildings encircling the great metropolis.

'You've heard of her before, have you?' he asked.

'Her family was known to mine. Back then. But I've only come into contact with her through the exhibition. What's she like? I only met her fleetingly in the Russian Club, remember?'

Derek shrugged, chary of self-revelation. 'What can I say? I understand why some would consider her a risk. She has a mind of her own. These days, in Russia, that isn't a good idea. She can communicate – speaks a few languages. She was once cultural spokesperson for a Ministry of Education.'

'Is that so? I heard what happened to her work. Dimitri told me. *Stalin's Dolls?* Now that would be explosive. She wasn't calling it that, was she?'

'The work hasn't been shown yet.'

'Even so, word gets out. Do you trust all the other painters? The Apostles, they call themselves, don't they?'

'Quite honestly, I've given up trying to understand the cabals of Russian politics.'

Goldman laughed, showing even white teeth. 'Join the club!'

'She is in a vulnerable position. I wouldn't want her to come to any more harm. If she'd been around when they raided her studio, I doubt she'd still be alive.'

'So, an exhibition of her work under her name in Paris would be a bad idea?'

'The very worst.'

The black Citreon drew into the villa grounds, crunching slowly over the gravel. Derek got out and sounded the bell. The same maid as before opened the door and showed them into the front reception room. Goldman glanced around, taking in the faded Gobelin tapestry over the mantle, opposite an early Matisse. 'An eclectic taste,' he murmured.

Anton Lensky appeared in a smoking jacket and velvet trousers. He had a tome of poetry in his hand, which he placed on an occasional table. Derek made the introductions. Lensky came forward and shook Goldman firmly by the hand. 'Thank you for taking the time to come here. When Monsieur Eaton explained the situation, I thought it for the best.'

'Of course.'

'Shall we?' he gestured towards the front door. 'Tanya Sergenevna is expecting our visit.'

The three men walked to the outbuilding that housed her work. Tanya was waiting for them. She turned to Goldman. 'I believe my grandfather knew yours?'

He nodded. 'I believe so.'

She had tidied up the space and ordered the charcoal drawings so they appeared in sequence. In her blue artist's smock, spattered with colours, and with her hair tied back, she looked every bit the working artist.

The central piece had been modified since Derek last saw it. Tinted lines drew the flying, fleeing figures together as if by rainbow gossamer. The effect was subtle but powerful: what formerly appeared dissonant and dispersed had become a symphony of related notes and tones. Goldman stood in front of it without speaking. Tanya, in turn, was eyeing him with an amused expression. 'Not quite my usual style.'

Still Goldman said nothing. He walked back to get a better view, then shifted from one side to the other. Next, he went towards the charcoal drawings. These he inspected one by one, without speaking. He walked round the space, looked at a couple of other paintings which were leaning by shelves and windowsills.

'Have you exhibited much in Russia?' asked Goldman at length. To which Tanya laughed.

'Why do you laugh?' asked Goldman solemnly.

'Painting is the last things on people's minds right now. Especially mine. You might say I've gone right out of fashion.'

'How come?' asked Goldman to Derek's surprise: did he really have no inkling? Tanya looked at Goldman askance.

'We are all moving together in the right direction into a bright future. The tractors are turning the soil, the ploughs are busy, the proletariat has taken over the means of production, the peasants are happy, relieved to be liberated from centuries of oppression. The leaders are wise and caring and rule by the highest standards of international law and justice…' Her voice as she spoke these last words was even and melodious so that one could be lulled into a sense that she believed what she was saying. She laughed again. 'So… in answer to your question: in recent years I have not exhibited in Russia.'

Goldman studied her face. 'You work with such urgency, it is vital that your work is communicated to others.'

She looked as though she was weighing something in her mind. 'My friends warn me I should balance personal safety with any such urge. But I am not willing to be intimidated.'

'Do you have any remnants of *Stalin's Dolls?*'

She started, then gave a long sigh. 'A few pieces remain. The remnants are jumbled up in sacks in the corner there.' She gave a dismissive wave of the arm.

'I'd like to see them,' persisted Goldman.

'As I said, they're just fragments and shards. I haven't even been through them. I was too upset by what happened. I'd need to piece them together to make sense of them.'

'Would you be willing to do that?' he asked quietly.

'Here and now, you mean?'

'In your own time.'

She looked thoughtful. 'To what purpose, might I ask?'

Goldman paced up and down, stared again at her centre painting, dug his hands deep into the pockets of his Savile Row suit. 'I like your work,' he said. 'It is bold, uncompromising. It is also playful. It has an almost transcendent quality about it – something that lifts it above the everyday temporal aspect of most other art pieces. I've never seen anything quite like it. I'm not sure what its commercial value would be. But right now that does not bother me. I'm interested in the statement they make about – what shall I say – the Russian psyche.'

She laughed again, this time without constraint.

'It's not even a statement, more a perception. A subliminal, visceral depiction of what's going on,' he continued.

'In that case,' she said, 'perhaps you should see some of the sketches and notes I've been working on for companion pieces to the work there.'

'You have more?' When she nodded, he moved towards her: 'Yes, I want to see them. I want to see everything you have done.'

Derek watched from the side-lines, fascinated by how Tanya was drawing Goldman in as surely as the gossamer threads of her painting held fast the disparate elements, which threatened to fly apart. Watching the two of them helped explain just why she was so dangerous, not only to the Russian state but to himself.

She walked over to a trestle table on which were stacked sketchbooks and painting materials. She cleared a space by dropping a pile of books onto the floor. Dust flew up in all directions. 'Here,' she said. She started leafing through the large pages. On each side were scribbles in Russian and English side by side with drawings. There were figures from a street scene, a café brawl, the river at night, but also demons, witches and caricatures with the bloated faces of Russian politicians.

Chapter Fifty *Lensky*

One way or another, Lensky was relieved to get away from Tanya Sergeyevna and Billancourt for a few hours. It was too tantalising to have her close, just round the corner as it were. As long as she was in the apple outhouse he would call by once a day, if he were not otherwise occupied, to invite her for a meal or just to see how she was getting on. More times than not he met with a rebuff. She was enjoying the solitude too much, she proclaimed. At night she was more than happy to hunker down on the makeshift field bed in the mezzanine floor above the main space. She was happy to eat bread and cheese. Happy to live like a nun. Everyday her eyes grew clearer and her determination stronger. He could see it in the set of her chin, the fire in her eyes.

He'd try to brush away Ludmila's tale of a stranger watching them in the park. She was sensitive and often imagined things. But every day the shadows were dancing closer. Another *enemy of the people* had been dragged off the street in broad daylight in Rue du Bac. Lensky did not know him personally or what his supposed offense was. He'd batted the news away like an irritating gnat.

With Tanya they were being more circumspect. She had had status and in many circles was still highly regarded. Admirers she attracted like butterflies in the sun. In artistic circles she was revered. Many still looked up to her, he gathered from Derek, when they spoke of her.

* * *

'We know what you're up to,' a low voice growled at him one night as he was leaving Scheherazade. 'We know where you live and what your family do. Ludmila is a very sweet girl. Serge is full of beans…'

Lensky started. He was just twisting the key in the padlock. He'd stayed on to lock up because the music had stirred him and he'd not yet been ready to face another night in Billancourt with an ailing wife. His mind was buzzing with the sultry tones of a Blues singer, the blast of a piercing trumpet. He turned but saw no one. Had he imagined it? And then the shadows separated, and he descried the hulk of a tall man in a long coat with a Homburg rammed slantwise over his face. It was not Ivan.

'What do you want?' Lensky snarled in Russian.

'I think you know,' said the other. He stepped forward into the oval of light thrown by the gaslight. He had pocked skin and a flattened boxer's nose. Lensky drew a sharp breath.

'Is this some sort of game?'

'You have helped us before. I am sure you are willing to cooperate. We are not looking for trouble. Have no intention of disturbing you, disrupting the *nice life* you've built for yourself.' He pronounced 'nice life' with the slow insinuation of threat. Lensky stared into the darkness, away from his assailant. Why hadn't they come after him in Billancourt? Why wait and accost him here, in the centre of Paris? Were they losing their nerve?

'Why here? Why now?' asked Lensky wearily. 'Why not come in daylight and show your face? This cloak and dagger stuff is too melodramatic.' He gave a forced laugh, yet his heart was pounding.

The other was momentarily silenced. 'We know you're shielding her,' he said at length. 'We are not thugs – unless we have to be.'

Ah, so that was it. Lensky and his wife were French citizens. Harm done to them would not go unnoticed, whereas a fugitive Russian emigrée, a subversive done away with would be of scant concern to the French authorities. There were used to feuds in the Russian camp. 'I don't know what you're talking about.'

'You know very well. Do you want me to spell it out? You are harbouring an *enemy of the people*.'

Out in the open now – the catchall phrase, the justification, the end justifying the means. Lensky stood his ground. 'So who are these *people* you speak so glibly of…?'

'Another word and I'll slit your throat,' said the other.

'So much for your lack of thuggery…'

'Shut it! I haven't got all day.' Lensky could sense the other concentrating, working out the best tactic. A couple of people were strolling down the narrow street, laughing. They walked close by, taking their time. The other drew back into the shadows, hid his face from the light. When the couple had passed, he moved back towards Lensky and continued in a conciliatory tone. 'We need to know where Tanya Sergeyevna is holing up. No harm will come to her. We need to ask her a few questions. She has been a spokesperson for an important cultural committee in the past. She is a worthwhile contact. There are things we need to learn from her, you understand.'

His attempts at persuasion made Lensky want to smile, but he dared not react. The other could shift from reason to brutality in a hair's breadth. He had the washed out, flat look of a hired assassin. He was wily, but his patience was growing thin.

'And if I told you I don't know what you're talking about. I am a night club owner, a musical impresario.'

'Monsieur Lensky, we know exactly who you are and where you come from, what you've left behind, who you choose to spend your time with. Cut the lies. You have been seen. Followed.'

'Is that so?' But not too well, it seemed, or else they would know exactly where Tanya Sergeyevna was spending her time.

As if reading his thoughts the other went on: 'Until yesterday she was occupying an outbuilding near your residence in Billancourt. She has not been seen since then. She is no longer there.'

Lensky looked at him sharply. What on earth was the man talking about?

Chapter Fifty-one *Derek*

Derek was surprised to learn that Tanya was back in circulation. With a curly blond wig, long felt green coat with black fur trim and matching green, strapped shoes, she looked much like any other chic Parisienne as she sipped champagne cocktails and smoked through a silver-chased cigarette holder. She wore her latest title: *enemy of the people* as lightly as her glittering silk stockings. He spotted her in the crowded, smoky interior of the La Coupole where she blended into the clusters of animation. Dimitri had informed him that she had pronounced, in no uncertain terms, that she was not to be bullied. Derek nodded, half in admiration, half in fear, while wondering where she had acquired her latest get-up. Her bedroom at Dimitri's place had been sparse, her clothes few. Better not to ask, he told himself: the webs of Russian connections were far too intricate and subtle for him to comprehend. Besides, he was keeping away from her: business only, from now on.

Trouble was, over the next couple of days he bumped into her again and again.

Every café he visited she seemed to be there, surrounded by artists and admirers, and not just The Apostles but denizens of other Montparnasse cafés, French artists of the Surreal school and the Spanish. She laughed. She teased. She held forth in voluble French and Russian. He thought for a moment of her trembling in his arms the night she'd been on the run from the dark forces of the Organs. Had that danger disappeared? What had changed?

The more he gazed at her from afar the more he was in awe of the audacity of her spirit. How dare she flaunt herself? He wanted to smuggle her back to Billancourt and the safety of the old outbuilding. When he asked Dimitri where she was staying, he did not get a straight answer.

After a couple of days he got a message from Goldman proposing a further meeting: time was pressing on and Goldman wanted to tie up a few loose ends. They arranged to meet in an expensive but deceptively simple restaurant on Boulevard Haussmann, not far from Goldman's hotel. When Derek arrived Goldman was seated opposite Tanya, who was wearing a Chanel suit of the latest cut. Her hair – her own this time – was caught up in a chignon, away from her face. It made her look older and more sophisticated. Derek felt at sea, no longer knowing what was going on with her or just how much Goldman and she had negotiated in his absence.

In a few words Goldman put Derek in the picture. Goldman had revisited her outbuilding studio where Tanya had reassembled several *Stalin's Dolls*. She'd also completed her work on the Russian émigré community in Paris. Derek caught the breathless excitement in Goldman's voice, caught the tinge of pure delight in his eyes. The art connoisseur had found what he wanted. The rest of the L'Atelier Blanc exhibition was background to this dazzling discovery. This talented, brilliant and beautiful artist was the star. So where did he fit in to this, he wondered, as Goldman waxed on about possible shows in New York, London, Berlin…

'I'm delighted,' he managed to say. 'I can't tell you how pleased it makes me to see Madame Sergeyevna's work appreciated by an art collector such as yourself. But have you,' he hesitated, wondering how to carry on. 'I mean, it's not as straightforward as all that, is it? These are provocative works. They will not sit easily with the …'

'We've gone through all that,' snapped Tanya. 'We need to move quickly. I'm keen to get out of Paris as fast as I can. You're right. It is not straightforward. I do not want to endanger my life any more than is necessary.'

What about those appearances in Montparnasse, Derek wanted to ask. Did she believe her disguise convincing? If she did, she was more naïve than he'd believed.

'We leave for America as soon as we can get her second passport and the visa sorted,' said Goldman. 'The works will be boxed up and transported. I've spoken to the shipping firm.' Derek was astounded at the speed with which Goldman had been able to move. Just weeks before Tanya declared herself inured to commercial considerations, yet here she was, done up to the nines, a cat with a saucer of the finest cream.

'You understand the urgency with which everything must now be done? I didn't want you to believe I'd abandoned interest in the other works. A little subterfuge is called for. I'm still keen to acquire your work and Kurovsky's. But it's not vital that those sales are completed now. I am willing to leave a handsome deposit. But the most pressing need is to get Tanya – Madame Sergeyevna – and her masterpieces out of the country.'

Derek's head was whirring. So why had Tanya come back and been seen out and about? Who was she trying to deceive? Goldman touched Tanya's hand, her pale, long-fingered artist's hand resting next to her glass of wine. She gave Goldman a sly smile. So that's it, thought Derek, with a spurt of fire twisting his solar plexus. She's captivated her rescuer; she's plotted her escape from the City of Light.

'Well, yes, I understand. These are troubled times,' he mumbled. 'There's a lot going on with the Russians right now. It's a good to have a well thought out plan, especially considering what happened to *Stalin's Dolls.*'

'I knew you'd understand,' said Tanya and turned her face towards him. Her expression was at once guileless and wise; but just for a fleeting moment he caught a shiver of fear glancing across her features. What an actress she was!

'Are we talking about days or weeks?' he asked.

'I know people in the Embassy,' said Goldman. 'These things can't always be rushed but there are ways and means. So, days, I'd say.'

'Things aren't looking too clever in the United States,' commented Derek. He'd read more of the crash on Wall Street, stocks and shares tumbling, the run on the banks. The whole US economy was reeling.

Goldman frowned. 'You're quite right. But one can't stop doing business. One can't give in to fear and panic.'

'Quite.' Derek guessed that the Goldman concerns would be spread over many commodities and interests. Their accumulated wealth would be less affected than many. 'Do you want another meeting with Kurovsky and Dimitri before you leave?'

'That's where you might come in. You've been such a splendid mediator…'

Derek raised his eyebrows. He had no need of smooth talk. What did the man want him to do? 'How did you want to leave it with Kurovsky? Have you spoken to him – or at least spoken to Dimitri about him? I've been out of the picture.'

Goldman glanced over his shoulder to attract the waiter and asked for the bill. 'I've paid half the asking price as deposit. The rest is earmarked. As soon as the paintings are despatched the money will follow.'

'Good. Then there's is little left for me to do.' Derek got to his feet and shook Goldman's hand. Tanya stood up and approached, put out her cheek to be kissed. He brushed it lightly with his lips. 'Madame.'

'Oh, do call me Tanya.' She clasped his arm. '*Au revoir*, my friend.'

Chapter Fifty-two *Mo*

In Scheherazade Mo took a deep breath, summoning courage. She'd be going over and over a song she heard on the wireless. It struck a resonance with her, and she couldn't get it out of her head. It was by Cole Porter. She knew he'd fallen in love with Paris and held court here for years before taking off for the palazzos of Venice. The song was a revelation, blending all that was suave and urbane, mixing jazz with romance in a way that teased and haunted. Porter had had his first Broadway success the year before with *Paris*. He flitted between New York and Paris. A revue here, a musical there: he was a creature of air and melody. She would like to have met him.

She looked at the tables of people, chatting, imbibing. Dare she launch forth with an unknown song that was just breaking into public awareness in New York? She might forget the words. She tossed her head. Why not? She recalled the joy of the words and tune as she'd sung on the balcony. At Scheherazade she'd rehearsed it once with the accompanist. She looked around at the upturned faces. When they noticed her standing there in silence, they hushed. She cooed gently towards them, stroking them with her voice:

> *I was a humdrum person*
> *Leading a life apart*
> *When love flew in through my window wide*
> *And quickened my humdrum heart.*
>
> *Love flew in through my window*
> *I was so happy then*
> *But after love stayed a little while*
> *love flew out again.*
> *What is this thing called love,*

This funny thing?
Just who can solve its mystery?
Why should it make a fool of me?
I saw you there
One wonderful day
You took my heart
And threw it away
That's why I asked the Lord
In heaven above
What is this thing called love,
This funny thing called love?

There was an embracing quiet as she drew to an end. In the front area, lit by stage lamps, she could see a glow of satisfaction on some faces. They might not understand all the words but they caught the mood, the basic sentiment of the song. If only Derek were here. He would be so proud of her, would note her growing sophistication. She smiled to herself. Why must he always figure so large in her thoughts?

She rounded off her slot by a Noel Coward song from: *On with the dance*. It was a favourite of hers, not least because it won her fame when she'd sung it at The Athena. The lyrics –with the sparkle of Coward wit undercut by chaos – seemed written for her.

Poor little rich girl
You're a bewitched girl
Better take care
Laughing at danger
Virtue a stranger
Better beware
The life you lead sets all your nerves a-jangle
Your love affairs are in a hopeless tangle
Though you're a child, dear
Your life's a wild typhoon.

She stepped down. She was glad she had ventured new material and bared her spirit to her Parisian audience. What was the point of art if one didn't leap into the flames? Tonight, though, there was no one to wait for her, no one to offer her a drink. She wondered whether Lensky would hear of her success this evening. Was audience satisfaction just run-of-the-mill for him? She would have to keep on her toes. Always there would be someone peering over her shoulder, ready to topple her if she stumbled. Derek said he had one last meeting with the Russians. The American art dealer was leaving for America soon and taking one of the artists with him. When Derek suggested they meet when his Russian rendezvous was over, she'd demurred, not wanting to tie either of them down.

She ambled back through the streets towards Marais. People were milling about, wandering from restaurants and nightclubs; always the streets had an animation, the city never completely at rest. The words of the Cole Porter song kept jangling in her mind: the up and down of emotions, the inconstancy of everything. Love came and went like a bird flying in and out of the window, free as the wind.

What could she really count on? She thought of Ma, the vibrant, carefree singer becoming the wasted woman with papery skin. All was sewn up before they left: Derek had made sure of that. And she couldn't blame him. The Mare's Head and Pa would swallow them whole if they allowed it. Yet she felt treacherous. Families did that to you. She hummed as she moved. Thank God for music. Thank God for art, for the creative urge which pulled you out of the morass. Families were fine but one needed to fly, and families could not do that for you. Rather they reminded you of where you came from and kept you tethered.

She wanted to go to the river. She loved to watch the columns of light dancing on the water at night, to see lovers strolling, the lone silhouette, the towers of the great mediaeval cathedral overshadowing all with its echoes of the centuries. The Seine reminded her of the Thames with its many bridges, the water a thoroughfare linking East and West. But for her the Seine was more romantic. It had witnessed the first flowering of their love and its renewal. Paris as the city of lovers was a cliché – yet there was truth in it. For her, it had become a gentler, more accepting place. She was beginning to view it as home.

The place was full of Americans fleeing who-knew-what. She wondered what would happen now. They knew only one or two, through Sylvia Beach. Would they hang on and try and make a go of it here, or rush back and rescue what they could? Pierre said *les années folles,* the decade of sizzle and fun, was nearing its end. Things were about to change. How did he know? Maybe it was just a clever thing to say. He often liked to pontificate.

She stood on Pont Neuf and pulled her coat round her. The water was churning in the wind, patterns darting and dancing across it, light fragmenting. It mesmerised her. She could not have been standing there for five minutes before a man came sidling up to her. 'Beautiful, isn't it?' he said.

She started, glanced sideways. The man was leaning over, gazing down towards the water. He was wearing a gabardine mackintosh, tied at the waist and had a hat rammed down over his forehead. He looked to be in his mid-twenties, maybe a little older. She went to move away. 'Don't worry, Madame. I mean no harm.' She glanced at him again. His accent did not sound quite French. She began walking towards Marais, not wanting to engage with him. She'd had enough of being followed in the night. When he walked behind her, she turned in irritation.

'Monsieur, please, do not ... bother me.' He held up his hands as if to say: what are you talking about? She quickened her step. He had drawn level with her.

'I think – if am not mistaken – you were at the *vernissage* in L'Atelier Blanc a few weeks back. Is that not so?' He was speaking in rather halting French, which she was just able to grasp.

'And what of it?' She took pains to hide her surprise.

He smiled. 'Forgive me, but I saw you perform tonight. Your face was familiar to me. It is only just now that I remembered where I knew you from.'

'Monsieur, have you been following me?' Her tone was sharp.

He laughed. 'This is my route home. I live on the other bank of the river. I am a friend of one of the painters.'

'You are?'

'She is not exhibiting. A sculptress. Tanya Sergeyevna. Do you know her?'

Mo hesitated. The image of the beautiful, gypsy-looking woman flashed before her mind. 'Not really. My husband does.'

'Your husband?'

'Derek Eaton. He's been working with the artists.'

'Ah yes, Derek Eaton,' said the man thoughtfully. He was studying her face. His expression was grave. He seemed to be hanging on every word she was saying.

'Well, *voilà!* I'd better be on my way. It's getting late.'

The man hesitated. 'I haven't seen Tanya Sergeyevna lately. She's been out of town.'

'Is that so?'

'You wouldn't know where she is staying, would you?' He spoke so carefully it sounded rehearsed.

'No, I wouldn't. I don't really know her. Met her just the once. You could always call by the gallery, I suppose.'

'The exhibition has finished now, hasn't it?'

'Well, yes, it has. *Bonne nuit*, Monsieur.' And with that she scuttled down into the street away from him, back towards the Marais. When she threw a quick look over her shoulder the man was still on the bridge, gazing in her direction.

Chapter Fifty-three *Derek*

'I got followed by a Russian,' said Mo in between spooning her café crème into her mouth. 'It's becoming quite a habit.' Often they would take breakfast together in one of the corner cafés if they both had a busy day ahead, it had become one of those little luxuries they allowed themselves.

'When?'

'When do you think? After the show.'

'What, you mean he was in the audience and tracked you down? Not again.'

She laughed. 'Only this one wasn't offering me work. I was on the bridge. Just taking the air. I was restless after the show.'

'I told you we should have met up. If you'd hung on at Scheherazade I could have picked you up. I'm not too happy about you wandering around on your own at night. I'm not sure how safe Paris is these days.'

She shrugged. 'You've said that before. No worse than the streets of London, I wouldn't have thought.'

'At least you know your way round there. Speak the language. Any way what did he want? Just pestering a pretty woman?' She laughed while he was aware of a growing unease in his gut. He should make sure she didn't walk home again unaccompanied. It was just too risky.

'Don't look so earnest. I can handle it. He wasn't being a nuisance. Just tried to engage me in conversation. He recognised me from the exhibition. He was one of the Russian party at the preview.'

'One of the painters, you mean. Why didn't you say so?'

'No, a friend. He was asking after Tanya. The one you introduced me to.'

He drew his breath in sharply. 'Tanya Sergeyevna?'

'Is that her name? The dark pretty one.' She eyed him with apparent nonchalance, but he could sense her measuring every flicker of his eyes, every shadow crossing his face. He sipped more coffee. 'Want another?'

She shook her head.

'So he said he was a friend? It wasn't Dimitri by any chance?'

'But I know Dimitri.'

'Of course.' He found himself floundering.

'Said he hasn't seen her lately. Wanted to know if I knew where she was staying. Anyway, I directed him back to the gallery. Said they'd know there.'

'Yes, they should know.' Derek began to regret he hadn't shared with her more of what was going on in the Russian community. But it was getting too enmeshed. Besides, she had enough of her own troubles to wade through without burdening her with his. 'So, how did it go last night?' He leaned back and peered at her, breathing deeply to expel the tightness in his chest.

'Oh good,' she dunked her crust of buttered bread into the coffee. 'I tried new material. From Cole Porter's latest Broadway musical.'

'It's not under copyright, is it?'

'Who cares? They're hardly going to come and arrest me, are they?' She chewed her bread and looked at him thoughtfully. It was hard to tell what was going on with her. But at least the spasm of self-recrimination had passed. She was looking clearer and more confident.

'Was Lensky there?'

'He doesn't come every evening. It was one of his nights off.'

'But a good audience?'

'Oh yes. But no roses or champagne.'

He laughed. 'Welcome to the real world.'

'True. But the main thing – they liked the song, even if they didn't have a clue what it meant.'

They parted company soon after. He watched her walk away. She was going back to Scheherazade to go over the new material with the accompanist and run through other songs. Knowing how fierce the competition was, she was determined to keep one step ahead. He ordered more coffee, wanting time to reflect. He had to get his pictures packed up for Goldman as well as preparing frames and canvases for the next paintings, already stirring within him.

What of this latest encounter of Mo with the Russian on the bridge? Who was he? Had the man lain in wait for her, knowing their connection? In many ways he was relieved that Tanya was trying for a new life in the States, even though it was not the most propitious time. Relieved, too, that she was directing her attention elsewhere, unlikely to turn to him unless necessary.

And yet the prospect of her going bothered him.

He lit a cigarette. Pondering Tanya was getting him nowhere. This was precisely what happened when he drew too close to the melancholy and fatalism of the Russian psyche. He smiled to himself. What was that they'd said about him being the cool-headed Englishman?

Later as he threw himself headlong into fashioning frames and priming canvases, he felt Tanya overshadowing him. He tried to shake her off. He cut and measured lengths, smoothed down the wood and placed finished pieces to one side, ready for glueing. He primed several canvases liberally with gesso, rubbing them till they were dry enough to work on. Today Pierre was out of town, visiting a cousin. He was thankful he could get on with his tasks without having to share the area. He was looking forward to taking up the offer of a mansard studio space nearer the L'Atelier Blanc, where he'd be able to embark on larger, more ambitious, canvases.

He found it hard to get that last image of Tanya out of his head – wearing a Chanel suit, with Goldman touching her hand. Already a new incarnation, a new optimistic, pragmatic self was emerging. He grunted with impatience. Tanya was an addiction to the impossible. Their paths had touched, he'd been able to help her and now she was on another trajectory, off somewhere where her work could appear and shine. He was truly glad for her.

Towards the end of the afternoon he stood back to survey what he'd achieved: enough for now. He went to the kitchen area where he brewed a mug of tea. He sat on the stool, stretching out his legs. A shadow fell across him. And there was Tanya, dressed simply in a black cape and dark skirt, her hair unrestrained. He started, convinced she was a chimera of his unquiet mind. She moved forward. 'Derek, I came to say goodbye.' She held out her hand. 'I didn't get the chance…'

'Tanya!' He gathered her up in his arms, not stopping to ask himself if he should or shouldn't. She nestled into him.

'I couldn't go off like that…'

'It's all right Tanya. I understand. I understand.'

'I have the permits. I can go…' Her voice was hoarse.

He smothered her mouth with kisses. 'I know. It's the best thing. The best.'

He crushed himself against her, his body burning. He half-led, half carried her to the back of the studio where there was a battered old sofa. They lay down on it. She let her cape slip off, slid out of her skirt, the high collared blouse she was wearing. He threw off his old work shirt, tore off his trousers. And there was nothing now between them. She pulled him towards her, kissed him tenderly on the forehead, the mouth, the neck. And he was lost. There was no pulling back, his body and mind were one, consumed by desire, consumed by desperation.

Afterwards they lay entwined on the sofa, feet dangling. He nuzzled into her hair, caught her familiar musky perfume, touched with his finger the delicate skin of her neck. She stroked his hand, his wrist. 'Better then that I go. It would not be possible.' He said nothing. Dared not speak. The light was fading.

They lay in silence as the darkness thickened around them. He was aware of a deep peace within. Whatever happened from here on he would have had this moment. At length he shifted, pulled back from her. 'And when do you leave?'

'In three days' time.'

'This could be the …'

'Shsh I know.' She put her fingers to his lips to silence him. 'It is better so.'

Chapter Fifty-four *Lensky*

Lensky went to the old apple store to see whether or not Tanya Sergeyevna was still there. He was not about to take as true what the shabby OGPU operative had muttered outside Scheherazade. He knew from experience they would lie to extract the truth, lie to confuse. Lying was like breathing to them. He thought it unlikely that Tanya would have disappeared without a word. They had an understanding, after all. He'd been in a position to shelter her, and she'd appreciated that; yet even as he told himself this, he knew it was self-deception. They might not say it, but both knew she was there on borrowed time.

He pulled open the wide doors and called out 'Tanya! Tanya Sergeyevna! Tanya Sergeyevna!' but he heard only the echo of his own voice. He strode forward and ripping open more doors discovered the empty store cupboard, bare shelves and one or scattered easels. He paced around, pulling out drawers, tipping them upside down. Only dust. He walked the length of the building, took the steps up to the old hayloft to see if she'd left any trace where she'd slept. Nothing. Nothing but a crumpled sheet and mildewed blanket. She had flown, migrant that she was.

* * *

For a moment he felt desolate. It was the same hollowing out as when he went back to the family home in 1905. The local peasants had turned against them. It was a time of reckoning. The damage was extensive: burnt out rooms, seared curtains, blackened stumps that had been furniture; everything upended, ransacked, despoiled. And outside the carcasses of thoroughbred horses in the paddock, the pitiful cow and calf slaughtered in the byre out of sheer rage. He and his sister had been away, studying; his parents were thankfully at their residence in the French

Riviera. The sight of so much dereliction dismayed him. But what he'd found worse, far worse, was that their own peasants had turned tail. Had his father not sought to better their lot, to teach their children the rudiments of reading and writing, arithmetic, and seen to it that they never went hungry even in the bitterest of winters, even when the crops failed? He shook his head. That was then. Forgiveness might stick in the gullet, but it was the wiser strategy in the long run.

Tanya Sergeyevna was a survivor, too. But it was out of his hands now. He could not help the OGPU discover her whereabouts even if he'd wanted to. Later that day he called in at the Scheherazade. He liked to show his face several times a week, take a look at the books and drop in when some of the singers were rehearsing. It was vital to ensure that standards were kept high. He knew of establishments that had gone downhill when the proprietor absented himself or sold it on. Good managers were hard to come by.

When he arrived he heard the strains of a Cole Porter song, familiar to him from the wireless. Mo Eaton's voice rang out with its sharp sweetness. He could tell her voice anywhere. It had that rare blend of the dulcet and the piercing. There was something almost virginal about it, yet it could slide in and surround the heart with such longing that it blotted out all else. How could a voice do that? Technically she still had a lot to learn. Sometimes she strained after notes or rushed where she might linger. Her phrasing was at times banal, her desire to please too obvious. Yet she had all the right ingredients. There was a lot of soul in her voice. He stood in the gloom of the lobby, not wanting to be noticed.

> *One wonderful day*
> *You took my heart*
> *And threw it away*
> *That's why I asked the Lord*
> *In heaven above*

What is this thing called love,
This funny thing called love?

'Brava!' he said, then: 'Could you go through it again? You're throwing some words away. You're rushing to get to the end. You need to tantalise your audience, keep them hanging. But you are also asking yourself these questions – so a little more feeling is needed.'

'Oh, it's you!' Mo seemed shocked to discover he'd been hovering out of sight. 'I was just …'

'You sang beautifully. But there is always room for improvement, is there not?'

'Of course, Monsieur Lensky.'

'Again,' Lensky directed the accompanist. 'A trifle slower, I think.'

Mo cleared her throat and raised her finger to begin. She is nothing if not keen, thought Lensky. Many a singer would be put off by such comments. The second time the poignancy and wit of the song were in better balance. She seemed to be straining less.

He gave a quick nod and went through to the office where he started checking recent revenue and outgoings. The bar takings were up on previous months, the number of clients passing through had doubled. He wondered fleetingly about the Wall Street Crash and what impact that might have. Already he'd heard that Americans were buying up tickets to cross the Atlantic. Some would stay on, but more would flee Paris, sensing that their party was over. In time, businesses in France would be affected but not yet, he hoped. Besides, few of Scheherazade clients were Americans.

It was mid-afternoon by the time he left the premises. Mo Eaton had long gone. He'd half hoped to take her out for lunch but there'd been too much of a backlog to sort through. He let himself of the building and wandered to a nearby café where he settled on a pavement table. He had not been sitting there long over his *croque monsieur*, newspaper and mineral water when a tall man stood above him, waiting for him to look up.

'Monsieur Lensky,' said the other. Lensky frowned. Did he know this person? Slowly it dawned on him that this was none other than his would-be assailant from the other evening. By daylight he looked just as pasty and unsavoury. He guessed he must have had smallpox as a child. At any rate he had the malnourished, drawn look of deprivation. Lensky almost pitied him. 'May I?' the man pulled out a chair and sat down.

'I suppose you'd like a drink,' said Lensky, keeping his voice even, determined to mask any hint of anxiety. He waved towards a passing waiter. 'What would you like?'

'Water,' snapped the other in Russian.

'Vittel or Vichy?'

'Whatever.'

Lensky smiled towards the waiter and placed the order, ordering a large cognac for himself. 'To what do I owe the pleasure?'

The other frowned, nonplussed by the unwonted courtesy. 'Tanya Sergeyevna,' he said curtly. 'You were offering her shelter. It would not look good to be known to be sheltering *an enemy of the people*.'

Lensky gave another slow smile though he felt a blockage forming in his throat. 'Last time we spoke, just there, if I am not mistaken…' – he pointed to a spot along the alley – 'you informed me that you just wanted to ask Comrade Sergeyevna a few strategic questions because of her former role as cultural representative…'

The other frowned again, as if unsure of his exact brief. It hadn't been the wisest choice to send his half-baked agent to question him. The other looked around to see if he were being observed. 'That is true. We wish her no harm. She will not be badly treated…'

'Of course not. If I were able to help I would, Comrade. But I haven't the slightest clue where this Tanya Sergeyevna is. What can you tell me about her? Why do you wish to see her? Is she to be recalled to Moscow, St Petersburg? I know little what her former role entailed nor why it is so urgent for you to find her now…'

The other leaned in. 'Cut the crap, Comrade. Just tell me where she is.'

Lensky pulled back. 'I haven't the slightest idea.'

'Comrade, you will help us find her or your family will suffer. Do you understand?'

PART 4

Chapter Fifty-five *Mo*

The rap at the door woke Mo in a second. Her heart beat strangely. She'd lain down after getting back from Scheherazade. Her session there had exhausted her, not least because there was new material to take on board. Lensky had put in an appearance and for that she was glad, glad too that he had commented on her performance. He was right, of course, she had been rushing and straining. She always did until she'd wrapped her voice around a song and made it her own.

There was another rap.

Her heart raced. It would be the landlord and what was more, she knew why. Just that night her mother had appeared to her. She was dressed in her favourite, velvet Music Hall robe and was smiling and twirling as she whispered. 'It's going to be all right Morwenna, my pet. It's going to be fine.'

Slowly she got to her feet, feeling sick, her hand shaking as she took the envelope he was holding towards her. She thanked him and closed the door. These days he always seemed to be the harbinger of doom. She had grown to hate the sight of his creased face, his constant air of disgruntlement.

'Ma died today' stated the telegram. She sat staring at the black angular letters, unable to move. The bald, undeniable, heavy fact of it. She stood up but sank swiftly back down: her head light as air. She stumbled to the kitchen to get herself a glass of water. Sipped, felt nauseous, sipped again. She took out her battered travel case and pushed a few clothes into it. Derek said he was working in the studio most of the day. She would find him there.

She put on her winter coat, rammed a hat down over her ears and headed off to find Derek, a numbness taking hold of her as she trod the familiar route through the twisting streets. A cat streaked across her path, startling her. Not heeding where she was going, she almost collided with a cyclist. He shouted at her and moved off. She came to the alley leading to the old house where studios huddled round an inner courtyard. It was dark now and she could see a light glimmering through the gloom. She approached the studio Derek shared with Pierre. The familiar smell of linseed oil assaulted her nostrils. The figure of a woman was hurrying towards her: slight, head bent, face covered.

Mo glanced at her as she passed. She seemed to be in some distress. Mo caught her breath. Surely this was the Russian woman from the preview? Confused, she pressed on. No time now … As she came into the studio Derek was framed in the doorway, his body silhouetted against the light. He was more tousled than ever. His face was distraught.

'Mo!'

A chaos of sights and thoughts, warring emotions. 'Derek,' she called and rushed towards him. She thrust the telegram into his hands without speaking.

* * *

Now she was sitting in the Victorian vestibule of the funeral parlour and eyeing the faded prints of barges on the Thames and the Tower of London as she waited for Derek to join her. Maisy Aurora, onetime singer and dancer, Ma Dobson, wife of Bert Dobson, publican, had been pronounced dead the day before. The doctors had issued a death certificate stating pleurisy and double pneumonia as the cause of death. But for Mo, it was as though Ma had died long before. Still benumbed, not quite able to function as she should, Mo was strangely at peace. It was over. Ma had passed on she knew not where.

She was relieved Derek was beside her; though he, too, seemed strangely absent. Seeing her state of shock, he'd insisted on sorting out the funeral details once she told him what the family wanted. He emerged from the dark little office. 'Next

Tuesday, the funeral directors say.' His voice was flat and matter-of-fact. 'I've got enough money put by so no one need worry about that.'

As expected, the funeral service took place at Saint Mary's church and the committal was immediately afterwards in the churchyard. Ma's grave was next to Timothy's. Half the punters of The Mare's Head had turned up in their finery, looking so scrubbed and solemn that she barely recognised them. Pa and her sisters stood in a line in the church porch shaking hands and wearing fixed smiles. She stared at the hole in the ground then glanced alongside towards Timothy's gravestone. She thought she was going to faint. The vicar's words offered solace and the promise of the life to come.

She shifted from one foot to the other. The grass about the graves was long and wet: her feet were getting soaked. Derek looked across at her. She knew she was the best of actresses and today she wanted to look bright and in charge. She smiled at him. But Derek would not be fooled for a moment.

Afterwards there was funeral tea at The Mare's Head, prepared by the neighbours. She couldn't stop thinking back to that last funeral tea here when she had been barely conscious. When all the neighbours had departed and the helpers had washed up and stacked the borrowed plates and cups in one corner, the family gathered in another, without speaking. Their linchpin had gone. They needed to sit in a circle and feel themselves a whole before they flew off to their various lives.

Her immediate task was to finish sorting through Ma's things. She wanted to be busy. She did not want to sit in the circle for too long. She excused herself and set about sifting through the remainder of Ma's belongings.

What she did not expect to find was a bundle of old letters tied with blue ribbon and wedged into the corner at the back of the drawer. She'd missed it when she'd done her initial sorting weeks before. Only her fingers sliding to the corners came across it. Gingerly she untied the ribbon, unfolded the top letter. When she looked at the date, she discovered it was just a few weeks old. Her heart pounded as she began to read.

Dear Maisy,

I have thought long about writing to you. My conscience tells me it is the right thing to do. I also enclose the letter I should have sent years ago and did not.

Coming back to London has opened my eyes. The war did that for me too. I can't speak of what I saw then. Most of us can't. I became an emotional cripple.

To see you the other night at The Athena theatre gave me a shock. It was the lightning striking. But you seemed afraid, timid – a shadow of the woman I knew. I say this not to be cruel, but because I was wrong to leave the way I did.

We have a daughter. The moment I set eyes on Morwenna Eaton, I knew her. Now I follow her from a distance. I spoke to her. And will again. I will not share the secret with her. I will not open the can of worms, as you say in England.

There are things I want to leave her. I say more later when it is clear. Money cannot make good the past. But I will do my best. I will contact you again.

    With respect and affection
    Yours Sandor

Mo put this to one side and read through the older, less legible letter.

Dearest M

When you receive this letter I will be far away. Leaving London was hard. So long there I am almost a Londoner. I did not expect to meet someone like you. I was used to being alone. Music is my passion – the reason I could break with my mother, Vienna and all the connections there. Some said it was crazy to leave Vienna. People offered me work. I had a feel for our great composers.

But I had heard the call. I try to explain. In Vienna I was always a poor Hungarian Jew. Everyone knew everyone in the music world. I didn't feel marked apart. By then the rules had changed and Jews were allowed into the arts. (You only have to look at all the men who were around then like Gustav Mahler and Arthur Schnitzler.) But I was fixed in the way people saw me and the urge to seek other opportunities was great. London offered that possibility.

I did not expect to fall in love. But our love is not possible. You are a wife and a mother. I offer you nothing but uncertainty. The wife of a musician is not for you. Family is important. You say you carry my child, but I cannot break what you have. You say your husband is a good man: honest, loyal. I am not. I am a nomad, I always long for the horizon. In time you will forget me. I hope you will forgive me. Know that I have been changed by you.

My dearest M., dearest heart, Goodbye. Leb wohl! I kiss you a thousand times.

    Your S O

Mo sat on the bed with the letter still in her hand. She noticed the paper was trembling; her hand and arm were trembling. She took a few deep breaths to calm herself, but questions torrented through her. Why was this letter tucked away here, out of sight, scrunched up along with others where it might never have been found? What had been going through her mother's mind when she received it? Had Ma sought to push it away like some loathsome thing, some toxin? Or was she just waiting her moment? Had Sandor and Ma met up again? Mo recalled a moment, just weeks before, when Ma had tried to tell her something and been unable to.

What on earth was she to make of it?

Over the next hour or so she could not stop thinking about the letters. Her mind went circling round them. People spoke to her and she had no idea what they were saying.

There was no opportunity to talk it over with Derek. But she became aware of a growing determination: she would find out what she could about Sandor Olmak as soon as possible.

She did what was expected of her in the family but made sure she found time to be alone. Derek was still keeping an eye on the running of The Mare's Head. From an old article she'd kept about The Athena fire she knew where Sandor Olmak had been living. Later that day she informed her family she had a business affair to attend to and made her way to Percy Circus.

Chapter Fifty-six

Like many parts of London, Percy Circus was an island of quiet. The Lloyd Baker estate with its neat railings and uniform façades skirted it to the south, while to the west were the bustle and frenzy of King's Cross and St Pancras. No 6 Percy Circus had seen better days: the tiny front space was ragged with broken glass and bicycle parts; the windowsills were flaking. But the house retained the grandeur of its original concept in the line of its architecture.

A woman opened the door to her, her hair bound up in a turban and wearing a slightly grubby apron. Mo told her she was an old friend of Sandor's. The woman raised her eyebrows. 'Not poor old Sandor again? I fought that was all done and finished with.' As Mo considered she was standing before the house where her father had last lived, she began to feel queasy

'D'you think I might have a glass of water?'

The woman looked startled, but said: 'Why, yes. Come in, why don't you?' She led the way down a dark, narrow corridor into a kitchen, which gave onto a square of garden where washing flapped on a line. 'Sit down.' She cleared space for Mo on an easy chair. Mo gazed round the cluttered kitchen, at a black cat dozing on the sill, at a pile of mending stacked in one corner. It reminded her of her sisters' places. The woman was staring at her with a mixture of concern and curiosity. Mo gulped the water. 'Did you know him well, Mrs ..?'

'Watkins.' She looked at the ground and then with a sigh sat down opposite Mo. ''e was here a few months. I was dead shocked at what happened.' She started rifling through a pile of mending. Mo thought of Ma, who would always have knitting or darning in her lap. Her voice faltered as she tried to explain again why she had come without divulging too much.

Mrs Watkins looked puzzled. 'The police was here already. Went through 'is things. After that publican come forward. You must've read about it? It was in all the papers.'

'I was in the fire.'

'You was?'

'I was in hospital. I missed what went on afterwards. That's why I'm here now.'

Questions were stirring in her, making her thoughts incoherent. She could see that Mrs Watkins was on her guard, in no mood to reveal what she didn't want to, especially to a stranger. For all she knew Mo might be a reporter or even a police officer in mufti. Mo read the reluctance in her tight mouth, her downcast eyes. 'What did you do with his things?' she surprised herself by asking just when she'd resolved to hold back.

'What's it to you, young lady? You ain't a relative or nothing.' Aggression had crept into Mrs Watkin's voice.

Mo sat looking at her hands and fingering her ring. 'I have a connection with him...' Her heart was beating in an erratic, frightening way. 'He knew I was there – he came to help. I heard his voice…'

Mrs Watkins let out a long sigh. 'I knew there was no foul play. I read about you getting out alive. And now – what exactly is it you are after?'

'I want to find out more... He knew my mother.'

'He was a strange one, all right' murmured Mrs Watkins. "E was no trouble. Often of an evening when he 'ad nothing better to do he'd sit with me over a cup of tea and listen to me yawing about this or that. Liked the company, see. 'E had friends, but I never got to meet them. I don't know if he 'ad lady friends. If he did he never brought them back here. I'd say, though, that 'e'd be one for the ladies. He had that air about him. Intense. Dark good looks.' She paused, gave a little sniff.

'But picky, I'd say. No riffraff. He went a few times a week to some music association. Over in Conway Hall. He'd go there to play the piano. Sometimes he give free concerts, for charity like. Other times he got paid. He invited me once. But I couldn't go. I had my sister coming.' She paused. 'When he disappeared I was dead angry. Another fly-by-night, I thought, just when I was getting used to him. Bloody foreigner, I said – though he spoke English like a gentleman. When I 'eard about the fire and 'is body being found by the police, I was that sorry.'

'You went to the funeral?'

'A string of us from here went and others from the Percy Arms and The Unicorn, a couple of theatrical types and all. But nobody from back home. They found out he come from Vienna, though I knew that all along 'cos he told me. He'd talk about it sometimes, describe the parks and concert halls. But he said 'e felt better here. Freer. Things were starting to grow ugly in Vienna. 'E didn't say why. But I guessed. 'E was Jewish, see, and they were starting up with all their rabble-rousing.'

Mrs Watkins looked at Mo wistfully. 'No, he was a gentleman, he was, though to me he remained a puzzle. You knew him, you say?'

Mo felt blood draining from her head. She sipped more water. 'He was interested in my work, my voice. He wanted to help me.'

'There's not much of his stuff left. After that publican come forward the police were round here like a shot. Asked questions. Wanted to rule out arson, I guess. London's had its fair share of trouble-makers. Once they realised he wasn't one of them and couldn't find nuffin in his room, they said the funeral could go ahead. Ben Tulston from The Unicorn saw to it. No frills. Him being Jewish a big church do wouldn't ave been what 'e wanted, but we gathered and had a few drinks in his honour.'

'When was that?'

'About three weeks after the fire.'

Mo wondered why no one had thought to tell her. Ma must've known. Knighton certainly. Maybe they just thought she wasn't up to it. Or maybe Ma didn't know. His name would've been in the papers but not necessarily details of his burial. 'I would like to have shown my respects.'

'Too late now.'

'Are there any people in Vienna who should be contacted?'

Mrs Watkins shrugged. 'I give away most of his clothes. Fetched a couple of pounds for his suits for the back pay in rent. There are music sheets and other bits and pieces. I've got no use for them. I was going to bin them – this week as a matter of fact. It felt disrespectful to do it earlier. Maybe it's a blessing you come. I put what's left into a cardboard box.'

Sandor Olmak had been Mrs Watkins' favourite lodger. She liked his connection with the world of music and art, though she would never aspire to that herself. She liked that he had manners and drank in moderation; that he had a way with words and could bring alive the places he'd been to, the concerts he'd played at. She liked that he was attractive but not vain. That he could have had many a lover but was discreet. And for all that he did not consider himself too good to sit in her back kitchen and listen to her. She missed him. She'd not been able to sleep for nights after she heard what happened. She kept on imagining the fire. She imagined him calling out and nobody coming to his rescue. She imagined him dying alone, far from the place of his birth.

Mo was unable to speak. She stifled the tears which threatened. After a while Mrs Watkins got to her feet and tidied the cups into the Belfast sink, signalling it was time for Mo to be on her way. Before she left Mrs Watkins handed her a medium-sized cardboard box stuffed with papers.

* * *

Alone in the small bedroom at The Mare's Head, Mo rooted in frenzy through the papers. Yes, there were musical scores as Mrs Watkins said. There were also what looked like poems in a foreign tongue. German, she guessed. There were letters in the same language. One or two of them looked official. She arranged the contents into piles. She would need help with this. Nobody she knew spoke German. She remembered that some of Derek's artist friends in Paris came from Bavaria.

Chapter Fifty-seven *Derek*

Mo was in a strange space. Though it was only to be expected, it made him uncertain how to be with her. Her eyes were glazed and faraway; she jumped every time he touched her. It was as if she were watching a silent movie reeling off inside her head. In many ways it was just as well, for he himself was still shaken from the twin shocks of Tanya and himself in the studio and then Mo appearing two minutes later. Just as well she'd been riven with grief at that moment or she would have sniffed out the truth of it. Though she might be off somewhere else in her head, she seemed to be taking the death of her mother in her stride, as if it had already happened long before. Cissy, Tilda and Pa were showing more obvious grief.

And then Mo had gone dashing off goodness-knew-where on the pretext of a business affair. What business? As far as he knew she had no business connections here. She had burnt her boats good and proper when she left with him for Paris. She couldn't possibly be going to look for work here or trying to renew contacts with any of the theatres. What then? Was she still chasing the Sandor Olmak link? He'd assumed that was dead and buried. In his view, it was pure folly.

He busied himself in Mo's absence casting a swift look over the running of The Mare's Head. He checked the ledgers, the order book and paying out books, the cash receipts. Tilda's input had made a big difference. It all looked relatively straightforward. After a decent period of closure due to 'Family bereavement' he assumed business would pick up and carry on. Pa worried him less than he had. The death had not been unexpected. Sadly, all things considered, it seemed inevitable. Ma Dobson had simply taken a turn for the worse, as the saying went. He understood there had been a rushed hospital admission after the relapse, but nothing the doctors could do. She had just given up, he suspected.

Pa and Cissy and Tilda and their families were hovering in the back parlour, making tea, and receiving visitors. He heard the constant rattle of crockery and hushed voices. He offered to fetch the groceries. He offered to fetch coal for the range. He made himself available. Cissy thanked him and told him they were fine. Until Mo returned there was little for him to do.

He decided to take a walk. As he wandered up and down Mare Street he grew dismayed at the dark windows marking failed businesses and decided to take a trip up West where the shops would be brighter and the people smarter. Like for Mo, the sight of too much penury stuck in his throat.

Drayton Gallery lay in one of the cobbled alleyways off Piccadilly. It was shut for the day. Derek pressed his face against the rounded windowpane. Through the gloom he made out stacked chairs and canvases propped against the wall. It was no longer thriving as it once had. He moved on to Seville Gallery in Argyle Street. One or two viewers were lingering over seascapes by the window. Derek passed by, recalling his last visit there, just before they left for Paris.

* * *

In his chartreuse neckerchief and sky-blue shirt, Samuel Quintock, the gallery owner, had held out his hand. 'Ah Derek Eaton. What a pleasure to see you. You haven't passed through here for a while.'

'I'm off to Paris. Just thought I'd call by before I go.'

He'd placed his portfolio onto the counter and slipped out recent sketches. He'd been playing with geometric shapes, to reduce objects to lines and relationships. Over his shoulder he heard a quick intake of breath as Samuel clapped eyes on them. Derek turned to face him and could tell straight away that the man was struggling. Surely, here, where he had sold and sold again there would be a positive reception for his ideas?

'They're rather – well they are certainly not run-of-the-mill. Quite unlike anything you've done before. You're experimenting, are you?' Derek was heavy with misgiving: Quintock was supposed to be a connoisseur. Was he quite ignorant of what had been going on across the Channel? 'What can I say? I know they're only sketches and so can't do justice to a work. But, well, I don't think the market is ready for this sort of thing – the unpredictability of the times is making buyers seek the familiar, back towards paintings that tell a story, show a landscape…'

'You could have fooled me,' muttered Derek. 'Have you been to Paris lately?'

'Mr Eaton, with all due respect, we are not in Paris. Mr Eaton – Derek – bring me some like the ones you had in here before and they'll fly out of here in no time. At a good price too.'

Derek had taken his leave soon after, remaining civil but making no promises to return to his earlier style. It was not the first time that he'd felt London shrugging him off.

He smiled to himself. They had been right to go to Paris, right to defy caution and embrace the uncertainty of creation. In the next moment his mind clouded, he felt a pain in his chest. Tanya would be gone on their return. She would be forever out of his reach. He wandered through Leicester Square and down to the water. He watched the barges coming and going, observed a leisure craft bouncing on the waves. It was as it should be. He would just have to suffer in silence.

Chapter Fifty-eight *Lensky*

His encounter with the OGPU left a sour taste in the mouth. Try as he might, Lensky could not shake it off. On reflection he was convinced he'd been sufficiently non-committal. He'd betrayed nothing. But pock face, as he dubbed his pursuant, was not giving up. Surveillance might be more covert here than back in Russia, but for all that it was not subtler. He doubted whether he would be bundled into a car and taken off to some dark forest and done away with, but the OGPU knew where he lived, where his children went to school, when and where his wife went to have a dress fitted or her hair cut. It was enough. Scheherazade they might decide to wreck but he could live with that. Harm to his family was of a different order.

Once, a long time ago, he'd told a local revolutionary committee the whereabouts of a particularly nasty and reactionary Tsarist officer: someone who, during the vicious civil war that followed the revolution, had thought nothing of slaughtering a whole village because it stood in his way. He'd killed every peasant, every last pig. Afterwards Lensky knew he'd acted unwisely in passing on such knowledge. He would be forever marked as a soft target, a potential informer. He had sealed his own fate without even realising it. At the time he'd just thought he was helping rid the world of one more brute.

Relieved that he could no longer inform on Tanya even if he'd been so minded, he attempted, once again, to push the matter out of his mind. He'd arranged for another couple of singers to come to the club for auditions. He could never have enough talent at his disposal. One was coming on the recommendation of a friend; another he'd heard at a dive in Pigalle. He wanted to hear her again. He wasn't sure about her. Jazz and the American flavour were still in vogue but with the chilly economic wind blasting across the Atlantic, he'd decided it would be prudent to encourage variety. Jazz would not go out of fashion any time soon. The Parisians loved Swing, the Blues. Josephine Baker might have stepped back from her outrageous banana act to re-style herself as a sophisticated *chanteuse*, Maurice Chevalier and Mistinguette might still win acclaim, but the excitement and stridency of jazz were now part of the intoxicating brew the Parisians craved. Being an impresario was nothing if you were not able to read the heart's desire. Right now, that meant an astute and flexible balancing act. Mo Eaton summed up the dichotomy well. With working class roots and steeped in West End musicals she could slide at will across the social divide. Sufficiently English to have a frisson of hauteur, she also understood the sentiment and guttural honesty of the *chanson réaliste*. And she moved like a dancer.

Now he was sitting over a glass of Bordeaux in the dim interior of Scheherazade. The singer recommended by the friend had come and gone. She was not for him. There was something too vapid about her. She looked pleasing enough. She could hit all the right notes. But she just didn't excite. He found himself wanting to glance at *Le Figaro* while she was performing. Then he'd pushed the paper away: it had too much of a rightwing slant these days. But he'd felt fidgety the whole time and kept wondering what he was going to say to her not to be hurtful and how he was going to square it with the friend. In the event she'd given him a pleasant smile and made haste to be on her way. She knew he wasn't interested.

He was surprised to hear a knock at the outside door. It was too early for the second singer. The accompanist had gone out on some errand. The barman, who was in to help check supplies, called through to him. He was surprised to see a different young woman on the threshold. He got to his feet and strolled over. It took him a moment to recognise her. It was Tanya's companion from the night of the *vernissage*. He'd noted her at other functions in the Russian community, but always from a distance. She was good-looking in a wide-cheeked, Slavic way and had good skin and teeth. She was tall and slender. He'd wondered fleetingly what she was doing in Paris and if she was attached to anyone. She came forward, held out her hand and offered her cheek to be kissed. 'To what do I owe the honour?' he said.

'I've heard good things about this place. I just wanted to visit. I'd heard you'd refurbished in the Bakst style.' She gave a little sigh. 'Sometimes one wants a little of the homeland.' She looked around. 'It's quite beautiful.'

He bowed his head in appreciation of her praise. 'May I offer you a drink. An aperitif? It's almost lunchtime. A glass of Bordeaux? Mineral water? Or Vodka?' he added with a laugh. He had forgotten what her name was if he'd ever known it.

'Badoit is fine.' Then seeing his glass on the table added. 'Well perhaps wine.'

He poured her a glass. 'Would you like to join me? I'm waiting for a singer to arrive.'

She sat at table slowly crossing her legs and smoothing down her silk dress. She really was rather attractive. He'd overlooked her before as she was always in the company of Tanya, who outdazzled any companion. Her dress, a delicate shade of peach, had a scooped neckline, which showed off her neck to perfection.

She gave him the whisper of a smile. 'I was rather hoping you could tell me where Tanya was. I haven't seen her for days. Last time I saw her was at La Closerie des Lilas, surrounded by admirers,' she added a little waspishly, he felt.

From the back office he heard the phone ringing. 'If you'll excuse me.' He returned a minute later. '*Voilà,* my second singer – the one I really wanted – has cried off with a cold.' She nodded. 'Perhaps we could take some lunch together?'

He could think of nothing better than to take this rather glamorous young woman out for lunch and find out more about her. Besides, it would be relaxing to lapse back into Russian. Though he spoke English and French to perfection there was nothing quite like the sound of his mother tongue. At home he spoke mostly French as his wife, though ethnically Russian, spoke the language poorly.

Karine Petrova – he'd meanwhile admitted to her that he didn't know her name – readily agreed. He took her a nearby bistro, which he favoured because of its convenience, its dark cosy interior and the *cassoulet*, which never failed to satisfy. As the first guests for lunch, they had their choice of table.

She had been in Paris for six months, he discovered. She came originally because she knew Tanya Sergeyevna from her student days. She worked with Tanya when she was still cultural spokesperson and stood by her when she fell from favour. He offered her a cigarette and she smoked it in a leisurely, languid way as if she were at a cultural salon being observed. He found it hard to place her socially. She spoke a correct but not expressive Russian with the hint of a Moscow accent. There was something closed about her.

The *cassoulet* was, as always, excellent; the wine, equally so.

* * *

It had not been his conscious intention to end up in her bed that cool November afternoon, but that is what happened. She had an apartment in Montparnasse off Boulevard Raspail, not far from the cemetery. After a long lunch, where bit by bit she started letting go of her reserve, they took a taxi there. As she climbed the steps leading to her apartment, he watched the gentle roll of her hips. He kept telling himself, this was just for now. It meant nothing: neither to her nor to me. It went with the good food and the wine.

And he was right. She was obliging rather than passionate. Physical release was not hard to achieve but he felt vaguely sad afterwards. His wife knew he was not unerringly faithful. She did not expect him to be. She had long cried off intimacy and even before her last difficult confinement he always felt she tolerated rather than enjoyed their love-making. But something in Karine's attitude made him feel he'd just played a set of tennis rather than made love to a desirable woman. Perhaps the fault lay with him. Or perhaps, like the singer he'd turned down, there was just no mystery about her. He stroked her shoulder and she nuzzled into his hand. He was thinking how he could extricate himself without appearing rude or ungrateful. She surprised him by biting into his shoulder. 'Ouch!'

She laughed and pulled his arm across her chest. 'You can't go yet' as if she were reading his mind. 'I make no demands. It is enough for me. But let's talk some more. I miss that. The artists are so bound up in themselves. They have nothing spare for anyone else.' She slid out of the bed and draped a silken peignoir around her. She ran her fingers through his hair. 'I'm thirsty. I'll fetch some water, yes?'

She left the room and he took a moment to gaze round it. The dressing tabletop was covered with scents and powders, Coty, Chanel and other French brands. There were a few books on the shelf. He ran his eye along them: a mixture of romantic novels with the odd volume of Tolstoy or Gorky. He wondered whether she actually read them. When she returned she laid the jug and glasses on the bedside table. She gazed at him with her grey-blue eyes.

'Don't be sad, my friend,' she said. 'I know you are missing Tanya. We shall find her. I will help you find her. When did you last see her?'

Chapter Fifty-nine *Mo*

Paris was wearing a shroud. Or so it seemed to Mo when they returned there. The late autumn sunshine had vanished, replaced by skies of metal and a bite in the wind. Leaving London had been a relief rather than a wrench this time. Ma was gone, no longer lingering in a sick bed, no longer pulling on her as she had done just days before. There was a sharp finality to the fact. Ma's passing released her. It crystallised her mind. It made her look to the future rather than the past. At the same time, she felt flat: grey and drab like the turbid water of the Seine and the heavy clouds over the city.

She pushed back. She would not succumb to melancholy. She would go right now and take up where she had left off. She sent Lensky a message telling him she would be calling by Scheherazade and could he make time for her. When she arrived there he kissed her lightly on the cheeks and expressed his condolences. She nodded. He, too, looked sad, or was she only imagining it?

'I'm glad you came. It must be difficult…'

'At home in the theatre we have an expression: Doctor Theatre. The best way through your – the tough times – is to keep working. I just wanted to assure you that I'm ready to go. I've worked on the Cole Porter. I'll be able to perform in a day or two, with your agreement.'

'Good, Mo. That's good to hear.'

They were sitting in the small room that served as his office. They talked for a few minutes about her growing repertoire, of how and when she might introduce some of the songs she'd been working on. The cleaner was in and Mo could hear her shifting chairs and tables as she mopped. Everything was being put in place for the evening. It lightened her to think there was a routine she could slot back into, that she would not need to spend too much time alone.

'I was wondering. I haven't spoken to your husband yet – I was rather hoping to see him. I didn't know you were back. We need to talk about some of the artists.'

'He's gone to meet Monsieur Goldman. Apparently there's been some hitch with the shipping of the paintings.'

Lensky stared into space. 'So I believe. But nothing that can't be sorted out.'

'Well, that's good. Thursday then? Is it possible for me to come in and go over more songs with the accompanist?' She gave him a quick smile.

'I'm sure that would be fine. I'll let him know.'

* * *

Mo left soon after. She was carrying Sandor's papers. She'd shown the letters to Derek. He'd raised his eyebrows, looked at her and said nothing. When she goaded him, he seemed reluctant to respond. From previous comments she gathered he found the pursuit of her parents' story futile. More than once he'd said it had little bearing on the present or who she was today. She begged to differ. But right now she did not have the strength to argue her case. She wanted to get through each day by doing what she needed to do.

Sandor Olmak would not go away. However fraught and entangled the connection, she could not let it go. Besides, there were the letters. Had he not mentioned that he was intending to leave her something? She cared little what that might be – monetary gain was not uppermost in her mind. It was more the living link with the man she sought. She loved that Sandor had thought of her and that he wanted to carry something over. Besides, if she produced something concrete, Derek would be talked round and no longer see the whole thing as romantic, wishful thinking on her part. Derek did not deal in dreams. Or at least the dreams he entertained were not hers. He wanted to entrench himself ever deeper in his work here. He wanted to paint and exhibit. To immerse himself in the eddy of artistic ferment that was Montparnasse. London was now out of favour. He had said as much on the ferry back.

* * *

Sylvia was busy, sorting books onto shelves. She smiled at Mo over her shoulder. An assistant was helping restore order: they'd thrown another launch party for an unknown author. When Mo showed curiosity Sylvia told her it was a satire on Prohibition and the powers-that-be. The author was not smiled on in Kentucky, his home state. No American publishers would touch his book. 'Another impecunious writer scraping by,' said Sylvia.

When Mo told her of her mother's death Sylvia gave her a quick hug. Mo went on to say she needed to get documents translated from German. Sylvia gave her the name of a man who might be helpful. He worked at the Jeu de Paume in the Tuileries. Mo found her way there without delay. The gallery, showing modern works by foreign painters, was a revelation. She wondered if Derek knew about it. She stared around at the large, incandescent canvases. Unfortunately, the man she was seeking, Dieter Neumann, was not working that day. The gallery owner said he should be in the next day. Mo vowed to return.

Chapter Sixty *Derek*

'Vanished?'

Goldman shrugged. 'Exactly what I say. She was staying here. I even changed hotels to be on the safe side. I thought this the most secure place for her given what I've learnt about her past and the people she's fallen out with. After a few forays around Montparnasse – in her blond wig – she took my advice.' His voice faltered. 'At least I thought she had.'

'Yes, I saw her. Wouldn't convince anyone. I thought it foolhardy at the time…'

'Well, she's a free spirit, after all. As I say, I put a stop to that. We were ready for our voyage. Everything prepared. She said she wanted to say goodbye to a couple of people and that's the last I saw of her. I waited and waited. Then gave the go-ahead for the transportation. Most of the pieces have been shipped by now. I thought I'd stay on and find her. But there was no point in rescheduling everything – shipping's a costly business at the best of times. They're going from Cherbourg. Will be in the States within a week. I chose the fastest route.'

'So the consignment consists of Kurovsky's and Tanya Sergeyevna's work?'

'Mainly Tanya's. One of Kurovsky's. But I'll be back. Probably early Spring. I'll take yours then and have a look at anything you've done in the meantime. And anything The Apostles have produced by then. As I said – I'll leave a serious deposit...'

Derek nodded. They were seated on plush mauve sofas in the lobby of the Hotel Napoleon on the Avenue de Friedland near the Bois de Boulogne. Goldman had shifted to a luxury suite here days before. Tanya had had the adjoining rooms.

Derek gazed around trying to ignore the cramp of anxiety building in his gut. Somewhere beyond the palms in copper pots and the Persian carpets a piano was tinkling Chopin. Waiters glided around discreetly serving tea or alcohol. 'I thought you'd both be gone when we got back from England.' He paused. 'Have you reported her missing?' he asked in a quiet voice.

Goldman raised an eyebrow, gave a wry smile. 'I hardly thought that necessary. This isn't Moscow.'

'You'd be surprised,' said Derek.

If Goldman was concerned about Tanya he was concealing it well beneath his usual urbanity. For not the first time Derek wondered if they slept together. Last time he was convinced they did, now he was not so sure. 'So what will you do now?'

Goldman sipped his lemon tea. 'I rather hoped you might be able to flush her out for me.'

Derek's neck grew warm in agitation: she was not some game bird to be beaten from its cover. But he said: 'I'll see what I can found out.'

* * *

Dimitri was none the wiser. Derek caught up with him at La Ruche. He glanced around. Getting a toehold here The Apostles must feel they'd really arrived, though theirs were probably the worst lit and most cramped of the ateliers. Dimitri was in the process of organising another exhibition. This time The Apostles were to be the sole exhibitors. The title of the show was *L'Exil.* He'd persuaded the owner of a Left Bank gallery in the Rue du Bac to grant them a week's grace. The gallery was small but located as it was in the hub of the Latin Quarter, they were hopeful. He was very taken up with the project.

'I'm looking for Tanya,' Derek repeated. 'She was due to sail to the States with Goldman. You must surely know that?'

'Yes, of course.'

'Then?'

'Oh, she was delighted about it – a bit apprehensive,

nostalgic. But she'd made up her mind. There is no way she wants to go back to Russia.'

'But…'

'We spent the evening together.'

'When was that?'

Dimitri scratched his head. 'Two nights ago, I think.'

'You're not sure?'

'I've had a lot going on. She said she was staying at Goldman's hotel and felt safe there – what with all the moneyed clients, concierges and doormen. She was happy. Gave me a twinge to think she was leaving. God knows when I'll see her again. But – well – I think it's for the best.' Dimitri seemed convinced that all was well. Derek wished he felt as confident.

'She was going shopping the next day with Karine. Wanted to go to one or two of the Maisons de Couture. Goldman must have given her an advance on the back of the paintings, which he swears will be of great interest to art lovers in New York.'

'Do you know where I'd find Karine Petrova?'

'She has a room near the cemetery. One of the others might know.'

'So you're not worried about her?'

'Who? Karine?'

'No. Tanya of course,' snapped Derek. He could see Dimitri was so preoccupied with this latest exhibition it had pushed all else out of his mind. 'Is Karine Petrova involved in helping with this exhibition?'

'I don't think so. She prefers the international scene. Anything purely Russian does not appeal to her.'

'Listen, let me know if Tanya puts in an appearance.'

Derek returned to the studio in Marais but was unable to concentrate. He sent a *bleu* to Lensky but received no response. He even called by Scheherazade, but Lensky was nowhere to be seen. One of staff at the nightclub said he thought he'd taken a trip to Fontainebleu and would be back the following day.

Towards late afternoon Derek decided to go home: he should not leave Mo too long on her own. Since their return to Paris she'd said little about her mother, but she still had a vague, vacant air about her.

As he entered the alley he saw the light above glimmering. He was glad she was at home and not meandering through the streets. November had brought a chill greyness to the place. It was less inviting to be outside. Candles glowed within restaurants, and he caught the whiff of smouldering chestnuts on street corners. This would be their first winter here. He wondered how they would fare.

'Darling, you're back!' Mo threw her arms round his neck and smothered him with kisses. He was a little taken aback. 'I've made us a lovely soup, so we don't have to go out again. It's a bit wintry out there, isn't it?'

He sloughed off his jacket and joined her at the table where she began pouring him a glass of wine. She was looking remarkably cheerful. Before he could ask her about her day she piped up. 'I saw Lensky. He's given me the green light to start on Thursday. And he's happy for me to choose what I sing. Couldn't be better.'

Derek sipped the wine and smiled towards her. 'That's good then. Was he at the nightclub? I called by this afternoon but he wasn't there.'

'I saw him this morning. But Derek – wait till I tell you. You're not going to believe this.' Her face was aglow.

'What then? You look very excited.'

'I've found someone who will help with the Sandor papers. Translate them for me. I'm sure mostly just bits and pieces but …'

'But what?'

'The letter to Ma – he talked about leaving me something.'

This was moving too fast. His brain was tired, his nerves jangling. He wanted nothing more than a quiet evening to think things through. But Mo was alight with hope.

'Who knows … could be a family heirloom, money.'

Derek's head was beginning to throb. He took a deep breath. 'It's possible, I suppose.'

'Is that all you can say?'

'Mo, I'd rather we take one day at a day.'

She tilted her head to one side, gave a long sigh. 'That's probably a good idea.' She spooned her soup slowly, looking thoughtful. 'It could be a godsend, Derek. Having a nest egg would give us security.'

Tired from the upheavals of recent days, they had an early night. Mo fell asleep within minutes. Derek slept then woke, unable to still his restless mind. Taking care not to wake Mo he made his way through to the balcony, where wrapped in an old coat he sat staring over the night sky, hearing the odd klaxon from the street below, catching the odd flash of light towards the river. His heart was pounding as he imagined all the dangers the city contained.

Chapter Sixty-one *Lensky*

Lensky did not go to Fontainebleu as he'd said he would. Instead, he arranged to have lunch with Karine Petrova, but at a restaurant some distance from Scheherazade. He enjoyed the ease of the connection with her. He hesitated to call it an affair. It did not yet have the furtiveness and constancy for that. It was just something that had sort of happened and was pleasant enough.

They were still searching for Tanya. He'd discovered through Dimitri that she'd been staying at the Hotel Napoleon near the Bois de Boulogne. He'd smiled to himself: that was a classy place – Goldman must be footing the bill. So Tanya was not all asceticism and devotion to her art.

He ordered a champagne cocktail as he waited: not his usual aperitif, but something bubbly and light, something to distract himself. After half an hour he decided Karine must have been delayed somewhere and went ahead and ordered himself partridge in red wine. He kept glancing towards the door. She knew where they were meeting; she might at least have telephoned. He felt piqued: she was taking their liaison a little too lightly. There, he had said it. Liaison. It was not the first and almost certainly not the last he'd have. He sighed. It was not uncommon in this culture at this time, but he did not admire himself for it and he'd hate to compromise his family.

The partridge in red wine smelled delicious and he tucked in with relish. All the aromas of humus, bonfires and well-hung game were there: the smell of autumn. He ordered a mature claret and settled into the sensuous enjoyment of his meal. By the time he'd finished he decided to take a stroll to La Ruche to see what the Russian artists were up to. He might even bump into Dimitri or Tanya. He'd been there before. He liked it. It gave you the sense that the creation of art was all-important, that wherever you came from and whatever your circumstances, you were welcome. A three-storey circular structure it resembled a beehive, hence its name.

He looked around. Today it seemed empty. The light was beginning to fade, he'd lingered over his meal longer than he realised. He wandered round the base of the building. Here and there a light glimmered from within. Some had the shutters and doors open, others had closed them to keep out the chill. Someone somewhere was scraping a violin and a melancholy Hungarian gypsy melody hung in the air.

For some reason it made him unutterably sad. It reminded him of all that was lost, of people being turfed out of their encampments, of bye-gone pogroms in Galicia and of the devastation of the Saratov countryside. It reminded him of the vulnerability of the artist, the performer.

He walked on. Round the next corner he saw that someone had lit a brazier and caught the smell of charred potatoes. Figures were huddling around it for warmth. One of them was poking the embers into flames. Peering closer he recognised the sturdy frame of Dimitri. He called out to him.

Dimitri raised his arms in welcome and made space for him round the glowing charcoal. 'What brings you here, my friend? Have you come to see what The Apostles are up to? Not many of them here at the moment– they're over at the club, trying to keep warm.'

'Just a social visit,' answered Lensky, putting his hands up to the fire. 'So how is *L'Exil* coming along?'

'Good. Good.'

'Maybe I'll come back another time when they are more of them about.'

'Most days they are here.'

'Have you seen anything of Tanya lately? Or Karine

Petrova?'

Dimitri glanced sideways at him. 'She was here a couple of evenings ago. Karine, too. They were making arrangements to go to a Maison de Couture. Tanya wanted something special for America. Haven't seen either of them since.' He frowned. 'You're not the only one asking.'

Lensky grunted and pulled up his jacket collar. He stifled the question he'd been on the point of asking. He feared to hear his concern expressed. He moved from one foot to the other. The violin music had stopped. It was time to be heading home.

* * *

He was woken next morning by a telephone call. The voice sounded urgent. 'Can you come?' It sounded half choked. Still muzzy from sleep it took Lensky a moment to realise that it was Dimitri. He was breathing heavily into the phone.

'What is it?' he growled, in no mood to be yanked awake. He glanced at his watch. It was seven thirty and barely light. 'What…'

But the other had already hung up.

Lensky dressed in haste, brushed his wife's forehead with a light kiss and was on his way. He wasn't even sure exactly where he was headed. Dimitri had not been specific. But he'd been upset, that was clear.

Lensky had a terrible sense of foreboding.

He made his way first to La Ruche where he found several Russian painters bunched round the embers of the brazier. They looked anxious and listless. One of them sidled up to him. 'They found a body. Someone's been fished out of the Seine. A woman. Here. This is the message he got from the police. It's a Russian for sure. But we don't know who. We've been looking round – to see who's missing this morning…'

Lensky nodded and made a note of the scrawled message. The gendarmerie would want help with the identification. As perceived leader of the group, Dimitri would be the obvious person to call on. Lensky felt sick to the stomach. He left the huddle and made his way by metro to the address given.

It was a tall grey, anonymous-looking building beside the river. Only when he rang the bell and was greeted by a solemn-looking police officer did he realise it was a morgue. He announced why he had come and mentioned Dimitri by name. They led him forward. They entered a cold, dark, echoing place with strip neon lighting. He shivered. At the other end he saw Dimitri. Crumpled and ashen, he was grasping his middle and trying to stop himself howling. Lensky's stomach turned over. He compelled himself forward. Dimitri looked up when he heard the steps approaching. 'It's her!' he shouted. 'They got her. They got her in the end.'

Lensky was level with him now. Behind him, laid out on a table, was a woman's body. As he looked more closely he thought he would faint. Hair plastered to her face, skin marble-white, eyes thankfully closed, she could have been asleep. But she was not. They had put her hands together as if in prayer, they had tidied her clothes. He wanted to shout out. He wanted to scream that it was a joke. This was not real. She was safe. He had been her protector. She had so much to live for, a golden future beckoned. But she was still as night, cold as stone. All that animated and drove her had fled.

'Oh no,' he whispered. 'Tanya, no.'

PART 5

Chapter Sixty-two *Mo*

In the café on Boulevard St Michel Mo carefully removed the documents from the buff envelope and pushed them towards Dieter Neumann. Dieter did not have much charm, but he was amenable enough. He'd said he was willing to be of service as Sylvia had asked it of him: she was always so helpful to him. In his mid-thirties and lightly built, he had an earnest air about him.

Sipping Stella Artois, he frowned over the papers. 'Was there anything else?' Mo was reluctant to show him the letters Sandor had addressed to Ma. They were too close, too raw. But the next moment, deciding she had to chase the truth wherever it led, she handed them over. He read. Looked up at her. Read again. He leaned back and stuck out his legs under the table, staring at the ground.

'Well?'

'I don't know quite where to begin.'

She pushed away her empty cup to conceal her agitation. 'Just say it. Whatever it is. You heard my mother died. These were among her things.'

'No, I didn't know.' He paused. 'I'm sorry...' Mo nodded in acknowledgement, turned to the waiter to order herself a glass of red wine.

'What do the documents say? Is it anything important?'

'You're sure they're genuine? Not someone's idea of a *blague*, a joke?'

'Monsieur Neumann, it's a long story. You've seen the letters. It was a huge upset to discover that my father was not the man I thought he was...'

'You've only just found out?'

Her glass was shimmering red and silver before her. 'A few

weeks ago.' She stiffened. 'It's a lot to take on board.'

'Yes. I imagine it is.'

'So what can you tell me?'

Dieter Neumann separated out the papers, folded the letters in English and placed them carefully back in the envelope. The other German papers he touched and sifted with his fingers. 'These are receipts. Nothing of importance, I don't think. There is correspondence with a bank in Vienna. And there is another receipt – for a painting. Now that is what intrigues me most.' He looked across at her, took a deep breath, half attempted a smile which failed.

'You're not going to believe this. Not only did your father know Gustav Klimt, but he is the legal owner of one of his works. A minor, lesser-known work – but a Klimt nevertheless.'

She stared at him, not quite taking in what he was saying. 'And now – now that he is dead?'

'That's where it starts to get interesting.'

He frowned, drew the documents nearer and perused them again, glancing up now and then. She felt herself growing tense. Slowly, pausing to make sure she understood every word and making sure he was not misreading, he went through the relevant documents one by one.

He confirmed that Sandor Olmak was the legal owner of a Gustav Klimt painting: *Autumn at Attersee*. There was correspondence with a lawyers' firm in Vienna: it was dated August of this year. Sandor had asked them to draw up a new will, bequeathing the picture to his daughter, Morwenna Eaton. There was also a copy of a receipt for storage in a bank vault. Other receipts were there, some in English, some German.

Mo paused, felt herself blanch. 'Can you go over what you just said?' Inside her head it was roaring. She thought she had misheard him. Slowly, almost pedantically, he repeated every statement he had just made. He continued to look grave. She barely moved, not knowing what to say or do.

'I guess you could say you've come into a fortune,' he said at length. Her first thought was to tell Derek. She wanted him here now so he could hear for himself was Dieter was saying.

She and Dieter parted company soon after.

She wandered down the street feeling light-headed, disassociated. She did not know what to say, how to behave. She wanted to throw her arms about Dieter Neumann for helping her, for unlocking the secret of her father's generosity, but he had already gone back to work. One moment she wanted to shout out to the world that she was a rich woman and would never be poor again. The next, she thought there had been some mistake and it was all a cruel joke. One minute she wanted to contact the lawyers' office straight away, travel down to Vienna and claim her inheritance; the next, she was shaking uncontrollably.

* * *

She needed to find Derek; before all else, she needed to speak to him.

Without further ado she made her way to the studio in Marais where she presumed he would be working. It was silent as she drew near, the courtyard deserted. Undeterred, she walked across it and banged on the door. She heard the noise echo through the space. She banged again. Finally Pierre emerged, looking fazed to see her there. 'Mo?'

'Oh, Pierre – sorry to disturb you while you're working – I was looking for Derek.'

'He was in this morning. Didn't stop long. He's been shifting his stuff over to the other studio.'

'Is that where I'd find him?'

Pierre shrugged a shoulder. 'Probably. He doesn't tell me what he's doing. Scarcely knows himself these days.' He paused. 'Or you could try La Ruche. A lot of the artists – especially the foreign ones – have studios there.'

'Where's that?'

He frowned as he gave her directions. She left the studio puzzled by his reserve. Were he and Derek drifting apart? The older man seemed peeved. Was it because Derek had attracted Samuel Goldman's attention and he had not? Jealousies amongst artists flared like firecrackers. But right now that was not her concern.

She decided to go to La Ruche first. Several of the Russians had studios there. Derek had spoken of the need to finalise things with Samuel Goldman. He was shipping Russian art works across to America: contracts needed to be signed, prices agreed.

She approached the pagoda-shaped building through a wrought-iron gate. It was like a little village in itself: an artists' colony. She could see half-finished statues, metalwork surrounded by bushes, scraggly trees hiding stone seats, an abandoned easel or two. Derek would feel at ease here, among the creators. She felt a glow in her body as she thought of the news she was bringing. It would ease their circumstances. They would be able to choose where they lived, where they took their holidays, what dresses she would buy. Never before had she felt the power of what money could bring.

The colony was strangely quiet, though. She expected to hear chisel on stone, the hammering of metal or to spot the odd artist at work. But all seemed still as the grave. It gave her an uneasy feeling. Finally, she came upon an artist who was shifting out broken canvases into a pile for a bonfire. 'Clearing out?' she said conversationally.

The other nodded. She wasn't sure whether to address him in English or French. 'I'm looking for Derek Eaton,' she said slowly.

He nodded again. Stopped what he was doing and looked at her directly. 'Today is a sad day,' he said.

'Oh.'

'We have lost our star,' he said.

'What do you mean?'

'Derek Eaton will be at the Russian club,' the other muttered and turned away.

Mo knew the Russian club, little more than a cellar bar by the river, was not far from L'Atelier Blanc. Derek had once pointed it out to her. Now she hastened there with a growing sense of dread.

* * *

She could hear voices as she approached. Low, murmuring voices, not the high shouts of jubilation or the ferment of squabbles; this was the Russians in a subdued mood. The door to the cellar bar was ajar. She pushed her way into the gloom. Dimitri caught sight of her. His eyes were bloodshot, his face glum. He took her hand. 'Our Tanya Sergeyevna is dead,' he said. 'My Tanechka.' The words sent the chill of ice through her. At just that moment she caught sight of Derek from behind. He turned round but had not yet seen her in the shadow of the door.

She gasped. His face said it all. He was stricken. He was as sad as she had ever seen him. Even the death of their son had not wreaked such damage. She barely recognised him. And suddenly the pieces started to slot into place: the wine glasses in their rooms when she got back from London, Derek crumpling and hiding the sheets, the woman fleeing from the studio when Mo arrived with the telegram about Ma. Derek loved Tanya. They had been lovers. They were in love. Passionately. Irrevocably. He might try to hide it, shield it from her. But that was the truth of it.

And just as suddenly she knew she could not bear to be near him. Could not bear that he loved another woman so fiercely, without reserve. She had to flee. She had to find her way out of this pain. She was riven in two. Her heart hurt as it had never hurt. She cried out. In the next moment she turned and fled. She did not know where she was going, what she was about to do, what the future held for her. All she knew was that she had to get away from him. She stumbled up the steps and nobody came after her. He had not seen her. Even now Dimitri might be telling him she had arrived here. She had to hurry. Clear out. Leave no trace or track behind. She was a deer speared by a hunter. She was the biggest of fools.

Chapter Sixty-three *Derek*

Dimitri touched him on the shoulder. 'Mo is here.' Derek looked at him and for a moment did not understand.

'What?'

'Your wife. She's here, looking for you.'

'Oh.' He turned around, looked towards the entrance but could not see her. 'Where?'

'Just there,' insisted Dimitri, pointing and squinting against the gloom. He scanned the area round the street door. 'At least she was.'

'Sure you're not imagining it?' Derek began to wonder why Mo might be seeking him out and found it unlikely. But his head started throbbing horribly. He had heard about Tanya along with the others when Dimitri came that morning to La Ruche and spluttered out the news. The others were incredulous. Surely this couldn't have happened? She was the favoured one. She was bound for America, that land of promise. The sun was at last smiling on her. It just could not be true.

Only he knew it was true. Instantly. A blinding shaft of lightning. An ice shaft bearing down on him. Of course, it was true. How else to explain her second disappearance? How else to put a stop to her brazen spirit? She was doomed the moment she came into the world. She was doomed with the touch of genius and the uncompromising drive that came with it. She was just too much. And certainly too much for Joseph Stalin, who was bent on eliminating his opponents.

Derek could not move from the club. Whether or not Mo had come looking for him, it could wait. She may have looked and decided he wasn't here. He did not want to see her. He did not want her to see the state of him. Try as he might he could not disguise what he was feeling. And he'd didn't even want to try. Better if she were not a witness to that. Dimitri shrugged and walked away: it was of little concern to him. Derek did not know what to do with himself. There were questions he wanted to ask, but that would take time and effort. He would need to be in a rational frame of mind when he posed them. Right now. Right now. There was nothing but the shock of it, the terrible beautiful logic of it. He was numb and dumb with it.

* * *

Lensky turned up, looking grave. He had been questioned by the police, not as a suspect but as someone whom they thought would know the ins and outs of the Russian émigré community. He took Derek off to a cafe to get away from the others. Later Dimitri joined them. They sat over wine without speaking.

'They wanted to know if it might have been suicide,' Lensky said at length. 'Wanted to know how stable or otherwise she was.'

The words fell awkwardly among them.

'What did you say?' replied Derek after a while.

'I told them I thought it unlikely. But what do I know?'

'She had too much to live for,' said Dimitri.

'Will there be a post mortem?' asked Derek.

'There were no obvious signs of violence.'

Derek began to feel sick. He recalled their recent fleeting love-making, the desperation of it, knowing perhaps more than they realised that it was to be their last. He recalled the musky smell of her, the softness of her wild hair against his chest. He sighed deeply. 'Someone must have given her away. Goldman was trying to make sure she kept within safe bounds,' he murmured. 'Does he know?'

'He does now,' said Lensky. 'I phoned him.'

'She was courting danger – before. Getting dolled up in a blond wig and all that. She was tempting fate…'

'What do you mean?' snapped Dimitri.

'I mean...' began Derek and wasn't quite sure what he did mean. It would be too crass to say she had a death wish. That wasn't even true. Her behaviour had merely been part of her defiance. 'I mean she didn't succumb to fear like the rest of us,' he muttered.

They sank back into silence. The more he thought about her, the more he thought he would choke. There was nowhere to go with the feelings he was carrying. He wanted to kick the nearest big mouth who said something stupid. He wanted to shout out the futility of it, the waste, the outrage. He wanted to smash the face of the nearest OGPU agent who came anywhere near him.

'Has anyone seen Karine Petrova?' asked Lensky in a low voice. 'She might know her latest movements.'

Derek went with Dimitri back to the club; Lensky retreated to Billancourt. He said he would be in touch. There were arrangements they would need to cover – not quite bringing himself to say funeral. That was a word that sat so ill with the vivacious Tanya. Some deaths seem more unlikely than others; though in truth everybody knows it as the great leveller. They embraced each other awkwardly.

'What of Karine Petrova?' asked Derek as they walked. 'How well do you know her?'

Dimitri shrugged. 'Not at all, to tell the truth. She just appeared with Tanya. I can't keep track of all her friends.'

'Has she disappeared too, then?'

'Quite frankly I couldn't care less about her,' said Dimitri. 'There are so many people passing through. You can't get attached to all of them.'

'I'm not suggesting you do. But she was her friend. She might know something. They were going shopping together, weren't they?'

Dimitri grunted. It was obviously too much for him to think about. It had been a long day. Derek sensed he wanted to get back to the club and drink himself to oblivion. Any other time he might have joined him. Now, slowly emerging from the frozen state he'd been in, he began to think more clearly. He should be getting home. It was time. What if it really had been Mo who came in search of him? Dimitri had no reason to lie. Earlier, distraught, he'd pushed away the possibility. Now it seemed feasible. But he wanted to clear his head. He wanted to walk and walk. He would take the route along the quay skirting the river. It was a couple of miles, long enough to order his thoughts. He looked at his watch: it was after eight. Mo would be wondering where he was. He should not take too long.

He walked briskly. Where he could he went beside the water, drawn almost to the last place Tanya had been. He allowed the tears to flow. He kicked out at bits of litter or stones in the way. He watched a launch slide by on the river, saw people dawdling over the bridges or walking arm-in-arm towards the restaurants and cafes that glowed and invited all along the Left Bank and over the other side, between the Tuileries and the art museums.

He crossed the Pont Neuf, wandered the length of the Ile de Paris, came to Notre Dame and heard the ancient chimes. He recalled Mo saying she'd gone inside and lit a candle, how it had helped her. He was not about to do the same, even if it had been open. But he wanted to linger in the shadow of its vastness. It had seen so much: plagues that devastated the city, fires, revolutions, massacres, the toing and froing, ups and downs of the volatile French civilisation. How small his life was in comparison. How transient his loves and hates. He had loved Tanya. He hadn't meant to. Didn't want to even. But we don't always get what we choose or even know what we really want. He sighed. Time to move on.

By the time he reached their alley he was tired. He rubbed his hands over his face, made himself ready to greet Mo. He looked up. The rooms were in darkness. He was baffled. Normally by this time she would be at home, cooking them a simple supper or getting ready for them to go out to one of the nearby cafés.

He let himself into their rooms.

'Mo? Mo, are you there? I'm back.' His voice echoed back to him. He climbed from the shared kitchen. 'Mo?' Everywhere was in darkness. He switched on the lights. Moved from one room to another. It wasn't till he entered their bedroom a second time that he noticed that the wardrobe door was wide open. He gaped at it. All her dresses and skirts were gone. Only her frocks for performance remained: black and shiny and tantalising. He wrenched open the top drawer of the chest-of-drawers, where she kept her lingerie. It was empty. And the next, where she kept her cardigans. Nothing. He checked to see if the ferry timetable was there. It had not moved. 'Mo – Mo where are you? Mo!' he was shouting now. He moved from one room to the next like a wild animal. He went onto the balcony. 'Mo!' he shouted. 'Mo!' His voice carried over the rooftops in a desperate plea.

Chapter Sixty-four *Mo*

Mo did not where she was going. Seized by an anger that tore through her, she'd had to move. To wait and hear his tread on the steps, to see his gloomy face would only confirm what she already knew. If not the anger, the sadness would destroy her. She'd gathered up her belongings, her passport, what money she had and fled the rooms. At any moment he might return. She did not know how she would react if she came face-to-face with him.

Out in the alley she looked up at the upper storeys leaning inwards, heard the clatter of evening meals being prepared. She hastened out towards Rue des Rosiers, lost herself in the tangle of nearby streets. It was not hard to do. In the penumbra of gaslight from the lamp posts shadows merged, danced away from each other. Her eyes were deceiving her, making her think she knew a corner when she didn't, leading her ever deeper into the labyrinth. She didn't care. Anywhere would do, anywhere away from him. She must keep going, one foot in front of the other, one breath following the last. That was how to survive.

On and on she went until she realised she did recognise some of the street names, the corners where saints would once, before the Revolution, have had their niches. She was in the vicinity of his studio, the one he was in the process of vacating. She paused to catch her breath. She had been rushing more than she realised. Far off she could hear the rattle of a tram, the metallic clink as it glided on its tracks.

She had given no thought to where she might spend the night. Now, growing tired, she admitted she could not wander all night in these darkened streets. She would have to find some corner to shelter, even if just for a few hours. She smiled to herself: the last place he would think of looking – if indeed he did go searching for her – would be his studio! It was such an unlikely place it was a brilliant solution. Unlikely, too, that he would return to work, though not impossible.

Arriving there, she eased through the side of the wrought-iron gates and crossed the courtyard. She heard something scuttling away. Leaves in the wind, a rat? She did not stop to investigate. The darkness was thick, not a glimmer anywhere from any of the ateliers. The moon and stars were shrouded in cloud. She struggled even to discern the outline of the roof against the faintest glow of the night sky. As she fumbled her way forward she tried to make out which door was theirs, which pot would conceal the big rusty key that would give her access.

With relief she let herself into the atelier, heard her steps echoing on the wooden floor. She lit a kerosene lamp at the back of the studio and sank onto the battered sofa drawing a blanket over her, hoping for sleep; but even as she went to settle down she realised she wanted to distance herself from the sofa. Who knew what had occurred here?

Pulling together two old cushions she attempted to make a nest for herself in the farthest corner. The wind, which she'd hardly perceived outside, came creaking through the floor, shivering down wall crevices and the chimney of the wood-burning stove. No matter. She would rest awhile. Even as she was churning the day's events exhaustion came. She drifted in and out of sleep, disturbed by ragged snatches of dreaming.

* * *

She woke with the light, shook her head, taking a moment to recall where she was and why. She got to her feet. Splashed cold water in her face at the corner Belfast sink where they washed their brushes or cleaned them with solvent and rags. Her head started to ache from the fumes of turpentine and linseed oil. She walked with determination towards the street door. She did not want to see any of Derek's work. Did not want to be here a minute longer than necessary. Outside on the street she made for the nearest café where she ordered coffee and croissants. She had not realised how hungry she was. As she sat licking the crumbs of croissant from the tips of her fingers a plan began to form in her mind. It involved laying claim to her inheritance. One way or another she needed to get herself down to Vienna and meet up with her father's lawyers.

It was a daunting prospect. She spoke no German and still felt completely at sea in the world of finance and the law. She spooned the last of the coffee into her mouth. She recalled Derek saying that Samuel Goldman spoke some German. He had cousins and connections in Austria. The more she thought about it the more she realised Goldman was the most obvious person to help her in her pursuit of the legacy. He'd also have a clearer idea than most what the picture might be worth and how she might go about selling it, if that was what she chose to do. Derek had mentioned in passing that he had changed hotels. He was now staying in the vicinity of the Bois de Boulogne. He'd said the name of the hotel, but she'd made no note of it.

She looked at the café clock: it was early yet and she doubted whether Derek would have fixed any meeting with Goldman at this hour. She paid for her breakfast and made her way by metro to the Bois de Boulogne.

Chapter Sixty-five *Lensky*

Lensky half expected to get another call, either from Dimitri or the police, to tell him another body had been fished out of the Seine. When no such call came, he began to ponder the fate of Karine Petrova. No one had seen her; several of The Apostles did not even remember her. Despite her physical attractiveness she had sunk into the shadows cast by the light of Tanya Sergeyevna, whom they all knew and loved and were now grieving in full measure. Karine had come and gone, always peripheral, her presence barely registered. It seemed Lensky was alone in being concerned about her welfare.

He went to her room near the cemetery, rang the bell and received no reply. He returned later but met with the same lack of response. The third time he called he bumped into the concierge. 'She's gone, that one,' said the scrawny old woman, eyeing him with an air of suspicion. If she recognised him from a previous visit, she gave no indication of it. 'Paid up last week. In advance. I thought it strange at the time. Gave no explanation. No forwarding address.'

Lensky walked away with a growing sense of disbelief. He entered the graveyard and walked among the tombstones as if they could provide, if not the answer, then a deeper perspective. The angels of deliverance on moss-covered stone, the crosses of forbearance stared back at him. Here and there the grass was long and threatened to obliterate the names and identities of the deceased. 'Loving wife and mother.' 'Much loved daughter.' No one ever wrote 'pleasure-giving mistress' on a gravestone. He thought of Karine. She hadn't given him that much pleasure, but he could get used to her.

At the time it had all seemed uncomplicated. But had she

wound him in and used him? Had she betrayed Tanya? Lured her to a place where the OGPU could dispose of her as they wished? While he could resist and outmanoeuvre the likes of pock face, Karine Petrova was another matter. How crafty of them to use a woman. How easily he'd fallen. How ready he'd been to drop his guard at the prospect of a fun-filled afternoon. But he'd given nothing away, they must have tracked Tanya down by another means.

Back at Scheherazade messages awaited him. Mo had phoned to say she would be away for a few days but back at work the following week. The call puzzled him. Surely she realised he and Derek were in frequent contact? Perhaps she didn't. Perhaps Derek had not told her of Tanya Sergeyevna's death. He shrugged. There was no accounting for what went on in another people's relationships.

The second message was from Dimitri, requesting a meeting as soon as possible: he wanted Lensky to accompany him to the police. He grunted. Of course, Dimitri would want to press for an enquiry. The third was from Goldman: he needed to see him urgently, that day preferably, to address the issue of Tanya Sergeyevna. So she had become an issue now, had she? Certainly there might be problems with her work already half way across the Atlantic. But he thought Derek had been seeing to all that. Maybe it was more complex than he'd been led to believe.

* * *

Dimitri looked as though he hadn't slept or shaved for a week. His eyes had the hollowed-out look of desperation. He declined Lensky's offer of lunch and stuck to alcohol. He fingered the base of the glass of vodka and stared at it.

'It wasn't suicide,' he muttered. 'There is no way Tanya would have done away with herself. Not now. Not since she's escaped the worst of it and had the promise of exhibitions. Sales. Places to exhibit her vision. She was on top of the world. Last time I saw her she was wearing that stupid wig and holding forth.

Promising all The Apostles she would see them right. As soon as she was established in New York, she would tell the world about what was going on – how many talented artists were being persecuted in Russia. Do you think someone in that position would jump into the river out of despair? I tell you categorically. It was not suicide.' Lensky nodded, watched the other's face spot red as he grew excited. 'I want you to come to the Gendarmerie with me. Let them know our views.'

Lensky suppressed an inner sigh. From his experience the authorities cared little about the bodies they dragged out of the Seine. These days there were just too many of them: natives of Paris driven to drown themselves out of hunger, depression or guilt at not being able to support their family; not to speak of the immigrants thronging the city. The gendarmes did little, unless pushed from above on account of the eminence of the deceased. Nevertheless, he owed it to Dimitri and his fellow Russians to make the attempt. So, having tied up any loose ends at Scheherazade and fixing a later meeting with Goldman and Derek, he accompanied Dimitri to the relevant *arrondissement*.

The meeting went much as he expected.

The officer in charge was civil, respectful even, but firm. There was no evidence to lead them to suspect foul play. Her body was intact: no signs of blows or sexual attack. Cyanide, the most commonly available poison, left traces in the body for only forty-eight hours. After that it would be impossible to detect.

'But – there are forces in the city,' began Dimitri. 'She was an artist. Someone who criticised what's going on in Russia.'

The officer raised his eyes as if to say. Not another artist! They were not the most stable group. Several foreign artists, chased by he-knew-not-what demons, had thought to curtail their lives and many of them used the Seine as their point of departure. He was not unsympathetic, and he understood how Madame – what was her name again? – had left many grief-stricken friends behind, but his superiors had not seen fit to grant permission for a state inquest. They were releasing her body forthwith and the honourable gentlemen should look to making the necessary funeral arrangements and contacting as many of her circle as possible.

'How did you know she was Russian?' asked Lensky as a parting shot.

The officer gave a wry smile. 'She was wearing a medallion inscribed with Cyrillic lettering. We got it deciphered. We will return it to you.'

Dimitri started at the mention of it. 'That was her mother's.'

The officer showed no further interest as he ushered them out of his office. After collecting the medallion, they left the building. Lensky was not in the least surprised by the outcome, but Dimitri looked so shaken that he took him to a café and spent an hour trying to calm him down.

Lensky had little stomach for Goldman after the day he'd been through, but he'd given his word. When he got to Goldman's hotel by the Bois de Boulogne he and Derek were well into a bottle of Sancerre, both looking grave. A pianist was playing Mozart: a light, lively piece he couldn't quite place. It fitted ill with the mood of the occasion. The two broke off what they had been saying to acknowledge his presence. He ordered tea with lemon from a passing waiter.

'A bad business,' said Goldman and looked at the ground.

'I've just come from the police,' replied Lensky. 'I spoke to the man in charge of criminal investigation for that area. They see no reason for an inquest. They'll record 'death by misadventure."' He paused. 'Actually, I just don't think they can be bothered. If it was a Grand Duke they might. But not for some obscure foreign female artist as they see it.' Derek grunted his understanding. Goldman glanced in his direction and nodded.

'So what happens now – to her assets, I mean? I presume you did actually buy her art? Or was it still all under negotiation?'

Lensky knew he was barging in where a greater delicacy of feeling was called for, but he feared Goldman just might disappear back to the States and assume undisputed ownership for all the shipped items. He himself was enough of a businessman to be willing to grasp that particularly unpleasant and burning nettle.

Goldman raised an eyebrow. 'I bought some outright. Paid into the account she asked me to. Other pieces were to go to auction. I was helping her on that front. The art world can be a snake pit.'

Lensky grunted.

Goldman leaned back, eyed them for a moment before reaching into his briefcase. 'I think you need to see this.' He laid a formal document before them. Lensky perused it, let out a long breath, then passed it to Derek. Tanya had drawn up a legal statement to the effect that in the unlikely event of her death all proceeds from her works were to be donated to the Fund for Russian artists, currently administered by Marie Vassieleva.

'She must have known,' whispered Derek. 'They were getting ever closer.'

'Does she have any next-of-kin?' asked Lensky.

'Not that I know of,' said Derek. 'You'd need to ask Dimitri. He was like a brother to her. And that female friend – what's her name? – she might know more.'

'Karine Petrova, you mean?' Lensky exhaled with a sigh. 'I have reason to believe that she's an agent of the Russian Secret Services.'

The others looked at him in shock.

Chapter Sixty-six *Derek*

Derek's head was tight with pain. He had not slept all night. The shock of Tanya compounded by the loss of Mo had driven him out onto the streets. He'd wandered the alleys and by-ways of Marais, searching for Mo. He'd drifted towards the river, back even to Notre Dame and sat on a bench, head in hands, clueless what to do. Knowing in an instant that Mo knew about him and Tanya, knowing that he would not be able to deny it even if he'd wanted to. He'd sat and sat, mind whirring, body aching, unable to move, unable to make any decision. At last, the bite of the cold night had got him to his feet and driven him home.

The one beam of light in all this confused gloom was the fact that Mo was still alive. And what was more she intended carrying on singing at Scheherazade. Lensky had dropped a casual remark at the start of their meeting to this effect, eyeing him strangely as he did so. Neither had said any more about it, Lensky astute enough not to mention how bizarre it had been to learn of Mo's wishes through a phone call. Derek was hugely relieved. Tanya's death had destabilised him to such an extent that without any difficulty at all he could see disaster all round – the world plunged at one stroke into random meaninglessness.

Nothing seemed to be resolved. The French police's refusal to investigate Tanya's death left a bad taste in the mouth. It made him feel powerless. He'd hoped that her rising status as an artist would mean something to the art-loving Parisians, and that knowing this, the gendarmes would investigate. Or, failing that, some big cheese in their ranks might show a passing interest in a young woman being stalked by the dark forces of the Russian state. But, no – it was perhaps true what Lensky maintained: the police were too busy struggling to contain the volatile political mix in the city. Unemployment was on the increase and with it, crimes of all sorts.

Hour by hour he was growing in the conviction that her death had been inevitable, especially if Karine Petrova was an informant. Through her, the Russian Secret Service would know the extent of Tanya's rebellion and of her resolve to fight for the soul of Russia, as she saw it. Until she went to stay with Lensky they would have had easy access. So what had they been waiting for? More evidence? An ideal opportunity to fake a suicide? Tanya was elusive, yet she had also been mocking them when she went into the cafés of Montparnasse. The moment was unimportant. It sufficed that they had not rested until she'd been destroyed. They'd accomplished what they set out to do. But had she herself harboured a death wish? The clarity of her intent to leave all the proceeds from her paintings to the Russian Fund for artists smacked of foreknowledge, foreplanning even.

He would never know.

But the hunt must surely be on for her work? That was the real danger. An artist lives on through their creation. Destroy her body they might, but her spirit would outlast it and shout her protest from the finest and biggest art galleries in the United States. Did they even know that her stuff, right now, was secure in the hold of an ocean-going vessel? Or was it? Had they infiltrated everywhere so even as now some sleuth on board the ship was ferreting out the offending items? It was too much to think about.

He needed to get rid of this pain in his head. It was as if someone was driving a chisel into his skull. He could not think straight. Later that evening he had another meeting with Goldman. The man had said he wanted to call New York in the meantime: he needed to make enquiries about tax and imported artworks and he needed to be in contact with other members of the company. Derek had stopped paying attention to what he was saying for he was beginning to feel out of his depth.

He thought of his own work. There were still some materials in Pierre's studio. He'd shifted the bulk over to the other studio but left his paints, brushes and a few canvases in Marais. Now he had the strong urge to get away from people, especially Russians – where it was all pain and tragedy. He wanted to throw off a sketch, mix a few colours and chuck them at the canvas, immerse himself in the parallel world of images. He relished the thought of being alone and unrestrained in the studio. No matter that daylight had now faded and he'd have to work by artificial light. It was the teeming in his head he needed to let go of. Only that way could he hope to restore equilibrium.

When he arrived there, he whistled as he swung open the door, shouted out: 'Anyone there?' just to make sure he was truly alone. He heard only the echo of his own voice. He took an armful of logs from the pile in the courtyard and filled the wood stove, watched as the blazing wood shifted and sent up sparks. He warmed his hands and prepared his easel.

His eye caught the battered sofa where he and Tanya had lain. He turned his back on it. He spotted a pile of cushions at the other end of the atelier. He couldn't recall them being heaped like that. He paused, not knowing why, but drawn towards this strange constellation of familiar objects. As he approached, he caught the slightest whiff of perfume. No, not Tanya's: this was fainter, more flowery – more like the eau de toilette, which Mo sometimes wore. He looked down on the cushions. They were moulded to the contours of a body and there, amongst them, lying like a silver snake, was Mo's scarf. He knelt and held it to his face. Mo wore it on chilly evenings. Again, he caught the smell of her, sensed her anger and desperation. He sighed. She had nowhere to go to get away from him and yet she had come here, to the heart of his work. No doubt she had spent the night here.

And tonight – would she come back? The more he thought about it the more unlikely it seemed. One night she could get away with, but not two. It had been clever of her to come here. She was making fun of him almost: playing cat and mouse. Only who was the cat and who the mouse? The drive to sketch had left him. He had to find her – but where on earth to start? She knew no one in the city apart from Pierre and Lensky. She often went to Sylvia Beach's shop. She'd been there seeking help with her father's documents. He became aware of an unpleasant twisting through his gut. Mo had every right to do what she wanted after she'd found out about Tanya.

He started pacing up and down the studio, muttering. He opened a can of crimson paint, dipped his largest brush in it and spattered it across a canvas. It was not enough. More colours, more rage, more chaos. He flung whatever was available towards the innocent blank until it was covered. He stood back. At last it resembled the confusion of his psyche.

He looked at his watch. He'd lost track of time. He needed to get a move on. Samuel Goldman would be waiting. No time to change out of his paint-smeared clothes. He'd have to do as he was. Goldman would want him to take charge of the Russian end of the deal, to tidy up the financial side as best he could. But right now Derek couldn't think his way through. His mind was a fug, his emotions a morass. He stood back. Breathed deeply. One day at a time, he told himself. That had been his philosophy after Timothy died. That would have to see him through now. He grabbed his coat, locked up and headed towards his meeting. He noticed as he walked that his headache was abating. That at least was something.

Chapter Sixty-seven *Mo*

Saint Stephen's cathedral loomed over the city of Vienna with its Gothic spire. Goldman had made Mo an appointment with the solicitors. With time to spare she made her way to Café Dorndt, where you could while away hours browsing over newspapers, sipping your choice of coffee and sampling the famed confectionary. People were dotted around her, munching and chatting in a clatter of dessert forks and laughter. She let a large wedge of *Sachertorte* melt in her mouth. Outside in the thin sunshine she glimpsed three ladies at a table, heads bent together like birds pecking crumbs. An elderly man crossed the square, nodding greetings and waving his stick.

The city had an old-world feel about it: horses clip-clopped over cobblestones; dark alleys off the cathedral square bore ancient wrought-iron work in their signage and balustrades. She straightened her jacket and glanced at her reflection in the glass of the window. Despite all, she smiled to herself. She had made it!

She would never ever forget the expression of sheer incredulity on Samuel Goldman's face when she showed him the letters and documents relating to the Gustav Klimt painting. It was almost comical. It wasn't the mouth falling open like a grouper or the raised eyebrows, it was more the way he stared at her, as though she were something blown in on a billowing, magical carpet. 'You gotta to be kidding me!' he said more than once. If he was supposed to retain a professional cool, he'd failed completely. For him it was a once-in-a-lifetime, he said: the reason he returned again and again to Europe.

Sensing her advantage, she'd jumped in straight away. She decided she could trust him as well as anyone – though to be sure she still doubted her ability to discern – and struck a deal. She would give him first refusal should she decide to sell the painting. Or, if it went to auction, he could be her agent. But he must keep absolutely *stumm* about the whole affair: no hint to either Derek or Lensky until she said so. He readily agreed then went even further. He said he'd ease her way. He'd call through to Vienna, arrange a meeting with the lawyers. He'd even organise for her to stay at a sumptuous hotel in the old town and foot the bill. She'd demurred. No, no, he insisted. It was the least he could do. He got a special rate as a regular visitor, he explained, and most of his expenses in Europe were tax deductible. She was in no frame of mind to argue. It just made her more aware how much this painting must be worth.

She glanced into an alleyway. It would be very easy to be taken in by Vienna. It was full of charm and so very far east. In the Baedecker guide she'd read that they'd had to beat off the Turks at the time of the Ottoman Empire. There were so many influences here: it remained redolent of a rich and cultured past. Yet the place made her uneasy. She wondered what town district her father had lived in. He'd come here from Galicia, now in Hungary. If only she had an address, some way of finding out. His mother took in washing, he'd once said. She wondered if he was ashamed of her, whether the rest of her family was... because of him. She looked out over the square, feeling sad, lost even.

* * *

Anwaltskanzlei Herber und Dolsch was situated on the edge of the central district, towards the commercial area. The office was in a modern, glass and chrome fronted building by a road junction and five storeys up. Luckily there was a lift. She was wearing the most sombre outfit she had: a grey dress with a matching jacket and hat, which made her look like a dame from the Home Counties. Rudolf Dolsch introduced himself and shook her firmly by the hand. He led the way into an office facing out over the street. Below, through an open window, she heard trams and cars stopping and starting.

'I believe you acted for Sandor Olmak?' she began when she learnt he spoke reasonable English. 'He died in London some weeks back.'

'Sorry to hear that,' said Rudolf Dolsch perfunctorily.

'Yes, well.'

Dolsch had assumed the dispassion of his trade, awaiting information, clarification.

'I have come to Vienna to carry out his last wishes.' As she reached into her handbag to retrieve the documents, he touched her hand to restrain her. She was puzzled. She wanted to get on with the business as quickly as she could. He explained that a legal clerk would be summoned to take notes. Some of letters might need to be translated. Her travel documents and passports would need to be examined in detail.

A pale-faced clerk came in, sat at one of the desks and proceeded to record the session. Mo handed over the documents. Dolsch told her they'd put a new filing system into operation, which might complicate the process. She was invited to have a coffee while she waited. Eventually a second clerk found Sandor Olmak's files. Dolsch looked carefully through them, glancing up at her now and then.

Mo began to feel impatient. Did they have an address for Sandor Olmak, the last place he lived, she asked. Rudolf Dolsch looked through the file he was holding and scribbled on a chit of paper.

Why was it all so protracted? Goldman had assured her he'd smoothed the way: it was just a case of them verifying the will and the picture would be hers. He mentioned that the ancient bureaucracy of the Austro-Hungarian Empire days could cast a long and pompous shadow over proceedings. But he'd done the best he could.

Finally, Rudolf Dolsch told her to return later that day.

Clutching the chit showing her father's last address she wandered off. Dolsch had told what tram to take to arrive at his former apartment. After initial frostiness he seemed keen to move things along as fast as he could. Now as she rattled along on a tram, she gazed out at passing buildings. They skirted the Donaukanal and after a few stops the driver turned to her to indicate that she should get off.

War had destroyed so much. In Vienna there had been huge upheaval. Though the edifices would be unaltered – as there had been no aerial bombing – nothing would have stayed the same. Sandor had lived in the Gonzagagasse, near the old Jewish quarter. Mo peered up at the grey five-storey building, pressed the bell, kept her finger on it and heard the sound reverberate inside. Silence. Nobody came to answer the door. She had a sensation of being forever shut out, abandoned in an anonymous street where the higher the building the longer the shadow it cast. It made her feel insignificant. She waited. Rang again. A woman passed her by, muttered something Mo did not understand.

Out on the main street she caught sight of a bunch of scruffy youths shuffling towards her. One was shouting out something in German. Others were waving the crooked sign she recognised as the swastika. Although few in number – perhaps just nine or so – there was a brutish, arrogant swagger about them. She backed into a doorway. Their boots echoed on the cobblestones. They cast around as if on the lookout. She stared at their pale, wasted faces, at their tatty clothing and broken shoes. One peered towards her. *'Was haben wir hier? Sie sieht ja jüdisch aus!'* There was a nasty leer on his sallow face. She caught the word *jüdisch*. It sounded like Jewish. She shrank back, heart racing. One of his fellow ruffians pulled him by his jacket. *'Komm doch!'* And they shuffled on. Frozen, she could not move from the spot.

After she'd made sure they were no longer around she made

her way back towards Saint Stephen's cathedral, glancing around as she went. She entered the mighty edifice, sidled down onto a back pew and looked up at the soaring arched pillars. She waited several minutes until she felt calm again.

She began wandering through the streets of the historic centre. All about her were the Baroque curl and twirl of buildings, a style harking back to a more elegant, highly decorative era, a time of court musicians and great music. She could not get the ugly mood of the shuffling youths out of her mind, their potential for random aggression.

With its interweaving strands Vienna entranced and confused her. There was the surface Vienna in the light, airy shapes, in the statues and sweep of wide streets and open squares, but there was the spiky world of discontent and poverty, that she'd just glimpsed. Even in the glory of the Hapsburgs there would have been subterranean catacombs and an underbelly of prostitutes and peddlars, ready to subvert the order of the hierarchy. Had her father been part of that lower realm? If she could not encounter the fleeting essence of her father through the last place he'd inhabited, perhaps she could grasp something of him in the work of Gustav Klimt.

* * *

The Secessionist building was striking: she admired the cleanness and simplicity of its lines. In the basement of this building was The Beethoven Frieze. Remembering the first time she'd come across an image of it, she was almost afraid of encountering it in life. She steeled herself as she went down the stairs. Narrower than she'd envisaged, the frieze surrounded her on three walls out of four. For minutes she was alone with it. She stood back, taking it in. She went closer here and there, mesmerised. The ingenuity and imagination of the frieze were hard to describe: the beauty of the colours, the gold, the ethereal disappearing forms, set against the dark forces of evil. How had Klimt contained all that? Klimt, who had painted the picture she was about to inherit. The very thought set her nerves jangling.

The second visit to the solicitors was productive. As the case was not a straightforward one, the office had taken copies of the letters, legal statements and deliberated further. They would need to go before a judge, *ein Richter,* Mo was now told, as the letter was not, in and of itself, a signed, certified will and therefore not strictly binding in law. Yet the letter did show clear intent and in view of the fact it was not being contested, would probably suffice.

'I'll represent your case,' said Rudolf Dolsch with the hint of a smile. He told her Sandor Olmak's circumstances had been further investigated, his former tenancy agreements and bank details called up for inspection. As he'd left the city some years previously, not a great deal was forthcoming. His bank account was dormant but not closed. He appeared to have no debts or outstanding contracts with anyone in the city. In effect, it appeared that he had made a complete break with the place until the sudden eruption of these letters.

The whereabouts of the picture in storage had been verified and a copy of the storage receipt located. The receipt was attached to a letter dated September 1927. The appointment with the judge was duly set. Dolsch, pleading urgency, had succeeded in having the hearing brought forward so they need only wait until the following day. He looked pleased with himself. As he shook her hand at the conclusion of the day's business, she began to feel he was on her side.

Exhausted, she was happy to retreat to the opulence and security of the Hotel Sacher near the Opernring. It was a grand, high-ceilinged place with cornices, chandeliers and maids in frilly aprons, fussing around, dusting and setting things in order. The air smelled of beeswax with a trace of wood smoke from one of the open fires. Mo had never seen anywhere so grand. The clerk at reception nodded *Grüss Gott* as she gave her name. He leafed through a large red ledger until he came to her reservation. A bellboy accompanied her to her room on the third floor.

She ate a supper of *Knödel* and *Kalbsfleisch,* dumplings and veal, served from a silver tureen in a secluded corner of marble dining room. The sommelier served her a local Riesling with much subtlety of aroma and taste. She found herself sinking back into the well-upholstered rococo chair. Later, in her well-appointed bedroom with its Biedermeier dressing table, she slumped onto the bed, gazing up at the intricate cornice and out through the long window overlooking the Ring, where horse carriages trotted up and down. She fell asleep within five minutes, the travails of Paris far away.

Chapter Sixty-eight *Derek*

On the morning after Mo's second night away from him, Derek received a telegram. He tore it open: *Gone to Vienna.* He slumped down as though punched, threw the telegram to the ground and stared at the crumpled paper – a declaration in no uncertain terms of her independence and right to rule over her own life. But at least she had communicated with him.

He gulped down the rest of his morning coffee and left their rooms. He had a full day ahead of him. He suspected she had written on impulse: to twist the knife deeper in but also to let him know he should not worry too much about her. If only it were that easy. Either way, there was nothing much he could do about it. He would just have to wait until she pitched up.

The Russian community had decided to go ahead with Tanya's funeral sooner rather than later. There would be no one attending from Russia, apart, he suspected, from the odd OGPU agent hovering to make sure she was well and truly buried and that her Parisian compatriots were not about to make a martyr of her.

The Aleksander-Nevsky Cathedral in the eighth *arrondissement* was the first Russian Orthodox place of worship built on French soil. Pablo Picasso had married Olga Khokhlova here, with Jean Cocteau and Guillaume Apollinaire in attendance. Ivan Turgenev, the writer, had had his funeral here. Tanya would be in good company, though Derek was not sure how much pomp she would have enjoyed. The chanting and the incense would appeal to her sense of the mystical, perhaps, if they were not too tainted with echoes of the Tsars.

Derek watched as both bedraggled and fine clad mourners filed into the pews. Lensky was there and Prince Yusupov. Half of the La Ruche artists trickled in. Even Kiki, the Queen of Montparnasse and singer of bawdy songs, was there. As was Marie Vassilieva, her archrival for that title. A one-time revolutionary, who kicked out many a Cossack dance at the Bobino Music Hall, Marie was a well-known figure about the place. She looked very buttoned up and dry-eyed. Samuel Goldman was there in a frockcoat, looking sombre and solemn. Tanya might even have found it amusing – seeing all these disparate elements of Russia squeezed in together to bid her farewell.

Karine Petrova was nowhere to be seen.

At first Derek felt curiously detached. He watched while people queued to file past the coffin, to kiss Tanya's cold forehead beneath a linen strip, as was the Russian custom. He hesitated, wanted to draw into the shadows, disappear into a side chapel and yet he was pulled, almost against his will, to take one last look at her. He found himself moving forward in the line. The deep tones of the choir had started up, the priests were chanting, a verger was swinging the censor so clouds of incense drifted upwards catching light through the high windows, circulating, filling the high vault.

Tanya, oh Tanya where are you? His steps slowed; his mind thick with the unthinkable: had she killed himself? Was she so thoroughly distraught by all she had been through? He tried to sweep aside the notion. What did it matter now? She was gone. Gone. And all this – so unreal, so solemn, so … as he drew level with the coffin, he found he could not move. The face was waxen but devoid of content. She was not there. This corpse was not the woman he had known. Yes, it was Tanya Sergeyevna – but it was not the vibrant, spirited creature he'd come to love. He could not bring himself to kiss her forehead. He touched her hand, which was intertwined with a crucifix. It was icy cold. More singing and chanting, prayers in deep voices and more clouds of incense – most of the service was in Russian – making it even more remote and exotic.

Now he wanted to get away from it. He did not trust his feelings. He did not want others to see his confusion. There were to be drinks and something afterwards, organised by Lensky, Marie and Dimitri. He supposed vodka toasts and maudlin speeches, tears. He wanted no part of all that. He was not entitled to it and did not want to be drawn further in. If he was to keep his wits about him, he needed to keep his distance.

He slipped out of the cathedral.

He wandered down Avenue Hoche towards the Arc de Triomphe. Cars whooshed by and the occasional horse drawn vehicle. He wanted to walk and walk. He wanted to still the unquiet thoughts and feelings moving through him. He wanted to bury Tanya Sergeyevna deep within him, never again to be disinterred. Crossing over into the Champs Elysées he attempted to brush away his turmoil. He gazed in at restaurants where they'd finished serving lunch and were preparing the tables for dinner. He watched a waiter flicking open a napkin and twirling it into the shape of a swan.

Chapter Sixty-nine *Mo*

The restaurant, Ilona Stüberl was on Braunerstrasse and accessed via an arched entrance. With its wooden panelling, lace tablecloths and coat hangers on hooks it had a homespun, friendly feel to it. Dolsch had suggested they have lunch together before the afternoon hearing: there were a few things he wanted to iron out. A waiter with a handlebar moustache brought a menu on parchment. From the kitchen came smells of roasting meat. She looked through the long, bewildering selection of dishes.

'Wonderful rich soups they do here,' said Rudolf Dolsch with enthusiasm.

'Why don't you order for me?'

She found it a little strange that were taking lunch together. 'A little Viennese hospitality,' he said as if reading her mind. Or was it just that she was about to become a wealthy woman, she asked herself. No matter, she could do with a contact in the city. He turned to the waiter, asked a couple of questions, and gave their order. 'It should be quite straightforward after all – the court and everything.'

'I hope so.'

'The protocol here can be bureaucratic – but, well, the legal system is there to protect…'

'I suppose so.'

'How have you enjoyed Vienna so far?'

She shrugged, unsure how to respond to this stab at friendliness. 'Early days,' she said then added: 'I've just scraped the surface of it. I believe there are many Viennas, just as there are many Londons.'

He leaned back, looking thoughtful, eyed her through his

dark eyebrows. 'You're right.' He sipped the wine, which had just arrived. 'Do you know what the nickname for Vienna is these days?'

She shook her head.

'*Wasserkopf.* Water head. You know it's a disease of the brain – when it has too much water in it and grows big? A big city with a hinterland that has shrunk to the size of a province?' He laughed.

She knew little of Austria and the might it had once wielded. All she knew from her father was the strictness of the hierarchy and what he'd said about being an outsider. Insider outsider it seemed. He got work, he'd said; knew all the right conductors and orchestras. But, nevertheless, felt restricted.

Rudolf Dolsch continued as if to himself: 'When a city has been the centre of a great empire for centuries … and then loses all that – it doesn't quite know itself.'

'Well, the British Empire is not what it was.'

'Vienna was a thriving metropolis under the Hapsburgs, a great centre of culture and music. Then the war came and all that broke apart. No more empire, no more subject peoples. No more attempts to knit together the varied traditions. After the war we had the Social Democrats. They tried to reform the city – new houses, streets, squares and better sanitation. But people are confused.' He gave a wistful glance around. 'Old Vienna has virtually disappeared.'

She thought of the street rabble from the day before, wanted to brush them aside. She half whispered. 'I'd love to visit the places my father knew. I tried his old lodgings. No one answered the bell.' She played with her wine glass. She could hardly explain how the loss of someone makes you want to track down every last corner where they have been, gather every word spoken of them as if panning silt for gold. She gave Dolsch a placatory smile. She didn't want to talk any more about it.

The court was a domed, echoing vestibule in a municipal building. The hearing had been squeezed in due to another case being adjourned. The judge, a man of sixty with jowls and a cast in his eye, looked jaded. Rudolf Dolsch laid the case before him. The judge asked if there was anyone contesting the claim and when assured that there was not, asked for proof of Mo's identification. He viewed her over his half-moon glasses with an air of indifference but granted in her favour. She was overcome with relief.

'Can I claim the picture?' she asked Dolsch.

'You need to produce your father's death certificate to do that,' he said.

'But that means going back to London.' She tried not to sigh. Deciphering exchanges in court when you understood no word of the language was impossible. She could be cheated her out of her legacy and be none the wiser.

'A copy would suffice.'

'I need to get back to Paris.' she said.

Rudolf Dolsch shook her hand and gave her a warm smile, as if genuinely gratified that they'd won their case without further ado.

* * *

That evening she dined alone. Anwaltskanzlei Herber und Dolsch would be in touch again. She gave Rudolf Dolsch's secretary her details and asked them to send the fee invoice to her in Paris. They would handle the handover of the painting and any further formalities once she'd obtained her father's death certificate.

Now she was in a Hungarian restaurant near the Hotel. As predicted, the goulash was outstanding: hearty and rich in tastes. She sipped the delicious wine and slipped her feet out of her shoes. Imbibing the warmth and cosy surroundings she found herself growing drowsy. She shrugged off any curious glances directed towards her.

She was on the point of retiring to her hotel when she saw three musicians emerging from behind a curtain by the kitchen: one was carrying a violin, the other a sort of xylophone and the third what looked like a clarinet. Ah, she thought: a little distraction. She sat back expecting to find it pleasant, but the music when it started up seared right through her.

The violin sang, it enticed, teased, pulled her away to other places. It was the air of the gypsies; it was the plaintive, plangent cry of the exile; it was the longing of love and its pursuit, its flowering and destruction. She could hardly breathe. She wanted to weep, she wanted to get up and throw back the tables and dance until she fell down; she wanted to take off on a white charger across the plains. Where on earth did this music come from? She felt she was about to break into a thousand pieces.

The piece came to an end and the musicians bowed their heads as a few diners clapped. Mo straightened her back, slipped her feet back into her shoes. Her throat caught. She did not want to pursue her thoughts. It had all been a bit much for her. Gradually she felt composure return. Music had always been her undoing. Now they had stopped playing she could start to think again. Despite any danger she would return to Vienna. She had to anyway. But the painting was almost secondary. She'd embarked on a journey with an unknown yet enticing destination. A visceral curiosity about her father had her in its grip.

The night train was late leaving Vienna. She settled into her seat, watched the bustling and rushing of porters on the platform; a family was making a last-minute dash to board. A whistle shrieked. Doors were slamming. The train started slowly forward. She watched the piled-up mail on trolleys, the crowds growing thinner. The steel girders of the terminus arched above and then came the night sky as the train slipped into the suburbs and ever westwards through thickening darkness towards Germany and France. Now she wanted to get back to Paris. She had so much to think about that she longed for respite and familiar surroundings. So much that had lain dormant had been stirred into life through her trip. And then there was the painting. She would need to find out how much it was worth, make sure she could get it out of Austria. And then what: sell it outright? Put it up for auction? She was swaying slightly with the movement of the train. It was time to rest. She'd booked a sleeping berth and was expecting to share with another woman, as was the practice, but when she got to the sleeper compartment she was delighted to find the other bunk empty. The last thing she wanted was to have to make polite conversation.

Chapter Seventy *Derek*

Now Derek wanted to look to the future, concentrate on work, patch up what he could with Mo. Mo had sent a telegram to Lensky, announcing her imminent return. But what would she be coming back to? Would she even speak to him? And what of her singing? Scheherazade was a fine venue. Away from the hub of Montparnasse it attracted a more varied audience, not just the American tourists and artists of Montparnasse; but it would never attract a crowd. It would never become *the* place. Lensky would rotate the singers as it pleased him. Besides, above and beyond all this, he had no idea what he was going to say to her.

He made his way to Goldman's hotel. Goldman had called himself, Dimitri and Lensky together. He was putting off his departure back to the States, he said, without giving the reason why. Derek knew better than to push him for an explanation. As Derek arrived the other three were sitting round a low table in the lobby of Hotel Napoleon, smoking cigars and drinking brandy and vodka. Dimitri looked morose and said little. Lensky looked strained. Only Goldman had something approaching his normal level of efficiency. Today no piano tinkled in the background so they could hear the soft shuffling of feet and muted voices from the reception area.

'Where did you get to after the funeral?' said Dimitri, by way of greeting.

Derek shrugged and decided not to try and explain himself.

'It's hard when you don't speak Russian,' said Goldman, easing Derek into their circle. It was apparent that the talk had been of Tanya Sergeyevna and Derek could see that Goldman was trying to steer it in a less emotive direction.

Goldman cleared his throat, took a sip of his brandy. 'I would like to come to some sort of arrangement today, if possible. I realise the legal side will need to be tied up and that will take time, but I thought if we could establish common ground that would be helpful.'

Lensky nodded. Derek said: 'Could you fill me in on what agreement you had with Tanya Sergeyevna?' Even as he pronounced her name, he felt his throat tighten. He tried to keep his voice even. 'As you know, I wasn't party to all that.'

'I paid her partly in cash for the recent drawings of the Paris Russian émigré community and partly it was a transfer of funds.'

'To where?' asked Lensky.

'The fund for Russian artists. She wasn't sure of the current situation with that organisation. We were looking into it when…'

'Yes, well,' said Lensky, looking across at him. 'That's where we need to take it up…'

'So what is the best way of doing that?' asked Derek.

'Not a problem,' said Lensky. 'I can look into that.' He was quick to jump in, thought Derek, and wondered why he was so eager to get involved.

'Given that Tanya Sergeyevna has no known blood relatives and that she made her wishes clear to me, I think we can follow her intentions quite easily. On more than one occasion she expressed her wish to help her fellow Russian artists. Actually, we discussed this at some length.' Goldman paused, looked round the table at each of them in turn. '*Stalin's Dolls,* however, is another matter.'

'Quite' echoed Derek. For a moment he was taken back to the attic studio where the outrageous mannequins lay strewn all about him. 'What remains of that exhibition must definitely see the light of day.'

'The question is where and how,' said Lensky.

'I've organised a showing at the Metropolitan Museum of art,' said Goldman.

Chapter Seventy-one *Lensky*

Lensky was unsure how much contact there had been between Marie Vassilieva and Tanya Sergeyevna. Not a huge amount, said Dimitri: Tanya had been to her atelier a few times but then Tanya had withdrawn. All the more surprising, thought Lensky, were her forays into the La Coupole and other Montparnasse cafes after she'd sold her Paris émigré sketches to Goldman.

Already Lensky knew a little about Marie Vassilieva. Above all, she served the artistic community well. She'd opened her atelier to all and sundry. Artists came pouring in. She liked to mingle the domestic with the professional, her doll portraits and furniture pieces with more ambitious Cubist paintings.

He found Marie in her atelier working on a doll portrait.

He was hesitant how to address her, not wanting to assume an automatic familiarity. She might indulge in wild Cossack dancing in the Music Hall Bobina, but she was still a serious artist. She looked over her shoulder and gave him a half smile.

'I'm not disturbing, Madame?' he said.

'Ah, Anton Lensky. To what do I owe the pleasure?'

He gazed at her work. He loved the meticulous attention she was giving it; the vivid colours reminded him of a vibrant peasant costume. He felt a pang of nostalgia. He hadn't seen the like in decades. He set about explaining Tanya Sergeyevna's legacy: how it was her dearest wish to help the artists of Montparnasse, especially the displaced and rootless ones. Marie listened without speaking, her eyes grave and thoughtful.

'Yes, we talked about it. She was here not long ago. A week before …' she paused looked at the ground and focussed intently on Lensky. 'I can think of many ways we might put that money to good use.'

Lensky gave her a broad smile, sensing that here was a woman of integrity, who knew how to get things moving. 'Excellent,' he said.

An hour later he returned to Scheherazade where he was taken aback to see Mo sitting on a barstool. Legs elegantly draped in silk stockings and smoking through a cigarette holder, she was chatting to the part-time manager. Lensky took her hand in his, raising it to his lips. 'The wanderer returns,' he said. 'I hear you were in Vienna?'

'News travels fast,' she replied. He was amused to note she was blushing. 'I had business to attend to there.' She inclined her head, as if uncertain how much to say. She took a long draw on her cigarette. 'Has Derek said anything?'

'About what?'

This seemed to rattle her. She flicked ash angrily into an ashtray. Lensky came to sit beside her on another bar stool. In fact, Derek had mentioned that she'd gone to Vienna even before he himself received a telegram to say she was on her way back to Paris. Derek had looked dreadful in the telling but displayed no signs of wanting to divulge more and Lensky had not pushed him. The two had obviously had a spat. How serious it was would be revealed in time. He knew better than to mix in where couples were concerned, and especially this couple.

You could see at a glance that they loved each other: the air was always electric between them, but then Lensky suspected Derek had had a distinct penchant for Tanya. He had looked broken by her death, looked even worse at the funeral, bottled up and distant, and he'd stayed well clear of the wake afterwards. Lensky assumed they had been lovers but did not know for sure. No, he did not want to get mixed up with all that. These were artists, after all. Their passions would be too deep for comprehension, too fiery for containment. Artists were mad, a species apart. It was bad enough trying to manage them, let alone trying to understand them.

'Actually,' said Mo, struggling for composure. 'I had a favour to ask.' She fiddled with the cigarette holder where the cigarette became dislodged. She was not a natural smoker and did it only to appear liberated, he suspected. She gave a little cough. 'I need … I was wondering if I might stay in the club tonight. If it doesn't inconvenience…' She was fumbling. He felt quite sorry for her. When he said nothing, she whispered: 'Derek didn't say anything?'

'I don't understand what's going on.' There he had said it. Instead of offering her free access to one of the rooms upstairs, no questions asked, he was getting involved.

'There's been a – a disagreement between us. I don't feel ready to see him right now.' Her face stiffened, seemed about to crumple. He felt the urge to put his arm round her, draw her close and tell her it was all right: above all else Derek loved her dearly, but he was an artist and artists did funny things, had strange drives. But what use saying all that? She was an artist, too, and would understand better than he ever could.

'Of course you may stay there. I'll get the cleaner to sort some bed linen out for you. I'll be seeing Derek later. There are things we need to settle…'

Again she seemed troubled. 'Would you mind not telling him that I'm staying here. I will see him. But not yet.'

He raised his eyebrows. 'Mo, I'll do as you ask. But Paris is a small place. How long do you intend hiding from him?' She straightened her back, glared at him for an instant but said nothing. 'He'll find out, one way or another.'

When Mo gave a defiant shrug, he decided it really was none of his business. He recalled, though, the trouble Derek had taken to ensure she got a good deal, that he'd been so keen she was accorded security, continuity. He had gone on to mention her fragility after the deaths in her life. Lensky hoped for both their sakes that this spat was a passing blast of discontent and that Mo was not teetering on the melancholy Derek hinted at. When asked if she was travelling alone, Derek had grimaced.

Lensky got up and touched Mo on the shoulder. 'Despite what you might think right now, Derek loves you. And he is a good man.' There he'd said it, poked his nose in, dropped the stance of the world-weary sophisticate. Those Russian doll portraits of Marie had a lot to answer for. Mo looked at him with big eyes.

Chapter Seventy-two

The cleaner had thrown open the shutters and windows of the small room. She'd made a hasty attempt to pile the clutter in one corner: music scores, old costumes, half empty cans of paint, one or two step ladders. The room was dusty and airless and smelled like a broom cupboard. No matter, the open windows were now wafting in fresh air and the sounds of the alleyway below. Mo was grateful for having a hideaway.

It was another day before she was due to perform. Tomorrow she could put through a call to London and set about acquiring her father's death certificate. She assumed it would be straightforward; Derek had seen to all that when Timothy and Ma died, wanting, she supposed, to save her the pain.

She spent a restless night on the narrow bed, unable to stuff her ears against sounds penetrating from below: Lisette's piercing trills, the guffaw of laughter, voices raised in enjoyment. Lensky had made sure she was provided with what she needed and stayed well clear. For that she was thankful. Hearing the last of the revellers moving off she drifted into a light sleep where she dreamed in snatches and had to keep drinking water from the bedside tumbler because she was parched.

The next night she got ready to perform. Luckily Lisette and she were the same dress size. All her glittering, dark gowns she'd left in Marais as her one small, battered suitcase had been unable to contain them all. Lisette was happy to oblige. The frock she offered was frayed slightly round the neck, but, no matter, in the subdued nightclub lighting few would notice. Mo's fingers trembled as she touched her cheeks with rouge. She tweaked a curl around her cheek, glanced this way then that at her image. She would do.

Would Derek be there tonight?

She thrust her chin forward, looked down her nose and squinted at herself.

She would try the Cole Porter again. She had had a quick rehearsal in the afternoon with the accompanist and Lensky had requested she perform it. 'It's a different crowd that comes on a Thursday. They won't have heard it.' That was fine by her, it meant less work and less to go wrong.

She stepped into the circle of light. Some voices hushed, others carried on. She opened her arms to the audience as if to embrace them and lost herself to the song. The time flew and already she was uttering the refrain:

> *One wonderful day*
> *You took my heart*
> *And threw it away*
> *That's why I asked the Lord*
> *In heaven above*
> *What is this thing called love,*
> *This funny thing called love?*

The audience loved it. They were hers. No one could snatch this from her. She bowed to accept their applause and then she was stepping away back towards the cluttered space that served as a dressing room. She had not been able to tell if Derek was in the audience. While she sang it did not concern her. Now, though, she was curious. Lensky came to find her.

'Derek is here,' he said.

She stared ahead.

'He is waiting for you. Will you come?'

She started cleaning some of the rouge from her face. It was far too bright and in normal light made her look like a clown. She nodded. 'In two minutes.' Her hand was steady now. She removed Lisette's frock and put on the day dress she'd been wearing.

As she made her through the tables as unobtrusively as she could, she recalled in a flash that earlier time in Brighton when Derek had sought a reconciliation. Then he had done everything in his power to win her round. She pictured him rolling out his towel on the pebbles and fetching a windshield for her. He'd even brought sandwiches, wrapped in grease-proof paper. She'd laughed when she saw that. She approached the water's edge. He had his bathing costume on under his trousers and it fitted loosely. He'd looked lean and strong. She'd found herself gazing at his body, remembering. He ran into the breakers, dived under a huge wave, disappeared, and then his black head was bobbing far out in the water. He was sounding the depths diving into the dark, swirling water. She'd watched him, anxious for his return. She'd seen him slicing the waves, moving up and down on the swell. He'd emerged, dripping, grinning, splashing her till she shrieked. He'd caught hold of her hand and dragged her up the pebbles, then throwing the towel towards her and offering her a ham sandwich roughly, playfully, like a huge untamed dog. And later he'd laid his head in her lap, stroked her calf. 'Mo,' he said, barely above a whisper: 'Have you thought any more – about us?'

That seemed a world away, a century ago. How many times could one forgive? Her eyes were searching him out. She found him at a far table. He got to his feet as she arrived. Took her hand, kissed it. 'You were superb.'

'I know,' she said.

'Can we talk?'

'I'd rather walk,' she said, for she did not have the patience for his explanations or self-recrimination. She did not want to hear about Tanya Sergeyevna or any of the Russians. She did not want to risk losing her temper with him. That would come. If there were to be any hope at all for them, she would need to vent her rage. But right now the words of the song, the warm applause of the audience were in her head.

'I'm too tired to think.'

They gathered their things and left. Derek nodded goodbye to Lensky. Mo felt him watching them.

They walked some distance in silence before she could contain herself no longer. 'I went to Vienna, as you know,' she began. 'I saw my father's lawyers. We went through his papers. He mentioned me in a letter. My father left me a picture and it needed to be attested. A Gustav Klimt picture.' She heard Derek's sharp intake of breath. She carried on without looking at him. 'Today I called about his death certificate. I have to send a postal order and then it'll be on its way. It's a matter of protocol. It's in the Public Records. I will go and claim my legacy and then decide what I am going to do.'

Her voice sounded calm, in charge. She stared ahead, intensively aware of his presence beside her, but unable to look towards him. She had pushed away her feelings, overcome by a sort of numbness. She listened to their steps sounding in unison on the flagstones. He touched her lightly on the arm. Still she refused to look at him.

'I was so worried,' he said. 'I can't tell you how relieved I am to see you.'

'I can't be second best,' she said. 'I can't wait till it happens again.' This time her voice was small and faraway. She sounded like a child. 'I will take my money and make sure I never have to depend on you again. It's the only way.'

'And what if you fall in love with the picture?'

'It's less dangerous than falling in love with a man.'

'A man? Any man?'

'You know exactly what I mean.'

They had reached a thoroughfare. She had forgotten its name. They were now only ten minutes from home. She was afraid to arrive there.

'I could've died thinking I'd lost you again.'

She snorted. 'Oh Derek, you are so full of lies.'
'It's the truth.'
'For now.'
'Now is all we have.'
'Derek, it's not a matter of forgiveness. It's a matter of self-protection. I don't know what went on between you and … that woman. You understand? But I can't stand by and wait for your next adventure. I just can't.'
'There won't be another.'
She quickened her step, moving away from him. 'I don't want to hear any more.'
'Mo,' he caught her by the arm, swung her round. 'You're the one. The others are just passing through.'

She snatched herself away from him, moving ever faster. Did he realise how much he had hurt her? Did he know? She supposed that at bottom he was just being himself. One way or another she had the choice: she could live with him and hope for the best or she could break away and find her own path.

But the choice was too stark.

Right now she wanted the animal warmth of his presence, she wanted his body next to hers. She did not want to be walking the dark streets of Paris alone. She would never ever possess him, but neither, she reflected, would he ever own her.

That, in itself, was a challenge and an awakening.

They reached their block in Marais. Derek led the way up the stairs. She watched him climb, watched him open the door to their rooms and was flooded, despite herself, with gratitude to have him in her life. She struggled against it. It was impossible. He was impossible. Their future was impossible. Where was her pride? Her independent spirit?

She did not want him to get off so lightly. Yet she remembered then, despite herself, all that he had done for her in recent weeks, the care he had taken over her family, the business at The Mare's Head. Was that guilt? He was humming to himself, affecting a calm, in-control demeanour. Was it to disguise *his* insecurity? She remembered her father. His remorse at running from commitment, connection. His eagerness to make amends. How the past had haunted him. What would Sandor have advised her now?

She and Derek entered their apartment and he took her coat from her, touching her gently on the neck. She was afraid to look at him. 'I bought some champagne,' he said, almost in a whisper, 'when Anton told me you'd be singing tonight. Shall we go through to the balcony?'

She followed without speaking, took two glasses from the kitchen and wiped them clean. He'd taken hold of a candlestick with a half burned out candle. He placed it on the wrought-iron table and fetched a blanket which he wrapped around her. 'I shall miss this place,' he said. 'We had a good start here.' Still she did not speak. She watched as he lit the candle, popped the champagne and poured into the glasses. She watched shadows flitting about the balcony, candlelight catching the bars of the balcony, the rim of the glasses, the bubbling liquid.

Start and finish, she was about to say, but could not. For this was not a death, however much she thought it might be. She could not walk away from him. The money would come to her or she would fall in love with the picture, the living link with Sandor Olmak, her father. That would all happen. Perhaps she might feel safer financially because of it; perhaps poverty would no longer stalk her. But Derek was another matter. What lay between them, what pulled them in and reeled them out had little to do with money. It had little even to do with their bodies and what they chose to do with them. She was not actually sure she what it was, this bond, this mysterious compact between them. It felt almost as though it had been decided elsewhere in some other sphere when she wasn't watching.

Was it true for him too? Was it true what he'd said: she was the one, the others were only passing through? And suddenly snatches from the Cole Porter song ran through her mind. For all the froth and gaiety of the lyrics the song had a kernel of truth. There was a wildness and unpredictability about the whole thing. There was passion, lust, irresistible attraction, that drew you along like a tide and dumped you where it would.

And then there was what remained behind.

The candle sputtered and died. Derek got up to fetch another from the kitchen. She stood up and looked out over the rooftops, drawing closer the blanket. Appearing intermittently between scudding clouds, the moon briefly silvered the towers of Notre Dame and filled the night with dancing shadows — shadows of things past and yet to come.

* * *

Derek stood alone in the kitchen, watching the shifting shapes as he lit and placed another candle in a bottle. He noticed his hand was shaking. Despite all, how fragile the connection between them. How easy to snuff it out. How easy to take it for granted. He would be lucky indeed to survive this breach of trust and he knew it. He walked slowly back upstairs, as unsure of himself as he'd ever been.

THE END

Coming shortly:

A Distant Call

In 1935 Mo and Derek are still in Paris. They have established themselves in the city, moved to a better apartment and are both succeeding in their careers. But all is not as it should be. Derek feels he has come to a standstill in his work. Mo has an assured status as a singer, but she longs for a family and is unable to carry a child to term. Paris seems to be shrugging them off. They move south, to the Riviera, where other artists and writers have preceded them. Here they flourish. But the world they know is crumbling. Extremism is on the rise: fascism and communism stalk society. When Mo falls pregnant again and all seems well, Derek has misgivings about the world they are bringing their child into. In Spain, an elected government is overthrown and supporters of democracy flock to its defence. Derek heeds the call.

THE EATONS, Vol 3

ABOUT THE AUTHOR

Brenda Squires grew up in London and Surrey and now lives in a restored Victorian Mansion in the deep countryside of West Wales, which she loves. Her background was in education, community work and psychotherapy but she has always had a passion to write. At first it was a background hum but it became ever louder, until irresistible. She was delighted and surprised when her first novel, **Landsker,** won the Romantic Novelists' New Writers Award. Her second book: **The Love of Geli Raubal** draws on her experience as a student of German and the exciting time she spent in a divided Berlin.

In the current trilogy: **The Eatons** she traces the ups and downs of a passionate relationship between two artists: a singer and a painter. She has always been intrigued by creativity: where it comes from, where it leads. Besides writing she has taken up painting recently and finds that the two art forms feed into each other. She likes learning foreign languages, walking in wild countryside and being by the sea. She helps run an arts and community centre in Pembrokeshire.

Printed in Great Britain
by Amazon